NO BIG RIP

ALSO BY JEANNE GLIDEWELL

A Lexie Starr Mystery Series

Leave No Stone Unturned

The Extinguished Guest

Haunted

With This Ring

Just Ducky

Cozy Camping

Marriage and Mayhem

The Spirit of the Season

A Ripple Effect Cozy Mystery Series

A Rip Roaring Good Time

Rip Tide

Ripped To Shreds

Rip Your Heart Out

Ripped Apart

Ripped Off

No Big Rip

The Grim Ripper

Soul Survivor

NO BIG RIP

A RIPPLE EFFECT COZY MYSTERY, BOOK 7

JEANNE GLIDEWELL

Book design by eBook Prep
www.ebookprep.com

May 2022
ISBN: 978-1-64457-244-3

ePublishing Works!
644 Shrewsbury Commons Ave
Ste 249
Shrewsbury PA 17361
United States of America

www.epublishingworks.com
Phone: 866-846-5123

Dedicated to the memory of one of the greatest loves of my life, our grey and white tabby, Dolly. She was the sweetest, most entertaining, and lovable pet we've ever owned and the inspiration for Rip and Rapella's cat of the same name. She brought so much joy to our lives for nearly thirteen years. My husband, Bob, and I were devastated when she was diagnosed with mast cell cancer in January of 2021. When she crossed over the rainbow bridge a year later she took a part of us with her. She will never be forgotten and forever remain in our hearts. The character named on Dolly's behalf plays a small part in solving the murder case in No Big Rip, and you can be assured my beloved cat's namesake will live on ad infinitum.

ACKNOWLEDGMENTS

I'd want to thank my editor, Hannah Phillips for her exceptional editing skills; and my proofreaders, Sarah Goodman, of Olathe, Kansas; Sheila Davis of Fairway, Kansas; and Cindy Travis, of Mission, Kansas, for their much-appreciated time and efforts.

Because my acknowledgments page somehow got omitted from my last release, *Ripped Off*, I'd like to express my belated gratitude to Sheila Davis. She has not only been my best friend since seventh grade but is also a financial advisor for Morgan Stanley. Her proofreading skills, as well as all of her technical assistance with everything related to financial investments, stock options, Ponzi schemes, and more, kept me from looking like a total idiot. And for that, I am eternally grateful.

I'd also like to thank Brian Paules, Anna Paules, and the rest of the eBook Prep and ePublishing Works team. We were all deeply saddened when the co-founder of eBook Prep and ePublishing Works, Nina Paules, passed away on August 9, 2021, at the young age of fifty-four. It was a huge loss for everyone who knew this multi-talented, creative, and absolutely wonderful human being. Rest in peace, Nina; you will be greatly missed!

FROM THE DESK OF JEANNE GLIDEWELL

Dear Reader,

This story involves substance abuse, a serious issue affecting many individuals from all walks of life. I've injected humor into the story, but please know it doesn't mean I find addiction a laughing matter. As is the case in this story, drug addiction can sometimes begin with a dependency on opioids following a serious injury or illness and then progress into more potent and dangerous narcotics.

I kicked the smoking habit in 2002 after over twenty years of nicotine addiction. In 2004, I suffered a pulmonary/cardiac arrest due to Acute Respiratory Distress Syndrome, or ARDS, which left me on life support for several days. The team of physicians who worked together to save my life told me I wouldn't have survived the ordeal had I still been smoking.

As tough as quitting smoking was, I'm alive today because I chose to conquer my addiction. I can't even imagine trying to beat a drug or alcohol dependency, but it too is often a life or death decision. If you find yourself in this position, please seek help through loved ones, rehab facilities, AA or NA programs, or other substance abuse assistance. It truly is a "one day at a time" journey toward recovery, but the effort's worth the blood, sweat, and tears you put into it.

Suicide also plays a small part in this story. Please consult a close friend, family member, or physician if you experience suicidal thoughts. There is also 24/7 help available through the National Suicide Prevention Lifeline by calling (800) 273-8255, which is the same phone number as the Military Crisis Line.

Thank you for choosing to read *No Big Rip*. I truly hope you enjoy it.

Happy reading,

Jeanne

CHARACTER LIST

Rapella Ripple – Rapella's a spunky seventy-one-year-old who can't help but get involved in murder cases that seem to follow her around like a stray kitten. She and her husband travel the country in a thirty-foot travel trailer she named the Chartreuse Caboose.

Clyde "Rip" Ripple – Rapella's husband, Rip, also seventy-one, retired from law enforcement nine years ago to hit the road with Rapella as full-time RVers. Rip is patient but wary of his wife's interference in homicide cases.

Dolly Ripple – Rip and Rapella's chubby grey and white tabby, who is treated like visiting royalty, plays a small part in solving the truth behind Lillian Sparrow's death.

Lexie Starr – Lexie, the fifty-three-year old co-owner of the Alexandria Inn, is Rapella's partner in crime-solving and is as anxious as her friend to get to the bottom of her next-door neighbor's death. But Lexie's also excited about the imminent birth of her first grandchild.

Stone Van Patten – Fortunately, like Rapella, Lexie has a patient husband too. Stone met Lexie on the East Coast and relocated to the Midwest to be near her. He purchased and restored a Victorian mansion, naming the new bed and breakfast Alexandria Inn after Lexie's given name.

Wendy Van Patten – Lexie's thirty-two-year-old daughter, Wendy, is the medical examiner for Buchanan County, Missouri, but she's on maternity leave and due to give birth any day.

Andy Van Patten – Wendy's husband, Andy, moved to the Midwest from the East Coast to be near his Uncle Stone. He fell in love with Lexie's daughter, Wendy, and married her the previous year. He's now about to be the proud father of their first child.

Lillian Sparrow – Lexie's next-door neighbor owns a historic Mediterranean mansion next to the Alexandria Inn. She is killed in an automobile accident two weeks before Rip and Rapella arrive in Rockdale, Missouri, to visit their friends.

Gary Sparrow – Gary was Lillian's second husband who died of electrocution in an industrial accident several years earlier.

Mickey Scott – Lillian's son from her short-lived first marriage is a disabled veteran who ends up homeless after his mother is killed.

Ruth Petschl –Ruth's an eighty-seven-year-old neighbor of both Lexie Starr and the victim. She can't help but join Lexie and Rapella in sticking their noses where they don't belong.

Judy Hamm – Lillian's youngest daughter from New Jersey is anxious to start a family, but her wife, Sammi, is showing signs of reluctance.

Sammi Hamm –Judy's wife has traveled to Rockdale, Missouri, with her spouse to help collect any of Lillian's belongings Judy wants to keep as mementos of her mother.

Rose Sparrow – Lillian's oldest daughter also lives in New Jersey and as the executor of her mother's estate she travels to Rockdale to take care of her mother's affairs.

Rowdy Noble – Rose's long-time boyfriend has accompanied her to Missouri to help her collect keepsakes from her mother's mansion, which is called *Casa de Hermanas*, or the House of Sisters. There's no love lost between Rowdy and Rose's half-brother, Mickey Scott.

Barron Buckley – Barron's an attorney who's interested in purchasing the victim's home to turn it into a lodging facility similar to the Alexandria Inn. He and his wife, Celia, own an expensive motor coach that's occupying one of the four RV hookup sites on the Alexandria Inn's property. Barron and the Ripples are neighbors in the small RV parking area.

Celia Buckley – Celia is Barron's wife. It's her dream to own her own bed and breakfast in the Rockdale area. When she learns about the *Casa de Hermanas*, she's determined to purchase it.

Narciso Garcia – Narciso was Lillian's groundskeeper with whom she'd appeared to have had a love-hate relationship.

ONE

"W hat the heck was that?"

"What was what?" My seventy-one-year-old husband, Clyde "Rip" Ripple asked. We were at a rest area outside St. Joseph, Missouri, on Highway 36 after filling up with fuel. Before proceeding to our destination of the Alexandria Inn in Rockdale, we had decided to eat an early lunch. We were in our thirty-foot travel trailer when suddenly an odd sound caught my attention.

"I heard a weird noise. It was kind of like the swoosh of someone making a three-pointer with a basketball, only louder."

"It's probably just your imagination, Rapella. I didn't hear anything."

"Of course you didn't!" I was aggravated because I knew I'd heard something unusual outside. "Hear that? I just heard another sound."

"Nope. Still didn't hear anything. Eat your lunch. I'm sure it's nothing."

"It's not 'nothing,' Rip. The last noise was the sound of five thousand bucks being flushed down a toilet. Why did we buy top-of-the-line hearing aids for you if you're never going to wear them?"

"I do wear them." *As seldom as possible,* Rip should've added. His next comment almost got his turkey sandwich slapped out of his hand. "I wear them whenever we go somewhere I'll want to know what someone's saying."

"Thank you for that endearing sentiment. At least you're honest about not giving a rat's behind about anything I have to say."

"What are we behind on that you have to pay?" Rip asked with an ornery grin. I knew he was trying to lighten the mood with some humor by pretending he'd misheard my remark. I whacked him on the head with my paper plate anyway, which prompted him to apologize. "I'm sorry. My hearing aid remark didn't come out quite the way it sounded in my head before I said it."

"Just promise you'll wear them while we're visiting with Lexie and Stone so you can keep up with the conversation."

"Yes, dear." Rip saluted me and took another big bite of his sandwich. "You have my word."

"Yeah, right. So I have your word. Why am I not very confident about you *keeping* it?"

We finished lunch and gave our tubby tabby, Dolly, a few of her favorite tuna-flavored treats. After straightening up the kitchen we were ready to get back in our Chevy truck to make the short and final leg of our trip. When we stepped out of the RV we were the only people left in the rest area. Or so we thought.

"Hey there, folks! Looks like you've got a flat!" A low-timbered voice exclaimed. Holding a buck knife in his right hand made it clear the tall, lanky owner of that voice, who had glazed eyes the color of periwinkles, was the cause of the ruined tire. It was also evident the dude was under the influence of some sort of illegal substance. On the upper right arm of the man holding the knife, I could see only part of a tattoo that read "RAH," which struck me as peculiar. I could think of no female name with those letters in it aside from Oprah, and he didn't impress me as a daytime talk show enthusiast.

My meandering mind was brought back to the present when the dude held the knife toward Rip in a threatening manner.

"Get back inside!" Rip immediately ordered me to retreat back into the trailer.

"But–" I began before I was cut off.

"Don't argue with me! Just do it!"

His last exclamation brought to mind a Nike commercial I'd recently seen on television, but it was his tone that alarmed me. It was one he'd last used with me when I'd gotten arrested at a protest in Rockport a couple of years prior. I quickly backed up the stairs and closed the door behind me. I hurried to the window and peered through a gap in the blinds. I saw a battered old motorcycle leaned up against a fence post. What I saw next scared the bejesus out of me. I watched the apparent owner of the decrepit bike—the knife-wielding, strawberry-blonde-haired man with several missing teeth, about a hundred tattoos, and a wiry build—lunge at Rip with the weapon.

Blood began to spread on the lower left sleeve of Rip's shirt and within seconds Rip brandished the handgun he carried in a small holster on his waistband. From Rip's years of experience in law enforcement, he was always packing and had a permit to do so. He'd known a confrontation with the hooligan was imminent when he'd ordered me back inside the trailer. I saw Rip's lips move as he spoke to his attacker. I imagined he was saying something like, "Didn't your mama ever teach you not to take a knife to a gun fight?"

I'd just recently purchased my very own cell phone and was prepared to use it to call 9-1-1 if Rip needed emergency assistance. I cracked the glass pane over the kitchen sink open and asked Rip if I should call the police.

Before Rip could respond, the young man bolted like a masked burglar who'd just robbed a liquor store. He was rolling the dice on not being shot in the back by my husband, who'd been a career lawman in our hometown of Rockport, Texas. Before Rip retired from law enforcement nine years ago, he'd served as sheriff of Aransas County for nearly a decade before calling it quits. We'd pulled up stakes at that time, sold nearly everything we owned, bought the travel trailer, and hit the road as full-time RVers. We'd been roaming the country and enjoying the wanderlust lifestyle ever since, having very few unpleasant incidents on the road—with this being by far the worst!

After Rip's assailant vanished into the woods, I opened the trailer door as Rip was reholstering his gun. "Are you all right? Do you need to have your forearm stitched up?"

"No," Rip replied as he held his left arm against his chest with his right hand. "It's not that bad. I jerked away just in time."

"If you'd jerked away just in time you wouldn't have blood dripping off your elbow right now. Why didn't you stop him when he ran off?"

"The only way I was going to stop him was to shoot him, and I might've done so had I truly felt my life was in danger. I'm certainly not killing some desperate drug addict for slashing a tire and attempting to rob us."

"How about one who's attacking you with a deadly weapon? The tire was the least of what he just slashed!"

"As soon as I drew my weapon, he was no longer a lethal threat."

"I suppose. So a punctured tire is what I heard earlier," I surmised.

"Yeah, that's what you heard," Rip replied with a sigh. "We've got a spare in the rear storage compartment under the trailer."

"That's good." I tried to leave it at that, but I just wasn't satisfied with Rip's handling of the assault against him. "I still can't believe you let him get away like you did."

"The only other option was to run the guy down and hold him at gunpoint until the police arrived. With my relatively new hip and recent cardiac surgery, I didn't think there was much chance of my catching a slender young man in his twenties who was probably high on meth."

There was absolutely no chance in hell of you catching him, I thought. *With, or without, the hip replacement and triple-bypass operations, it'd have been like Aesop's "Tortoise and the Hare" fable. Only this time, the rabbit would've left the poor turtle choking on dust in its wake.*

"Well, I suppose I'm glad you didn't shoot him or try to run him down," I said. "But don't you think we should report the incident? You could've been killed."

"But I wasn't."

"I see that. The point is it could've ended tragically had you not been carrying your gun. The little thug needs to be caught and taken off the streets. Reporting the crime isn't a sign of weakness on your part, you know. We'll have to wait for the Triple A serviceman to come change the tire, anyway."

"I can change it myself. Don't go calling Triple A. We could be sitting here on our thumbs for two hours waiting on them."

"I highly doubt it. They get exceptional online reviews for quick arrivals and expert service."

Rip shook his head. He was your typical man: proud, hard-headed, and insanely oblivious to his age and physical condition. He might've just thwarted an armed robbery, but that didn't mean he wouldn't heave up his turkey sandwich after the exertion of changing a truck tire.

"I guess the Triple A membership is kind of like your hearing aids then, isn't it?" I didn't like letting the punk who'd assaulted my husband get off scot-free, and I liked even less not taking advantage of a service we religiously paid for every September.

"How's that?"

"It's nice to have, even if we've no intention of ever using it."

"I'm not in the mood to bicker, Rapella." Rip was irritable and aggressive, like a wounded dog. I couldn't say I blamed him.

"You're right. I'm sorry, honey. I'll call Lexie and Stone and tell them we'll be a little later than we'd anticipated while you change the tire."

"Good idea. But just tell them we've had a flat. I don't want them fawning over me when we arrive."

I nodded, wondering how he planned to explain the gash in his arm. "We'll need to replace the spare while we're in Rockdale."

"I realize that, Rapella."

"I still think we should call Detective Johnston when we get there. A violent attack like that shouldn't go unreported." Wyatt Johnston, a close friend of Lexie and Stone's, and now a friend of ours as well, had served on the Rockdale Police Department for nearly twenty years. He'd know what to do.

"It's really no big rip."

"It might be no big rip to you," I began, "but it might be to the dude's next victim, who might not be as fortunate as you. His next mark might not be packing and end up robbed and injured, or worse."

"I guess you do have a point, dear." Rip consented, although I felt as if it was just to appease me and get me off his back. The feeling intensified when he said, "I'll think about giving Wyatt a call and asking him if he'll stop by the inn while he's out on patrol."

"Thank you." I knew thinking about it and actually doing it were two separate things. "Let me dress your wound before I help you tackle the tire."

"Well, all right." I was surprised Rip agreed to let me assist him. There was either a chink in his armor or his arm hurt worse than he was letting on. On the other hand, I realized he could have just agreed with me to shut me up, as he was wont to do.

I retrieved the first aid kit from the storage compartment under our queen-sized bed, which was scarcely able to handle a wound the size of Rip's, but I made do with what was available. As I wrapped a roll of gauze around his forearm, I prayed the terrifying incident wasn't a sign of how our visit at Alexandria Inn was going to go. After the recent murder case we'd gotten involved in while we were visiting our granddaughter, Tiffany, and her husband, Chase, in Albuquerque, I was ready for some rest and relaxation. But then, I was ready to win a million dollars in the lottery too, and that wasn't apt to happen any time soon, either.

TWO

"Well, look what the cat drug in," Lexie exclaimed good-naturedly, as she embraced me in her arms with a warm, welcoming hug. "You are most definitely a sight for sore eyes, Rapella."

"It's so nice to see you too, Lexie," I returned with a second hug. Lexie's given name was Alexandria Marie Starr, but everyone referred to her as Lexie. Even though she and Stone Van Patten had married several years earlier, she'd not taken his last name. She joked she was too lazy to order new checks, but I knew she preferred the surname of Starr. Her first husband, Chester Starr, had died of an embolism many years ago when their daughter, Wendy, was only seven.

Lexie had stayed single for a couple of decades before even dating again. Stone's first wife had passed as well after a bout with cancer. Lexie met Stone on the East Coast while doing some research on Wendy's first husband, Clay Pitt, who'd been a suspect in his first wife's death. Wendy had not been privy to the fact Clay was married before, much less that his previous wife had been brutally murdered. It should come as no surprise that the marriage ended in an annulment. Wendy was now happily married to Stone's nephew, Andy Van Patten. Andy and Wendy were expecting their first child together and Rip and I planned to be around for the birth of the baby. We'd been present for the marriage proposal and wedding the previous year, so we weren't about to miss this milestone in their lives either.

Just then, Stone entered the kitchen where Lexie and I stood arm in arm. Lexie repeated her first remark. "Stone, look what the cat drug in!"

"So good to see you, Rapella," Stone said. "Speaking of cats, how's Dolly?"

"She's fat and sassy, as always. Her Majesty is out in the Chartreuse Caboose. Rip is working on hooking up to the electricity, sewer, and water. It was so nice of you to add a few full hookup sites on the property."

Stone gave me a quick hug and smiled. "You know we were always happy to have you stay in one of the suites here in the inn as our guests. We love having you—"

"I know," I interrupted. "And we love staying here with you in the inn. But with Dolly to tend to, and everything we need in the trailer, it's just easier this way. Plus, we hate the idea of taking up a suite you could be renting out instead of filling it with a couple of freeloaders like us."

"You and Rip are hardly freeloaders," Lexie said. "I don't know what we would've done without you the several times you've stayed with us. You've been very instrumental in helping us get to the truth behind a couple of serious situations. For gracious sakes, you even got me sprung from jail when I was locked up for a murder I didn't commit."

"Well, yes, but . . ."

"No buts about it." Stone was adamant. He hugged me and added, "Lexie's absolutely right. At Rip's suggestion, we've added a total of four RV sites now and, as he predicted, they've been a blessing. Having the added amenity of RV hookups has proven very beneficial to our lodging facility. They've been popular since the day we put them in."

"So popular, in fact, that Stone's considering adding a few more," Lexie said.

"I think I'll start with two and might add additional sites later on," Stone explained. "Did Lexie tell you we have a new member of the family?"

I must have looked crestfallen, because Lexie laughed and said, "No, not the new grandbaby. Wendy's delivery date is still a few days away, not that the baby couldn't arrive at any moment now. Our new family member is of the feline variety. A couple of weeks ago a stray calico showed up on our doorstep, looking for a free meal, a free room, and—"

"And a couple of servants to wait on her hand and paw," Stone cut in.

"And you gave her a forever home. How sweet," I said. "I'll bet she's adorable."

"I don't know about 'forever,'" Stone replied with a chuckle. "I almost kicked her to the curb ten minutes after finding her on the porch. The first thing she did was bite my ear and then she followed it up with slapping me across the face. She left a large scratch on my cheek that's just recently healed. When Lexie asked me what we should call her, I told her we should call Uber to get her a ride to the next county. I wasn't naming her anything until I decided if I wanted to keep her. But luckily for the kitten, she's cute as a button and the little hellion weaseled her way into my heart. When Lexie asked me a second time if I had any ideas what to name the kitten, the first thing that came to mind was 'Trouble.'"

"So you named her Trouble? How cute is that?" I asked rhetorically.

"I wonder what Dolly would think of Trouble if we introduced them," Lexie mused.

"Not a good idea. Her Majesty is queen of the Caboose, and I can guarantee you she'd rip Trouble a new one if the two were to come face to face." I thought it best to warn Lexie so she didn't show up at the doorstep of our trailer with the new unsuspecting pet in her arms. Dolly was never one to share, whether it was food, attention, or even space. At her age, she didn't tolerate any change in her routine. As with humans, she was most certainly a creature of habit. Trouble would be reduced to a bloody pile of fur and bones within seconds.

"You're probably right. Cats can be very territorial, can't they?" Lexie asked.

"Most definitely," I answered. "That's especially true of cats like Dolly who are a little past their prime. An older cat who's been the ruler of the roost their entire life usually has no intention of being demoted."

Changing the subject, Stone asked, "Reckon Rip can use a hand hooking up the trailer?"

"It'd probably be a good idea." My voice broke a little as I replied. "Under normal circumstances, he can hook everything up with his eyes closed."

"What do you mean by 'under normal circumstances'?" Stone asked with concern in his voice, having picked up on my anxiety.

"Is everything all right?" Lexie asked before I could respond to her husband. "Has he had another cardiac scare?"

"No, thank goodness. His heart is fine, as far as we know. It's just that we had a frightening incident at the rest area just outside St. Joseph on Highway 36."

Lexie immediately looked worried. She put her arm around my shoulder. "What happened?"

"Rip's a bit lackadaisical about it but I'm shook up by the whole thing. In fact, he's got a laceration on his arm that I think needs to be looked at by a doctor."

Now Lexie looked downright distressed, and Stone wore a nearly identical expression of angst. He asked, "What in the world happened? How'd his arm get cut?"

"It got sliced by a knife-wielding thug who would've injured Rip even worse, perhaps critically, if Rip hadn't been packing his old service revolver." My voice trembled as I spoke. The thought of what might've happened caused a shiver to run up my spine. The last time I'd experienced that feeling was when Lexie, Wendy, and I nearly got electrocuted in an RV park's swimming pool in Cheyenne, Wyoming, a couple of years prior. It was the first time we'd become acquainted with Lexie, Stone, Wendy and Andy, and we'd been fast friends ever since. I guess there's nothing like a shared brush with death to enhance bonding.

Lexie opened her mouth to speak, but nothing came out. *Trouble must have her tongue*, I thought.

"Son of a bitch!" Stone exclaimed, more than able to put his thoughts into words. He appeared frantic as he asked, "Where is the guy now?"

"Do you mean Rip or the knife-wielding thug?" I asked inanely, not operating on all cylinders again yet.

"The man who attacked Rip, of course," Stone replied impatiently. "You already said Rip is out—"

"Oh, yeah," I waved off Stone, not letting him finish his remark. "Sorry, I'm still on edge."

"I can well imagine," Stone said consolingly. "I would be too."

"The last I saw of Rip's attacker—a young, strung-out, scrawny dude I'd guess to be in his late-twenties—he was high-tailing it into the woods behind the rest area's bathroom facilities. Rip pointed his gun at the creep, but didn't fire." I knew I sounded disappointed by my last statement, but wasn't surprised when Stone nodded in agreement.

"No, of course not." Stone seemed oblivious to my displeasure. "Rip would never shoot an unarmed assailant."

"He had a knife!" I said in protest. "He'd just slashed Rip with a deadly weapon!"

Lexie nodded in agreement, but Stone cleverly changed the

subject again. "I'm going to go check on Rip. Why don't you gals go join Andy and Wendy in the parlor? They're anxious to see you and Rip. Wendy can look at Rip's wound as soon as he comes inside."

Lexie grabbed my arm, as if helping a centenarian across a busy street. She led me into the parlor where Wendy and Andy leapt to their feet in unison to greet me. Being just days away from delivering a baby, Wendy's leap to her feet was more of a painstakingly slow, cautious rise but her enthusiasm in seeing me was still apparent. Andy hugged me, and Wendy, whose belly was in the way, kissed me on the cheek instead.

"It's so nice to see you again, Rapella," Wendy said.

"The feeling is mutual, sweetheart. Do you know what the gender of the baby is yet, or are you two waiting to be surprised?" I asked.

"Andy and I know, but we haven't told anyone, not even Mom and Stone. We want it to be a surprise for them, and for you and Rip too." The gleam in Wendy's eyes was that of a woman with a delicious secret she couldn't wait to share.

"If you've kept your baby's gender to yourselves this long, a few more days should be easy-peasy," I said with a warm smile.

"It's been a challenge to keep it to ourselves, but we're determined not to spill the beans. Thank you for coming. Andy and I are thrilled that you and Rip wanted to join us for the birth of our baby."

"We wouldn't miss it for the world! We've been here to see you two get engaged, and then married—your wedding took two attempts, you know—, so we couldn't *not* be here for the arrival of your first child."

"Thank you. It means the world to us," Wendy said with emotion in her voice. She wiped a tear from her eye and then looked around. "Speaking of which, where's Rip?"

"He's getting the trailer set up and will need you to take a look at his fresh wound when he comes inside."

"Fresh wound or flesh wound?" Wendy asked.

"Both."

"Oh, no! What happened?"

"What happened?" Andy asked in unison with his wife's query.

Before I could explain what had taken place at the rest area, everyone turned to watch Rip amble into the parlor with Stone trailing behind him. The welcoming hugs and kisses began anew. This time the greeting was less rambunctious out of concern for his recent injury.

"I'm going to call Wyatt," Stone said. Rip had just described the frightening incident that had resulted in the gash in his forearm. He made the confrontation sound as if it was an everyday occurrence, and nothing to be upset about. But Stone was having none of it. "Wyatt needs to follow up on this assault."

"There's no need to call Detective Johnston. I barely sustained a scratch." The look on Wendy's face, who was examining Rip's wound as he spoke, said otherwise.

"A scratch?" Wendy was clearly astounded by his nonchalance. "This is hardly a scratch, Rip. It's a laceration. I'm not sure it shouldn't be stitched up. Otherwise, it's going to leave a nasty scar."

"I'm not worried about a scar. I'll just have Rapella apply some more antibiotic cream on it later on and put a fresh Band-Aid on it."

"It needs more than a Band-Aid, Rip," Wendy replied before turning to her husband. "Andy, would you go get my medical bag out of the truck?"

Wendy, who served as the Buchanan County medical examiner, explained she carried the bag everywhere she went, in the event she happened across someone injured in a car accident or anyone else in need of emergency medical attention. She then looked at Rip and said, "You're lucky the gash wasn't any deeper. But for the grace of God, a major artery wasn't cut."

"That's what I told him," I interjected. "He just responded that it was 'no big rip.'"

"Did you say 'no big rip,' Rip?" Wendy gazed directly into her reluctant patient's eyes as she applied antibiotic cream on his wound which was still oozing blood. "Had an artery been cut, you could've bled to death."

Rip had the decency to look as if he'd been admonished. But his next remarks made it apparent his opinion about the seriousness of the attack was unchanged. "I know. But I didn't. The punk made the mistake of picking on a guy who spent his entire career in law enforcement and never leaves the house without his service revolver."

"What if he doesn't make that mistake next time?" Stone asked softly. He was clearly reluctant to pile on and aggravate his friend. "What if he picks on a defenseless old lady who can't defend herself the next time? Suppose it was Rapella he had attacked rather than you."

The look I shot Stone was that of someone who'd just been told she was as helpless as a newborn puppy. My irritation was not lost on him, either.

"Sorry, Rapella. No offense," Stone said in an effort to smooth my ruffled feathers. "I didn't mean to imply you were old."

"I *am* old, Stone," I replied. "Or, at the very least, I've been around the sun a lot more times than you have. But I'm hardly defenseless! Like Lexie, I've brought down a number of killers with my cleverness, spunk, and fearless determination. Sometimes brains are more effective than brawn when you're in a sticky situation."

"Ain't that the truth?" Lexie turned to me with her right hand raised and I slapped it with mine in a high-five manner. "If I had to pick someone to stand in my corner during a crisis, it'd be Rapella."

I smiled at Lexie in gratitude, and Stone fell all over himself apologizing to me. "My mistake and I hereby stand corrected. You both are totally right. I wasn't thinking when I spoke and I'm very sorry. Please forgive me, Rapella."

"You're forgiven, Stone." I chuckled and gave him a big hug as I continued. "No worries. I still love you. Just don't make that same mistake again."

"I won't. I promise. I love you both too." Stone looked at Rip as he added, "And that's why I'm so concerned about what happened at the rest area."

When Rip didn't respond, I added, "I agree with you whole-heartedly, Stone. The next time this punk attacks someone, the outcome could be much grimmer."

"Absolutely!" Lexie, Wendy and Andy responded in stereo.

"All right, all right, I give up. I'm clearly outnumbered." Rip looked at each of us in turn, nodding in concession. "I'll call Wyatt. After all, I couldn't live with myself if I didn't report the incident and someone else was injured by that same kid."

I wanted to say the brazen brute was hardly a kid, but I remained silent. Rip considered anyone under sixty a kid. Besides, I didn't want to annoy him after he'd just come to his senses and agreed to file a report on the frightening and potentially life-threatening attack.

THREE

S tone called his friend, Wyatt Johnston, and the forty-something detective arrived within fifteen minutes. We were all in the parlor drinking coffee and helping ourselves to a platter of sausage, cheese and crackers Lexie had brought out from the kitchen. She was the ultimate hostess, which had helped make the lodging facility a resounding success.

Lexie handed Wyatt a cup when he walked into the room. I'd watched her add several teaspoons of sugar and about half a cup of creamer to a mug that contained very little coffee. She clearly knew precisely how the police officer liked it. She then poured about three tablespoons of the creamer into a small bowl for Trouble, who'd been batting around a twist-tie off a loaf of bread on the hand-scraped hickory floor. With a heart shaped patch of orange fur on her chest, she was absolutely adorable.

Afterward, Lexie walked around and refilled every coffee cup in the parlor. I'd learned long ago that Lexie had a caffeine addiction and unconsciously over-caffeinated everyone in her presence. I fully understood why Wyatt did his best to limit the amount of actual

31

coffee he was ingesting at the Alexandria Inn. He had a dangerous job to perform and he couldn't afford to be jittery while doing so.

I explained to the detective what had occurred at the rest area. I didn't want to give Rip another opportunity to make it sound less traumatic than it'd actually been.

"Do you remember anything distinguishing about the assailant?" Wyatt asked, looking from Rip to me and then back to Rip. "For instance, did the man have a scar, body piercing or tattoo?"

"There was one thing," Rip began, "when he ran off into the woods, he moved with an awkward gait, as if he had a leg injury."

"Okay, good," Wyatt said as he made a notation in a small notepad he'd removed from his shirt pocket. "Can either of you recall anything else about him?"

"Rip ordered me back into the trailer, so I didn't get as good a look at him, but I do remember he had long strawberry blonde hair, bad teeth and lots of tattoos. In particular, I noticed a tattoo on his upper right arm. I couldn't see all of it but the last three letters were R-A-H, as in 'Oprah' or 'hoorah.'"

"Oh, no," Lexie mumbled. Her face drained of color as she continued. "You were close, Rapella. The tattoo actually says 'Oorah' as in the Marine's battle cry. I'm afraid your attacker's name is Michael Scott, but he goes by Mickey."

"What? What are you saying? You know this punk?" I was shocked Lexie not only knew the assailant but also seemed to be very familiar with him. The sadness in her voice indicated she even had a certain amount of fondness for the dude. "Are you sure, Lexie?"

"Yes, I'm sure, Rapella. I've seen that tattoo. Mickey's always been very proud of it. He had it inked on his arm the very day he enlisted in the military, which was the day after he graduated from high school. He'd wanted to serve his country since he was barely out of diapers, and dreamed of being a Marine as soon as he was of age."

"Are you one-hundred percent sure it's him?" Hearing what

Lexie had said about his patriotism, I didn't want to believe it was this Mickey she was referring to.

It was clear Rip didn't either when he said, "I'm sure a lot of Marines have 'Oorah' and/or 'Semper Fi' tattoos, even though the Marine Corp is very particular about where the tattoos can be located on their bodies."

"Yes, I'm sure they do," Lexie replied. "But when you mentioned the long strawberry blonde hair, and that he was scrawny, I was thinking it might be him. The 'bad teeth' made me more sure, because like many drug addicts, he's in need of some serious dental work. But when Rip mentioned he had a limp and you described his tattoo, I was positive; or at least ninety-five percent certain. As you mentioned, Rip, he also has 'Semper Fi' tattooed on his chest. Mickey's older than he looks. I'm not sure exactly how old he is, but somewhere in the neighborhood of thirty-seven or thirty-eight."

"Really?" I asked. "He must have found the fountain of youth. I would've guessed him to be at least ten years younger than that."

"Yeah, me too," Rip chipped in. "You'd think a man in his late-thirties would know better."

"Mickey didn't used to be so reckless. He's always had a baby face; even after all of the tragedies he's experienced." Lexie looked sad as she explained. "Mickey served with the Marines in Afghanistan. He was injured in a rocket attack on a military base in Helmand Province, along with a number of his comrades. His left leg was shattered and he sustained a brain injury. He hasn't been the same since, as you can well imagine. Not to mention, he acquired an addiction to opiods following his injuries, which quickly escalated to barbiturates, meth, and other illegal narcotics."

"Oh, my!" I exclaimed. "That's terrible, and, sadly, all too common."

"Yeah, and it seems to be getting more widespread all of the time," Lexie agreed. "It's a sign of the times, I guess. Mickey was released from the military with an honorable discharge due to his injuries. He'd married his high-school sweetheart, who was nineteen years old, while on a two-week leave, but the marriage dissolved soon after he was injured. After he came home from the war, he moved in with his mom, Lillian Sparrow, and lived with her until just recently. Mickey's wife was a sweet girl, but young and immature. She couldn't handle all his issues and it wasn't all that easy for his mom to deal with them either."

"Did you say his mom's last name was Sparrow?" I asked. "As in the bird?"

"As in Captain Jack Sparrow?" Rip asked at the same time. I guess it says a lot about our interests that Rip would instantly think about a character from the Pirates of the Caribbean motion picture series, while a common visitor to the bird feeders I used to hang in our yard in Texas would spring to my mind.

"Yes to both."

"Does Lillian live here in Rockdale?" I asked.

Lexie pointed to the window next to the massive fireplace. "She used to live in that big white house next door. The Mediterranean-style mansion is an even more imposing structure than this place. She must've rattled around in it like a piece of gravel inside a hubcap."

"Did she move?" Rip asked.

"No. She died recently in a tragic car accident."

"That's unfortunate. How recent was the accident?"

"It was only a couple of weeks ago, Rip. The crash occurred on October twenty-second, to be exact."

Lexie's words sent a chill up my spine. Her next-door neighbor had died on our granddaughter's thirtieth birthday. Rip and I were in Albuquerque to surprise Tiffany on her special day, which turned into quite a memorable experience that landed me knee-deep in another murder investigation.

I regained focus when Rip nodded at Lexie's response. "I can see that the loss of his mother may have been a trigger for Mikey's aggressive behavior."

Lexie knew Rip had a bad habit of forgetting names as soon as he heard them. She didn't bother to correct Rip and tell him the young man's name was actually Mickey. I, however, couldn't overlook it. His failure to pay attention was a constant source of irritation for me. "Focus, Rip. The guy's name is Mickey!"

Rip's only response to my reprimand was to roll his eyes, but everyone else in the room looked amused. I was almost glad Rip had screwed up the man's name as it had erased the sadness on Lexie's face. She couldn't contain her amusement, and when she stopped giggling, she said, "You gotta admit, Rapella, that was closer than Rip usually gets. He once called me Marsha, for goodness sakes! How does one mistake the name Lexie for Marsha?"

"Sorry about that, Lexie." Rip had the decency to look embarrassed. "I'm sure that was back when we first became acquainted."

"Actually, it was the last time you were here." Everyone laughed out loud at her remark. Then she turned to Rip and apologized. "Sorry, but I couldn't resist teasing you. I find your difficulty remembering names rather endearing."

I groaned dramatically and the parlor erupted in laughter once again. Afterward, Detective Johnston said, "I only realized that Mickey Scott was Lillian Sparrow's son after her accident. Until then, I'd thought Lillian only had two daughters that both live in Egg Harbor Township, New Jersey. I remember hearing about him on the local news after the tragic incident in Afghanistan and knew Mickey personally from responding to a few police calls involving him, but I never realized he was Lillian's son until recently. Wendy, didn't you have to handle the next-of-kin death notifications after her death?"

"Yeah, I did," Wendy replied. "It was rough telling them their mother had passed away. I recall Mickey being the most distraught of Lillian's three children."

"Yes," Lexie began, "Mickey had a hard time accepting his mother's death. He was Lillian's first born. She got pregnant during her junior year in high school. She ultimately married the father, a young man named Michael Scott, but the marriage only lasted a few years. Their son was named after Michael, but they called him Mickey so it wouldn't be confusing."

"Was he close to his biological father?" I asked.

"I assume so. Mickey lived with him from the time he was twelve until he went into the military. While he was in Afghanistan, his father was diagnosed with throat cancer and passed within six months. Sadly, it was while Mickey was deployed."

"It seems odd that the boy didn't live with his mother after she divorced his dad." Rip had taken the words right out of my mouth, but Lexie soon explained the situation.

"He did for a while. But a few years after Lillian and Michael's divorce, Lillian married Gary Sparrow and they bought the property next door a couple of months later. Mickey didn't get along with Gary and began to feel invisible when Lillian and Gary devoted so much of their attention to their two young daughters. Mickey has mentioned to me it was his fault more than his stepdad's. He couldn't understand how his mother could replace Michael so easily and it didn't make it easy for his new stepdad to get along with him. Unfortunately, it caused mother and son to be estranged when Mickey was about twelve."

"I can understand how he felt," Wendy said. "I'm not sure I wouldn't have felt the same way had Mom hooked up with another guy shortly after Dad died. I'm sure I would've been angry that a man had taken away from the undivided attention I had grown to expect from my mother. No doubt Mickey felt the same way. As it turned out in my case, I was beginning to think Mom would never even look at another man the rest of her life. At that point, the undivided attention had become somewhat of an albatross around my neck."

"What?" Lexie appeared aghast at her daughter's last remark. "You never told me you felt that way."

"No offense, Mom. You did a wonderful job raising me alone

and I knew you were only trying to protect me. But by the time I was in high school, you'd become somewhat of a helicopter parent." Wendy spoke in a kind voice. I had never heard the term she'd used, but she soon explained it. "Having your mother hovering over you at school dances, parties, and sporting events, as well as chaperoning you on dates, hardly makes you the most popular girl in your class."

"Well, maybe not," Lexie said defensively. "But you still had a lot of great friends, like Mattie Hill and Joy White. More importantly, it helped keep you from becoming a pregnant teenager like Lillian was. I didn't date again until you were grown because I wanted to be there for you at all times."

"That's my point, Mom! You were there at *all* times, like a shadow I couldn't sneak away from," Wendy teased, before reaching over and squeezing Lexie's hand affectionately. "Didn't you ever wonder why I tried to hook you up with my science teacher, a friend's divorced father, and even our mail carrier?"

"You mean the pimply-faced dude who called me Ms. Starr, was twelve years younger than me, and delivered our mail to the next-door neighbor's house at least once a week?"

"Hey!" Wendy exclaimed. "I was getting desperate at that point."

We all laughed at her remark, and then again after Stone said, "It just took your mom a long time to find the perfect guy. Handsome, kind, successful men like me don't come along every day, you know. Not to mention, I was a jeweler. I won her over with diamonds."

"Actually," Lexie said, gazing at Stone, "you won me over with your compassion, charm, and intelligence. But the diamond earrings and necklace didn't hurt your cause any."

When the laughter died down, I asked Lexie, "So what do you know about Lillian's daughters?"

"Judy Hamm is the youngest of the siblings. She and her partner, Sammi, moved to the East Coast when Sammi was transferred there and got married in October of 2013, on the very day same-sex marriage became legal in New Jersey. Lillian told me she flew back there for their wedding."

"So the two have been together for quite a while," I mused out loud.

"Yes," Lexie said, "they met at the San Francisco Pride parade in 2012."

"Small world," I replied. "I'm almost positive my brother, Billy, and his partner marched in that parade too. They attend the event every year. So, Lexie, what do you know about Mickey's oldest half-sister?"

"Rose followed in her mother's footsteps and worked as a legal aid for a few years. She graduated from high school in 2008, the same year as Wendy."

"You and Rose were classmates?" I asked Wendy.

"No, I graduated from Shawnee Mission West in Shawnee, Kansas," Wendy replied, "and Rose went to school here in Rockdale. I've never actually met her."

Lexie nodded, and continued. "Rose is now unemployed and lives with her boyfriend in his father's garage in the same small township as her sister. The sisters have always been close, which is why Rose moved out there shortly after Judy did."

I was beginning to feel sorry for the man who'd attacked my husband just a couple of hours earlier, and the change of emotion wasn't setting well with me. "I'm sure it was traumatic for Mickey to lose his father while he was stationed overseas."

Lexie nodded. "He expressed to me he felt like an orphan until he patched things up with Lillian. It was only after his stepdad, Gary, died from electrocution on a large high-rise construction project that Mickey and his mother reconnected and became close."

"Oh, goodness. The entire family has had to deal with more than their share of tragedy. What about Judy and Rose?" I asked. "Do they get along all right with Mickey?"

"According to Lillian," Lexie began, "they'd never really had any issues with Mickey and thought their dad was too judgmental when it came to their older half-sibling. From what I gathered, both Judy and Rose were glad when Mickey moved in with their mother after their father died."

"That's good that he didn't have to deal with a lot of drama concerning his half-sisters. Blended families sometimes come together like oil and water. I'm glad that wasn't the case with Lillian's children. It sounds as though Mickey had enough to deal with." I now felt even more compassion for Mickey. "Apparently, Judy and Rose didn't hold his substance abuse issues against him."

"Well," Lexie began, "to be fair, there'd just been an incident that frightened the entire family."

"What happened, Lexie?" Rip asked.

"An intruder was sneaking around Lillian's house, peeking through her windows while she was inside. Fortunately, he was scared away when a neighbor's dog began barking, or God knows what might have happened."

"My partner and I responded to Lillian's 9-1-1 call that night," Wyatt broke in. "We couldn't track down the alleged intruder and encouraged her to have cameras installed around the exterior of her home."

"Did she?" I asked.

"No. Unfortunately, it looks as though she asked Mickey to move back in with her instead," Wyatt said.

"Why was that unfortunate?" I had to wonder if the detective felt Mickey was responsible for his mom's death when he shook his head in response. He finally elaborated on his choice of words. "I just feel like she might still be alive today had she had a security system."

I was still pondering his remarks when Wendy said, "I'm not sure it would've made any difference, Wyatt. If someone was determined to harm her, nothing would've stopped them. Besides, I thought Lillian's accident was just that—an accident!"

"Yeah," Wyatt said, "I'm sure you're right."

Wendy nodded, and replied, "Not only did I have to notify her family of her death—thanks to you, Wyatt, for declining to do it—I also performed the autopsy on Lillian. It was extremely gruesome."

"I know. Thank you for handling the next-of-kin notifications, by the way. I was just too emotionally involved, Wendy. I was the first responder to arrive on the scene of the fatal accident and found her mutilated body lying face down on I-29. Her corpse was nearly unrecognizable."

"Don't I know," Wendy said in agreement.

Wyatt met Wendy's eyes and gave her a warm smile before continuing. "So, as I was saying, if there actually was an intruder, he was long gone by the time we arrived and we were unable to apprehend him. We suggested to her it might have just been her imagination, but she was adamant that someone was on her porch, peering through the glass in her front door. Lillian said she was too far away to make out his features but was nearly positive it was a relatively short, older man. The next thing she knew he was looking through a window in her dining room when the neighbor's dog began to bark. I think knowing this Peeping Tom, as she referred to him, was still in the wind made Lillian even more apprehensive about living alone."

"It did," Lexie said. She obviously already knew what Wyatt had just related to the rest of us. She continued with her story. "She told me as much, and I would've felt the same way. Because of that close call, Lillian's daughters felt comforted their mom would have a man in the house to look after her. I think they actually encouraged her to ask Mickey to move in with her. I'm sure they thought it was a win-win situation for both Lillian and their half-brother, who was bouncing from one friend's house to the next, never staying too long in one spot."

"It sounds like it was the perfect solution. Too bad she was killed in a car accident." *If it was an accident,* I thought. *Wyatt appears to have some doubt about it.* I turned to Lexie, and asked, "How are her daughters handling the loss of their mother?"

"I don't really know. I saw them both at Lillian's memorial service, but not since. Naturally, at the funeral both girls were beside themselves with grief. Rose has never been married. If not for the fact she'd been involved with a guy named Rowdy Noble for a number of years, I think she would've moved back to Rockdale to take care of her mother. Lillian talked about Rose and Rowdy the last time I chatted with her. She said Rose was over the moon about the dude, claiming she'd finally found the love of her life."

"How'd Lillian feel about this Rowdy guy?" I somehow knew the information would be important to me in the future.

"Lillian didn't seem happy about the relationship but I got the impression her distaste for Rose's boyfriend was based more on his first name than anything else. Lillian said his last name of Noble could not have been any less fitting."

"I'm sure Rowdy was just a nickname from his youth that stuck, like with Rip," I said in the boyfriend's defense. "As you all know, Clyde is his given name, but when all the kids in grade school began calling him Rip, he was just as happy to let it ride. He was relieved the moniker stuck, having never liked his real name."

"I was named after my great-grandfather," Rip explained. "I always associated the name Clyde with an old man I barely knew who was in his eighties when I was born. I met my namesake exactly two times; on the first occasion he totally ignored me, and the last time I saw him he told me he'd stuff a greasy old burlap bag in my mouth and a fireplace poker in my new puppy if we didn't quiet down and sit still. He said, 'dogs, like children, should be seen and not heard.' I was seven at the time. He died when I was ten and I didn't bat an eye at his passing."

"Good grief! No wonder you didn't like your given name," Wendy said, as she rubbed her belly. The expression on her face indicated the baby was treating her internal organs like soccer balls.

"So what caused Lillian Sparrow's accident?" I asked, looking straight at Wendy. Her earlier comment about the autopsy being gruesome had piqued my curiosity, and the fact Wyatt found the deceased lying dead on the interstate had made me even more inquisitive.

"I don't think it was ever determined for sure what caused it, but Lillian's car plowed straight into a bridge abutment." Wendy's face paled as she spoke, as if the memory had made her nauseous. "According to the police report, there were no skid marks, which indicated she'd never even applied the brakes. It was almost as if the crash was deliberate. I suppose it's possible she passed out, or something, even though I found nothing during the autopsy that would cause her to lose consciousness."

"Oh, no!" I put my hands on my cheeks in horror at the image Wendy's words painted in my mind.

"It gets worse," Wyatt assured me. "Mrs. Sparrow was ejected through the windshield of her Volvo. Her body came to rest in the middle of I-29 where a bus containing prisoners from a chain gang out of the state prison in Lansing ran right over the top of her. Thankfully, Wendy determined she was dead on impact with the pavement and didn't feel a thing. Originally, it was assumed she fell asleep or was distracted by her phone. As of yesterday, however, Mrs. Sparrow's death has been reclassified as a probable suicide."

"What?" Lexie exclaimed. "Why didn't you tell me about that, Wyatt?"

"Because I knew the news would distress you."

"Yes, it would've upset me to know my friend might've killed herself in such a horrible manner, but I'd still have wanted to know. Has Mickey been notified of the updated classification?"

"As her next-of-kin, he was informed of the update yesterday, this time by the sheriff. The reclassification hasn't been released yet to the general public though," Wyatt replied. "Mickey was insistent his mother would never have taken her own life."

"I don't believe it either, Wyatt," Lexie said. "Lillian told me she'd received a very generous offer to purchase her property but turned it down because of her disabled son. She was determined to help Mickey defeat his demons. She felt as if he was making progress the last time we spoke. Obviously, any progress he might've made is down the toilet now. But as long as Mickey was living with her, Lillian felt needed and as if she had a purpose. No way would she've left him to fend for himself."

"Mickey said nearly the exact same thing," Wyatt remarked. "Then the detectives told him they'd discovered his mother was on depression medication. Apparently, she'd never shared her mental status with her son. I'm sure she felt Mickey had enough to deal with and didn't want him to think her depression could have anything to do with his situation."

"I found traces of an antidepressant in her system," Wendy said in clarification. "Naturally, all findings have to be notated in my report."

"Why didn't you tell me about the results of the autopsy you performed on her?" Lexie asked her daughter.

"Because I knew the news would distress you." Wendy repeated Wyatt's reply to nearly the same question her mother had asked the detective.

Lexie let out a long dramatic exhalation in response. "I'm not fragile, you two. You both should have been open and honest with me."

"No, you're not fragile, Mom, but you were already distraught about Lillian's death and neither I nor Wyatt wanted to further upset you."

"And, by the way," Wyatt began with a shake of his head, "Wendy and I should not be releasing this information to anyone, not even to you all. So please keep these details to yourselves."

After everyone agreed to keep mum on the information the detective and medical examiner had shared, Lexie said, "Okay, Wyatt. I understand your concern. You mentioned that Lillian was on an antidepressant medication. So what? Who isn't on depression medicine these days? It doesn't necessarily make her suicidal. I was on Zoloft for a number of years after Chester's death, and I never had any inclination to take my own life. Besides, I had Wendy to raise and look after. I could never have done that to my child. Lillian wouldn't have done that to Mickey either, especially not when he needed her the most."

"I agree, Lexie. I don't believe she committed suicide either." Wyatt shrugged. "The sheriff was only going off what Lillian's former groundskeeper said when he spoke to him on the phone. Narciso Garcia told them his employer had mentioned wishing she was dead on a couple of occasions when he questioned her about why she was so down in the dumps. Garcia said she even threatened to kill herself one day when she was in a really dark state of mind."

"I find that difficult to believe," Lexie stated.

"Why would the gardener have any reason to lie about it?" Wyatt countered.

"I don't know. Even if Lillian said that, I know she would've never carried out that threat." Lexie thought for a second, and asked, "So, Wyatt, why did the sheriff question Mr. Garcia in the first place?"

"Mr. Garcia showed up for work on the afternoon of Tuesday, October twenty-second. It was payday so, according to Garcia, he knocked on Lillian's front door to collect his check. When she didn't respond to the doorbell, he knocked again, louder this time. It was to no avail, so he tried to call her, but she didn't answer the phone either. Her garage was locked up so he couldn't see if her car was parked inside. After a few hours of being unable to contact her, he got concerned and called the police department to request a wellness check on Lillian. The sheriff told him she'd died in a car accident earlier in the day. Mr. Garcia asked if they'd ruled out suicide and explained why he suspected it. The sheriff didn't seriously consider the idea until he read the autopsy report and realized Lillian had been on prescription meds for depression - two different medications, to be exact."

"I still don't believe it." Lexie looked glum, and yet, defiant, as she spoke. I could tell she didn't want to even think about the fact her friend might've intentionally drove her car into a bridge abutment. "And I'm sure Mickey feels the same as I do about it."

"You are correct," Wyatt replied, "but I *do* believe being told yesterday his mother had likely committed suicide could've definitely triggered Mickey's aggressive behavior this morning. His brain injury was fairly severe and he was diagnosed with post traumatic stress disorder. He's been known to react to upsetting situations in a violent manner."

"When was that?" Lexie asked with a hint of anger in her tone.

Wyatt grimaced before responding. I sensed he was debating with himself whether or not to offer an example to his already anxious friend. "After Mickey failed to call in sick or show up for work three days in a row, he lost his job stocking shelves at Pete's Pantry. In retribution, he slashed all four of the tires on Pete's Dodge Caravan. He hasn't been able to land a job since, as far as I know. Pete was sympathetic to Mickey's struggles with PTSD, but he had no choice but to let him go."

"I understand," Lexie replied solemnly with her eyes fixed on her entwined hands which were resting on her lap.

Andy spoke up for the first time in a long while. "In a small town like Rockdale, it doesn't take long for news to get around. I'm sure his reputation of being unpredictable and having a hair-trigger temper is not going to make folks stand in line to hire him on as an employee."

"Poor guy; it seems as though he's had a hard go of it his entire life," Wendy murmured. I agreed wholeheartedly with her remark.

Andy exchanged a glance with his wife and they seemed to reach an unspoken agreement. After Wendy nodded at him, Andy said, "We could use a hand on the ranch. If the guy would admit himself into a rehab facility and get some psychological counseling, we'd be willing to give him a chance to redeem himself and get his life back on track. With a little one on the way, Wendy's going to need my help taking care of him—"

"Andy!" Wendy shouted as everyone in the room gasped at the revelation.

"Oh, damn!" Andy responded. He glanced at Wendy in dismay. "I'm so sorry, honey."

"No worries." Wendy was petting the calico kitten curled up beside her. Trouble looked up at Wendy and hissed after her next remark. "I actually thought it'd be me who'd accidentally let the cat out of the bag."

Andy hugged his wife, causing Trouble to jump on top of the coffee table and swat at something only visible to her. Andy then whispered something in Wendy's ear. She giggled and said, "Well, as you all know, it was supposed to be a surprise. But, I have to admit it was becoming a really difficult secret to keep. I've wanted so badly to tell you all that Andy and I are having a son."

The room erupted in congratulatory exclamations. Hugs and kisses were exchanged with the happy couple. The tears running down Lexie's cheeks made my eyes mist over, as well. I had to laugh when Wendy said, "Mom, now you can quit trying to trick me into revealing the gender of your first grandbaby every chance you get."

We all laughed, and then snickered even harder when Andy said, "Oh, I thought it was just me she was doing that to because—"

"Because she knew you were the weak link in this secret-keeping chain?" Wendy finished for him.

"Exactly!" Speaking to all of us, Andy added, "When Lexie was planning Wendy's baby shower, she told me that along with the crib Stone was making for the baby, she wanted to get some sheets to complete the present. She asked me what color I thought she should purchase. I told her a green or yellow would work well, and she replied, 'You don't think it'd be better if her crib looked more feminine?"

When the laughter had calmed down, I asked, "Have you thought about a name yet?"

"Well, um," Wendy was obviously hesitant to reveal the baby's name. After a moment of consideration, she said, "Oh, what the heck! You already know it's a boy so I might as well tell you his name, as well. We're naming him Chester Sterling after both of our fathers. Since Chester sounds a little old-fashioned, we're going to call him Chet."

I loved the name, and it was obvious everyone else did too. The hoopla intensified as we all soaked in the information. Lexie's eyes filled with tears once again. I knew having her grandson named after her first husband meant a great deal to her. More than once, I'd heard her describe Stone as the "second love of my life." Even Stone seemed to appreciate Wendy and Andy's decision. Sterling was his late brother and Stone had once told us the two brothers had always been thick as thieves.

After his dad's death, Andy had become even closer to his Uncle Stone - so much so that he moved to the Midwest to be near Stone and purchased a cattle ranch outside of Atchison, Kansas. He'd given up his job as a pilot in Myrtle Beach to pursue his dream of being a cattle rancher. Now Andy and Wendy both lived on the ranch and even she seemed to love the lifestyle.

Wendy commuted to St. Joseph every day for work, except for right now while she was on medical leave pending the birth of Chet. She'd stopped going into the lab soon after Lillian was killed and planned to have her assistant take her place until Chet was six weeks old. It was about a thirty-minute commute to the autopsy lab, but Wendy didn't seem to mind. The last time Rip and I visited Rockdale, Wendy had told me, "The drive home gives me time to unwind from some of the atrocious things I've seen that day while slicing up cadavers as if they were honey-baked hams. I never want to take my work home with me, and the half-hour commute makes that goal more achievable."

Thinking back to that exchange, I said, "I can only imagine how troubling this case must've been for you, Wendy."

"Some cases, like Lillian's, are more distressing than others," she replied. "But every person I perform an autopsy on is someone's parent, friend, spouse, or loved one, so all are disturbing to some degree."

"No doubt."

Wyatt left to respond to a call about two teenage boys vandalizing a fountain in the local park. The rest of us continued to visit in the parlor. After much discussion about Chet's upcoming arrival, Lexie, Andy, Wendy, and I were discussing how helpful it would be to have a ranch hand at Wendy and Andy's disposal when Lexie's phone buzzed. She stepped into the foyer to take the call so she wouldn't interrupt our conversation. Rip and Stone were discussing something called fish tape, a new artificial bait they wanted to try out. A friend of Stone's owned a boat and had already offered to take the two men out fishing while Rip and I were in town.

When Lexie stepped back into the room a few minutes later, her face was so pale you'd have thought she'd just returned from a two-year stint on the International Space Station. It was immediately apparent the phone call she'd taken was not from a friend asking her if she was going to bring her famous ambrosia salad to the next potluck dinner at their church.

"What's wrong?" Those two words echoed around the room as we all asked her the same question at the exact same time.

"That was Wyatt." She took a moment to catch her breath as we all looked on in rapt attention.

"Was he able to catch the unruly teenagers?" Rip asked.

"Yes," Lexie replied. "But that's not what he called about. It looks as if the new classification of 'Probable Suicide' regarding Lillian's death didn't last long."

"They've been able to ascertain she didn't kill herself?" Stone asked.

"In a matter of speaking, yes they did. They've been able to determine that someone else killed her instead."

"What?" It took a moment for her words to sink in. We all looked on in stunned silence. Wyatt's earlier skepticism about Lillian's death being an accident sprang to mind. I finally asked, "Are you saying her death's now been reclassified as a homicide?"

"That's precisely what I'm saying. Wyatt said they found a note from an anonymous sender that had been taped to the front door of the police station. The note read, 'Do a thorough check of the wreckage from the Lillian Sparrow crash, which will prove she didn't kill herself.' So they did."

"And?" We all asked in stereo again when Lexie paused to collect herself.

"Wyatt said that two of the four brake lines on Lillian's Volvo had been intentionally severed. They were clean cuts by a blade, not from the wear and tear of time and usage. She'd just stopped at the bank and gone inside to get into her safety deposit box. The teller who waited on her told the detectives she'd seemed to be in a very jovial mood." Lexie stopped talking to wipe tears from her eyes and blow her nose.

When she didn't resume talking immediately, I said, "Go on."

"A few minutes later she was on I-29 headed toward St. Joseph when the brakes failed. That's why there were no skid marks. After they discovered the cut brake lines, they went to the bank and found a good-sized stain on the concrete where she'd parked that day as the brake fluid was slowly draining out of the lines. Unfortunately none of the bank's security cameras picked up that area of the parking lot. Although they hadn't had time to check yet, the detectives were confident the lines were cut before she left her residence that morning."

After speaking, Lexie flopped into a chair as if she'd just finished a marathon. She appeared exhausted, and like the Volvo's brake fluid, completely drained. She pulled the used tissue out of her jeans pocket and blew her nose again.

"Are there any suspects?" Rip asked gently.

"Not yet, according to Wyatt."

I was pretty sure everyone in the room was thinking the same thing I was when there was a long moment of silence. I decided to say it out loud. "How do you reckon Mickey's going to react to this new classification? If he freaked out when they said his mom had likely committed suicide, how do you think he'll feel when he discovers she was the victim of murder?"

"I don't even want to think about it," Lexie said. "This news could push the poor guy completely over the edge. I was convinced Lillian would never have killed herself, but her son is a different story altogether. He's most definitely a suicide risk. Someone he trusts who sincerely cares for him needs to be the one to tell him, not the sheriff or a homicide detective."

"You might be right," Stone said.

"I know I'm right. I know him better than most people because I was a close friend of his mother's and interacted with Mickey on many occasions. I asked Wyatt if they'd let me notify him rather than the police department. He told me he didn't know if the sheriff would approve my request, but they couldn't say anything if I acci-dentally ran into Mickey before they did," Lexie explained using air quotes to emphasize Wyatt's use of the word 'accidentally.' "The sheriff told Wyatt they were going to bring Mickey in on Monday morning and notify him then. Wyatt was relatively sure they will then interrogate him as a prime suspect in his mother's death."

"That's all the boy needs," I said earnestly. "That could well be the final straw in Mickey's will to live."

"Yes, it could." Lexie's voice broke as she spoke. "It's Saturday, so that gives us tomorrow to hunt down Mickey and break the news to him in a more compassionate manner than the homicide detectives are likely to do if they consider him a suspect."

It was clear Mickey Scott had been through a lot in his young life. Despite the fact he'd slashed both the tire and my husband's arm and ruined a perfectly good dress shirt in the process, I felt sorry for the guy. Rip, not so much. His distrust was evident when he said, "I can understand why they might think it could've been Mickey who cut the brake lines on his mother's car. He's proven to be very handy with a knife and seems to enjoy slashing tires." He held up his newly bandaged arm as he spoke. I thought Rip was being cold-hearted, but I knew I tended to assess situations with my heart while he reviewed them with his head, due mostly to his experience in law enforcement. I didn't comment because I didn't want to butt heads with my husband, who'd been attacked by the man in question just a few hours earlier. Not to mention, I felt certain Lexie would put her two cents in. My instinct was correct.

"I can't imagine he'd do something like that to his mother. He adored her. He might've been a bit volatile since returning from the war with his severe brain injury, but he never impressed me as being mean-spirited, or in this case, pure evil. I believe his attack on you earlier was just a one-time anomaly. I realize he suffers with PTSD as well as the physical injuries he sustained, but Lillian's been his rock since he returned from the war. She's whom he always turned to when he needed to find peace and balance."

"That may be, but he's also afflicted with an addiction now. Addicts have been known to throw their own mothers under the bus to get their next fix." When Rip noticed the expression on Lexie's face, he remembered how her friend had died. "I'm sorry. I didn't mean that literally. It's just that during a long career in law enforcement, I've seen the hold drugs can have on people. Some will do about just about anything that would enable them to acquire drugs."

Lexie paled. "Oh, dear. I know what you're saying is true, Rip. I just pray that wasn't the case this time. Mickey was really a good kid growing up. He was interested in performing magic and before the Covid-19 restrictions he would occasionally go to the VA Hospital in Leavenworth and do tricks for patients there, just to cheer them up."

"That was very admirable of the young man," I said.

Lexie nodded in agreement. "Lillian told me he was a better-than-average student with a 3.2 grade point average, and he was a baseball star in high school. He was highly recruited by several colleges as a top-notch pitcher with a ninety-five mile-per-hour fast-ball but he was dead set on joining the military instead. He also ran track and still holds the school record for the 100-yard dash and the 440."

"He did skedaddle awfully fast out of that rest area," I said in concurrence. "Even with that bum leg."

"Having a gun pointed at him might've had something to do with that," Rip joked.

I didn't laugh. Neither did Lexie. I thought about how I'd originally chided Rip for not shooting at the thug who'd slashed his arm, even if it had only been a warning shot. "I'm really glad now you didn't use your gun to stop him. It sounds like Mickey just needs some help and guidance. Finding justice for his mother would be a big help to his psyche too."

"I agree," Lexie said. The look of sorrow was gone from her face now, and one of determination had taken its place. "Mickey needs rehabilitation and emotional support to get his life back on track. I hope it works out that he can work as a ranch hand on the kids' property. I still can't imagine he'd harm his mother in any way."

"I sincerely hope you're right," Rip said.

I'd originally wanted the dude to be caught, then tarred and feathered for his attack on my husband, but I'd had a change of heart. Now I wanted his mother's killer apprehended and arrested. Lillian deserved justice, and it might bring Mickey at least a little bit of closure. And maybe, as Lexie mentioned, he could find help for his destructive instincts and addictions. The guy had earned a stable, safe, and satisfying life, for his service to our country if nothing else.

As you may realize by now, me wanting a killer brought to justice is never a good thing. I prayed Mickey had no part in his mother's death and that the individual who *did* cut Lillian's brake lines would be identified quickly. I also prayed I wouldn't feel obligated to stick my nose into another murder case. The one we'd just recently gotten into the middle of in Albuquerque was still fresh in my mind, and I hadn't come to terms with the results of it yet. Rip would balk at my interference and the last thing I needed was to get involved in a case I had no business being involved in while quarrelling with my husband for doing so. I should've known my fellow sleuth, Lexie Starr, would have other ideas.

FOUR

I wasn't surprised when the detective returned to the inn after his phone call to Lexie. Wyatt surely sensed how his news had affected her. After giving her a warm hug, he said, "Once Mickey is located, I'm going to suggest he turn himself in at the police station. If he doesn't agree, I'll arrest him and haul him to jail myself."

"What?" Lexie exclaimed, shoving Wyatt away from her. You'd have thought the detective said he'd immerse Mickey's head in a vat of liquid nitrogen and count to ten. Lexie glared at Wyatt. "What on Earth are you talking about?"

"No matter what happened to his mother, it doesn't give Mickey a legal right to attack an innocent person at a rest area, probably with the intent to commit armed robbery. I need to file a report and charge Mickey with assault and battery against Rip."

"No, wait," I replied. Lexie had shot me a pleading look. I knew what she was thinking. And I, too, felt the compassion she was clearly feeling.

"I don't think that's necessary at this juncture." Rip spoke before I could continue, nodding at Lexie before turning to the detective. He'd accurately read her expression too. "Mikey has enough to deal with at the moment without getting him into legal trouble over this little scratch on my arm."

"His name is actually Mickey, Rip, not Mikey," Wendy reminded him. She appeared less amused this time.

Welcome to my world, young lady, I wanted to say, but Wendy was still talking. "Like I said before, it's hardly a scratch. And it could've been much more serious. But I agree we shouldn't pile on the guy right now. The young man needs help, not a rap sheet that'll follow him around the rest of his life."

Andy and Stone nodded their consent. Wyatt shrugged. He looked at Rip and said, "Well, the decision's not mine to make. It's totally up to you and Rapella."

"Let's just drop it for now," Rip said. "Is there any way you could sit the boy down and have a talk with him, Wyatt? Mickey needs to know help is available and it would be in his best interest to seek assistance. Maybe we could make it conditional; we won't file charges as long as he gets some counseling."

"Or better yet," I interjected, "he admits himself into a rehabilitation facility."

"That's a great idea!" Lexie exclaimed. We all nodded in accord.

"And, like I said before," Andy added, "a successful stint in rehab is also a requirement for the ranch hand position we're offering him."

"Of course," Lexie replied. "But, Wyatt, if it's okay with you, I think it'd be better if we didn't drag the law into it at all. It may trigger more irrational behavior on his part. Mickey knows and trusts me, and I know he wouldn't hurt me. How about if I go out to the rest area and try to rustle him up? I'll let him know his mom's death has been ruled a homicide, and then tell him about the conditional offer to not file charges for the assault on Rip in exchange for him seeking help for his mental instability and addiction issues. I think it would yield better results than if he was approached by a cop."

"I would be happy to accompany you." I glanced at Rip, who suddenly had no visible irises because his eyeballs were rolled back so far in his head. "After all, it would be Rip and me offering him the 'get out of jail free card' option."

Lexie smiled at me and then turned to Rip. "Don't worry. Rapella will be in no danger as long as I'm with her."

"That's right," I said with a nod. I was impressed Lexie could say such a thing with a straight face. Even I knew investigating a murder with Lexie was inherently fraught with peril. Impending danger was a premonition I just couldn't shake as hard as I tried.

When Rip didn't immediately respond, Stone reached out and patted his buddy on the back. "I'm with the ladies on this one. I know the young man personally, as well, and am confident he wouldn't do anything to injure Lexie or Rapella. I think his behavior this morning was totally out of character for him. He's not normally a violent guy."

You mean other than slashing our tire and attacking Rip with a deadly weapon after slashing the tires on a former employer's car with the same knife most likely? I could've asked had I not wanted to adversely affect Rip's agreement to let me accompany Lexie on her mission.

Wyatt agreed, and Rip nodded. "All right, but I want you to take your pepper spray with you, Rapella. Okay?"

"Yes, of course, Rip." We'd purchased the pepper spray to use as a deterrent against bears during a trip we'd made to Buffalo, Wyoming, the previous year. I assumed it was still functional. The sales clerk had told me a can of it was usually good for two years. I felt more comfortable knowing we'd have some form of protection with us because I didn't quite trust Mickey as much as Lexie apparently did. I then made a comment I regretted making the second my lips stopped flapping. "Mickey might be able to give us some clue as to who might've wanted to harm his mother, or kill her, as it turned out."

"Oh, yes," Lexie said softly. "I'm anxious to talk with him about—"

"No!" Everyone else in the room shouted in complete harmony.

The single word reverberated around the parlor as if it'd been broadcast through a megaphone and was followed by a chorus of comments on the order of "You two are not going to get involved in Lillian's death!"

Wyatt summed up the unanimous opinion of the group with, "Let's leave the investigation to the homicide detectives. I don't want you and Lexie putting your necks on the line."

"Again!" Wyatt, Stone, Wendy, and Rip added, again in stereo. Only Andy had the decency to remain mum. Of course, that could've been because Trouble had her tiny but razor-sharp claws buried in his ankle at the time.

"Do you two remember what happened the last time you were here, Rapella?" Wyatt asked. I did remember and I wanted to remind the detective how it'd been because of Lexie and me that the truth behind the situation had been brought to light. But I instinctively knew it wouldn't be in my best interest to argue with the detective. I remained silent, even when he added, "So you two need to stay out of this murder case. That's why some of your tax dollars are spent on paying folks like me. Okay?"

Lexie nodded at Wyatt and then shot me a look that spoke volumes. She was even more single-minded than me when it came to determining who killed someone she cared about. Her easy-to-decipher expression made the hair on my arms stand on end because I knew I couldn't bail on her. She would've never opted out if it was my friend who'd been murdered. I gave her a barely detectable nod and she smiled in return. I knew the nod she'd given Wyatt after his last question was not meant as a solemn vow, but rather as a way to end the conversation before he demanded a promise from the two of us.

Wyatt left to return to duty once again after we'd come to a decision on how to handle the assault situation. Wendy and Andy left soon afterward. With the arrival of their baby looming, Wendy tired easily and said she needed to get home and put her feet up "before they swell up like a road-killed possum."

The last two hours had been an emotional roller-coaster from happiness and exultation, to tears and sadness, to laughter and delight, before starting the ride over again. I was exhausted from having my mood go up and down like the tide. With just Stone, Lexie, Rip and me left in the parlor, the conversation shifted to a less volatile subject as we discussed our current health statuses, recent maladies, and overall health concerns, as older folks often do. Stone had an ingrown toenail that was bothering him and his dermatologist had removed a suspicious mole on his back that, according to the pathology report, was not malignant. Lexie had recently been diagnosed with acid reflux, and now both she and her husband were taking the same popular heartburn medication. Rip blathered on about a routine nuclear stress test his cardiologist had performed to ensure the three arteries he'd had bypassed were still functioning as expected. The entire exchange about health woes was nearly as benign as Stone's mole and it gave my nerves a chance to settle down.

When there was a lull in the conversation, Rip and I excused ourselves to get settled in the Caboose. Dolly would be pissed off enough already that her afternoon snack was not served on time. There's nothing worse than a disgruntled cat that thought the sun rose and set on her two best friends. And before you think I'm referring to Rip and me, who have always put her on a pedestal, we're only the servants who dish up her BFF's, Kit and Kaboodle.

"Dinner is at six this evening," Lexie informed us as we stood up to depart.

"You don't need to wait on us like we're Ben Affleck and Jennifer Lopez," I said. "Or treat us like paying customers, for that matter. We have some leftover barbecue chicken from last night's supper in the fridge. That will suit us just fine."

"First of all, I wouldn't pander to Bennifer just because they're celebrities, unless they were guests of the inn, of course, and secondly, the chicken will also suit you for lunch tomorrow." Lexie made it clear she wouldn't take "no" for an answer. "I'm slow-cooking a large enough roast to feed an army, and the last time I looked there was no army staying in the inn right now. In fact, we only have two guests and they have plans to dine with family members at the Hoof and Horn steakhouse in St. Joseph tonight. I also prepared Rip's favorite dessert: strawberry shortcake with delicious fresh strawberries and pound cake. So, get some rest and we'll see you at six."

"Yes, ma'am," Rip said quickly. I knew he didn't want me to have an opportunity to object again. He was a pushover when it came to strawberry shortcake. He asked Lexie, "With whipped cream on top?"

"Of course, Rip! Have I ever let you down?" Lexie laughed. "I've made homemade whipped cream, in fact!"

I could see our cholesterol levels shooting up like an outdoor thermometer on Independence Day in south Texas. Good thing we didn't have appointments with our primary physician any time soon. Dr. Herron, who worked us in whenever we were back home in Rockport, could be absolutely terrifying when our lab work made it apparent we weren't following her orders the way we should be. She was the only woman I'd ever known who could make Rip, dressed only in a paper gown and stocking feet, cower like a scolded puppy.

I gave Lexie another hug and stepped outside onto the front porch of the beautifully restored Victorian mansion. I gripped Rip's good arm, the one without bandaging, for support as we followed a cobblestone pathway around the building to where our trailer was parked.

Rip had pulled the Caboose into the very first RV site, and an ultra-fancy motor coach was parked in the fourth site which was the furthest one from the inn. I had to fight back the green-eyed monster inside me as I wondered who owned the fancy-pants RV with no less than four slide-outs. Even the rear-end of the motorhome slid out, making the forty-foot unit even two feet longer. *I bet it has a washer/dryer combo and a built-in fireplace*, I thought. *The high-falutin' owner must have won the lottery or be operating a fraudulent vehicle warranty phone scam.*

———

The weather in western Missouri could not have been any more ideal than it was that day. To enjoy the mild temperature, Rip and I decided to lounge outside under the awning later on in the afternoon. We hauled the chairs around with us in one of the undercarriage storage compartments of the Caboose. We were drinking the once-a-day alcoholic beverages Dr. Herron allowed us and talking about how exciting it was to find out Wendy and Andy were expecting a son. I knew they would've been just as content with a daughter and neither Stone nor Lexie had any preference on which gender their first grandchild turned out to be. But it was still fun to find out, even if it it'd been an accidental slip of the tongue on Andy's part.

"It's nice they're going to honor both of their fathers by naming the boy Chester Sterling. I love the nickname Chet too." I would repeat the upcoming arrival's name numerous times in the next few days in hopes Rip wouldn't refer to the baby as something like Chandler Stanley, or worse yet, Chip, in front of the baby's parents and grandparents.

I took a long draw of my cold drink and wiped condensation off the bottom of the quart canning jar with my shirt sleeve. I always served our drinks in the large jars because Dr. Herron had limited us each to the one drink per day but hadn't mentioned how large those drinks should be. I erred on the side of liking my tequila sunrises a little too much. And, as you can imagine, I got no complaints out of Rip on the size of his Crown and Coke. I could serve his in a fifty-five gallon drum and he'd still down it and ask for a refill he knew would be denied him.

"Sterling's an odd name," Rip mumbled. I wanted to remind him that not every Tom, Dick, and Harry was named Rip either, but he was rubbing the injured arm as if it was aching.

"Like Stone, his dad was a jeweler, and both he and his brother followed in their father's footsteps. The chosen names for the two boys reflected his line of work, as if he and Stone's mother knew from the time of their sons' births they'd grow up and become jewelers, as well."

"Yeah, I suppose. I guess it's better than sticking them with names like Ruby and Opal." Rip chuckled at his remark and continued to rub his arm. "It'd be like Johnny Cash's *A Boy Named Sue*. Have you noticed most gems tend to be feminine sounding?"

"Is your arm bothering you, honey?" I asked, knowing he was just babbling to keep his mind off the throbbing injury.

"It's a little sore, but not too bad. This whiskey will help. It'd feel better yet if I could get a refill just this once."

"Well, all right. But just this once," I conceded even as I wondered if I was being played.

I looked out the kitchen window of the trailer as I refilled Rip's drink, and saw a Lexus pull up and park next to the large motorhome. The coach had a car dolly on the back so I assumed this luxury car was towed on it when the owner was on the road. A tall, well-built gentleman wearing creased jeans and a suit jacket emerged from the car's driver's seat and briefly glanced Rip's way. He'd been alone in the shiny black vehicle. He had thick dark hair and the fedora hat he wore reminded me of the one worn by James Spader in his role as Raymond Reddington on the show *Blacklist*. *Blue Bloods* was still Rip's favorite television series, but *Blacklist* was a close second, and Rip never missed an episode.

"Afternoon," the gentleman said in a southern drawl as he tipped his hat at Rip.

"How ya doing?" I heard Rip say in response as their voices had drifted through the screen door into the living room. The man looked affluent. It may have been my imagination in overdrive, but I felt as if he was looking down his aristocratic but slightly bent nose at the sight of our chartreuse-colored RV. I thought the sunflowers I'd added enhanced the trailer's classy appearance, but Rip felt differently. He'd long since gotten over his embarrassment concerning the unique paint job, however I felt as if it'd given the other man a sense of superiority over him.

I have to give the guy credit. He *was* extremely handsome. Even the crooked nose that looked as if it'd been broken in a bar brawl at one time, or an MMA bout, only seemed to give his face character. He definitely had the muscular build of a cage fighter.

Without replying to Rip, the man unlocked the door of his RV and stepped inside. *Man of few words*, I reasoned.

I exited the trailer and handed Rip his drink. "I saw you met our neighbor."

With a nonchalant shrug, Rip took a sip, responding with a "Yep" as he set his drink down. He wasn't exactly Chatty Cathy either. I settled back into my chair and pulled my iPhone out of my back pocket. I wanted to see if I could find anything on the Internet about the crash that had killed Lillian Sparrow. I was disappointed there wasn't much to be found about the accident I didn't already know. I was surprised I recognized her in the photo accompanying her online obituary, but couldn't place where I'd seen her before. It would eventually dawn on me, I was certain. Things like this usually came to me at three in the morning and woke me from a dead sleep.

That evening, after a delicious supper of roast, garlic mashed potatoes, a tossed salad, and sourdough dinner rolls, we lounged on the front porch of the renovated inn and chatted with Stone and

Lexie. Our hostess asked me if I'd help her dish up dessert about an hour later. I joined her in the kitchen to plate up the strawberry shortcake with a healthy dollop of whipped cream on top. On Rip's plate, Lexie added a second dollop. She winked at me, and said, "I made him a promise."

I realized why she'd asked me to join her in preparing the dessert plates when she said, "Let's plan on leaving for the rest area about nine tomorrow morning."

"Nine sounds good."

"And don't forget to bring the pepper spray. Not that we'll need it to protect ourselves from Mickey, but you never know what might pop up."

"I won't forget. I agree it's better to be safe than sorry."

Little did we know at that time that something *would* pop up and we'd both be very grateful that Rip had suggested we take the pepper spray with us—for a brief moment, anyway!

FIVE

s expected, at two-fifty-four the next morning, according to my alarm clock, it felt as if a grappling hook had grabbed the front of my pajama top and yanked me up into a sitting position. I'd been sound asleep in bed when it hit me where I'd seen Lillian Sparrow before. She had attended Wendy's surprise thirtieth birthday party nearly two years ago, as had Rip and I. Unfortunately, another party guest had been killed during the celebration and we'd become embroiled in the murder case. During our stay at the Alexandria Inn following the surprise party, Wendy and Andy had gotten engaged, which had been exciting for all of us who'd witnessed the proposal.

What I remembered most about Lillian was that she was thin, elegant, and very proper - exceedingly beautiful in an old-fashioned way. She gave the appearance of being aloof, standoffish even, and almost as though she was uncomfortable being out in public. Her nervous manner gave me the impression she'd rather be home vacuuming her carpet. Although she'd been friendly and engaging when I'd made small talk with her, I'd had the feeling she was holding me at arm's length. Her responses to my shallow questions were short, no more than one or two words.

Finally, I'd attempted to break the ice by talking about the beverage I was holding in my hand at the time. "What do you think of Sheila Davison's punch? I tried but I couldn't get her to divulge the ingredients. My guess is there's at least half-a-dozen different types of liquor in it. Have you sampled it yet?" In response, Lillian had picked up a red solo cup off a nearby table, took a sip, and nodded with a condescending smile. It'd made me feel awkward, so I'd kept the exchange light and brief. As soon as it seemed socially acceptable, I proceeded to mingle with guests who were less taxing to converse with.

After being jarred awake by the memory of Lillian, I couldn't get back to sleep. I quietly got out of bed and tip-toed into the living room. Dolly was asleep on the back of the couch but instantly awoke and struggled to get up on all fours when I approached her. She was a chubby kitty, but it was hard not to feed her when she looked at you with her adorable pleading eyes and pouty lips. I knew Rip would indulge her with a full bowl of cat food as soon as he was up and about. I gave Dolly just a few tuna treats to hold her over and turned on the coffee maker.

I felt on edge, like one might feel while sitting in a lavish lobby waiting to get called back for an IRS audit. Usually, the notion of spending time with Lexie made me very happy. But for some reason I couldn't quite put a pin in, the idea of going back to the rest area in an attempt to track down Mickey had me feeling anxious. Considering what had occurred the last time I'd seen the guy, I suppose it wasn't surprising that meeting up with him again had me second-guessing my hasty agreement to join Lexie later that morning.

While the Columbian Supreme dripped into the carafe, I began searching for the can of pepper spray. I recalled placing it in one of our junk drawers, but I didn't remember which one. I don't know what it says about me, but there are only five drawers in the travel trailer's kitchen and two of them are filled with miscellaneous junk. They are the two largest drawers, no less. There was a drawer the length of the bench seats under each side of the kitchen table. If you removed the top of the table, and the center metal pole holding it up, you could lower the tabletop, use the padded seat backs as a mattress, and create a child-sized bed. It was similar to an interactive toy called a transformer.

We had never had an occasion to transform our table into a bed. However, the over-sized drawers were sure handy. I stored everything from extra batteries to bottles of Crown Royal and Jose Cuervo, to Tupperware bowls and lids—none of which matched— to an old Butternut coffee can full of various and sundry keys. One key actually had "VW" engraved on it, clearly belonging to the Volkswagen Beetle I'd owned many years ago. The VW Bug had long since been scrapped and probably recycled into things like the Butternut can its key was now stored in. Not a key in the lot appeared to unlock anything we currently owned, but I couldn't force myself to throw any of them away. In the back of my mind, I feared we'd suddenly find a crucial lock we'd forgotten about and the key to open it was amongst the three or four dozen in the coffee tin. It was totally illogical, but a matter of human nature, I reckoned.

I finally found the pepper spray behind a motion-sensor critter cam I'd picked up at a garage sale in Buffalo, Wyoming. I'd thought it was a frivolous purchase and the waste of a perfectly good twenty-dollar bill until it helped solve the murder of one of the owners of the RV park we were staying in. I'd used it again while investigating a murder in Seattle, Washington, where we'd stayed while Rip underwent a triple bypass and the rehabilitation therapy that followed. No way would I dispose of it now, never knowing when it might come in handy in the future.

With the pepper spray tucked into my purse, I tried to relax by working on a crossword puzzle. When I couldn't come up with a four-letter word for "mundane," I decided to look for something less *dull* to do until Rip arose and was ready for breakfast.

I was looking on Amazon for possible baby gifts for Chet when Lexie knocked on the trailer door at precisely nine. "Ready?"

"Yep," I replied. "So, what's the plan?"

"I don't know his phone number, so once we arrive at the rest area, I'll start calling out for Mickey, letting him know we're on his side and there to help. If that doesn't work, I guess we will just have to comb through the woods behind the restrooms and hope we can locate him. Do you remember the direction in which he ran off after slicing Rip's arm?"

"Of course, but what if we don't find him?" I could sense the "inherently fraught with peril" premonition coming into play.

"Guess we'll just have to cross that bridge when we come to it."

Will that bridge be made of tattered rope and swinging over a pond filled with hungry alligators? I wanted to ask. Instead, I nodded as I fastened my seat belt and settled back into my seat for what would undoubtedly be an adventure.

As we entered the rest area, a man driving a blue Ford F-150 was exiting onto the interstate and a woman was walking back to her white SUV without picking up the pile her mastiff had just left behind in the grass. *Some people should not be allowed to be pet owners,* I thought. *There's a pet waste station dispensing dog poop bags not ten feet from the dog's calling card. How lazy and inconsiderate can one be?*

With only the SUV in the parking lot, Lexie pulled up in front of the building that housed the restrooms, a lobby with area maps displayed behind glass fronts, and adult and kid-sized water fountains. We both used the ladies' room before standing behind the facilities and hollering out for Mickey. By then the tactless dog owner had left the rest area. I let Lexie do most of the yelling because hers was a voice the young man would recognize. We continued to call out for him for fifteen or more minutes, stopping only temporarily when a young family stopped to use the restrooms.

"I'm going to be hoarse if I holler any longer," Lexie said. "Either he isn't here or he's intentionally not responding."

"I guess it's time we begin our hike through the woods." My response sounded hesitant even to my own ears. The thought of meandering about in the woods brought back frightening memories of the time we spent in the Big Horn Mountains of Wyoming while trying to solve the mystery behind the RV park owner's death. Even though I knew the chances of encountering a bear in these particular woods were slim to none, I was hesitant.

"Yeah, I guess so." Lexie sounded even less thrilled about the idea than I had. She took a deep breath and began walking towards the heavily wooded area behind the facilities. I followed directly in her footsteps. If she didn't step on a snake, I most likely wouldn't either. We walked back and forth for at least fifteen minutes before Lexie spoke again. "He may not be camping in these woods after all. It could've been merely a coincidence that he was here when you two stopped to eat lunch. It's possible Mickey just stopped in to use the restroom too."

"You're probably right. Does he own a motorcycle?"

"Yeah, kind of a forlorn-looking bike that he spent much of his time working on in Lillian's driveway."

"That has to be the one he had with him yesterday morning. Maybe we should—"

"Look!" Lexie interrupted me as she stopped and pointed toward something that'd caught her attention. "Isn't that a tent I see?"

I looked in the direction she'd pointed. A small, camouflaged tent made of canvas had been erected next to a tall sycamore tree and blended perfectly into its surroundings. Had Lexie not spotted it, I would have never noticed the tent. On the other side of the tree was a fire pit with barely discernible wisps of smoke emitting from it. "Yes, it's definitely a tent. And considering the fire in the pit hasn't been completely extinguished, the tent's owner must be nearby. How reckless would it be to leave and not put the campfire out?"

Lexie gave me a look. I instantly felt a little silly for assuming whoever called the tent home would be conscientious about something of that nature. In my defense, I said, "Well, you wouldn't think Mickey, or whoever owns that tent, would want to burn down these woods if it's the only place he has to call home."

"That's true." Lexie shook her head. "If it *is* Mickey, I have to wonder why he doesn't just stay in his mom's house."

"I reckon that's something we should ask him when we locate him."

Lexie agreed. We approached the area tentatively. When we were within ten feet of the tent, we heard a rustling sound.

Please let the noise be coming from Mickey and not someone who makes Mickey look like a pillar of society, I prayed.

"Mickey? Is that you?" Lexie asked. "It's Lexie. Lexie Starr. Is anyone inside the tent?"

When her inquiry was met with silence, she repeated herself. There were more rustling noises, but no verbal response. Lexie motioned for me to follow her as she walked toward the zipped-up canvas structure and reached for the zipper. I was reluctant, knowing someone was obviously inside the tent, but not responding. I thought again it could very well be someone beside Mickey. And if it *was* Mickey, he clearly didn't want to be disturbed. After hesitating a moment, I followed in Lexie's footsteps like a snow goose following the flock's leader as they migrated north in the spring.

I watched as Lexie opened the tent flaps and peered inside. "Mickey's bike's in here but he's not. It's definitely his tent though."

She let loose of the flap then walked around to the other side of the tent.

"Bear spray! Bear spray!" Lexie shouted. I'd convinced myself the odds of confronting a bear in northwestern Missouri were infinitesimal, but the sheer terror in her voice made my blood run cold. She continued to shriek as I clawed at my clothes trying to recall where I'd stuck the can of spray. I located the can in my purse just as she hollered, "Hurry!"

I handed her the can and stepped around the tent. I was scared spitless, but I wasn't going to let my friend face her attacker alone. I was shocked to find her in the midst of a staring contest with a large bobcat. Unlike bears, the medium-sized cats, also referred to as red lynx, were extremely prevalent in the area.

The menacing-looking creature began snarling ferociously from about ten feet away. The bobcat appeared to be ready to pounce at any second. Lexie pointed the pepper spray at the animal's face and pulled the trigger. Nothing came out. She tried again. Nothing. Nada. Zip. Not a frigging drop squirted out of the useless canister of spray I'd paid good money for at the Wyoming campground. In desperation, Lexie threw the small container at the bobcat and missed it to the left by at least two feet.

The bobcat apparently took the black object whizzing by its ear personally and moved several yards closer to us. I knew we were in deep doo-doo when two kits skittered from behind a tree to follow their mama. One looked woozy, like it'd just been beaned in the head by an empty aerosol can.

It's the innate nature of any mother to defend her offspring and I knew this mama bobcat was no exception. As the twin kits engaged in horseplay, swatting at each other and rolling around in the dirt, their mother advanced on us even further with her fangs bared. The animal was within spitting distance when Lexie asked, "Should we attempt to outrun her, or at least try to get into the tent?"

"I don't know about you, dear," I said in a trembling voice. "But

I'm seventy-one. I haven't been able to outrun a bobcat since . . . well, *ever*!"

"Don't move!" A voice hollered from behind us. "You don't want to look like prey."

Just then I heard something zip by my head. It was a large, round rock that struck the bobcat squarely between the eyes. The animal let out an eerie yelping sound and quickly retreated into the woods, followed closely by its offspring. I was glad the bobcat was just stunned and not severely wounded, but I'd never been so relieved to see something disappear in my life, except maybe for the funnel cloud that had formed right above my brother's house a few years back when we were visiting him in Edmund, Oklahoma.

I turned around to see the guy I now knew to be Mickey Scott. He appeared even scrawnier and filthier than he had the previous day. Even though he was around six feet tall, his jeans and shirt hung on him as though they were two sizes two large. It was obvious he'd recently lost a lot of weight. Both he and the clothing were in dire need of being introduced to some soap. His wild red hair looked as if it hadn't been combed in days and what was left of a cigarette clung to his lips. I'd once wanted the dude dead. Now I wanted to kiss him for keeping me and my friend from being injured, or worse, from a possibly lethal attack by the protective feline. I recalled Lexie saying he was a high school standout as a baseball pitcher, and I was thankful he hadn't lost his touch.

"Oh, thank God!" Lexie exclaimed. "I'm so glad to see you, Mickey! You showed up just in the nick of time. Is this your tent?"

"Yeah." There was no inflection in Mickey's voice. He clearly wasn't terribly keen about his current living conditions. Perhaps he was humiliated to have Lexie discover he was residing in a canvas tent, as well. After all, Lexie was staring at him in obvious repulsion.

"Didn't you hear me hollering out your name?" She asked.

"How could I not?" He replied sarcastically. "I'm sure half the county heard you."

"Then why didn't you respond?" Lexie sounded more hurt than annoyed. "We only came out here because we want to help you."

"I don't want any help and I don't need any either. How'd you even know where to find me?"

"The Ripples told us where you were yesterday and likely today, as well," she replied.

"Who the hell are the Ripples?" Mickey spit out what was left of his cigarette. It had burned down to the filter. He ground the butt into the dirt with the heel of his right boot. Mickey was scrutinizing me as if trying to recall where he'd seen me before. He turned back to Lexie, and asked, "Who's your friend?"

"This is Rapella Ripple, Mickey." Lexie spoke tentatively, as if afraid of setting Mickey off. But she didn't mince any words when she added, "It was her husband you sliced with a knife yesterday in the rest area's parking lot."

Mickey immediately hung his head, clearly ashamed of his actions. "I'm sorry. I didn't really mean to hurt anyone, but I was in dire need of a fix and I didn't have enough money to score a rock."

"A rock?" Lexie asked.

"Crystal meth," he simply replied. "It looks like a rock, and—"

"Hence the name, I assume?" Lexie asked.

"Yeah."

"And how about now, Mickey? Are Rapella and I also in danger of being victimized by you?"

"No, of course not. I would never hurt you, Lexie. You've been too good to me. Besides, I'm okay today. I took the bike back to ma's house yesterday afternoon, got a diamond ring out of her jewelry box and hocked it."

"I can't believe you'd do that, Mickey," Lexie looked and sounded disappointed.

Mickey shrugged. "Hey, you knew I was an addict. Losing my ma didn't change that. In fact, it made it worse. I'd been sober for almost two months before she died. Losing Ma caused me to have a relapse. Then yesterday I discovered she'd been murdered and—"

"You've already heard they've reclassified your ma's death as a homicide?" Lexie interrupted him, stunned by his statement.

"I'm the one who figured it out yesterday morning and left a note at the police station. I told them to examine Ma's Volvo for signs of sabotage as I had just done at the salvage lot they'd towed it to."

It dawned on both of us then that it'd been the victim's son who'd first discovered the severed brake lines on his mother's Volvo. He'd resisted the idea she'd take her own life and had been on a mission to prove it. I admired his resolve. When asked by Lexie if he had any idea about who might've wanted his mother dead, he shook his head and said, "I can't imagine anyone who'd want to harm Ma in any way, much less kill her."

"Me neither," Lexie said. She slipped an arm over his shoulder when his eyes filled with tears. Hers immediately followed suit. "But, Mickey, you have to know her murder doesn't give you the right to exact revenge on an innocent bystander who had nothing to do with your ma's death."

"It wasn't an act of revenge. I just badly needed a fix and had about thirty-seven cents to my name. I was hoping the old dude had a few bucks in his wallet I could scare him out of."

His callousness ticked me off and I tore into him. "That old dude is my husband and it'd take a lot more of a man than you to 'scare him out of' whatever he had in his wallet."

"I'm sorry." Mickey looked away, unwilling to face me. "I didn't mean to be rude."

We both remained quiet after Mickey spoke. He seemed to take our silence as a sign of disappointment or maybe condemnation. When the silence became deafening, I asked, "You do realize you could've killed my husband, don't you?"

"I'm sorry," Mickey repeated. "I really didn't mean to hurt him. I just wasn't in my right mind at the time. You ladies have no idea what I've been through. You'd never be able to understand why I am the way I am or how it feels to crave a fix so desperately you would claw your eyeballs out and sell them if it would help you achieve that goal."

More silence ensued. Neither Lexie nor I could come up with a response. A sense of foreboding enveloped me like hot, humid air would when stepping out of an air-conditioned building near the Florida Everglades.

"Maybe not," Lexie finally said. "But there are folks out there who *would* understand. They'd be able to help you turn your life around before it's too late."

"I told you I don't want any help."

"Whether you want it or not, you desperately need it." Lexie shook her head in sadness. "This is certainly not the kind of life your mother would have wanted for you. Do it for her memory if you won't do it for yourself."

"I'm really not proud of anything I've done in the last couple of weeks." He glanced at each of us in succession and then quickly averted his gaze. I sensed he was mulling over what Lexie had said about his mother wanting better for him, and *from* him, no doubt. "I'm sorry for what I did yesterday. I'd just figured out Ma had been intentionally murdered and wasn't handling it very well."

"We understand that," Lexie said in a soothing tone. "The news upset us, as well. We want to make sure she gets the justice she deserves."

Mickey's face brightened at Lexie's remarks. "Thanks. I want that too. Ma didn't deserve what happened to her."

"No, she didn't," Lexie replied.

Mickey turned toward me but didn't make eye contact. He stared at my ever-expanding waistline as he said, "I hope your husband isn't too seriously injured. As soon as my ma's house is sold, I'll pay you back for his shirt, the ruined tire, and any medical bills."

"There were no medical bills. Wendy bandaged him up and Rip refused to go to the hospital for stitches, because he's stubborn as an old mule. And the shirt is of no consequence. I probably paid a quarter for it at the Good Will store, if I wasn't able to negotiate the clerk down to a dime." Lexie was snickering and Mickey was now looking me in the eye with amusement. The amusement on Mickey's face faded like a poolside umbrella when I continued. "But I do expect to be reimbursed for the tire. It only had a few thousand miles on it. And, by the way, what you did to Rip is considered a felony - assault with a deadly weapon. You could do some serious time for a crime like that."

"I know," Mickey replied. He appeared resigned to his fate as he added, "And I'm ready to go with you to the police station to turn myself in. I'm sure they'll want to question me about the note I left anyway. If they haven't already figured out I'm the one who discovered the severed brake lines, they will sooner or later. I might as well be the one to tell them."

"Yes, you should be," I said. "I'm sure they will want to question you, but that's just standard homicide protocol. Murder's often committed by a family member of the victim, but that doesn't mean they believe you had anything to do with her death. They'll be curious as to why you decided to study the mangled vehicle. I have to wonder why they didn't discover the evidence of sabotage themselves."

"My point exactly!" Mickey exclaimed. "Why didn't they? Seems like pretty sloppy police work to me."

It did to me too, but I didn't want to denigrate the department Detective Johnston worked for. To change the subject, I said, "Rip and I are prepared to make a deal with you regarding your assault on him in the parking lot yesterday."

"Oh, yeah? And what would that be?" I hadn't even spelled out the details and he already looked as if he'd rather have fought off the bobcat with his bare hands than agree to any deal I had to offer. This didn't go unnoticed by Lexie either. She stepped in then to appeal to him.

"Mickey, you have way too much going for you to continue going down the rabbit hole you've recently fallen into. There are a lot of people, including Stone and me, who care about you and want to see you get help for all of these demons you've been fighting."

"I'm not fighting any demons."

"Say what?" Lexie looked as if he'd slapped her, but I thought Mickey sounded more reconciled than defiant. I soon discovered I was correct when he clarified his response.

"Rather than fight them, I'm just sitting back and letting them win. Letting them beat me down into submission. Lexie, I'm sorry, but I just don't have any fight left in me. I really don't feel as though I have a hell of a lot left to live for."

"That's not true and you know it. You were a gifted athlete, a decorated Marine, a good son who was wise enough to go scrutinize your mom's car to determine what really caused the accident that took her life. And you know she wouldn't want you to just give up because she's gone. Because you know she's not truly gone, Mickey. Your mom's with you all of the time." Lexie placed her flattened hand on the left side of Mickey's chest. "She's right here and she's in heaven watching over you. I know you want to make her proud. And we want to help you do so."

I chipped in with, "You have a full team of folks on your side, willing to lend a hand and help you reach your potential. You really should take advantage of what we have to offer."

"And what's that?" He repeated, still skeptical of anything Rip and I would agree to offer him. I understood his wariness because, after all, the Earth had yet to make a full revolution around the sun since he'd sliced my husband's arm open with a knife.

Lexie went on to explain the deal I'd mentioned to Mickey earlier, including our decision not to charge him with assault if he sought treatment for his addiction by admitting himself into a drug rehabilitation facility. Mickey quickly agreed to our proposal and also accepted Andy's offer to take him on as a ranch hand, supplying him with room and board after he was released.

"That actually sounds like it'd be right up my alley. Thank you for caring," Mickey said as he stared directly into my eyes. "I appreciate you giving me a chance to turn my life around. I know it's not going to be easy, but I'd rather be dead than dependent on drugs the rest of my life—"

"Which will probably be cut terribly short if you continue to abuse narcotics," I said, butting into his response.

"You're right, ma'am," Mickey said. "Right now, I want to be clear-minded so I can try to find out who murdered my mom. I want justice for the most important person in my life."

"We want the exact same thing, Mickey," Lexie said. "Rapella and I were already planning to dig into the case."

We were? Why didn't you tell me we were planning to dig into the case? I wanted to ask Lexie. *I thought I was planning to resist the urge to interfere in order to avoid being at odds with my husband.* I shrugged involuntarily. I knew from the very beginning I would cave in at the slightest hint of pressure. The pretense of Lexie and I not getting involved in Lillian's murder case had been destined from the beginning to dissolve faster than an igloo in Kuwait. I remained silent as Lexie spoke to Mickey.

"You are welcome to stay in one of our suites after you're released from the rehab facility, at least until we can get you settled in at Wendy and Andy's ranch near Atchison. I would feel much better if you were there instead of out here where you could accidently stumble across that bobcat again. If she caught you unaware, you could be shredded like pulled pork before you even knew it."

"The cat could then cook you right up on that campfire you've still got going," I said as I tilted my head toward the smoldering ashes in the fire pit. I knew he got my drift when he responded.

"Thank you both so much for your generous offer. After I finish adjusting the carburetor on my bike, I will grab what I need from the tent, make sure the fire is completely out, and then head into town. Fortunately, most of my stuff is still at my ma's place. I promise I'll look for a therapist and sign up for Narcotics Anonymous in the next few days. I will admit myself into a rehab facility later on—"

"No!" Lexie exclaimed. "This deal stems on you admitting yourself into a rehab facility immediately. After you are released from rehab, you can sign up for NA meetings and a therapist."

"But I want to be free to help you investigate Ma's death." Mickey looked stunned as though Lexie had spat a wad of chewing tobacco on his tattered boots.

"We can find out all we need to know from you in a matter of minutes and carry on from there while you're receiving treatment. I'm sure if we have any questions for you, they'll let us speak to you. At the very least, they'll let you communicate with Detective Johnston." Lexie's tone was firm when she added, "If you don't admit yourself into rehab, the detective will arrest you on an 'assault with a deadly weapon' charge and you can sit in a jail cell while Rapella and I work on the case."

"Well, okay," Mickey muttered. Lexie had left him no choice, and he knew it. "I will admit myself into the Serenity Meadows Rehabilitation Center in St. Joseph. I checked it out right before Ma asked me to move in with her because she was afraid to be alone in her house. The rehab center had great reviews."

"I know. I checked it out too," Lexie replied. When Mickey raised his eyebrows, she clarified her statement. "For you, not me, of course."

After an amused chuckle, Mickey said, "I assumed as much. I look forward to working on Andy and Wendy's ranch after I get out. I want to be the best ranch hand they've ever hired."

I didn't want to set the bar low by telling him he'd be the first ranch hand they'd ever hired. Instead, I said, "That'd be a great goal to aspire to, Mickey, along with sustained sobriety."

"I agree, ma'am." With a forced smile, Mickey nodded at me and hugged Lexie tightly.

"Serenity Meadows has an excellent reputation and I've heard they have the best success rate around," Lexie said while still in Mickey's embrace. I could tell by the way she'd wrinkled her nose that the young man stank. He then turned to me with a questioning expression. I wasn't anxious to be that close to the grubby, smelly fellow, but shrugged and opened my arms. He walked right into them. Mickey reeked of perspiration, cigarette smoke, and oddly enough, a hint of sage. He must have recently taken what is known as a "Marine shower," using cologne to mask body odor in lieu of actually bathing. After a warm embrace, Mickey said, "Again, I'm sorry, ma'am. Please pass my apologies on to Rip."

"I'd prefer you called me Rapella rather than ma'am."

"Yes, ma'am. Sorry, I meant yes, Rapella."

I smiled and continued. "You'll need to apologize to Rip yourself, but I forgive you, Mickey. Just don't let us all down."

What he did next surprised me. He dug a hole in the ground with the heel of his motorcycle boot, right beside where he'd stubbed out the cigarette butt, and from his front jeans pocket pulled a small plastic bag containing the "rock" he'd mentioned "scoring." After removing the meth, as if to say farewell to it, he studied it for a moment and put it back in the bag. He placed the bag into the indention in the ground and covered it up with the dirt he'd unearthed with his hands. He then covered the area with leaves, making it hard to distinguish where the bag had been buried. It was a promising gesture, even though I knew a lot of promising gestures don't end up producing the desired results.

Mickey chose to walk us back to Lexie's car, lest we be threatened again by the "rascally cat." He spoke as if the crazed bobcat was as dangerous as Dolly when her lunch was served five minutes late. I knew better. Dolly might glare at Rip and me as if she's considering replacing us as her chief servants, but she wasn't likely to rip our faces off if we displeased her. The bobcat, on the other hand, had looked at us as if she was fixing to rearrange our facial features.

There was no sign of the protective mama on our way back, but something Mickey said as we chatted in the rest area's parking lot made the hair on the back of my neck stand on end.

SIX

"Can you repeat that?" Mickey spoke into what appeared to be an inexpensive pre-paid cell phone. Leaning against Lexie's Jeep, Mickey quickly enabled the speaker mode. I sensed he knew we wouldn't believe what the individual on the other end of the call had just told him if we didn't hear it with our own ears.

"Yes, of course." We heard the voice of an older woman emanate from the phone. "I said there are no vacancies at the moment, but one is scheduled to open up next week. If that's not acceptable, I can recommend other facilities in the vicinity."

Mickey looked at Lexie with a questioning expression. After a moment of consideration, she said, "I hate to have you put it off, but it's only a week and they *are* the best around. I'd suggest you sign up to fill the vacancy when it becomes available. You can stay at the inn for the time being. It might be advantageous to have you there while we investigate your mom's death."

While Mickey gave the lady pertinent information to confirm his reservation, Lexie and I waited silently. After he ended the call, we thanked him for escorting us to the car. Lexie said, "I'm happy you are signed up for rehab, Mickey, but we'll want to get you settled at the ranch immediately after you're released. Andy will want to get you up to speed as soon as possible so he'll be freed up to help Wendy with little Chet."

"I'm anxious to get started. I'll need to keep busy so I'm not tempted to cave into my cravings. The lady at the rehab center told me stays at the center typically last between thirty and ninety days. I'm shooting for thirty." After appraising Lexie's dubious expression, Mickey added, "But I will stay as long as it takes. Just don't give my ranch hand job to someone else in the meantime."

"We won't," Lexie replied. "I promise. I can help Wendy out with Chet until you're released and Andy is freed up."

"Thank you. I appreciate it." Mickey's openness and honesty surprised me. I'd known addicts in the past who did all they could to hide and deny their alcohol and drug dependencies. That wasn't the case with Mickey. He owned his addiction, which made me think he meant what he said and would give sobriety his best shot. "You have given me hope and I'm determined to beat this."

The only things I've ever been addicted to are malted milk balls and *The Walking Dead.* One fattened me up like a Christmas calf and the other creeped me out. Both disgusted me at the same time I was unable to deny myself those guilty pleasures. I'd guess it was very similar to how Mickey probably felt about his addiction. It was probably a blessing I'd never had a reason to be prescribed pain pills. If I couldn't say no to a malted milk ball, how would I ever have been able to beat an opioid addiction? I prayed Mickey could succeed at it, but I had no illusions it'd be easy or without relapses. "I think the trick is to want to get your life back on track more than you want to scratch that particular itch." *Who am I to give advice to an addict?* I thought.

By the expression on Mickey's face, it was clear he didn't think I was qualified to give guidance to a drug addict either. It wasn't a whole lot more ludicrous than me telling Elon Musk how he should build a spaceship to fly to Mars. Instead of responding to my remark,

Mickey said, "There's something we need to do tomorrow, if not tonight."

"What's that?" Lexie and I asked in unison.

"Find the threatening note my mom found on her front porch the day before her accident and confront the sender."

Lexie froze in her tracks, and I was left speechless, as well. When Lexie could finally find her voice, she asked, "What'd the note say?"

"Who was the note from?" I asked in quick succession.

"I don't know the answer to either. Ma wouldn't give me any details, although I asked both questions repeatedly. I should've pushed harder. I stopped by the morning after her cousin's wedding and she was in the process of making tuna salad for a book club meeting she was attending that day with Rose. I asked her how the wedding went, and she seemed giddy about being asked out on a dinner date with some guy she'd met at the reception. Before I could ask more about this dude, Ma told me that not long before I'd arrived there'd been a knock at her front door."

"Does your ma use mayonnaise in her tuna salad?" I asked inanely as I tried to wrap my head around what Mickey had just told us. "I've discovered plain Greek yogurt is not only tastier, but also healthier."

Mickey stared at me in disbelief and shrugged while Lexie looked at me as if I'd just asked the young man if I could strip-search him. She rolled her eyes at me and returned her attention to Mickey.

"Who was at her front door?" Lexie asked, clearly not interested in whether Lillian used mayo or yogurt. It was obvious Mickey's ma could have used drain cleaner in her tuna salad for all Lexie cared at the moment. I was embarrassed at having had one of those "Squirrel!" moments I'm prone to on occasion.

"Good question, Lexie! Who was at your ma's front door, Mickey?" The lame attempt to hide my humiliation only left me feeling more embarrassed.

"No one. When Ma opened the door, there was nobody there,

only an envelope partially tucked under the welcome mat containing an unsettling note from an anonymous sender. When I begged her to let me read it, or at least tell me what the note was about, she declined, saying it was no big deal and nothing for me to be concerned about. I realize now she was afraid of how I'd react because of the condition I was in. It's my fault she's dead. I might as well have just cut the brake lines myself."

Did you? I wanted to ask. But then I realized he couldn't be that accomplished an actor and not have a shelf full of little golden statues to his credit. It was quite apparent that Mickey was beyond furious with himself. The look on his face could've made a crocodile spit out a baby zebra in terror. He began to shake as moisture formed on his upper lip. I felt we needed to calm Mickey down, lest it trigger him to fall off the wagon he'd only just decided to climb back up on. It was already a tenuous balancing act without him finding excuses to dive off the wagon headfirst.

Lexie must've been thinking the same thing. She said, "Mickey, it's possible your mom wasn't just trying to keep from worrying you. Perhaps she thought it was such a silly annoyance that she was embarrassed to tell you the details. It truly might have been a minor deal, not a death threat or warning of violence to come. Who could possibly want to harm your mom?"

"Obviously *someone* did!" He responded angrily.

"Possibly the killer mistook your mom's car for someone else's. It could have been a case of mistaken identity. Or perhaps the note was from a friend that irritated her for some reason, a personal affront of some kind. Maybe one of her friends requested she not bring her tuna salad to the book club meeting because her recipe was a bit on the sour side. That'd be just the kind of insult a mother wouldn't want to share with her son."

Maybe the sourness was from the drain cleaner she put in the tuna salad? I thought. Not only did I feel as though Lexie's remarks were even more idiotic than my mayonnaise question had been, I thought she'd used too many adverbs like possibly, perhaps, and maybe to convincingly voice her premise. Mickey just shook his head in denial as he replied, "No. Trust me, ladies; it was more than just a silly tuna salad slight. I'd bet my life it was no coincidence Ma died the day after she received the note."

When neither Lexie nor I responded, he added, "Besides, my ma's tuna salad was delicious: it was not one bit sour."

Lexie assured him she was not insulting Lillian's tuna salad, as she'd never even eaten any of it, but was only using it as an example. She went on to tell him she knew Lillian to be an excellent cook and was sure her tuna salad was just as delicious as everything else she'd ever tasted that his ma had prepared. I just rolled my eyes behind Lexie's back. Mickey caught it and gave me a knowing look that indicated he wasn't buying Lexie's hypothesis any more than I was. What mother was afraid her grown son would lose sleep over the fact her tuna salad recipe had been snubbed by one of her so-called friends? More likely, if the knife Lillian's friend had plunged into her back had cut that deeply, Lillian would want to vent about it, not refuse to tell anyone willing to listen the details of the offensive remark.

"Lexie, if you'd been there, you'd know it was something more alarming than what you just described. It was clearly a threatening message. Ma was on pins and needles. I hadn't seen her that uneasy since I brought home a baby raccoon I'd found trapped in the maintenance shed when I was ten. I wanted to keep it as a pet. After Ma spoke to Gary about it, he told me I could 'want in one hand, and you-know-what in the other and see which one filled up first.' I knew Ma wasn't thrilled about having a baby raccoon around the house because of their destructive nature and the fact they often carry rabies. But she still argued with my step-dad on my behalf about letting me keep it. When he refused, she told him that he'd have to take it to Dewberry Park and release it. I think the jerk took it up the street and shot it because he returned home too soon to have relocated the coon to the park, which was fifteen miles from the house.

And Ma gave him the silent treatment for several days afterward so I'm sure she felt the same way, even though she denied it when I asked her about it."

Mickey smiled at the memory, but the smile didn't reach his eyes. He hadn't forgotten the incident or forgiven Gary. Lexie and I shook our heads in commiseration. I could see why Mickey didn't care for his stepfather. Because of his lack of compassion, I despised Gary too, and I'd never even met the man.

"So, anyhow," Mickey began, "Ma told me if I stopped by early the following day, she'd make me breakfast. I think she was trying to mend fences with me, so I jumped all over the offer. While the biscuits were baking on that morning of her death, she went out on her front porch to collect a new phone book that'd been placed on her welcome mat. When she returned to the kitchen, she had another note in her other hand."

"Was it another threatening message from the same person?" Lexie asked.

"No, it was just an invite from Rose to meet Ma for coffee and brunch at a Starbucks in St. Joseph. I think that's where Ma was headed when her brakes gave out. They'd gone to a cousin's wedding together two days before that. I realized Ma was telling me the truth because of the relief on her face after she'd read it and realized the note was from Rose and not the person who'd left the intimidating note the previous day. She was excited to join Rose for brunch that morning, but I knew she'd been on the brink of a nervous breakdown due to the nasty note she'd received the previous day."

"I would've been uneasy too," Lexie replied, as I was wondering why Rose didn't just invite her mother to coffee and brunch in person or send her a text. "Do you have any idea where the threatening note is now?"

"Nope, but I'm almost certain it's somewhere inside her house."

"So, what do we do about it? Report it to the homicide detectives?" Lexie asked.

"Heck no!" I exclaimed. Mickey followed up with a similar retort, only his response was much more vulgar.

Mickey took the words out of my mouth when he added, "This afternoon the three of us should scour the house for it. I've searched and searched and come up empty every time. But I refuse to give up. When I heard she'd died in a car accident, I had a bad feeling her death was connected to that threat by an anonymous source. Knowing Ma, I'm nearly positive she wouldn't have thrown it away and trying to locate it is not a task we want to drop into the laps of Rockdale's homicide detectives. Have you ever been inside Ma's house?" Mickey inquired, looking straight at Lexie.

"No, I never have. Your mom always preferred to come over to the inn to visit with me rather than for me to go to her place."

"I'm not surprised. You'll understand why I feel this way when you see the house. Ma would've kept the note as evidence if nothing else. But, as you know, it's a huge home and we don't have much time."

"Why do you say that?" I asked.

"My half-sisters were contacted by a gentleman who's interested in buying the house. Judy and Rose are anxious to sell the place and cash out their shares of the estate. I'm not in any hurry for my third, but I'm outnumbered. The prospective buyer is a lawyer from back east named Barron Buckley. Judy told me he was born and raised in Tupelo, Mississippi, but is now living in Atlantic City, New Jersey, where his office is located. He'd also told her it would be a cash deal with immediate possession. A turnkey type of transaction so he doesn't have to deal too extensively with having the place furnished. I'll need to get out everything I want to keep before he looks at the place so my personal property doesn't become part of the sale. Although much of Ma's stuff is just crap, there's a few things I want to keep that are sentimental to me and shouldn't be sold off as if they were thrift store items."

"Absolutely," I said in agreement, thinking the prospective buyer's name sounded very snobbish, like the type of guy who'd wear a three-piece suit to a one-year-old's birthday party just to make the other attendees feel less worthy. My guess was that this Barron Buckley was a personal injury attorney, who was in the business of filing lawsuits against folks after their neighbor's unsupervised six-year-old son climbed up their clematis trellis to the roof and jumped off, breaking his arm in three places.

I came out of my reverie when Mickey nudged my shoulder. "Rapella?"

"Oh, sorry," I said. "I was daydreaming. Anyway, I think you should keep anything of hers that means something to you. Her personal items shouldn't be part of the sale either. I'm sure your half-sisters would appreciate if you held back a few sentimental items for them as well. For instance: her jewelry, photos, meaningful knick-knacks, journals or diaries, and electronic devices, just to name a few. Some rich East Coast attorney doesn't deserve to have those types of things thrown into a real estate deal. That goes for valuable antiques and collectibles, as well."

"I agree. That's why I've already moved a bunch of things I think Judy and Rose will want to keep. I stored items like you just mentioned in a friend's basement. I don't want any of that stuff, but I'm sure my sisters will want them as keepsakes."

"No doubt. When's this Barron Buckley supposed to look at the house?" I asked.

"The showing is scheduled for ten tomorrow morning. A local real estate agent named Sherri is going to show it to him. She's out of the Winnett Group Realty office in town."

"Oh, sure. She's fantastic." Lexie nodded. "I've met Sherri. She's as nice as they come, and a very successful realtor. She could sell a brothel to a nun, so we better act fast. Let's plan to go through your mom's house as soon as you arrive at the inn, Mickey. Rapella and I can try to sniff through the house room by room for the note Lillian received in the mail while you deal with rounding up all the stuff you want to keep."

"That'll just take me a few minutes, but you two can get a head start. You'll need all the time you can spare to 'sniff' through Ma's house."

Although I felt akin to a blood hound following Lexie's and Mickey's remarks about sniffing through Lillian's house, I agreed to the plan, unfazed by Mickey's implication the task wasn't going to be as easy as Lexie had made it sound. I was as keyed up as a child being led into a candy store at the idea of locating the note that could bring a killer to his knees. This kind of quest was definitely in my wheelhouse.

Mickey's nerves are clearly on edge, I realized. *We'll have to handle this young man with kid gloves if he's going to be of any help to us in tracking down his mother's killer, while at the same time, trying to keep him from racing back to the rest area and digging up the drugs. I can just visualize him running amok through the woods like a hungry chipmunk looking for the nuts it'd buried.*

Mickey arrived at the inn about twenty minutes after Lexie and I finished visiting with Rip and Stone over lunch. I wondered if the burying of the bag of drugs was just for show and he'd already retrieved them before heading back to Rockdale. I'd hoped the gesture was made out of a sincere wish to conquer the addiction, but I wasn't overly confident. For just that reason, I'd left a tell-tale marker behind at the "burial site." I even thought about returning to the area and utilizing the motion sensor critter cam I had stored in my junk drawer, but decided it would serve no point. If Mickey dug up the drugs after we left, or went back for them at a later time, there was nothing we could do about it.

Lexie had made roast beef sandwiches for our noon meal which she served along with freshly-sliced tomatoes and air-fried tater tots.

There'd been plenty of roast beef left over from dinner the previous night. Lexie wasn't lying when she'd told us it was big enough to feed an army. We topped the scrumptious meal off with leftover strawberry shortcake. It was a rare treat for Rip and me since we usually limited ourselves to two meals per day, a light breakfast and a full supper.

Three squares a day would pack pounds on both of us because we just didn't work off the calories like we used to when we were younger. Whoever invented the phrase "golden years" ought to be stripped naked, covered in honey, and tied to a stake on a huge ant hill. There was nothing golden about getting old. They should've named the post-Medicare period as the "tin foil" years, because that's about how fragile I feel on occasion. I could now bump my forearm on a throw cushion and end up with a hematoma that looked like I'd been pistol whipped by a carjacker.

At our last checkup appointments, Dr. Herron had warned us both if we got any fatter we'd be inviting type 2 diabetes, worsening cardiac health in Rip's case, and several other serious medical issues into our lives. Naturally she said this in a slightly less insensitive way, but not so subtly that we couldn't read between the lines. She even mentioned we might have to do away with our daily highballs, but recanted the threat after seeing the looks of horror on both of our faces.

At the time Dr. Herron mentioned our increasing waistlines, I'd assumed she'd included me so as not to embarrass Rip by singling him out. After all, I didn't consider myself to be overweight but felt he could definitely stand to lose twenty or so pounds. However, when I couldn't get the zipper zipped on one of my favorite pair of capris the next day, I thought maybe it wouldn't hurt me to lose a few pounds too.

I'm gonna get right on that weight loss mission just as soon as we get to the truth behind Lillian Sparrow's death, I vowed. *I might even try to persuade Rip we should forego our daily highballs, even though my efforts would be as futile as trying to talk a grizzly bear into foregoing his annual hibernation.*

As I stood beside Lexie and Mickey, I admired the scene before us. The *Casa de Hermanas* was truly a sight to behold. The property surrounding the Mediterranean-style mansion had a park-like quality: concrete benches and bird baths, large shade trees such as oaks and maples, several flowing fountains, and beautiful lilac bushes and crepe myrtles bursting with colorful blossoms. There was even a large koi pond next to the front porch that now featured several dead and bloated fish. Clearly, the poor things hadn't been fed since Lillian passed, if not before.

"Your mother's groundskeeper had a lot of responsibility keeping her property up to snuff, didn't he?"

"For sure. She kept her precious koi fish fed but hired a man named Narciso Garcia to work on the lawn two days a week. They seemed to have a contentious relationship," Mickey said. I already knew about the groundskeeper, but let Mickey keep talking. "He always complained she didn't pay him enough and she argued he was so slow that any other lawn maintenance guy could do in one day what it took Narciso two days to accomplish."

"Is Narciso still taking care of the lawn?" I asked Mickey.

"Ma had just let him go before she died. She was probably in a snit about something at the time and would've rehired him after she'd gotten over it like she had a couple of times in the past. I would've asked him to return to work after her death if I could've afforded to pay him. I came by about a week ago to mow and trim a couple of bushes but quickly realized I could never keep up with all the different things that need to be constantly maintained. I think Narciso worked a lot harder than Ma ever gave him credit for."

"Do you reckon you could find time in your schedule today to toss some fish pellets into the koi pond?" I asked. "I also have some lettuce you can shred for them. A puddle of water with upside down fish floating on top is not a good look when you've got the property on the market. Besides, your ma would turn over in her grave if she saw the current condition of her precious koi fish."

"Yeah," he began, "I know. I'll give the fish some food today."

Despite his remark he'd quit trying to keep up the property, the grounds were still as beautiful as the land Alexandria Inn sat on. But it'd only been two weeks. If the property didn't sell soon, the place would become overrun with weeds, grass, and untamed foliage in no time. In its prime, I could tell this property was just as nice as Stone's and Lexie's, if not nicer. *If the outside of this home is this amazing, I can only imagine how extraordinary the inside is,* I thought as we walked toward the mansion's front steps.

Mickey was strolling a few yards ahead of us, studying the house with a curious expression as he mechanically put one foot in front of the other. I had to wonder what he was thinking. I'd imagine he was consumed with memories of his mother as he gazed at her beautiful home. He looked so absorbed in his thoughts; I didn't want to bother him.

"Have you really never been inside?" I whispered to Lexie.

"No, I truly haven't," she responded just as quietly. "Lillian always came to my house. At first, I thought it was odd, but then I decided it was because she felt I needed to be readily available should any of our guests find themselves needing something from me. Needless to say, I'm dying to see the interior."

"Me too," I began, "because the outside is incredible."

A minute or so later, Mickey motioned for us to follow him up a dozen alabaster stairs to a wide porch flanked by pillars that complemented the steps. We stood behind him while he lifted up the welcome mat, plucked a key off the wooden plank below it, and unlocked the door.

"Your mom kept a spare key to her house under the welcome

mat?" I asked. *Is that not the first place a burglar would look for one?* I thought. "Not the most strategic place to hide a key."

"I tried to tell her that, but she refused to hide it somewhere else."

"Why?" I asked Mickey.

"It was not only placed there for me to use because she claimed she didn't have another key to give me, but half the folks on this street know where her spare key is hidden, as well. She'd given a spare to the lady across the street a few years ago, but got tired of having to go borrow it every time she locked herself out, which she did on a regular basis."

Mickey stepped aside as Lexie walked into the foyer with me just behind her. I noticed her flabbergasted expression before anything else.

"Oh. My. God." Lexie looked as if she'd just walked into a saloon and saw Pope Francis slamming back a shot of tequila while getting a lap dance from Mother Teresa. After a moment to gather her thoughts, she said, "Now I understand why Lillian always wanted to come over to the inn rather than have me come here to her place."

I'm sure my expression was very similar to Lexie's. Scanning the room, I couldn't find a place to set down my purse. I turned to Mickey. "And I understand now why you were so certain she wouldn't have thrown that threatening note away. I doubt your mom ever threw anything away." He just shrugged and shook his head in response.

With a rueful expression, he said, "And I'd guess you both understand now why I need help in scouring through this place for the note. I loved my ma to death, but—" Mickey stopped speaking abruptly. Before I could ask if he meant that last remark literally or figuratively, he continued. "Sorry. That was a bad choice of words. The thing is, my mother was the sweetest woman I've ever known, but the woman was a habitual hoarder. While searching for the threatening message, I found one chest of drawers that contained every cancelled check she'd written from 1985 through 2004."

"Why'd she stop saving them in 2004?" I asked purely out of nosiness.

"Because her bank stopped returning the cancelled checks after the Check 21 Act was passed," Mickey explained. "At that point they began mailing out scanned images, and trust me the bottom drawer of that dresser held sheets of paper with the scanned images of her checks from 2004 on. She couldn't let go of a single thing. Wait until you see the attic. It's full of junk like old computers and monitors that no longer work, three cast iron skillets that have turned to solid rust, an electric skillet with no cord or lid, at least a hundred half-empty rolls of wrapping paper, and every single greeting card and letter she'd ever received."

"Did you search the attic for the threatening note?" Lexie asked.

"Of course," Mickey replied.

"What would possess a person to keep all of that stuff?" I asked.

"You got me!" Mickey exclaimed even though my question had been rhetorical. "What would possess a person to keep a stack of spam e-mail messages she'd printed off of her HP laptop? There's not a single item up there that shouldn't have been pitched in a dumpster rather than stored in the attic. Trust me, that note she received the day before her death is still in this house somewhere, but I'm pretty certain it's not in the attic."

For a few moments, Lexie and I just glanced around the living room in disbelief. There was a small path that led from that front room into a hallway, surrounded on both sides by piles of miscellaneous stuff. Worthless, useless crap would be a more appropriate way to describe it. *Where does one start to search for a single piece of paper in this mess?* I wondered. I considered turning around and walking out of Lillian's house. I felt awash in frustration and disillusionment.

"Guess we better get started," Lexie said, a positive lilt to her voice. She clearly was a glass half-full kind of gal, while I was a glass completely empty type of person from having downed every drop of the tequila that had been in that schooner to begin with. I needed a stiff drink right now, in fact, to bolster my enthusiasm for the task of finding a needle in this proverbial haystack.

I sighed loudly and dramatically before nodding my head and picking up a box that contained empty McDonald's Happy Meal boxes. I lifted the top one out of the box to show to Lexie and Mickey.

"Wow." Mickey shook his head again. "I kind of figured she kept all the toys I'd collected from those kids' meals, but not the boxes. Ma had it bad, didn't she?"

Yep! Real bad! I thought to myself while Lexie tried to be tactful as she spoke her affirmation out loud. "I'd say she just really loved her possessions; so much so that she was unable to part with them."

They're empty Happy Meal boxes, Lexie! I wanted to shout. *How can anyone love "possessions" like that? Crazier still, love them to the point of being unable to part with them?*

Mickey appeared oblivious to Lexie's remark. He was deeply entrenched in his own thoughts and memories of the past. He cut in to say, "Ma used to let me grow my hair long when I was younger, even though Gary was opposed to his stepson looking like a 'sissy.' That was before I moved in with my dad, of course. I think she let me grow it out just to aggravate Gary. Well, one time, after the guy at the window of a McDonalds drive-thru glanced at me sitting in the back seat of the car, he gave me a happy meal with a girl's toy in it. I was crushed when I got an Ariel the Mermaid doll rather than the plastic Big Mac that transformed into a dinosaur. Ma says I sat on the front steps of this house and cried for two days. I begged her to cut my hair after that so I'd never be mistaken for a girl again."

"Your hair's long now," I said, admiring his pinkish blonde locks.

"I got over it! I haven't gotten it cut since getting discharged from the military." He snickered at the horrifying memory of being given the mermaid doll. It was obviously an incident that had totally traumatized him at the time it occurred, but after many years had passed, he could tell the story and laugh about it. Although I thought the anecdote was humorous, the thought of having to also go through boxes of Happy Meal toys didn't amuse me at all. Mickey gave me an apologetic look before adding, "Sorry about that."

"No big deal," I replied. "But do I really need to sort through a box of empty Happy Meal boxes? They smell like old grease."

"Yeah, I'm afraid so. If I knew my ma, she'd have hidden the note in a place she felt sure I'd never think to look."

I knew at that moment it was going to be an extremely long day.

SEVEN

By nightfall, we hadn't even cleared the living room yet. There had to be at least fifteen or more rooms in the historic mansion. The closest thing I'd found to a menacing note was one that looked as if it'd been written to Lillian in grade school by a boy named Olaf.

LILY, WELL YOU GO WITH ME? CHEK YES OR NO. IF YOU CHEK NO I WELL SPIT ON YOAR TRAY IN THE LAUNCH ROOM. OLAF.

"Olaf was a brazen young man, wasn't he?" I asked after reading the note out loud.

"Olaf?" Mickey appeared surprised by the name of the note's sender. "Olaf Dudley was my dad's best friend when they were older. In fact, he became my godfather. Unfortunately, he died in his mid-twenties from a brutal beating outside a Leavenworth bar."

"Had he spit in his attacker's beer?" I asked before realizing how insensitive it sounded.

I was relieved when Mickey laughed loudly. "Probably so. Olaf was a loose cannon, always looking for a fight. Unfortunately, he found one that night with a guy who was the undefeated champion of the Jackson Brothers Boxing Club in St. Joseph at the time. Olaf's face was unrecognizable when his folks went to the morgue to identify his body."

"Oh, my!" I exclaimed. "That's terrible. Please excuse my stupid quip. It wasn't humorous at all."

"No worries." Mickey flashed me a rare smile, which showed more empty space than teeth. "Actually, I thought your remark was funny. Olaf would've thought so too."

An hour or so later, I was opening up a box marked, "Better Homes and Gardens, 2012-2015" when Mickey apologized for the fourth or fifth time. "I'm so sorry you two ladies have to waste your time going through all this junk."

He was sincere and obviously embarrassed by his mother's inability to throw anything away. I wanted to lighten the emotional load which was clearly heavy on his shoulders. "No need to apologize, Mickey. It's only a waste of time if we fail to locate the note. Besides, it's kind of fun."

"Fun?" He asked with a snort.

Sure, I said under my breath. *Fun like prepping for a colonoscopy. Fun like stepping in a dog's calling card just before you walk inside the church for Sunday's service. Fun like splitting your pants when you lean over in the middle of Wal-Mart to tie your shoes. You know, Mickey, that kind of fun.*

Out loud, I said, "It's like going on a treasure hunt. Besides, to us a lot of this stuff might seem like pure crap, but to your ma it was her personal possessions. I'm guessing she was very sentimental. Even things like those Happy Meal boxes brought back fond memories of you as a child. And although your ma was a hoarder, she was an extremely organized one. Every box, basket, shelf, cabinet or drawer is clearly marked with the nature of its contents. Her attention to detail will undoubtedly be helpful."

"Yeah, I guess you're right. She *was* very sentimental. And as well as being a hoarder, Ma was kind of obsessive compulsive." I was relieved Mickey seemed pleased with the backhanded compliment I'd made about his mom. He confirmed it when he said, "I suppose its fortunate the OCD made her pretty organized. But then, I guess she had to be to get a lifetime's worth of 'personal possessions' into a house with only twenty-one rooms."

Twenty-one rooms? The painful reminder we had barely scratched the surface hit me like a Louisville Slugger to the breadbasket. After Mickey took in my exasperated gasp and the look of dismay on Lexie's face, he said, "You ladies haven't seen anything yet! But you're right about Ma marking everything to make a particular item easier to locate. I sure wish there was a box marked 'threatening notes' sitting by itself in the middle of the kitchen table. This basket I'm getting ready to sort through has a post-it note taped to it that says 'entertainment.' What in the world could be in here? It doesn't look like DVD's, board games, or puzzle books."

I looked up just as Mickey reached into the basket, dropped whatever he'd grasped as if it was a coiled-up cobra, threw his arms up in the air, and shouted, "Oh, my God!"

"What?"

"What is it?" Lexie and I both shouted questions at him. Mickey now looked as if he was on the verge of puking.

"What'd you find? Is it something that has rotted and turned rancid?" I asked. When he failed to respond, Lexie and I took turns launching possibilities at him in rapid-fire succession.

"Is it the note?"

"Is it a gun?"

"Another kind of weapon?"

"A snake?"

"A rat?"

"Dead rat?"

"Is it petrified dog poop, or what? Come on, Mickey! What in the hell is it?" I finally asked, running out of ideas and already out of patience.

"It's none of those things. Although, I wish it *was* petrified dog poop!" Mickey finally exclaimed. "Instead, it's one of those female things."

"Female things?" I asked the young man who had turned as red as the McDonalds Happy Meal boxes. "What kind of female thing? Are you referring to a box of tampons?"

"Um no, although I did have to go into a pharmacy and ask for a box of those for Ma when I was about eleven and it was a traumatic experience that nearly scarred me for life. But this is, you know, um, well, um, well, um, um," he stuttered but seemed incapable of making eye contact with either me or Lexie. "It's a, um, you know, a toy."

"A toy?" I had a feeling I knew what he'd found in the basket but couldn't resist making Mickey feel even more embarrassed about what he'd accidently happened upon. "You mean like your Ariel the Mermaid doll?"

"No. It's not at all like that." Sweat had broken out on Mickey's forehead. I hate to admit I was enjoying his discomfort a little too much. He was staring at the floor when he said, "You know, a female sex toy. Ewww. . ."

I knew immediately I'd been correct about what he'd found in the basket marked "entertainment" and found myself amused at his overwhelming revulsion and disbelief that his mother had ever engaged in a sex act. With herself, no less! I'm sure he thought his birth was like that of Jesus, the result of an immaculate conception. Lexie was openly laughing and I couldn't help but join her. Even though it didn't seem possible, Mickey turned even redder. I decided to cut the guy some slack. In case the basket held other items that would equally repulse him, I said, "Tell you what, son. I'll finish sorting through that basket, if you want to look through this box of four dozen *Better Homes and Gardens* magazines."

He couldn't trade places fast enough, which pleased me, as well. Mickey's "toy" basket was surely more interesting than a box of periodicals. It took a good ten minutes for the blood to return to his face and nearly as long for Lexie and me to stop giggling about his morti-fying discovery. We continued to search for another twenty minutes before calling it a night. Supper was already overdue and Rip could be as grumpy as Dolly when a meal was delayed. I often wondered if he married me for my cooking prowess or my good looks and charming personality. I wasn't certain I wanted to know the answer to that question, though.

"I knew I was being overoptimistic thinking we'd be able to track down that note tonight. We'll just have to hope the potential buyer isn't interested in buying this place after seeing it firsthand. He's already indicated he wants immediate possession." Mickey spoke in a defeated tone, but I couldn't see how he'd think anyone would be interested in buying his ma's house in its current junk-filled state. If the structure were to belch, a thousand cancelled checks would explode like a volcano out of the chimney top. It would be like confetti being shot out of a cannon. I basically said as much to him.

"You don't understand." Mickey sounded resigned. "He was warned about the condition of it and the fact the owner was a hoarder. Apparently, he told this realtor lady that his wife, Celia, wanted to turn it into a bed and breakfast like yours, Lexie, and she didn't care about all the junk inside, or really what shape the house was in. He and Celia planned to hire a company to restore and remodel the old mansion before opening it up as a lodging facility. It sounds as if the Buckleys are dead set on buying the property."

"It also sounds as if the Buckleys are looking for a tax write-off," I said.

Both Mickey and Lexie nodded before Lexie began to speak. "Maybe we can appeal to the Buckleys for a reasonable amount of time to sort through the place before he takes possession."

Lexie's idea sounded fair to me, but Mickey soon made it clear the request wouldn't pass muster with the prospective buyer. "No. Like I said, Buckley's made it abundantly apparent he wants immediate possession. And as an attorney, I'm sure he knows how to get around all of the red tape to make it happen."

"Have you met the realtor showing Buckley the house tomorrow morning?" I asked him. "I've forgotten what you said her name was."

"It's Sherri, with the Winnett Group Realty office," Mickey replied. "And no, I've never met her or even spoken with her. Sherri's been communicating with my sister Rose, who acts as though she wants this place sold yesterday if not sooner."

"Uh-huh," I replied absentmindedly. I had an idea and felt I had just enough gumption to make it work. "I think I can buy us some time."

"How?" Mickey asked, appearing just as confounded as Lexie.

"I might not be a trained real estate salesperson, or any good at selling a house. But I think I'd be great at not selling one." I glanced from Lexie to Mickey and paused for the meaning of my last comment to sink in. My eyes were fixed on Mickey as I added, "All I need is for you to call Sherri and tell her you're Barron Buckley and have changed your mind about wanting to see or buy this house. I will handle the rest."

"If she's spoken with Buckley on the phone, which she most likely has, wouldn't she be able to tell the difference between our voices?" Mickey asked.

"Good point." I hadn't thought of that potential problem. "Then tell her you are Buckley's agent, or business partner, and he asked you to contact her and cancel the showing."

"Well . . . ." Appearing skeptical, he finally said, "All right. I'll call Sherri right now."

Lexie and I stood on Lillian's front porch as Mickey called the real estate office and locked up his mom's house. I explained to my friend how I planned to dissuade Buckley from purchasing the house. Lexie was excited about my ruse, as I knew she would be. This kind of deceit was just as much up her alley as it was mine. I was actually looking forward to my attempt to pull off the clever hoax.

Now if I could just pull it off without landing us both in the doghouse with our husbands. Or worse yet, landing myself in the *big* house.

When I answered the knock at Lillian Sparrow's door the next morning at straight up ten, I was taken aback by the man on the front porch. It was our neighbor at the inn, the handsome man who owned the luxury coach that looked as if it cost more than all of the homes we'd ever owned combined. *He hasn't actually seen me yet. He's only met Rip. But the fact we're staying in such close proximity to this man might not bode well for me,* I thought. I didn't realize it at the time, but it was a prophetic reckoning and would indeed come back to bite me in the keister.

"Howdy ma'am," he drawled, habitually tipping his hat in greeting. "I'm Barron Buckley, here for my ten o'clock showing."

"It's nice to meet you Mr. Buckley. I'm Sherri . . ." I paused when I realized I hadn't asked Mickey for the realtor's last name. "Um, well, you can just call me Sherri. My surname is too difficult to pronounce."

With confusion etched on his deeply tanned face, he said, "Didn't you tell me on the phone your last name was Lee?"

Crap! I thought. *Of course he knows Sherri's last name even if I don't.* "Well, lookie there! You pronounced it correctly on your first attempt."

Buckley's eyebrows were raised as I extended my hand. He grasped it in a firm but not overpowering handshake. "It's nice to meet you, Sherri. I'm anxious to take a quick tour and get the paperwork wrapped up this morning."

"You better see the inside before you start writing out that big check," I said in a teasing manner.

Mr. Buckley laughed politely. Looking around, he said, "The grounds here are incredibly gorgeous."

I quickly scanned the front lawn. I was glad Mickey hadn't gotten around to feeding the fish in the koi pond or removing the dead ones. Bloating and floating, the fish made for just the kind of first impression I'd hoped for.

"Yes, of course. Come on in." I noticed the gentleman glance up at the etched wooden sign above the entry way that read *Casa de Hermanas*, which I knew from my one semester of Spanish in high school translated to House of Sisters in English. My first thought when I'd seen the sign the day before was that naming a house was absurd. My second thought was that I was a fine one to ridicule someone for naming their residence. Talk about throwing stones at glass, silly-named, houses. I'd named our travel trailer the Chartreuse Caboose, which most folks probably considered equally ridiculous. "Welcome to the *Casa de Hermanas*, Mr. Buckley!"

He nodded in response. I'd expected the man to insist I call him Barron, but it quickly became apparent he felt calling him by his first name was above my station. His nose wrinkled in dismay as he stepped inside. "Good grief. What's that smell?"

"I've been wondering the same thing," I replied. "Although it actually smells better today than it usually does. Don't worry. You'll get used to it eventually. Most of the time you won't even notice it over the reeking smell of the seeping sewer lines."

"The seeping sewer lines?"

"Yes. After replacing the leaky roof, you'll probably want to replace the entire septic system before doing any remodeling."

"Leaky roof?" As Buckley spoke, he peered into the living room and saw a couple of five-gallon buckets, half full of water and strategically placed around the room. As we'd scoured that room the previous evening, I'd cleared off those areas by stacking boxes in other areas even closer to the ceiling to make room for the buckets.

"I hadn't really planned to invest in any structural work, just cosmetic upgrades. I may have to re-evaluate my offer." Barron looks discouraged, which was just the emotion I was hoping to induce in the potential buyer. I tried not to let my delight be evident on my face.

"No problem, as long as your offer meets the reserve price, of course."

"Reserve price?" he asked. "Are you saying the sellers have set a minimum price?"

"Of course!" I replied as if I couldn't believe he didn't already know all the particulars. "You don't seriously think they'd take a chance on this cream puff being sold off too cheaply, do you? But before you worry about the roof and septic system, I'd be more concerned about the foundation. The cracks are becoming more of an issue than they were when this property last sold many years ago." I didn't want to be too detailed about dates as I had a feeling Buckley already knew when the Sparrows had purchased *Casa de Hermanas*.

I glanced at Buckley, who was jotting down notes on a pad of paper. The refillable fountain pen he was using had a green ink cartridge in it. The pen reminded me of the one my mother had given me for Christmas one year when I was in high school and had become interested in learning the decorative writing style known as calligraphy. It was nearly a lost art. Kids these days had a lot more choices when it came to amusing themselves. I dare say not too many millennials would choose calligraphy over playing *Grand Theft Auto* or *Candy Crush*. Even I was no exception when it came to enjoying an hour or two of crushing candy every night while Rip watched "shoot 'em up bang-bangs" on the television.

"Should we get started by looking at the living room?" I asked. "Or at least what you can see of it. I assume you've been told the former owner was a hoarder?"

"Yes, you told me that when I called to schedule this showing. I must say your voice sounded much deeper on the phone."

"Oh, yes, so I did tell you about the hoarding," I shook my head at my forgetfulness and then cleared my voice as if to rid myself of a big wad of phlegm parked in my throat. "Thank goodness I'm finally over that horrible cold I was plagued with and have my normal voice back."

"I must say, that was a quick recovery, as I only called yesterday."

"I'm a fast healer; a medical miracle, my friends like to call me. But, back to the former owner; she's gone now. I think she might've passed in the master suite, but I'm not positive."

"She was killed in a one-car accident." After Buckley had corrected me, I quickly ushered him out of the foyer, away from the closet where I'd placed a bag of rotten potatoes. I'd found the ten-pound bag in one of our undercarriage compartments where I'd put it in July and then forgot about it for several sizzling hot months. Now it was November and the smell of the putrefied spuds would gag a maggot. Rip had discovered my oversight earlier that morning while getting a small patio table out of the compartment. He'd complained the smell nearly caused him to upchuck the oatmeal he'd had for breakfast. Buckley must have never had something similar happen to him or he'd have surely recognized the nauseating, rancid stench of decaying spuds.

Buckley looked around the room and shook his head. "I really hadn't expected the task of cleaning out this place to be quite so overwhelming. I had an aunt that was a hoarder, but her home was nothing like this. Her closets were a bit Fibber McGee and Molly-ish, but you could at least see if the floor was tile, carpet, or wood."

"This house has a nice mixture of all three; there's some hideous tile in the kitchen and outdated shag carpeting in a few of the bedrooms, but most of it is hardwood that needs to be refinished. I do know what you mean, however. Cleaning out all twenty-one rooms, each as equally cluttered as this one, is going to be either a massive expense or an even more humongous task if you choose to do it on your own. I'm afraid it'd be a deal breaker for me." As I spoke, I noticed Buckley cross his arms across his chest and rub his hands up and down his arms. It was the perfect time to bring up the faulty heating system. I faked a shiver and said, "Brrr . . . I'm glad I wore a cardigan over my blouse. The HVAC unit in this house is clearly old, undersized, and inefficient. I'm guessing a house this size needs two or three units, at the very least."

"Somehow I'm not surprised the HVAC needs to be replaced," Buckley said, in a tone as dry as Death Valley in August.

It had turned abnormally cold overnight and I'd turned the heat off in the house the evening before, turning it on again just before Barron's ten o'clock arrival. I'd wanted to ensure it was uncomfortably cool in the house during the showing.

We continued on through the rest of the structure in the same manner. I pointed out every negative thing I could see: wood rot on several window sills, a hole in a base board that looked like an ideal portal for a rat, and a crack in a bedroom wall that "I swore wasn't there the day before, but with the foundation shifting they seemed to be popping up everywhere."

I even pointed out a few things that weren't visible, probably because they were issues that didn't actually exist: black mold along the rafters in the attic, a termite colony of notable size in one of the dining room walls, and a soaker tub in a first-floor bathroom that was but a bath or two away from crashing through the creaky floorboards, landing the tub and the bather in the "spooky" basement below.

"Just out of curiosity, do you know the story behind the name of this historic home?" I asked him as we moved on to the master suite, one of two bedrooms on the main floor.

"No. I only know it's been dubbed *Casa de Hermanas*, which means the house of sisters in Spanish."

"Correct," I said. "The house was originally owned by three

sisters who were all spinsters and rumored to be witches. After they were burned at the stake during the days of the Salem Witch trials—"

"The Salem witch trials?" Buckley interrupted in a disbelieving manner. "Those occurred in the late sixteen-hundreds. According to the MLS listing, this house was built in 1881."

"Oh." I felt as if I'd just stepped in a big pile of horse manure with both feet and had to quickly think of a way to get out of it without making a bigger mess. *Note to self: do your homework next time.*

"The sisters couldn't have been—"

"You're right. I misspoke. I was thinking of another house in town." *Actually, I was thinking the witch trials occurred in the late eighteen-hundreds because everything I learned in my high school history classes, I forgot before I hit twenty.*

To stall for time while I thought of another fictional story with an "ewww" factor, I pulled out my phone and pretended to Google the name of the house. Finally, I said, "Oh, yeah, that's right. Now I remember. The three Hispanic sisters were murdered in their beds while they slept on the night of Dia de los Muertos, or Day of the Dead in English. The Mexican holiday is also known as All Souls' Day. Since their gruesome deaths, this place has been rumored to be haunted by the sisters. Folks swear they hear their footsteps walking from bedroom to bedroom on the upper floor. I'm sure I heard foot-steps walking those hallways myself the last time I showed this place."

"This place was just listed yesterday," Barron pointed out.

"Of course, it was." I spoke with an impatient tenor to my voice. Buckley was seriously getting on my last nerve. "The couple I was showing it to last night heard them too and couldn't have escaped out the front door fast enough. They raced up the sidewalk to their car as if they were being pursued by a cannibalistic tribe in Papua, New Guinea."

"Fascinating story." His tone was not only impatient, as mine had been, as well, but also exceedingly cynical. He shook his head so raucously his fedora toppled off his head, nearly taking his toupee with it. It was only then I realized his thick black hair was a rug and the dashing gentleman was actually bald as a newborn kangaroo. After awkwardly readjusting his hairpiece, Barron mumbled, "But your story is clearly a fairy tale."

As "fascinating" as the tale may have been, he didn't believe one damn word of it, which was disappointing to say the least. I'd been right proud of the fable I'd concocted at the drop of a fedora hat. You can't imagine how much it ticks me off when my fabricated stories aren't given the respect they deserve.

Embarrassed by his incredulous reaction to my haunting narrative, I couldn't have segued into another subject fast enough. I cleared my voice and asked, "Shall we proceed to the kitchen? I know that at least two of the major appliances are malfunctioning, but I'm not sure which ones. You'll likely want to buy all new ones anyway. Just as avocado-colored appliances were popular in the seventies, white appliances were all the rage in the eighties. Not so much in the twenty-first century."

"Uh-huh. I'm sure Celia will want to replace them with stainless steel models." His tone was so dry now that I'd swear I saw a cloud of dust escape from his mouth as he spoke.

We made quick work of the kitchen as every available space in the large room was taken up by boxes of nonperishable food, paper products, cases of water, and other essential items needed to survive a natural disaster that might've kept Lillian trapped in her home for years on end. She had left nothing to chance, I realized, when I opened a broom closet to reveal several large oxygen bottles I'd noticed during our search the previous evening.

Mickey had confirmed at the time his mother had not been afflicted with asthma, COPD, or any other breathing problem, but kept the oxygen on hand in case one of those afflictions cropped up unexpectedly, or at an inopportune time. That kind of foresight sounded like OCD on overdrive to me, and I'd jokingly replied, "Where did your ma keep her crutches and wheelchair in the event she became unable to walk?" I had abruptly stopped giggling when he'd rolled his eyes and responded, "In the basement with her hospital bed, portable toilet, and the rest of her emergency medical equipment."

To explain the oxygen bottles to Barron, I said, "I'm pretty sure the previous owner was on oxygen to avoid inhaling particles of the black mold that coats the inside of the structure's interior walls. I hope you and your wife aren't smokers. This place could go up like a bottle rocket at the flick of a cigarette lighter. Good thing the gas stove is inoperable. It may have a gas leak, however."

Buckley shook his head and turned to head toward the parlor. As soon as he turned his back to me, I opened the door to the back yard to let cold air in as it was already beginning to warm up in the house. *The HVAC unit in this monstrosity must actually be super-efficient*, I thought.

The next room we weaved our way through was the parlor. Buckley placed a hand over his nose as we neared the wall of drapery-covered windows. "Egads! This room smells even worse than the foyer. What in the world could make this room reek so badly?"

"I don't know. I have no earthly idea what makes this house so stinky, but I can see where an unfinished turkey sandwich, or even a pet poodle, could get buried in the rubble without the owner even realizing it. By the time a few months had passed, either one would likely get pretty rank."

"Uh-huh. I'm sure they would."

"As you can imagine, in these massive old homes, the parlor is where company usually gathers. The same holds true for guests when the home is turned into a lodging facility. If you were to purchase this place, you'd probably want to pinpoint the source of that putrid stench before welcoming guests to the *Casa de Hermanas*. Either that, or change its name to *Casa de Hermanas Apestosas*, which stands for—"

"I know what it stands for!" Buckley's retort was curt. He clearly saw no humor in my attempt at levity. "It's Spanish for 'Stinky house of sisters.'"

"Actually, it's 'house of stinky sisters.'" I laughed. Buckley did not. In fact, he looked as if he'd just learned his new puppy had been flattened by a dump truck. Or, worse yet, his pet poodle had been buried in a mountain of twenty-year old magazines.

"Let's just get on with it, Ms. Lee," Buckley said brusquely.

How delightful, I thought. *Barron Buckley's mood seems to be deteriorating more and more the longer we make our way through this remarkable home. As George Peppard used to say in his role on the "A-Team" television show, "I love it when a plan comes together."*

I'd drawn the heavy navy blue drapes in the parlor completely closed, and exchanged the seventy-five-watt bulbs in the light fixtures with twenty-five-watt bulbs earlier that morning, so it'd look dark and dungeon-like in the large room. This was fortunate because it made the self-satisfied smile on my face less noticeable. I had to suppress a laugh when Buckley banged his shin on an old steamer trunk. The expletive he made under his breath was unrepeatable. The parlor was so jammed with furniture, knick-knacks, and insignificant stuff, it made the rest of the house look downright bare in comparison.

At one point, while viewing the parlor, as much as one could in the dark and cluttered room, Buckley asked me if I had anything positive to say about the residence. It was though he felt I was underselling the property. Imagine that! I paused for a spell, as if racking my brain to come up with something encouraging about the place.

Finally, I nodded. "Absolutely. Like I said before, this house is what we call in the business a cream puff. Sure, there are some drawbacks, but what house doesn't have a few of those? If I sound as if I'm not anxious to sell you this wonderful home, it's just that I believe in being totally transparent with my clients. I want them to know exactly what they're getting into, not be upset later because I didn't point out a potential problem to them during the showing."

"How admirable," he mumbled sarcastically.

"Thank you," I replied as if I'd been given high praise. "Truthfully, I think the *Case de Hermanas* would be a great investment for you. Even though the real estate taxes and insurance are ridiculously high, as are the utilities in a house this size, I still believe if you pour enough cash into this place, it will make a perfectly adequate lodging facility."

"Good to hear," he said, with his western drawl and a heavy dose of derision intertwined. "'Perfectly adequate' is just what my wife and I were looking for."

"There you go!" I exclaimed as if his sarcasm had flown over my head like a cluster of birdshot. "This particular piece of property is just about as 'perfectly adequate' as a house can get."

"I don't want to sound rude or unappreciative, but I'm not sure selling real estate is your true calling, Ms. Lee. Have you ever considered retirement or pursuing a different occupation?" Barron asked, sounding *both* rude and unappreciative in my opinion.

"For a while I thought about becoming an actress," I replied, doing my best to sound sincere. "My granddaughter says I look just like Jamie Lee Curtis. And you be surprised at how gifted I am at playing a role, pretending to be someone I'm not. But, after careful consideration, I decided I was too good at moving houses to change cows in mid-stream."

"Horses."

"Horses?" I gasped dramatically. "Oh, no, sir, I'm nearly positive there's some kind of ordinance preventing folks from keeping horses, or livestock of any kind, within Rockdale city limits. Perhaps you should look at purchasing a farm outside of town rather than this rickety old monstrosity. I'd be happy to show you a few that just recently came on the market."

Barron looked at me as if I'd just morphed into Casper the Ghost and offered him a Snickers bar. "Uh, well, never mind about the horses. Can we move on to the bedrooms upstairs?"

"Of course." Standing at the base of the staircase, I looked up toward the top step. "Can you just imagine the lawsuit that would ensue if a guest were to fall down these steep stairs?"

When Barron just stared at me in silence, I added, "Oh, yes, of course you can! After all, you are an ambulance chaser yourself, aren't you?"

"No, I'm afraid not. I probably have more disdain for personal injury lawyers than you do." Buckley looked contemplative when it seemed he should have been offended by my remark. He went on to clarify what type of law he practiced. "I practice family law."

"Oh, I see. So, you're basically a divorce attorney." I then joked, "Maybe if you practice long enough, you'll get good at it."

"We also handle custody cases, adoptions, and restraining orders, among other family issues." Barron looked perturbed. I could tell he didn't feel as if he should have to justify his profession to a real estate agent who should've already taken down her shingle and retired; not only because she was old, but also atrocious at her chosen occupation. "Let's just carry on with looking at the house."

"Fine with me." We proceeded to go upstairs and walked down the hallway, between stacks of old magazines and newspapers, peering into each bedroom and bathroom. There was no need for me to point out faults in any of the third-floor rooms because they were blatantly apparent. The bathrooms were plain and colorless, the bedrooms, small and unremarkable. Each bedroom had a tiny closet and dated wallpapering, peeling off the walls in strips in some instances. Barron shook his head, and muttered, "We'll have to start by tearing down non-load-bearing walls to combine several rooms into one suite. It's going to take a lot of time and money to turn these dreary rooms into rentable suites, isn't it?"

It was basically a rhetorical statement not really demanding a response. Feeling inordinately pleased with myself, I replied anyway. "Hopefully, like most lawyers, you've swindled a gazillion bucks out of your clients."

Buckley showed no reaction to my barb as though he hadn't

heard a single word I'd just said. His next remarks proved otherwise and wiped the grin from my face as if it was a mathematical equation being removed from a blackboard with an eraser. "Let's not waste any more time. I have a lot on my plate today. Let's go downstairs to the kitchen, clear off the table and a couple of chairs so we can sit down and draw up a purchase agreement. I need to get this property under contract so I can get home and concentrate on several cases I have on the court's docket next week. It looks as though I might need to swindle another gazillion bucks out of my clients to afford the restoration of this place. I'm going to offer the seller's asking price so there's no issue with the reserve. It'll still be less than my initial offer to Ms. Sparrow before her untimely death."

I can honestly say I felt more gobsmacked than I had in ages. I'd timed out as soon as I heard the words "Draw up a purchase agreement." I swallowed hard. This was one contingency that hadn't occurred to me. I repeated his words back to him as I followed Buckley down the staircase. "You're going to offer the seller's asking price? And you want me to draw up a purchase agreement so we can get this property under contract?"

"Yes. I want this building despite all the handicaps that come with it. I need some substantial tax deductions and this place will definitely help me accomplish that goal."

I'd been correct in my initial assumption that Buckley was looking to buy the property as a write-off. I waited until we were halfway down the stairs before I exclaimed, "Oh, darn! I left my briefcase at the office. I don't even have a blank real estate contract with me. I guess I just couldn't imagine anyone actually wanting to purchase this property."

Annoyance was evident on Buckley's face. He sighed loudly before pulling his notepad out of the breast pocket of his suit. He hastily wrote down his offer with the fancy fountain pen, along with the date, the address of the property, his personal address, and other pertinent information. I noticed he wrote in cursive, a practice slowly becoming extinct. He ripped the page out of the notepad and handed it to me. "Here's the info you'll need. Get the purchase agreement drawn up as soon as possible and call me with the seller's response to my offer. Although the two mansions are quite different in style, I guarantee you that eventually this imposing structure will be every bit as nice as the inn next door."

I'd been so confident I could talk him out of wanting to purchase the property and was now floundering for an idea on how to dig myself out of the gaping hole I'd just dug. I excused myself on the pretense of making sure I'd turned off all the lights upstairs. At the top of the steps, I sent Lexie a text. I then waited for Buckley to grow impatience and holler up the staircase, questioning what was taking me so long.

I descended the staircase as slowly and unsteadily as I could, and looked at Buckley with a befuddled expression. "Who are you? Why are you in my house?"

"What?" Now his expression was even more bewildered than mine, although *his* confusion was authentic. He placed his hand on his forehead as if someone had just snatched the badly-fitting hairpiece off his slick noggin. "What are you talking about?"

I was saved from having to respond by Lexie rushing into the room. She was panting from the exertion of sprinting across the wide expanse between the two mansions. "Oh, thank God! There you are, Me-Maw! What am I going to do with you?"

While I stared at the wall as if watching a fresh layer of paint dry, Buckley was staring at Lexie equally intensely. Stunned, he asked, "Ms. Starr? Is Sherri your mother?"

It was then Lexie pretended to recognize the potential buyer as one of her RV site guests at the inn. "Mr. Buckley? I had no idea you were in town to look at the Sparrow property! I'm so sorry, but my mother wanders off on occasion and it scares me half to death. This is the second time this month they've had to issue a silver alert for her."

"But, but, but," Buckley began to stutter. "I thought she was a realtor. She was just showing me this house. Not well, but showing it to me all the same."

Lexie shook her head in a forlorn fashion. "Mother hasn't been in real estate for over thirty years, I'm afraid."

My head jerked up as though I was Rip Van Winkle waking up from a long nap. "Yes sir! I'll get right on that contract."

Lexie and Buckley exchanged a look that was easy to decipher; predominantly pity and sadness. Lexie patted me on the shoulder. "I'll take care of it, Me-Maw."

"If you insist, dear," I replied. "I need to help Granddad take the pigs to market this afternoon anyway."

Lexie then turned to Buckley. After the pair exchanged another knowing look, she said, "I'll take care of it on your end, as well, Mr. Buckley. I will get with the Winnett Group Realty office and reschedule a showing with the actual agent who has the home listed. I'm so sorry about all of this."

"No need to apologize. I understand completely. My mother's in an assisted living facility in Boston. Her dementia has gotten so bad she rarely recognizes me now when I go to visit."

"I'm so sorry to hear that and it's something I realize is looming on the horizon with my mother that I'm absolutely dreading. Alzheimer's, or any kind of dementia, is just a gut-wrenching condition. More for the family than the person who's afflicted with it, I think."

As I walked toward the Alexandria Inn behind the two, who were commiserating over the mental conditions of their mothers, my mind was racing. I was already trying to conjure up ways to buy Lexie, Mickey and myself some time to do more searching. It wasn't until Buckley spoke next that the reality of the situation hit me so hard, I gasped in alarm.

"Are you all right, Me-Maw?" Lexie asked with genuine concern, to which I responded with an incoherent grunt.

"No need to call the real estate firm, Ms. Starr," Barron said. "I'll give them a call from the coach. You need to concentrate on taking care of your mother."

It had slipped my mind that Barron Buckley owned the high-dollar Newmar motorhome, the only other RV currently staying on the inn's grounds. I was relieved I'd been inside the Caboose when Rip had exchanged greetings with Buckley the previous afternoon, but how was I going to avoid running into him in the future? Not an easy task when our home on wheels was merely yards away from Buckley's.

Crap, crap, and double crap! I said to myself in despair. *And that's exactly what's going to hit the fan when news of this debacle reaches Rip, which it undoubtedly will.*

And it did. Unfortunately, it reached him even sooner than I'd expected.

EIGHT

I lagged behind Lexie and Barron as they discussed some news about Alzheimer's research Barron had just read about in an AARP publication. Once we reached the inn, Barron excused himself, saying he had to drive over to the realty office to speak with the broker, Jerry Winnett. I didn't like the sound of that and wondered if I'd be behind bars before Lillian's killer was arrested. Lexie assured me Barron seemed like too kind of a man to get her "ailing mother" in legal trouble.

I stayed in the inn with Lexie until I saw Buckley's Lexus pull away from the curb. Just then my phone dinged. It was a text from Rip.

I need you to come home from wherever you're at. Dolly's missing and I can't find her.

Did you look behind the recliner? I replied.

I looked everywhere. She's not in the trailer. I must've left the door open while I was setting up the patio table and chairs. I even crawled into the undercarriage compartment I'd removed the outdoor furniture from and nearly had to call for Detective Johnston to come yank me out. I could tell Rip was in panic mode when he allowed auto correct to take over. *I think Dolly might have waltzed down the path to Innsbruck.*

I sent him a return text saying I'd be right there, resisting the urge to assure him it would've taken significantly more time for Dolly to have danced her way to Austria.

I was relieved to discover Mr. Buckley's fancy car was nowhere to be seen when I arrived at the Caboose. Hopefully, he wouldn't be returning to his even fancier motorhome anytime soon.

Rip and I engaged the help of Lexie and Stone and the four of us searched the entire grounds of the inn twice before convincing ourselves our chubby cat had meandered off the property and into the surrounding neighborhood. She may have just been curious, but more likely she'd wandered off in search of food. One look at her and you'd know overeating was apt to kill her a whole lot quicker than curiosity.

We'd just returned to the trailer to regroup and scour every inch of the trailer one more time. It'd occurred to me she might've jumped up into the storage compartment Rip had searched, but crawled in between the gas grill, empty propane tank, and two spare tires, where Rip couldn't possibly have crawled close enough to see. Had he tried, it would've taken more than Wyatt's brute strength to pull him out. It would've required the Jaws of Life.

In my concern over Dolly, who had Rip and me wrapped around her furry little paw, I'd forgotten completely about Barron Buckley until his black Lexus pulled up beside us. The panicky aura of our group must've been evident because he asked, "Is everything okay, folks?"

Rip nodded, even though he was obviously upset. Dolly was definitely a daddy's girl. "We're just trying to find our cat. She got out of our trailer when I wasn't paying attention."

"Oh." It was obvious Buckley was too esteemed an individual to give a cat's ass about our missing pet. "Well, good luck finding her. I'll keep an eye out for—" His voice trailed off as soon as he made eye contact with me. I'd been trying to hide behind Lexie which proved difficult since I'm at least a half-foot taller than she. He turned back toward Rip, and asked, "Are you Lexie's father?"

"No." Rip smiled at Lexie and then turned back toward the attractive gentleman. "Although I would've been honored to have Lexie as a daughter, she and Stone are just good friends of ours."

"But I thought your wife was Lexie's mother."

It should come as no surprise that after the confusion about my identity was straightened out, I was forced to explain my subterfuge to Mr. Buckley, Stone, and my infuriated husband, while Lexie did her damnedest to maintain a low profile.

After introducing myself using my actual name, I spelled out all the details of why I'd pretended to be the real estate agent Sherri Lee. I concluded with, "I'm truly, truly sorry, Mr. Buckley. I knew you wanted immediate possession and I was only trying to buy us time to find an envelope containing a note that might help lead us to the individual who sliced Lillian Sparrow's brake lines. As you can imagine, in a hoarder's home such as Lillian's, it's like finding one particular grain of sand on Waikiki Beach."

To my astonishment, Buckley laughed out loud. He was clearly amused by my explanation. Rip and Stone, not so much. I did my best not to make eye contact with either of them. Buckley laughed again, and said, "I have to admit, I was beginning to get suspicious when you told me the home's original owners were burned at the stake during the time of the Salem Witch Trials. In fact, I found the entire showing a bit mystifying. I've never met a real estate agent so determined to *not* earn a hefty commission on a real estate transaction."

I did catch Rip's eyes then and instantly wished I hadn't. His normally green eyes were the color of volcanic ash—and still smoldering. I quickly averted my gaze back to Buckley and fell all over myself apologizing. "I'm so sorry, Mr. Buckley. I really—"

"But," Buckley interrupted, "when Lexie explained you were her mother and had dementia issues, I thought the mystery was solved. I'm not sure I see the resemblance to Jamie Lee Curtis, Rapella, but I *do* believe you missed your calling as an actress. I wish you'd just told me that story when I first arrived at *Casa de Hermanas*. I would've been sympathetic to your plight and allowed you as much time as necessary. And please call me Barron, rather than Mr. Buckley."

"Thank you so much for understanding, Barron. I'm sorry you'll have to contact the real Sherri Lee to draw up a contract for you. I'd appreciate if you didn't mention me to her."

"My lips are sealed. Now, what can I do to help you in the search for your missing cat?" I was stunned at Barron's show of compassion. Maybe he did give a cat's ass about our missing kitty, after all.

"She's definitely not in the storage compartment," Lexie said. "I crawled all around inside of it and there was no sign of her."

"Thanks, Lexie." I turned my attention back to Barron, relieved I'd been granted a respite, even though I knew I had a severe scolding from my husband to look forward to in my not-so-distant future. "Her name's Dolly, she tips the scales at twenty pounds, and she's primarily grey with white paws and belly. We think she must have wandered off the Alexandria Inn property."

"At twenty pounds, she should be easy to spot."

"Yes," I began, "but don't tell her that. She's very sensitive about her weight."

Rip rolled his eyes while everyone else in the group chuckled. He could be such a grumpster when he was worried about the furry love of his life that was missing, and upset with his wife, who was currently acting like a numbskull in his opinion.

After the laughter died down, Barron asked Rip, "How long after Rapella left this morning did you leave the trailer door open?"

"It was immediately afterward. Rapella wasn't even out of sight. I presumed at the time she was going to the inn to visit with Lexie."

"Is it possible she could've followed Rapella to the property next door?" Barron asked no one in particular.

We all agreed it was a distinct possibility. Dolly would follow me to hell and back if she thought her efforts might be rewarded with a snack.

Barron nodded. "Then I'm almost positive she's in the house next door. She likely came in the back door when you left it open to let the chilly air inside, Rapella."

As I was blushing at the idea he'd observed me purposely opening the back door of *Casa de Hermanas*, Barron continued. "I was walking through the parlor to exit the house when I heard a rustling noise that I assumed at the time was caused by one of the rats you said used the hole in the base board as a portal. At that point, I was not beyond wondering if you'd actually hired rodents to scare me off the property."

I could not have been more humiliated. Barron was not making it easy on me. If he kept adding fuel to the fire the scolding in my future was going to be a humdinger, possibly the worst on record as far as I was concerned. He winked at me then, and said, "Sorry, I just couldn't resist. I figured out fairly quickly in the showing that you didn't want me to buy the property. I just didn't know why at the time. I'm glad it wasn't because you had a personal objection to me."

"Of course not," I replied. "You are the ultimate gentleman, Barron."

Mickey joined us and we walked as a group to the *Casa de Hermanas*. I still had Mickey's key to the house in the pocket of my cardigan. As I nervously fiddled with the old-fashioned skeleton key, I could never have imagined our cat would be the one to break Lillian's murder case wide open.

When the six of us walked into the kitchen of *Casa de Hermanas*, we found Dolly sitting in the middle of the stove, licking the outside of an envelope. She had knocked over a large roll of *Bounty* on the counter next to the stove. Presumably the small envelope had been tucked underneath the unopened roll of paper towels. Rip snatched up Dolly and hugged her as though he hadn't seen her in a week of Sundays. I asked Mickey, "Didn't you say your ma was making tuna salad at the time the note was delivered? Dolly loves tuna."

When he confirmed my query, I picked up the envelope and sniffed it. Although faint, I could definitely detect the scent of tuna. I looked at Dolly in amazement. "And people thought African elephants had a strong sense of smell!"

I handed the envelope to Mickey. If the envelope contained what we all hoped it did, I felt it was his right to read the note first. If he wanted to share its contents with us, he would. If he didn't, I'd just have to figure out a way to weasel it out of him. Fortunately, he saved me the trouble and read it out loud. "It says, 'This will be your one and only warning. I've got my eyes on you so you better watch what you do.' That's it! That's all it says. And there's no signature."

Rip took the note from Mickey and studied it before speaking. "Although it was sent anonymously, Lillian may have known, or at least suspected, who the author of this note was. What could the person behind it possibly be talking about? What could Lillian have done to make someone leave a message like this on her porch?"

"I don't think Lillian knew who left it on her porch," I countered. "The fact that it's typed makes me think whoever wrote it didn't want Lillian to recognize his writing. If she did know who wrote it, she could've taken the threatening note straight to the police so they could pay a visit to that person. I'm surprised she didn't do that anyway."

"That doesn't surprise me at all," Mickey replied. "Ma was very independent."

"I can totally see her not wanting to get the police involved,"

Lexie said in agreement. "Do you think she knew what was behind the note?"

"I don't think Ma had a clue what the message was referring to or who wrote it. She appeared to be totally baffled by the threat, even though she wouldn't tell me what the note said. Personally, I feel like it might have been related to the person who was looking in her windows that night she called the cops. Why? I don't know. But it just seems as though someone is trying to scare her for some reason."

"Yeah, I'd have to agree," Rip began, "that the person who wrote the note wanted to remain unidentified and had some reason for wanting to frighten Lillian. But I think she *did* know who likely was behind it. To me, it seems as though there had to be some kind of contentious interaction between Lillian and the person who typed this note before leaving it on her doorstep."

I could see Rip's point. I reread the message and studied it and the envelope that'd enclosed it. It was with nostalgia I thought about the first typewriter I ever owned. It was an Underwood model. I used it for years, and finally pitched it when the "b" key stopped working. I thought for a while I could get by without using any word with that seldom used letter in it, but began to realize it was in more words than one would think. The typewriter used to produce this message to Lillian had a similar defect. The "y" type bar, or striker, was misaligned and printed a barely detectible twenty-five percent higher than the other letters. There were seven "y's" in the message and all of them were out of kilter with the rest of the letters. After I came out of my reverie, I said, "How ironic that such an intimidating message was typed on the inside of a blank 'thinking of you' card."

"Intentional sick humor, no doubt," Rip replied. "Now let's make like geese and get the flock outta here! I'm not normally claustrophobic, but this place is giving me the heebie jeebies!"

Walking back to the Alexandria Inn, I whispered to Barron so that Mickey couldn't hear what I had to say. "The *Casa de Hermanas* is available for your possession now that we've located this card. If you run across another threatening note, please bring it to our attention. But we can't hold you up any longer."

"Celia and I are not in such a hurry we can't give Lillian's children a few days to collect anything they want to keep out of the house. The more they take, the less I have to dispose of," he said.

"That's extremely kind of you," I replied. "I do want to let you know there's not really a reserve price set on the property." I didn't want the Buckley's to overpay for *Casa de Hermanas* because of anything I'd said.

He smiled at me and nodded. "I've got an offer in mind, but I appreciate your honesty."

I felt bad that I'd been anything but honest with him when I'd tried desperately to dissuade him from wanting to purchase the property. However, I reminded myself that all's well that ends well and the sense of guilt that'd been plaguing me vanished like a Saharan mirage.

When the six of us reached the Alexandria Inn, Barron excused himself to return to his motorhome. He told us he needed to call the realtor in order to reschedule the showing he'd been forced to cancel due to "something that popped up unexpectedly."

Mickey had made arrangements to drive out to the ranch and introduce himself to Andy and Wendy. Andy had promised to show him the lay of the land and give him an idea of what his responsibilities would consist of as a ranch hand. Lexie offered her Jeep to Mickey for the trip to Atchison, but he declined, preferring to take his chances of becoming an organ donor by riding on his relic of a motorcycle. To make a point, I asked, "By any chance, was that bike the very first Harley Davison to ever come off the assembly line? It's kind of a hot mess."

Ignoring my concern, he said, "Speaking of hot messes, my half-sisters, Rose and Judy, and their partners, are en route to Rockdale and due to arrive early tomorrow morning. They plan to stay for the closing, if one is imminent, and load up the items I stored in my buddy's basement on their behalf in the meantime. I recommended they stay at the Alexandria Inn during their visit, so you can expect one of them to call today to book a couple of suites."

"Thanks Mickey," Lexie said, draping an arm warmly across his back. "I'll set the two couples up in our nicest suites. It should be a quiet weekend, so I'll see to it the four of them have the top floor to themselves."

Mickey excused himself a few minutes later, leaving Lexie and I alone with Rip and Stone. I'd noticed Mickey had seemed to be agitated, twitching and blinking too rapidly. He was sweating profusely and it was barely sixty degrees outside. I looked at Lexie. "Is Mickey okay? Did you notice how oddly he was acting?"

"Yeah," she said, clearly concerned. "Should I go after him?"

Rip shook his head. "I don't think that'd be a good idea. The boy is probably jonesing."

"Jonesing? What's that?" I asked.

"It's just slang for craving a fix," Rip explained. "It's too bad Mickey couldn't get into rehab right away. In the meantime, he's going to be erratic, both mentally and physically. I wouldn't suggest getting into the middle of his addiction. The folks at the rehab center are better prepared to deal with this sort of thing."

I watched Mickey enter the front door of the inn and prayed he didn't have any drugs in his possession. I'd hated to see him walk away from the group because the scolding I'd been expecting commenced the moment he was out of view. Rip tore into me and Lexie like a badger might rip into an unsuspecting pocket gopher. To help keep my own temper at bay, I thought about what to fix for supper while he carried on, asking questions like, "What were you ladies thinking?" and then answering them himself. "You weren't thinking, and that's the problem!" Lexie wasn't spared either.

"Haven't you learned by now that Rapella is bat-shit crazy when it comes to things like this?"

Lexie knew responding to a question like that was a no-win situation, so she remained silent to let Rip blow off steam without interruption. Before he could begin venting again, Stone turned to him and said, "Going along with any of Lexie's harebrained ideas is rarely ever a good idea either."

"Touché, buddy," Rip replied to Stone. "Is there anything else you'd like to add?"

Stone shook his head. "Not much. I think you've about covered it, Rip. Besides, I have to sleep with my wife tonight and doing that with one eye open is next to impossible."

Then, as if he'd had second thoughts, Stone turned his attention toward Lexie and me. "But I will say that Rip is right in that you gals need to be more cautious. You both have a penchant to jump into dangerous situations without considering the potential pitfalls. When you're working in tandem, that impulsive tendency only seems to intensify. It's as if the two of you believe you're invincible when you team up. Guess what? You're not!"

"We know that, honey," Lexie began in a pleading tone. "We are just appalled about what happened to Lillian and want her killer brought to justice."

"I know you do, sweetie. So do Rip and I. We just don't want anything bad to happen to you because in your fervor to figure out who killed your friend, you've acted recklessly. Could you at least run your ideas past us, so we'll know where you two are and what you're doing? This is particularly crucial when your ideas are as preposterous as having Rapella pretend to be a real estate agent, and then, a victim of Alzheimer's when she realized the gig was up. Could the two of you really not foresee all of the potential pitfalls in that absurd gambit?"

"I'm sorry, Stone," I said. To defend Lexie, I added, "It was totally my idea."

Stone's eyebrows arched in obvious skepticism as he said, "Even if that were true, and I highly doubt it, Lexie went along with it. I'm really not trying to pile on or take the wind out of your collective sails. I'm just trying to keep the two of you from suffering an unanticipated catastrophe: physically, legally, emotionally, psychologically, or even financially. I'm sure Rip would agree he and I would be willing to help in any way we can, but we all need to proceed with caution and stay within the boundaries of the law."

I heard Lexie mutter under her breath. "Gee whiz, for not having much to add, Stone sure seemed to natter on for a long time."

"And that's another thing," Rip said, having not heard Lexie's derisive remark because his hearing aids were safely stored in his toiletry bag. "I'm not sure what crime you committed by impersonating a real estate agent, Rapella, but I'm sure it was at least a misdemeanor. You're lucky Barron is such an understanding fellow. He could've just as easily chosen to press charges against you."

Lexie and I made rash promises to keep Rip and Stone in the loop and to use more discretion. Finally, our husbands' white-hot rage began to simmer down. I thought it was an opportune time to ask, "Is it just me, or are the rest of you ready for a stiff drink?"

Over cocktails, Lexie and I decided to have a cookout for supper that night. Rip and Stone could grill hamburgers while she and I put together some side dishes. Lexie had already prepared a fresh blueberry pie for dessert. She said, "I got the recipe for this easy-to-make pie from Lillian. She told me she got it from Ruth Petschl, our neighbor across the street."

We invited Barron to join us along with two couples who were currently renting suites at the inn: Norma and Johnny Lozano from Texas who were celebrating their fortieth anniversary later that week, and Dave and Sharon Nicholay from Minnesota who had just arrived that afternoon and were in town to attend a family reunion.

The Alexandria Inn offered both breakfast and supper to its paying guests, just one of the ways they went above and beyond the normal duties of a B&B establishment. Lexie would need to feed the two couples anyway and thought this was an easy way to do so. All four were fun and friendly and it made for an interesting chat fest.

During one particular exchange, Barron informed us he had put in his offer which had been accepted by Lillian's daughters. "Mickey told me his sisters were coming into town tomorrow morning for the closing later this week. I told him I'd be happy to give them several days before I took possession so they'd have time to go through the house and see if there was anything else they wanted. I'd consider extending the time if two or three days aren't sufficient. The same goes for you folks. There's not a single item in the house I care about. Anything that isn't salvaged by all of you will end up in the local dump. I think emptying out the house, gutting it, and starting from scratch is the best plan of action. It'd be expensive, but I can always swindle a few more clients if need be."

Barron looked at me and winked. I glanced at Rip, who just shook his head and said, "I don't even want to know what he meant by that remark."

Barron laughed and continued. "I'm positive my wife will want to replace all of the appliances and furnishings anyway rather than store them during the remodeling process. Besides, as someone mentioned to me, white was a popular color for appliances in the eighties, but not so much now. So, if there's anything in *Casa de Hermanas* any of you want that Lillian's children aren't interested in, get it while the getting's good."

Before Barron even finished talking, I already had designs on a bedspread in one of the guest suites. It was perfect; a yellowish green hand-stitched quilt with a large embroidered sunflower in the center of the spread. I assumed the quilt was purchased in the seventies, but it looked clean and in excellent condition. Not only could it not have matched the Caboose's exterior paint job any better if it'd tried, it was also queen-sized like our bed in the trailer. I'd wanted to replace our current bedspread for a while but hadn't found any yet I felt were worth their seventy-five to one-hundred dollar price tags. If none of Lillian's children snatched the sunflower quilt up, I would. I had a sneaking suspicion it wouldn't be a top priority for any of the three siblings. However, if any of them did appear interested in it, I might have to make a nonchalant comment about how hideous the half-century-old quilt looked.

NINE

M ost of the conversation at the cookout that evening involved politics. With half of the group being registered Republicans, and the rest Democrats, it made for a lively discussion that bordered on contentious at times. At one point when it looked as if an all-out brawl could develop between the Nicholays and the Lozanos, Lexie made a deliberate attempt to change the subject. "What do you all think about this green bean casserole? I made a slight adjustment to the recipe that I found on the fried onions container."

The spirited debate between the two couples came to a sudden halt as the foursome stared at their hostess as if she'd just announced she'd put anchovies and metal shavings in the casserole. I jumped in to assist Lexie in her quest to lighten the mood which had gotten uncomfortably tense. "The green bean casserole is delicious, Lexie. But I did notice something slightly different in the flavor. I can almost detect a hint of bacon."

"That's it!" She gave me a look of gratitude as she continued. "When I was at the *Dollar General Store* the other day, I discovered Campbells now offers a Cream of Bacon soup, which I substituted for the usual Cream of Mushroom the recipe calls for. I think I actually kind of prefer the casserole with a bacon flavor rather than mushroom."

Rip had picked up on the tension between the guests and recognized Lexie's desire to put out the fire the political exchange had started. "As do I, Lexie. But then, what doesn't taste better with bacon in it? Rapella makes me eat oatmeal for breakfast most mornings. I'd probably add bacon to it if she'd let me."

"And I would, Rip, if the bacon wouldn't cancel out the health benefits of the oatmeal and exacerbate your already sky-rocketing cholesterol level. Bacon was probably somewhat responsible for the triple bypass you underwent, and will be equally to blame for the lethal heart attack you'll likely have if you don't cut saturated fat completely out of your diet."

"Hey!" He exclaimed in defiance. "I eat what you put on the table. So whose fault is it that the last time my cholesterol was checked, the result was but a few points away from a perfect game of bowling?"

"Good grief, Rip." Lexie remarked. "Your cholesterol level is almost 300?"

Before she could ask me why I didn't cut saturated fat out of my cooking, I said, "I go to a lot of effort to serve meals that are as healthy and wholesome as I can. I can't help it if he sneaks Big Macs, French fries, and chocolate long johns behind my back at every opportunity. I'm beginning to believe if I'm not with Rip, it's physically impossible for his truck to pass by a doughnut shop without the brakes engaging."

"How long have I been trying to tell you I can't be held responsible for the poor decisions that naughty Chevy makes?" Everyone chuckled politely at Rip's pathetic attempt at humor, except me and Stone. By that point, I'm pretty sure Rip was wishing he hadn't tried to help us divert the conversation away from politics.

"That's not funny, Rip," I said.

"She's right, buddy," Stone said in agreement. "Lexie and I think the world of you and Rapella. We want to keep you around for as long as possible. I sincerely wish you'd take your health a little more seriously and do all you can to get that cholesterol level—"

"And triglycerides," I interjected. "He's already been diagnosed with a fatty liver due to high triglycerides."

"And your triglycerides level," Stone added, "under control. Do it for those of us who love you if you won't do it for yourself."

"Um, well." Rip had the decency to look ashamed. His next remarks were sincere and spoken from the heart. "Thanks, Stone, I needed that. I truly did. I appreciate your concern and for giving me the kick in the caboose I needed to get back on track. Sometimes I lose sight of the fact that if something happened to me, it's not just me who'd be affected. Family and great friends like you and Lexie, not to mention my beautiful bride, would be affected, as well."

Rip turned to gaze into my eyes as he'd voiced his next remarks. "I apologize, and especially to you, Rapella. I promise to start making my health one of my main concerns, second only in precedence to your safety and well-being. You will always be my number one priority."

I reached over and kissed Rip's cheek, touched by his sincere vow, which I knew he would do all he could to keep. I would make it a point to thank Stone for backing me up. After a brief moment of silence, Johnny Lozano mentioned he'd recently had to have a couple of cardiac stents inserted after experiencing chest pains at a cocktail party. He made a similar vow to Norma to be more conscientious about his health. Then Dave Nicholay promised Sharon he'd have a dermatologist check out a mole on his back she'd been concerned about for several months.

The topic of conversation had successfully changed from politics to a harmonious discussion about all of the health issues the group contended with, which conversations among older people usually do. No further disagreements took place to dampen everyone's spirits during the remainder of the cookout. And frankly, how could anyone not agree that an irritable bowel syndrome flare-up was anything but pleasant?

Before asking to be excused because he had a lot of business calls to make, Barron pulled Lexie and me aside. "I'm not sure what I could possibly do to help out with your investigation into the death of Lillian Sparrow, but if you think of anything, I'd be more than happy to assist. I'm certain Celia would be too once she arrives."

I got the impression it was said in the same vein as you might ask a hostess at a dinner party if she'd like help washing the dishes. You are more than willing to lend a hand if she answers affirmatively, while secretly hoping she doesn't. Still, I thought it was a generous offer by the kind man, especially considering the hoax I'd pulled on him. I thanked him again for his kindness and indulgence and congratulated him on his purchase of *Casa de Hermanas*.

Lexie congratulated him too, and said, "It will be a pleasure having you and your wife as our new next-door neighbors."

"The feeling is mutual," he replied. "I hope you don't mind the competition."

"On the contrary, I welcome it. It would be nice to have a nearby lodging facility to send business to when we are full or want to go on a trip. Stone and I are hoping to do a little more traveling in the future, but it's hard to get away. It'll be easier to free up our time if we can direct guests to the bed and breakfast next door."

"That's great to hear. We will undoubtedly do the same thing when we want to get away for a vacation. It will be advantageous for all four of us if we can work together. But, for now, I don't intend to spend a lot of time in Rockdale. Unfortunately, my business is based on the East Coast and requires the majority of my time. You'll probably see my wife, Celia, much more often than me. For now, anyway, we're planning on having her run the B&B until I retire in a couple of years."

Lexie spoke up then. "I'm anxious to meet Celia and look forward to getting to know her."

"You'll like her. It was she who was determined we buy the historic mansion and turn it into a business that'd continue to produce income during our retirement years. Celia's the kindest, sweetest woman I've ever met, and I'm not just saying that because her perseverance in getting what she wants often scares the living hell out of me. She's like a bulldog with a bone; one-hundred and ten pounds of pure tenacity. She told me I'd better get this deal sewed up, or else! And I believed her." Barron laughed along with Lexie and me, tipped his hat at the entire group, and before heading back to his motorhome, thanked everyone for a wonderful meal and an entertaining conversation.

I was so used to having to yell so Rip could hear me, I'd forgotten Stone's hearing was akin to a barn owl's until he asked Lexie, "Did I hear Barron offer to help you and Rapella investigate Lillian's death?"

'Yes," Lexie admitted as she looked straight into Stone's eyes. "You know I can't just sit idly by while the person who killed our friend and neighbor walks free among us."

"That sounds a bit on the dramatic side," Stone replied. "But I do understand why you'd want to see that she received justice for her death, and I suppose find closure for Lillian's children. I assume you and Rapella were going to run any plans you've made by Rip and me. Right?"

"Of course," Lexie and I said together.

"Just promise me you two won't get into trouble the way you have in the past."

"I promise," Lexie said, "we will be as careful and sensible as possible."

"I don't think that was the answer Stone was looking for," Rip said. He then turned to Stone and asked, "When was the last time you've seen these two wanna-be detectives show any sense or discretion when it comes to murder cases?"

"Never," Stone responded. "But when was the last time you've seen these two 'wanna-be detectives' listen to a word we've said when we've pleaded with them not to get involved? I figured trying to dissuade them was a lost cause."

"I see your point." Rip then looked straight at me as he said, "But please exercise caution and stay out of trouble, as Stone requested."

"We will!" Lexie and I exclaimed together.

Lexie and I left Stone and Rip to discuss plans to go fishing while we carried food and dishes from the picnic area into the inn. Now that we had the reluctant approval of our husbands, we discussed our next move in our investigation of the murder. We felt as if we'd made headway by locating the anonymous note Lillian had received the day before her death but agreed it didn't put us any closer to determining who typed it. We had yet to confirm whether the threat and the victim's death were connected.

We decided we needed to come up with a list of potential suspects. Who might want to harm Lillian and why? If we were able to scrounge up suspects, we needed to determine if those people had alibis. That would be a tricky task because the alibis need not cover the time of Lillian's death, but rather the time the brake lines were cut, which we had no clue about.

It seemed to me that nowadays a video account of every accident, crime, or unusual event eventually surfaces. Not only were there often security cameras in doorbells and strategically placed locations on the exterior of many homes and businesses, but traffic cams on streetlights were now nearly routine. People also habitually used their cell phones to video everything from police interactions with civilians and individuals acting bizarrely or uncivilly in public, to events as innocent as puppies chasing their tails on the sidewalk.

Perhaps our first course of action should be checking if the individual was somehow caught on tape tampering with the Volvo the day prior to the accident that killed Lillian, I thought. I ran my notion past Lexie.

"Great idea," she said. "We might even be able to find a video of the killer driving up to her house, placing the envelope under a corner of the welcome mat, and driving off."

I nodded my head even though I thought the chances of the murder case being that easily solved were remote. I admired Lexie's optimism, however.

While Judy, Rose, and their partners were scouring through their mother's house for keepsakes the following day, Lexie and I would be scouring the neighborhood for video cameras that might offer some sort of inkling to the identity of the murderer. We would run our inspiration by Rip and Stone so as not to instigate another long-winded sermon by the pair. As it'd turn out, they'd be so wound up about trying out some fish tape on the fishing trip they were taking the following day with Stone's friend, Ray Franklin, that they'd have no objection to our plan.

Rip and Stone headed out early the next morning for their fishing trip. Ray had a new boat he wanted to try out, and a honey hole he guaranteed would produce their limit in crappie. He got Rip all hyped up for the trip with just one sentence. "I once caught an eight-pound largemouth bass in that exact spot."

Rip took along the rod and reel combo he'd purchased in Rock-port to go wade-fishing with our son-in-law, Milo Moore, the previous year. He also took along his well-stocked tackle box, along with some crappie jigs, rattling lures, fish tape, and a half full jar of stink bait in case they decided to fish for catfish. I hoped Rip caught at least one nice fish because we already had hundreds of dollars invested in it.

Lexie and I were anxious to get started on our mission as soon as the men left on their much-anticipated fishing excursion. Getting into Lexie's vehicle was more difficult than I'd realized it'd be. I had to firmly grasp the "Oh Shit!" grip on the door frame and heave my well-padded rump up into the seat while Lexie hoisted me from behind. It was almost comical and made us both giggle uncontrollably. This was one scene I prayed did not show up in a video on social media.

Lexie's light green Jeep Wrangler was brand new and nearly the same color as the Chartreuse Caboose. The cute vehicle looked as if it might actually glow in the dark. It definitely would be easy to spot in a Wal-Mart lot, just as our travel trailer was a cinch to pick out of a crowded RV park.

Our first stop was the local Missouri Department of Transportation office. It didn't take long for us to discover we didn't have carte blanche access to the security cameras mounted on Rockdale's traffic lights, of which there were far fewer than we'd expected. The snotty blonde behind the counter stopped filing one of her fingernails long enough to respond, "Bring us a subpoena from the District Attorney's office, or better yet, take your concerns to the Rockdale Police Department."

I really don't want to repeat what my response was to the thirty-something employee. It was vile and beneath me. Rather than apologize I just turned and walked out of the building, feeling remorseful already. I would hate to be in a position where I had to deal directly with the public again. I'd been in a position like that years ago and my employment hadn't lasted a full day.

Once we were back on the sidewalk, I did apologize to Lexie about my rude retort to the clerk. She laughed and replied, "I was getting ready to say something much worse, but decided your response was sufficient."

Our next plan of attack was to check for doorbell cameras in the neighborhood, preferably close to *Casa de Hermanas*. My granddaughter Tiffany and I had used Ring doorbell videos in our investigation into the death of her friend in Albuquerque just a few weeks earlier. Although the videos hadn't exactly helped to solve the murder case, one did get Tiffany's husband released from jail where he was being detained as the prime suspect.

Luckily, we found a doorbell camera directly across the street from Lillian's home. Lexie said, "That's where my friend Ruth lives. She won't mind us looking through the videos her doorbell camera has taken."

When we pulled up to the curb in front of Ruth's house, we noticed Barron Buckley's black Lexus and several other vehicles in the *Casa de Hermanas* driveway across the street. Barron and a slender well-dressed woman we deduced must be his wife, Celia, were standing in the front yard having a lively debate. It appeared to us as if they were having a spat. Celia had the same slender build and classy appearance as Lillian Sparrow had and wore a waist-length fur and knee-high boots. She gave off a celebrity status vibe. I was surprised there wasn't a Maltipoo, Shih Tzu, or some other kind of status symbol pooch peeking its head up over the top of her open satchel.

"What do you reckon Barron and Celia are arguing about?" I asked.

"Probably that he offered full price for a place that allegedly has so many issues: mice, abhorrent smells, nonfunctioning HVAC unit and appliances, leaky roof, and enough worthless rubbish to overload a landfill, just to name a few." Lexie couldn't help giggling at her own joke. I couldn't either, because her laughter was contagious.

We returned our attention to the cars parked in Lillian's driveway. We guessed the red Porsche with the white convertible top belonged to Celia, and the Chevy HHR and brown Ford Taurus belonged to Mickey's half-sisters, or their partners, all of whom had arrived earlier that morning as Mickey had said they would. Both the HHR and Taurus looked as if they were on their last legs. I couldn't imagine making it to the local post office in either of the cars before the engine blew up like a bowl of chili left too long in the microwave.

We pulled into the driveway across the street from Lillian's property. According to Lexie, the owner of the two-story Tudor house was the neighbor who'd given her the blueberry pie recipe. A highly skilled artist, Ruth Petschl was an eighty-seven-year-old bundle of energy. Lexie told me Ruth often joined her in the morning for a chat over coffee after the elderly lady had finished her four-mile daily walk. The last time I'd walked that far was several decades ago. My car had broken down along a barren highway and the closest pay phone was at a small gas station nearly five miles down the road. I admired the woman's fortitude and told Lexie so. I recalled a Ruth Petschl original hanging in the Alexandria Inn's parlor.

"Isn't the hummingbird painting in the inn's parlor one of hers?" I asked.

"Yes. Great eye, Rapella! Even at eighty-seven, Ruth still paints regularly. She is incredibly talented and exhibits some of her work at the Rockdale Art Center. She particularly excels at painting wildlife."

"The hummingbird painting is fantastic! The tiny bird looks so real you'd expect it to fly off the canvas if you tried to touch it."

"Ruth gifted me with that painting last Christmas," Lexie said as she rang the bell. I could tell Lexie had forgotten the Ring doorbell was videoing us as she continued to speak. "I gave her a stupid set of coasters, but she's so sweet she pretended to love them."

A lady with beautifully-coiffed white hair and strikingly blue eyes opened her front door. She immediately invited us inside. She and Lexie shared the same short stature and I felt like a giraffe looming over them. Lexie and the spry older woman exchanged a quick hug before Ruth excused herself to go turn the burner off under something she didn't want to burn.

Lexie stopped talking abruptly as we both laid eyes on a set of coasters on Ruth's coffee table with photos of whooping cranes, snowy egrets, an osprey and a flock of roseate spoonbills on them. As

I recall, they'd been featured in a Rockport Center for the Arts advertisement in the *Rockport Pilot* newspaper a few years prior. Lexie swallowed hard and stared at her shoes. I could barely make out her words as she said, "Oh, I forgot you gave me those coasters two Christmases ago. I'm so sorry. I hope I didn't offend you."

"No offense taken," I said with a hearty laugh. "I'd received those coasters from a friend in my Bunko club named Gracie Parker the previous Christmas and had no use for them in our tiny trailer, so I decided to regift them to you. Truth be told, Gracie had originally been given those coasters from another Bunko club member, Adelaide Hall, who volunteered for years as a docent at the art center. As conservative as I am, I can appreciate the fine art of regifting, and am not insulted one iota you saw the benefit of it, as well. The fact that Ruth has them on her coffee table and enjoys painting wildlife scenes make me think they finally, after a number of Christmas exchanges, ended up with the right person."

"Yes, I guess you're right. Still, I feel bad about it."

"Well, stop it!" I said, as I back-handed Lexie's arm in mock punishment. "To be perfectly honest, the set of milk glass serving bowls Rip and I gave Wendy and Andy as a wedding present was a prize I'd won in a Chinese Raffle the previous February. Since our home on wheels is often bouncing down rough roads, I don't want to have any dishware in the trailer that doesn't remain in one piece when ejected out of a cabinet and slammed to the floor. Most of our dishes are *Melmac*, which can be dribbled like basketballs without sustaining any damage. But keep that to yourself. I don't want to offend the kids."

"Wendy loves those bowls," Lexie said. "No way would knowing you won them in a raffle offend her or Andy. But mum's the word, none-the-less." I could hear a lot of clanging and shuffling in the kitchen, and Lexie took the words out of my mouth when she asked, "I wonder what's taking Ruth so long?"

Before I could respond, Ruth reappeared in the living room. She apologized for making us wait so long, and we both brushed her apology off with a wave of our hands. After Lexie made an introduction between her neighbor and me, she explained why we'd shown up on her doorstep unannounced and uninvited. Lexie offered an apology of her own. "Sorry, I didn't call first to make sure you weren't busy."

"You are welcome here any time, Lexie. I am never too busy for you. I hope my Ring videos can be of some help to you ladies. I'd love to see the person who killed Lillian nailed to the wall by his thumbs just as much as you two would." Ruth had ushered us into her kitchen and was pacing the floor and fiddling with her cell phone as she spoke. I found it peculiar that there was no pan or skillet on the stove, or evidence of any food being prepared.

The three of us huddled over the kitchen table as Ruth brought up the videos on her Ring app one by one. There had to be thousands of them, as if she hadn't deleted a single video since having the special doorbell installed. It took a while, but she finally got to the videos taken on the day before Lillian's deadly accident. After about two dozen video clips, Lexie said, "I didn't know we lived on such a busy street, Ruth."

"Me neither, and according to the time stamp, it wasn't even eight in the morning yet in the last video we looked at." Ruth brought up the next video, and pointed at the back of the lady walking across the street toward the Sparrow home. "Oh, look! That's me walking over to Lillian's house. Wow! Does my butt really look that wide?"

"I'm sure a lot of thirty-year-olds would kill for your figure," Lexie replied. "As would I."

I leaned in closer to view the video as it showed Ruth walking toward Lillian's house carrying a small white card or envelope in her right hand. As she neared Lillian's front stairs, we lost sight of her because a large crepe myrtle tree in Lillian's yard blocked the view from that point on. It was autumn and the tree had lost most of its leaves, but was still dense enough to hide the front porch. After just a few scant moments, Ruth popped back up on the phone's screen at the edge of Lillian's yard. Both hands were now empty. She looked both ways several times, her head going back and forth as if she'd been watching a tennis match. She then stepped back down off the curb and sprinted back to her own home. She could not have crossed the street any faster had she'd been in danger of being run down by a semi. When the video ended, Ruth shook her head and said, "Even though the speed limit is twenty miles-per-hour, people drive down this street like they're racing in the Indianapolis 500. We need speed bumps in front of our homes."

"Amen to that," Lexie agreed. "Wyatt ought to sit in our driveway and run radar. He'd hand out speeding tickets like they were Halloween candy."

"Was that a white envelope you were carrying in your right hand, Ruth?" I asked once the two ladies were through gabbing about speeders.

"No. It was a recipe card." She sounded defensive. "I was taking Lillian a copy of a broccoli-cheese casserole recipe she'd requested earlier that morning."

"You sure didn't stay long!" I did my best not to sound as if I was accusing her of leaving a threatening note on Lillian's front door, rather than a recipe, although that's precisely what was going through my mind.

"Well, no." Ruth looked remorseful as she went on to explain. "Knowing now what would happen to her the following day, I feel bad about not knocking. As much as I adored her, I didn't have time that morning to listen to every little minute detail about a cousin's wedding she'd attended the previous day with her oldest daughter, Rose Hamm. You see, Lillian had a bad habit of jabbering on and on. Am I not right, Lexie?"

"You are spot on, Ruth."

"On two separate occasions I have nodded off while she was

explaining something to me, only to wake up to find her still talking, unaware I'd taken a power nap." Ruth smiled at the memory.

"That happened to me one time too," Lexie said, wearing an expression of fond remembrance. "I even told that story at her memorial service and everyone laughed. A few told me later they'd had a similar experience with her. Lillian, God bless her soul, rarely came outside of her home. But when she did, she could be quite chatty, and could talk your arm off if you'd let her. It once took her twenty minutes to tell me what she'd made herself for breakfast after I'd gone to her house to borrow some *Bisquick*. Meanwhile, I had seven hungry guests at the inn waiting to be served their own breakfast."

"Oh, no," I said in amusement. "What did you do?"

"I stood on her porch and listened politely to her ramble on. I checked my watch every couple of minutes, but she didn't get the hint. Try as I might, I couldn't get away until she'd described every facet of her meal. I still remember her saying, 'I put three pats of butter on my pancake, which incidentally was shaped like a watermelon. Not one pat, not two, but three pats of butter. And do you know why I put three pats of butter on my pancake, Lexie? Because I could. That's why!' I was getting very impatient by that point, and probably came off as annoyed, but I find it an endearing memory now."

Ruth laughed at Lexie's high-pitched imitation of Lillian's voice. "I had a fresh loaf of bread in the oven at the time I ran the recipe over to her. I didn't want the crust to burn so I left the recipe under her welcome mat and sent her a text telling her where to find it. I feel guilty now and wished I'd taken the time to visit with her. It's not like I couldn't have delayed baking the bread for an hour, which is at least how long it would've taken Lillian to describe the bride's wedding gown."

We all chuckled at Ruth's last remark, which was spoken in an affectionate manner, not a critical one. I watched as Ruth's laugher ceased and sadness replaced it. I tried to comfort her. "Don't beat yourself up over it, dear. It's understandable you'd feel that way now, but hindsight's twenty-twenty, as they say. You had no way of knowing what would happen the next day."

"I know. You're right, Rapella." Ruth grabbed my left hand and gave it a warm squeeze. I smiled at her before speaking again.

"Let's continue on to the next video." Although I spoke as casually as I could, I couldn't help but notice how clandestinely Ruth had appeared in the video we'd just watched. She'd glanced around before racing across the street, both coming and going, in a very anxious manner. It was as if it was a common occurrence for a pack of wild dogs to roam the neighborhood and she didn't want to be caught unawares and get attacked. Moreover, it was as though she didn't want to be seen by the neighbors while the "pack attack" was occurring. If I hadn't known the woman's age, friendly personality, and the fact that she was a close friend of Lexie's, I might've put Ruth on my personal suspect list. Surely her show of grief wasn't merely an act. *Or was it?* If she turned out to be the perpetrator of this heinous crime, it wouldn't be the first time it was the last person I could've imagined committing it.

I might put her on my list anyway, I decided. *I told Ruth she had no way of knowing what was about to happen to her neighbor. Now I have to wonder if I misspoke.*

Lexie had taught me the first time we'd met at a campground in Cheyenne, Wyoming, to carry a small notebook so I can make notations in it I might need to look back on later. The habit had proven very handy in past murder investigations I'd unwittingly gotten involved in. *I will have to dig around in my night stand for that notebook when I get back to the Caboose. I have a lot to write down in it, including my reservations about Lexie's friend and neighbor.*

That's plum silly, I then argued with myself. *Ruth could no more sabotage her neighbor's Volvo by severing its brake lines than I could install a new carburetor in that same vehicle. For starters, I'm not certain I could tell the differ-*

ence between a carburetor and a catalytic converter, or a toaster oven, for that matter.

I had talked myself out of adding Ruth to my suspect list when another thought crossed my mind. *On the other hand, the aging artist could've had a very compelling motive we haven't uncovered yet, and a competent accessory to carry out the crime. One could practically be on life support in prison and hire a hit man, for goodness' sake!*

In the end, I won the debate with myself and would start off the list in my notepad with a potential but very unlikely suspect. *After all, I reasoned, I have to start somewhere.*

We watched another half-a-dozen video clips which showed nothing to stir our interest. Two of the six were of Mickey arriving on his motorcycle and leaving thirty minutes later, which was to be expected.

Ruth sped by a dozen or more videos before coming to an intriguing video clip time-stamped at 09:38. It was light outside and we all watched as the video showed what appeared to be a purple Chevrolet HHR drive slowly under two street lights before pulling into Lillian's driveway. I recognized the model because my grandson's first car was a 2007 Chevrolet Sunburst Orange HHR, a retro-styled panel wagon. Dusty had told me the HHR stood for "Heritage High Roof," as crazy as that sounds. I also recognized the car because there was currently an identical one parked in Lillian's driveway. Before the HHR even rolled to a stop in the video clip, a large brown delivery truck parked in the street, obliterating our view of the purple sedan and Lillian's house entirely. We saw the driver walk toward the camera with a medium-sized package to leave on Ruth's front porch. Immediately after the UPS truck pulled away, with the driver motoring up the street to make his next delivery, the HHR backed out of the driveway and followed suit. The elapsed time was less than a minute.

"Dang it!" I exclaimed. "Because of that UPS truck, we didn't get to see who was driving the car, or what they did while they were at Lillian's."

"The package UPS delivered contained a few kitchen utensils I'd ordered from *Crate and Barrel* with a gift card my daughters, Cindi and Lori, had given me for my birthday," Ruth explained, even though no one had inquired about the package's contents.

In deep thought and ignoring Ruth's remark completely, I thought out loud. "But clearly the HHR belongs to one of Lillian's daughters, or their partners, who are all here in town for a few days to scour through the house for keepsakes."

"Which makes it a moot point," Lexie began, "because neither Judy nor Rose would harm their mother. I've met both ladies and they were sweet, thoughtful, and appeared to be very close to Lillian."

"Have you met Rowdy or Judy's wife?" I asked.

"No, I've never met Rowdy or Sammi. But I've heard a lot about them from Lillian. Why do you ask?"

I merely raised my eyebrows at Lexie. She got my point and said, "No, I really don't think either of those two would do anything to harm Lillian either."

"Even to cash in on their significant other's share of the estate? According to Mickey, both Judy and Rose are anxious to get their mom's house sold so they can 'cash out,' as he put it."

"Yeah, I know. But still . . ."

"You don't think we shouldn't at least question the girls? Maybe we could simply engage them in a conversation in order to judge their reactions to a few sensitive remarks. I'd be happy to do the talking and spare you from possibly antagonizing Lillian's daughters."

Although Ruth was nodding in agreement to my queries, Lexie remained noncommittal; indicating she didn't want to appear suspicious of their intentions when they'd just lost their mother to a murderer. She knew as well as I did that a murder victim's closest family members, most commonly one's spouse, were often the number one suspects. I brushed off her objection to questioning Lillian's daughters and their partners, but I wasn't going to give them a pass, even if I had to speak to them myself while not in Lexie's company. My suspect list was growing and yet Lexie hadn't put a single name on hers.

Perhaps she's too close to the forest to see the trees, so to speak. She's lost someone close to her at the hands of an evil killer. I totally understand she's emotionally involved in Lillian's murder case and doesn't want her buddy's death to have been brought about by a greedy relative. I would feel the same way if I was in Lexie's shoes. I don't have the emotional aspect to deal with and I don't want to do anything that might make the hurt Lexie feels even more painful. I'll have to be diplomatic, but diligent, so as not to overlook a prime suspect in my efforts not to upset my already grieving friend.

TEN

The cookout the previous evening had gone over so well, we decided that Stone and Rip would host a fish fry that evening for everyone staying at the Alexandria Inn, as well as Ray and Cheryl Franklin. It was Ray's nineteen-foot Bass Tracker deep-V boat they'd taken to the lake to fish from. He'd just recently purchased it from Bass Pro's headquarters in Springfield, Missouri, and had been anxious to try it out. All three men seemed impressed with its features and comfort and praised the performance of its 150 XL Four-Stroke motor.

Between the three fishermen, they'd caught a dozen crappie, six nice bass, three catfish, and two large sun perch. Rip was on cloud nine from having reeled in a fourteen-pound blue cat just as their day of fishing on Smithville Lake was drawing to a close. Ray had cleaned all the fish earlier. Rip seasoned and battered the filets while telling a few questionable fish tales and Stone cooked them in a sizzling pot of peanut oil. Stone explained to the crowd that peanut oil didn't burn like vegetable oil was wont to do, a useful tip I stored in my memory banks for future reference.

Stone then lowered a basket of "crab puppies" into the sizzling oil. The hush puppies stuffed with crab meat were a creation of his. "It's a crowd pleaser," he declared. Stone winked at Rip as he added, "Along with the deep-fried fish and French fries, it's guaranteed to be a meal that'll delight your taste buds and clog your arteries."

Along with the three fishermen and their wives, attending the fish fry were the Lozanos, Nicholays, Judy and Sammi, Rose and Rowdy, Mickey, Barron and Celia Buckley, and Wendy and Andy. It was a beautiful November evening and nothing but a light jacket was needed to keep comfortable. Everyone appeared to be in good spirits and was sipping on the adult beverages they'd each brought along for their own enjoyment. As far as Rip and I were concerned, Dr. Herron's one alcoholic drink per day rule was tossed out the window like a dead cockroach. What she didn't know wouldn't hurt us, or at least not lecture us until she was blue in the face.

When Lexie mentioned she was going into the inn to retrieve a big bowl of potato salad she'd made that morning, I took the opportunity to draw Mickey aside for a quick exchange.

"How's it going?" I asked.

"It's tough, but I'm doing all right so far," he replied. I hadn't specifically asked about his attempt at sobriety, but he'd sensed that was what was behind my inquiry.

"I'm glad to hear that. Does someone in your family drive a purple HHR?"

"Yes," he replied. "That old car belongs to Rose's boyfriend, Rowdy, but it's usually Rose who's driving it. Rowdy usually drives his bike everywhere. Why do you ask?"

"I was just curious. Lexie and I checked out some neighborhood doorbell camera videos and saw a purple HHR stop by your mom's house for just a few short moments the day before her death. We couldn't see what the driver of the vehicle did while he was there, but now that I know the car belongs to Rowdy, I'm not as concerned. For that matter, it could've just been a coincidence that the car matched his."

Mickey laughed. "Oh, come on, Rapella. You don't believe that any more than I do. How many purple HHR's do you see on the road these days? They stopped making them about a decade ago. There weren't too many purple ones manufactured to begin with and that was quite a few years ago by now. I remember when Rowdy first bought that car from an ex-girlfriend. He was showing it off to me, and I asked, 'How old *was* this girlfriend anyway? I thought only old ladies liked the color purple.'"

"What'd he say?"

"He said, 'It ain't purple, dude. According to Chevrolet, the color is called Majestic Amethyst Metallic'. And I replied, 'It sure looks purple to me.' It ticked him off real good."

"It looks purple to me too, Mickey, and it's a hell of a lot easier to say than majestic amethyst metallic." We chuckled a moment before growing serious again. "Did you know Rose and Rowdy visited your mom the day before she died, or at least stopped by her house for a few scant moments?"

"Yeah, I knew Rose was here for a few days to attend a cousin's wedding with Ma and was still in town when Ma was killed. The bride was actually a second cousin to Rose and Judy. It had to be Rose in the HHR you saw in the video. I'm not surprised to hear she drove Rowdy's car rather than catch a flight. Flying has never been one of her favorite things to do. In fact, the very thought of flying has always terrified her. I only saw Rose for a couple of minutes during her visit, but Rowdy wasn't anywhere to be seen. I really don't think he tagged along. Which is fine with me because the bast—" Mickey stopped mid-sentence to apologize for the language he almost used.

"No worries. We are both adults. So, why were you and Rowdy at odds with each other?" I asked, as if it were any of my business. He had no obligation to answer my nosy inquiry and I'm not certain I would've had our roles been reversed. Fortunately, his longing to see his ma's killer brought to justice outweighed his desire for privacy.

"I just don't trust him. His real name's Rodney, but it's no surprise he was given a nickname like Rowdy when he was younger. I know I'm no prize, being an addict and all, but Rowdy Noble takes the cake when it comes to being a troublemaker." Mickey brushed his straggly hair out of his eyes and studied my expression for a moment, accurately sensing how badly I wanted to ask him if that wasn't the pot calling the kettle black, before he continued. "I swear my attack on Rip was a once in a lifetime thing. I've never done anything like that before and never will again. I still feel awful about it. I was totally out of my mind from having just learned Ma's death had not been an accident and was in bad need of a fix. I literally wanted to stone myself to death that day."

I almost said, "It's *literally* impossible to stone yourself to death, or at least as difficult as it is to stab yourself in the back." But then it dawned on me it was a different type of stoning he was referring to. "I understand, Mickey, and I'm glad you didn't. Go on with what you were saying about Rowdy."

"He's been arrested more times than I can count, mostly for burglary and armed robbery. Once for shooting a liquor store clerk in the leg when the guy couldn't open up the safe fast enough because he was too shook up to get the combination correct. I think he did thirty days in the county jail for that one but soon after the arrest was expunged from his record, according to Rose. She told me it all happened back in his younger days and he'd turned his life around by the time she met him. She may be right. I can't see her having anything to do with him if he was still as wild as he used to be. To give credit where credit's due, Rowdy does seem to be very conscientious about taking care of his ailing father."

"I guess that's one bright spot in an otherwise dark past. Rowdy's first name might suit him, but his last name of Noble sure doesn't."

"That's exactly what Ma said. She had absolutely no use for him."

"Why is a low-life like him not behind bars?"

"Mainly because his dad retired as the Atlantic County attorney and before he became senile, he once wielded a lot of power in Egg Harbor Township, which has a population of around forty-thousand residents, according to Judy." Mickey suddenly became quiet and began toying with his drink, which I noticed was a Mountain Dew. *Plenty of caffeine, but no alcohol,* I thought. *Good for him!* Just then I felt a presence behind me, looked up and discovered the reason behind Mickey's curious behavior. Rowdy Noble had walked up behind me.

"What's up, bud?" The man asked Mickey after nodding casually at me. The greeting was casual, but the tension in the air was anything but.

"Not much," Mickey responded. I could sense he wanted to remind Rowdy that the two of them were not buddies. "What's up with you?"

"Just anxious to get the stuff Rose wants out of your mom's house loaded up so we can head home. Work has been crazy busy recently."

"Your lawn maintenance business has been crazy busy in November? Glad it wasn't so hectic you couldn't get away a couple of weeks ago to visit Ma here in Rockdale." There was sarcasm in Mickey's voice and he was making no effort to disguise it. "What was that visit all about?"

"Ah, you know how it is," Rowdy replied. I was impressed with Mickey's presence of mind to devise a way to determine if Rose's boyfriend *had* tagged along on the trip after all. I can't imagine Rowdy would've been all that anxious to attend the wedding of his girlfriend's cousin whom he'd likely never met, but perhaps he'd had other reasons for wanting to come to Rockdale. Rowdy stalled for time by bending down and retying an already well-tied shoestring. It seemed to me it was taking him a long time to come up with a reasonable response to Mickey's query.

"No, I don't," Mickey said after a long pause in the conversation, waiting for Rowdy to elaborate on his remark. "Why don't you tell me how it is?"

"Your sister just had a hankering to visit your mom and attend that wedding with her. Who am I to deny my girl something like that?" Rowdy had the audacity to make himself sound like boyfriend of the year material, when in actuality, it was obvious even to me there was more behind the visit than he was letting on. "Actually, I was a little annoyed at the time because I didn't want to leave my sick dad just so Rose could attend the wedding of a second cousin she'd only met twice in her life."

"So why did you?" I asked. "Couldn't Rose have made the trip here by herself?"

"She actually begged me to stay home to take care of my dad," Rowdy replied. "But I didn't like the idea of her traveling across the country alone in my old car, which has one-hundred-and-eighty-thousand miles on it. I'm pretty sure it's on its last legs."

"Why don't you replace it with a newer, more reliable car?" I know I sounded derogatory, but I really didn't care. There was just something about Rowdy that turned my stomach.

"Don't you think I would if I could afford to?" Rowdy's tone was discourteous, but I suppose my questions were just as offensive in his view. "As it turned out, I'm glad I insisted on coming along and that we came when we did, with your mom's death occurring two days later. We were already here for the funeral, which saved us a trip back to Rockdale."

"How convenient that must've been for you." Mickey's remark was as insincere as it could possibly get, but Rowdy didn't seem to pick up on the irony in his voice. "I thought you'd flown in from New Jersey for the memorial because I hadn't seen you at all that week."

"Nope. I was already here, in a room at the Quality Inn. I never did see your mom on that trip–alive, that is– because I entertained myself while Rose visited with her. You know as well as I do your mom didn't care for me much."

"Yeah, she pretty much despised you." Mickey certainly wasn't one to beat around the bush. "But I'm sure you had no trouble entertaining yourself while you were in town. I'm surprised you found the time to attend her services with Rose."

I was certain Rowdy *did* pick up on Mickey's sarcasm that time. How could he not have? But he refused to react or respond to it. "Had Rose and I only known what was about to happen, we might've been able to somehow prevent the terrible accident. But you know what they say about hindsight being twenty-twenty."

Yes, I thought, as Mickey glared at Rowdy. *I do know what they say about hindsight. I just used that tired old cliché myself a couple of hours ago. But when I used it, I wasn't trying to dodge the truth. And, by the way, Rowdy, you and I both know there was nothing "accidental" about the accident that killed your girlfriend's mother.*

Rowdy walked away after speaking, clearly not thrilled about being questioned by Mickey and then grilled by some old lady he didn't even know. I had several other questions I wanted to ask the guy, but they would have to wait.

I looked up just as Lexie walked out the back door of the inn with an armful of food and condiments. An unopened bag of potato chips swung from her clenched teeth. I raced over to lighten her load by grabbing the chips from her mouth and jars of tartar sauce and ketchup that were teetering on top of a foil-wrapped bowl of potato salad she was balancing in her left hand. In her right hand she carried two round Tupperware containers stacked one on top of the other. Inside the containers were freshly baked pecan pies for dessert.

We could debate on whether to pronounce the word pecan as "pee-can" or "puh-kahn" until we'd driven ourselves *nuts*. As far as I was concerned, the latter was correct. A pee-can was a five-gallon bucket my dad always brought along when he took me and my five brothers on fishing trips. The bucket was for my benefit alone; I was the only one in the boat who couldn't just "hang it off the side of the boat" to take a leak.

"Thanks buddy!" Lexie said, as I took the two pies from her right hand, freeing it up so she could place the potato salad on the serving table.

"I didn't realize you had so much stuff to get from the kitchen. You should've asked me to help you!" I scolded Lexie. I'm sure she was thinking, "You should've offered!" In normal circumstances, I would have automatically joined her without even asking if she needed assistance. But, in this instance, I didn't want to waste my chance to speak to Mickey alone. In retrospect, it was a very informative conversation and I'd be adding one more name to my list of suspects. In fact, Rowdy Noble had just taken over the number one spot.

I'd considered keeping the information I'd garnered from the conversation with Mickey and Rowdy to myself - temporarily, at least. But it felt wrong to keep such incriminating details from my partner in crime-solving. Although I knew Lexie was determined to find a suspect outside the victim's family, I decided to tell her what I'd learned, but do so with discretion and diplomacy. Those are two things that do not come naturally to me, as you shall see.

"I think Rowdy Noble cut Lillian's brake lines so he could capitalize on Rose's share of her mother's estate," I stated, mincing no words. Lexie stared at me as if my eyebrows had grown together in the few minutes since she'd last seen me. I swiped my right hand across my forehead to make sure I hadn't actually sprouted a unibrow without realizing it.

"What in blazes makes you think that?"

I reiterated the short exchange between myself and the two men that'd just taken place. "I can't say for certain, Lexie, but I got the distinct impression Mickey believes the same as I do. You had to be here to feel the tension between the two men, but it was so thick you couldn't have cut it with a chainsaw."

"To be fair, Rapella, as much as I care for Mickey, it's difficult for me to come to that kind of conclusion based on Mickey's opinion of the guy. Truthfully, the two dudes may repel each other like oil and water, but they're as alike as lard and tallow: basically the same thing but derived from two different animals. I have an idea that Lillian's dislike for Rowdy was not *only* based on his nickname, but also from the disparaging remarks Mickey frequently made about the guy."

"I agree wholeheartedly," I replied. "But I'm not basing *my* opinion of Rowdy on Mickey's. We watched every video recorded on Ruth's Ring doorbell app from the day before Lillian's death. Right?"

"Yes."

"It was fairly early in the day when Rowdy's car was seen arriving at Lillian's house. Agreed?"

"Agreed; it was nine-thirty-eight in the morning, I believe the time-stamp read."

"Does it not seem odd to you, Lexie, that Rowdy drove Rose here from New Jersey to visit her mom, but they only stayed at her house less than a full minute?"

"Well, yeah, now that you mention it."

"Only the driver got out and walked to the front door and then returned to the car. We couldn't tell if both Rose and Rowdy were in the car, but wouldn't you think if the pair had driven that far to visit Lillian, only to find her not home when they arrived at nine-thirty-eight in the morning, they'd return later in the day?" I asked. "Besides, in a house the size of Lillian's, it might take her longer than a minute to answer a knock at the door."

"Yes, but supposedly Lillian and Rose had attended the cousin's wedding the day before the 'thinking of you' card was left on her porch. Rowdy didn't say so outright, but he definitely implied that Rose had gotten to spend some time with her mother the day before her mother was killed, as well. According to the videos we looked at, that implication doesn't ring true."

"'Ring true'?" Lexie asked with a grin. "Was that supposed to be a pun?"

"Nope," I replied with a wink. "It was an accidental play on words. But do you see what I'm getting at?"

"Yes, my friend. I do see." I watched Lexie as her mind went into overdrive. I could almost see smoke escaping from her ears as thoughts flitted about in her brain. "I do recall that whenever either or both of Lillian's daughters came to visit, with or without their partners, they always stayed in a local hotel called the Quality Inn. At the time, I always thought that was odd. Having been inside her home, I now understand why they didn't stay at *Casa de Hermanas*. Twenty-one rooms in the house and yet, there is nowhere for a guest to sleep. Every bed in the place is piled high with 'stuff.'"

"Well, not *every* bed," I replied. "The bed upstairs with the chartreuse quilt on it had nothing, or very little, on top of it or I wouldn't have been able to see the sunflower in the middle of the bed covering. Is it possible Rose decided to stay at Lillian's house that weekend for a change? Rowdy could've just stopped by to bring Rose something she'd requested he drop by her mom's house, which would explain the 09:38 video."

"That's possible, I suppose."

"And wanting to spend some time alone with her mother could be why she didn't want her boyfriend to join her on the trip. She might have wanted to vent or cry on her mother's shoulder about a rift she and Rowdy were having in their relationship."

"That's certainly possible," Lexie agreed. "When Chester and I had our one and only falling out during our first year of marriage— after a critical remark he'd made about my first attempt at homemade lasagna, no less—I ran straight home to my mom to cry on her shoulder, knowing she would commiserate with me."

I smiled. "And she did I presume?"

"Oh, hell no!" Lexie responded with a laugh that came out as an unladylike snort. "She told me to march my sniveling butt back home and make up with Chester. She said, and I quote, 'No daughter of mine is going to get divorced over a stupid batch of lasagna, one of the toughest and most foolish dishes to attempt when you barely knew how to make toast yet.'"

"Your momma sounds like a hoot, and remarkably like my own." I laughed at her anecdote, and then returned to the original subject. "Chances are Rowdy was alone in the car in the video. If not dropping off something for Rose, he might've been going to visit but had a change of heart once he stood on his mother-in-law's doorstep. He made it apparent he knew she didn't hold him in very high esteem."

"Oh, yeah," Lexie agreed, "she made her contempt for him quite clear. We need to look at that particular video again. I think we should send it from Ruth's cell phone to mine so we can study it closer when we have more time."

"It might be a good idea to forward it to your phone anyway," I said, "just to have easy access to the clip later on if it's needed as evidence."

Lexie nodded. "We also need to look through all the videos on Ruth's Ring app from the day of Lillian's death and send any pertinent videos from that day to my phone, as well."

"All right. What are we going to be looking for in the video with the HHR?" I asked out of curiosity.

"Well, we know the driver got out and returned to the car less than a minute later, so it didn't appear as if Rowdy dropped Rose off to visit with her mother. If the driver *was* Rowdy, that is, which is something else we need to try and confirm. I'm not sure we'll be able to determine what the driver did during that time with that UPS truck blocking our view."

"Well, it won't hurt to give it another look," I said. "As far as any videos from the day of her death, there should be one of Lillian leaving her house sometime before ten to head out on her fateful trip to meet Rose at Starbucks in the sabotaged Volvo."

"Yes, and prior to that video, there should be one of someone stopping by to cut the two brake lines. I would think they'd have had to be cut fairly shortly before Lillian left in her car." Lexie's response was brief, but we had to get to work arranging everything on the serving table for the evening's fish fry. Stone had just announced the fish would be ready in five minutes. We still had to bring out the paper plates, silverware, and dinner napkins and the starving natives were already getting restless. We hastily agreed we needed to return to Ruth's house the following morning and continue our investigation from there.

Stone yelled, "Soup's on!" and once the platters of fish were placed on the serving table, Lexie asked that all of the dinner guests hold hands for a quick prayer.

"Lord, thank You for the food before us, the family and friends beside us, and the love between us. Amen."

"Amen," the group echoed in unison, just seconds before total chaos ensued.

Just as we all raised our bowed heads, we saw Mickey let loose with a haymaker that rendered Rowdy unconscious. As blood flowed freely from Rowdy's nose, Rose broke her bottle of Miller Lite over Mickey's head in retaliation for her half-brother's assault on her boyfriend. Judy jumped in between her siblings to prevent further injury and instead took an errant elbow to the eye socket. Sammi shook her head and popped a crab puppy into her mouth in apparent disgust. The dinner party had gone downhill faster than any social gathering I'd ever attended in all of my seventy-one years. I only wished I'd thought to video it with my cell phone.

ELEVEN

Rowdy regained consciousness as the ambulance pulled into the circle drive. The head emergency medical technician, or at least the fellow who appeared to exude the most authority, quickly began to assess the injuries. The handsome EMT, who looked like Paul Newman in his prime, declared Mickey had a laceration on his head and possible concussion, Judy had a black eye, Rowdy had a broken nose, and Sammi, whose throat was quickly swelling shut, was experiencing anaphylactic shock. I'm not sure what she thought Stone had stuffed the hush puppies with, but she was apparently unaware the *crab* puppies contained crab meat. Other than Sammi's shellfish allergy, I'd had all of those diagnoses nailed down before Lexie had ended her call to the 9-1-1 dispatcher.

After the paramedics had strapped an oxygen mask on Sammi and given her an epinephrine injection with her own epi-pen, they suggested someone drive Mickey to the local urgent care clinic for stitches. They then recommended Judy put a bag of frozen peas on her rapidly swelling eye and that Rowdy lean forward and pinch his nostrils together for ten minutes to help stop the bleeding. Ten minutes after their arrival, the EMT's left the scene with the unspoken promise of a nine-hundred-dollar invoice for their services to be mailed out soon.

I'm not disparaging the first responders, mind you. In my eyes, they are all heroes, and I can't imagine where we'd all be without them. If not for EMT's, Rip might have bled to death after being shot in the hip a couple of years ago and my daughter might still have an uncooked lima bean embedded in her left nostril. In this instance, however, I'd thought it was unnecessary to call 9-1-1 in the first place and had said so. I'd been outvoted. The EMT's had made it apparent they agreed with my assessment, but had acted as professionals all the same.

Lexie glanced my way as they waved and drove off. I shrugged and she gave me a thumbs-up gesture to indicate they should've all listened to me when I told them calling for an ambulance was a waste of time and money. If emergency services had to respond to every little dust-up between two alpha males, there wouldn't be enough ambulances left to respond to real emergencies, like heart attacks and cutting one's finger off with a circular saw. I suppose the epinephrine injection was beneficial for Sammi, although she could have just as easily utilized the epi-pen in her jacket pocket herself. It's conceivable the idea of injecting herself made her uneasy, but I would've been happy to stab the needle in her upper thigh had she only asked.

Rowdy and Rose retreated to their suite in the inn with a wet rag over Rowdy's nose and Judy held a bag of frozen veggies to her eye as she and Sammi followed suit. Lexie had been unable to produce a bag of frozen peas, but we all agreed frozen corn kernels would suffice. That left Stone to haul Mickey off to get his coconut sewed up. The fish fry resumed, but it was a much smaller group and more subdued affair following the mêlée.

I helped Lexie clean up after everyone had eaten and the remaining guests had dispersed. On the walk back to the Caboose with Rip, we discussed the skirmish. I brought up what had transpired before Mickey punched Rowdy's lights out and Rose used her Miller Light to put a hole in his head in retaliation. Rip, who clearly wasn't impressed with either combatant, replied, "It just seems like a waste of a perfectly good bottle of beer."

The following morning found Lexie and I back on Ruth's front porch. Ruth quickly ushered us inside and asked us if we'd like a cup of French Roast. As I was about to decline the offer, having already downed three cups in Lexie's kitchen before we walked across the street to Ruth's house, Lexie replied, "Absolutely!"

I was already trembling like a six-week-old puppy that'd been swatted on the rump with a rolled-up newspaper for peeing on my owner's house slippers. *What could one more cup hurt?* I decided.

According to Ruth, we had arrived just as she was in the process of figuring out how to delete all of the videos on her Ring app. "I had no idea there were so many on my phone, sucking up memory like a Shark vacuum!"

"A shark vacuum?" I repeated, confused by her comment. "I didn't know they made vacuums designed to suck up sea creatures."

"No, silly, not sea creatures. More like dust bunnies. It's a technologically advanced vacuum cleaner with really powerful suction," Ruth replied, as if explaining trigonometry to a toddler. "I'm shocked you've never heard of them. Have you been living in a cave the last two decades?"

"I haven't shopped for a new vacuum cleaner in years." I hoped my response didn't sound defensive, but I felt as though Ruth was making fun of my naivety and I didn't appreciate her mocking tone. My fondness for Lexie's neighbor was fading faster than a t-shirt made in China. "My twenty-year-old Hoover still sucks sufficiently enough for the two-hundred-and-forty square foot living space inside our travel trailer."

"Two-hundred-and-forty square feet living space?" Ruth asked, aghast at the idea of living in such cramped conditions. "A cave would actually be more spacious! I have more room than that in my living room. How do you or your husband turn around without bumping into each other?"

"We manage."

Ruth was oblivious to my increasing irritation, but it didn't go unnoticed by Lexie. Sitting between Ruth and me, she patted us each on the forearm simultaneously and said, "Let's get back to the matter at hand. Ruth, are you saying you've already erased some or all of the videos taken by your Ring doorbell on the day before Lillian's death?"

"No, I never figured out how to delete them. I'm afraid I'm not very tech-savvy. Where's my four-year-old great-grandson when I need him?"

Lexie and I both laughed at her response. I could definitely relate. Rip and I had just figured out how to record a show on our VCR when they went obsolete. We decided we weren't even going to mess with trying to learn how to use a DVD player as they would undoubtedly be dethroned by some higher tech device about the time we had it down pat. But kids these days practically emerge from the womb with a smart phone in one hand and a fancy game station in the other. It was just a sign of the times.

It was fortunate Ruth hadn't been able to delete any of the video clips on her Ring app. We were surprised to discover the fifth or sixth video, time-stamped at 06:25 a.m., showed a vehicle pulling into Lillian's driveway. Light rain had been falling at the time and it was still dusk outside when the video was filmed. We couldn't recognize what kind of car it was other than it was a sedan.

"Why would they not have their headlights on at six-twenty-five in the morning?" I asked. "Especially since it was raining and before sunrise."

"I don't know. It seems very suspicious to me," Lexie replied.

"Me too," I agreed.

The driver's seat door opened briefly, illuminating the interior of the car as the driver stepped outside and vanished into the darkness. In those few moments before the door eased shut, we could make out what might've been three additional individuals in the sedan. The murky, low-resolution image made it difficult to determine accurately what was recorded on the video clip, which ended shortly after the driver disappeared from view. The next clip, time-stamped at 06:27, showed the driver reentering the vehicle and driving away in the same direction from which it'd come.

"The driver looks to have a similar height and build as Rowdy," I said, sharing an observation.

"You mean 'average?'" Ruth asked. "Average height and weight is a description that fits about a zillion and seven people in Rockdale alone."

My fondness for Ruth was now about equal to my fondness for sushi. If God had wanted us to eat raw fish like we were an eagle or a blue heron, he'd have given us wings and wasted no time creating fire. I was tempted to point out to Ruth that Rockdale's population hovered around ten thousand residents, even though I realized her "zillion and seven people" remark was meant to be facetious. I also wanted to make it clear my question had been directed toward Lexie in the first place, not her. I squelched the urge and instead personalized my next inquiry.

"Did that look like Rowdy's HHR to you, Lexie?"

"No, it appeared to be too streamlined to be an HHR, but it's hard to make it out very clearly. I'm not even positive there were other passengers in the car. It might have been an optical illusion. But if there *were* four people in the car, it begs the question of whether or not Judy and Sammi were in collusion with Rose and Rowdy. Perhaps they were in town too but laying low in an area motel. Although, truly, Rapella, I still can't visualize any of the four being involved in Lillian's death."

"According to Mickey," I began, ignoring her last comment, "both sisters were anxious to get their money-grubbing hands on their share of their mother's estate as soon as possible. Although Mickey hadn't mentioned Judy being in town to go to the cousin's wedding with her sister and mother. Like you said, though, if they were in town to participate somehow in Lillian's death, they'd certainly not want it to become common knowledge."

"That's true. It's possible they were all in Rockdale at the time, but I'm pretty certain it was only Rose who attended the wedding with her mother and Judy and Sammi flew in from New Jersey the day after Lillian's death. Not to mention, we can't be positive the driver wasn't acting alone, and the sole person in the car. One thing we know for certain is the driver was gone from the vehicle for only about two minutes. Would that be enough time to cut the brake lines on Lillian's car?" Lexie asked.

"It actually could've been any amount of time from two minutes up to three. Besides, I'd think you could sever the lines in a matter of seconds, but the killer might have had to break into the garage first. Plus, he would've been moving slowly and cautiously to avoid making any sort of racket that would've alerted Lillian or her neighbors."

"True. I think it's definitely the killer who got out of the car though. Don't you?"

"I don't think there's any doubt about that!" Ruth exclaimed before I could respond. Handing her phone to Lexie, she asked, "Do you want to send this video to your phone so you can take it to the police? They have fancy imaging equipment these days and may be able to enhance the video enough to make out the license tag number on the car, or perhaps even identify the driver."

Lexie and I both agreed with Ruth that we should do just what she suggested. On our way back to the inn, however, we also both agreed that was the last thing we wanted to do at that juncture. Neither of us truly believed the grainy, dark video could be enhanced enough to identify the driver or make out the tag number. Simply put, we didn't want our investigation to be squelched by the Rockdale Police Department because we were interfering with an investigation we had no business being involved in.

Back in the inn's kitchen, Lexie poured me yet another cup of coffee. My bladder was already so full I'd nearly sprung a leak on the walk back from Ruth's house. "This has got to be my last cup today, dear. Any more caffeine and I won't sleep until next Thursday."

We'd replayed the 06:25 video several times that Lexie had sent to her phone from Ruth's. We were discussing it at length when Mickey wandered into the room in nothing but a pair of sliced-up jean shorts. Not cut up in such a way that turned a twenty-dollar pair of shorts into a forty-dollar pair, but in a way that suggested the shorts had been worn so many times they'd deteriorated into rags held together only by a few still-functioning threads.

"Good morning, ladies! I apologize if the thumping inside my head sounds as loud to you as it does to me. I haven't had a headache this intense since I woke up on life support a week after that rocket attack in the Helmand Province."

"Maybe some breakfast will help," Lexie said. She grabbed a carton of eggs out of the fridge before Mickey could even sit down at the table. A roll of gauze was wrapped around his head, securing the bandaging over his recent wound. I could see a strip of hair down the center of his head had been shaved to limit the chance of infection while applying sutures. As Lexie stirred together the ingredients she needed to prepare an omelet, I volunteered to shave the remainder of Mickey's head after the stitches had been removed. Otherwise, it'd be like mowing the middle third of your lawn and leaving the rest to grow into a jungle.

"I'd be happy to cut your hair for you, Mickey," I said. "I've been cutting Rip's hair for decades. It doesn't take long now that there are only about two dozen of them left."

"Thanks," he mumbled with a chuckle. "I might have to take you up on that offer. It probably does look a little silly now."

It looked silly before they made a reverse Mohawk out of it, I wanted to say. Out loud I said, "Well, it would definitely look better if it was all the same length."

With her left hand rubbing her lower jaw, Lexie ran the fingers on her right hand through what was left of Mickey's hair hanging out from beneath the bandage, which was the color of vanilla and strawberry ice cream stirred together. "It'll be a shame to have to whack off all these pretty locks, Mickey. But I guess that's what you get when you go punching people in the nose."

"Or snot locker, as my daddy used to call it." I smiled at the memory my comment had invoked. "My daddy had a way with words, as you can tell."

"So, you came by it naturally, Rapella?" Lexie asked with a giggle.

"I reckon so." I laughed along with her, as I knew she was only teasing. *Or was she?*

Only after Lexie inquired about what had preempted the knuckle sandwich to Rowdy's face the previous evening did Mickey explain his actions.

"That was his fault, not mine."

"Are you saying Rowdy hit you in the fist with his face?" I asked Mickey.

"Well, no, of course not." He looked at his hand, which must've felt tender that morning from its collision with Rowdy's skull. "But if he hadn't said what he said, I wouldn't have had to deck him."

"Which was?" Lexie inquired. "What did Rowdy say to you?"

"He said, 'Now that you found a way to cabbage onto a bit of extra dough, maybe you can invest in some porcelain.' I *had* to hit him for basically accusing me of killing my own ma."

168

Is that what happened? I wanted to ask. *As insensitive as Rowdy's remarks were, you should definitely heed his advice about getting new teeth. Meth won that battle, unfortunately, and the jack-o-lantern smile it left you with is offsetting.*

As much as I hoped Mickey had nothing to do with Lillian's death, I couldn't bring myself to eliminate him from my suspect list. Not yet, anyway. There was still too much we didn't know about what happened. The young man was as agitated by Rowdy's comment now as he had been at the time it was made the evening before, which made me think the remark had affected Mickey deeply. Rose's reaction to his assault on Rowdy clearly did too. "I still can't believe my own sister busted a beer bottle over my head."

Half-sister, to be more accurate, I wanted to respond to Mickey. *And not only is blood thicker than water, so is love. Rose was defending the man she loved from the brute, half-brother or not, who had just punched his lights out. She'd reacted in the same manner I might've after you attacked my husband in the rest area had I had a gun and acted out of sheer instinct.*

I was tempted but decided against reminding him of that incident. Instead, I remained silent as Lexie spoke softly to Mickey to calm him down.

"Would a pain pill help?" She asked as she removed a prescription bottle from the front pocket of her shorts and offered it to him. When he reached for it, she pulled it back as if a light bulb had just switched on over her head. "Maybe I should get you some ibuprofen instead."

"Good idea," he said, although the look of disappointment was evident on his face. "Pain pills are what got me in this position to begin with."

I recalled Lexie mentioning his addiction began after being treated with pain medication for the injuries he sustained while serving in Afghanistan. As Mickey rubbed his temples in a circular motion with his index and middle fingers, I said, "I'm proud of you,

Mickey. I know it's tough, but it's important you hang in there and be even tougher."

When I asked Lexie why *she* was carrying around a bottle of the pills, she said, "I woke up with a terrible toothache in my lower left jaw. It's getting worse by the hour. I have to call into my dentist, hoping to get in to see him today. Fortunately, I had about fifteen or sixteen Oxycontin left over from my carpal tunnel surgery last winter, which I keep in a bottle in my nightstand."

"I'm so sorry to hear you have a bad toothache. I wondered why you were rubbing your jaw earlier. I haven't had to go to the dentist since 2012." That was the year I'd had all my teeth pulled due to a serious case of periodontal disease that had my teeth falling out of my gums like dried up pine needles. I wanted to advise Mickey to consider getting a set of fake chompers himself, which were a far sight better than what he had now. "There *are* a few advantages to having false teeth."

Lexie and I sat in relative silence for several minutes while Mickey wolfed down the four-egg cheese omelet, which luckily didn't require a lot of chewing. I'm sure when Lexie chose what to make him to eat, she had in mind the effort it'd take Mickey to gum a breakfast steak or pork chop to death. We didn't have all day to waste on watching the guy eat, after all.

Finally, Lexie turned to Mickey. After waiting for him to put his fork down and groan at the persistent pounding inside his head, she asked, "Do you believe Rowdy, Rose, Judy, and/or Sammi could have played a hand in your ma's death?"

"Frankly, I don't know what to think about who might've killed Ma at this point." Mickey stopped speaking long enough for Lexie to take a bag of cut green beans from her freezer and hand them to him to hold against his head. "Thank you. You know, I can definitely imagine Rowdy having a hand in Ma's death, but it's a lot harder to wrap my head around either of my half-sisters being involved. If either of them was involved, it was against their will. They'd have had to be forced at gunpoint to hurt the woman who gave them life and always put them first. Ma definitely put their well-being and happiness ahead of mine, her first-born."

"I'm sure your ma loved you more than you could ever know, Mickey," Lexie said, "but I agree it's hard to imagine either of the girls harming their mother in any way."

"How much do you know about the financial status of both couples?" I asked when Mickey failed to respond. He obviously didn't agree with Lexie's remark. I'm sure he felt as though his mother chose Gary and her daughters over him when he went to live with his biological father at such an impressionable age.

"Well, not much," Mickey began, "but I do know Judy and Sammi are hoping to have a child. Judy has some kind of issue, a 'congenital uterine condition,' she called it, and so they've opted to go the 'rent-a-womb' route."

"Are you talking about surrogacy?" Lexie asked as I was still trying to make sense of his remark.

"Yeah, but rent-a-womb is how Sammi referred to it," Mickey said with a chuckle. "She told me they'd already frozen some of Judy's eggs and have selected a sperm donor, as well as a gestational surrogate. They opted for the in vitro fertilization route."

I looked at him in surprise and he read my expression perfectly. "Trust me, ladies, having talked with both Judy and Sammi on the phone the last few months, I've learned way more about IVF treatments and surrogacy than I ever wanted to."

"Isn't IVF pretty costly?" Lexie asked him.

"Uh-huh. According to Judy, the entire process will cost in the neighborhood of a hundred grand, maybe more, and that's assuming the IVF treatment is successful on the first attempt."

"Wow!" I exclaimed just as Lexie said, "That's crazy!"

Mickey nodded in agreement to our reactions. "It's a very expensive and unpredictable undertaking. Judy told me on the phone last week they were still a ways off from having saved enough money for the IVF procedure to commence. I can't figure out why they bought that high-dollar Porsche 911. It cost nearly as much as the new baby would have."

"That sports car belongs to Judy and Sammi?" I asked. Lexie and I had assumed the expensive sports car belonged to Celia Buckley. It was hardly the first time one of our assumptions had been wrong.

"Not to mention it's not really the ideal car to be driving around with a newborn or even a toddler on board," I said. "Priorities, I guess, even if they sound illogical to me."

"They sound stupid to me too," Mickey said. "As the self-proclaimed black sheep of the family, I use more sense than those two do sometimes. It's hard to save up money for IVF when you're making big-honking car payments."

True, but there's a motive there, I thought. "What about Rose and Rowdy?"

"All I know is that they're currently living in Rowdy's father's garage in Egg Harbor Township. They both seem content enough although Rose did mention something about wanting to buy their own place. I'm sure she meant after Rowdy's father was gone. Rose is anxious to buy a new car too because she's had to rely on using Rowdy's car, which is old and unreliable. It's left her stranded more than once. As Rowdy admitted himself, the 2007 HHR is likely on its last legs."

"Are they paying rent or helping his dad out with the mortgage payment?" I asked.

"No, the old man has lived there forty years, so the house was surely paid off years ago. I'm almost positive they live there rent-free because he would be helpless without them there to care for him. He's wheel-chair bound and has advanced dementia."

"Then you'd think Rowdy and Rose could afford a reasonable car payment. He runs a lawn maintenance business and they can't possibly still owe anything on that old HHR."

"I'm sure they could have afforded a second car, Rapella,"

Mickey agreed, "had he not just purchased a brand-new special edition Harley he's making hefty payments on. For what that bike cost, they likely could've afforded an apartment to get out from under his dad's roof if they'd wanted to. And I'm sure they could've found live-in nursing care or found an assisted living facility to put Rowdy's dad in. I'm not sure how much dough Rowdy rakes in with his business though. Not a whole lot, I'd guess. He's almost too lazy to pick his own nose. If you asked me, I think he'd hire it out if he could."

I didn't ask you, but thanks for the visual. "That's disgusting, Mickey, especially now that you've rearranged that nose for him. I do have to applaud Rowdy for putting his dad's best interests before his own," I said honestly. "As much as I love my daughter, I'm not convinced Regina wouldn't book me a room at the Peaceful Acres Nursing Home the moment it became apparent I couldn't live alone should Rip predecease me. She may have a room reserved for me as we speak, just in case the situation arises."

Mickey knew I was kidding and laughed at my attempt at humor before emitting a long moan. I could tell he was miserable. His head was undoubtedly throbbing mercilessly, the pounding probably similar to that of a ten-year-old with a new drum set. The fact he had reached for the bottle of pain pills before Lexie regained her senses didn't give me a lot of confidence that he could, and would, break his addiction to drugs.

I left Mickey alone to nurse a cup of hot tea Lexie had steeped for him and told Lexie I needed to go back to the trailer to fix Rip something to nibble on as well. "I'm sure by now his stomach thinks his throat's been cut. Let me know if you get in to see the dentist and if there's anything I can do to help out while you're gone."

"Okay, I'll give you a buzz when I hear from Dr. Schultz."

"Speaking of buzzes," I said. "Don't forget, Mickey, I'd be happy to give you one too whenever you're ready to say goodbye to what's left of your hair."

"Okay, thanks, Rapella," he replied. "I've got to psych up for being bald first!"

"Look at Rip, Mickey," I said in encouragement. "He's nearly bald and he's still hot as any Chippendale dancer."

"Yeah, well," Mickey said with a barely discernible roll of his eyes. "Like I said, I'd have to psych up for it first."

Walking back to the Caboose, I ruminated over all we'd learned that morning. I felt like both of Lillian's daughters, along with their partners, had viable motives to commit murder. I couldn't imagine how anyone could slay their own parent, but I knew for a fact it happened more than one would think. How many cases had we heard about on the news where a parent had killed their own children: drowning them in a car, smothering them and placing their tiny bodies in an oil tank, or some other murderous act that's just as sadistic? Was there any crime harder to envision? I hated to even think Lillian's life had been taken for no other reason than a child wanting to hasten their inheritance. But I couldn't ignore the fact it was a possibility. Money truly is the root of all evil, after all.

My suspect list was growing longer by the day. And I still hoped to get a chance to delve into any potential motive Ruth Petschl might have to want her neighbor dead. It wouldn't be an easy task, I realized, because Lexie's affection for Ruth was evident. I didn't want to alienate Lexie or damage our friendship by openly questioning Ruth about her whereabouts on the morning of Lillian's death.

Darn it, I thought suddenly. After reviewing the video showing a car pull into the victim's driveway at six-twenty-five, we hadn't thought to look at any of the other video clips from the day of the fatal crash.

Even as this thought crossed my mind, I had a feeling it was too late. Ruth had been in the process of trying to figure out how to delete the Ring doorbell videos on her phone when we'd showed up on her doorstep that morning, which I found suspicious. My guess was that she'd completed the task as soon as she could after we'd left her house just over an hour earlier, even if she'd had to make a visit to her great-grandson's house to find out how to delete them. Lexie and I should have told her not to delete any video clips from her phone in case they were needed as evidence later on. I had to wonder. *Was Ruth truly concerned about the memory the videos were taking up in her phone or is there another more malevolent reason behind her wanting them gone?*

TWELVE

My phone rang an hour later. It was Lexie telling me she'd been able to get an appointment with her dentist due to a last-minute cancellation. "I have to be there in twenty minutes, so I can't talk long. While I'm gone, can you go see if Ruth still has the videos from the morning of Lillian's death and send the ones of any interest to my phone?"

"Of course."

"Dr. Schultz said it sounds like I may have an abscessed molar which might require a root canal, so it could take a while."

"No problem. Good luck with your appointment. I'll see you later on."

"Okay. Thanks." I felt sorry that Lexie had a painful dental issue, but glad to have been presented with the perfect opportunity to speak to Ruth alone.

I told Rip I needed to go speak with the neighbor at Lexie's request and explained why Lexie had to leave for a while. I was out the door before he could even finish chewing the bite of leftover pecan pie he'd just stuck in his pie-hole and respond to me.

"Good morning, Rapella," Ruth greeted me. "Where's Lexie?"

She looked around me as if I might intentionally be blocking Lexie from her view. I sensed she was seriously hoping her neighbor was with me and she just hadn't spotted her yet. I knew her mind was whirring as she tried to think of an excuse not to invite me inside. So, I stepped around her into the home's foyer. Although it was a mild, sixty-four-degree morning, I rubbed my hands together and said, "Chilly out there. I need to get my fingers thawed out before they snap off like icicles."

"What can I do for you?" Ruth asked warily before repeating her earlier question. "Where's Lexie?"

"She had a dental emergency and asked me to come over and see if I can look through the rest of the videos your doorbell cam took on the day of Lillian's death."

"All right. Let me get my phone."

All right? Did she really just say "all right?" I would've bet big money—okay, ten bucks—that she'd have already figured out how to delete every last one of the Ring doorbell videos. Maybe I'd misjudged Ruth after all.

After we forwarded the 06:25 video clip from the day before Lillian's death to Lexie's phone, we began reviewing the videos from the day she died on Ruth's Ring app one by one. I played the fifth video several times. I was hesitant to ask Ruth to send it to Lexie's phone because it showed Ruth crossing the street to Lillian's. It was dark outside and like before she moved stealthily like a parolee who'd just broken into an ATM machine. And, once again, she carried a small white card.

"Another recipe?" I asked.

"Yep!" She nodded. "When Lillian called to let me know she'd found the broccoli-cheese casserole recipe under her welcome mat, she asked for my coconut and banana cream pie recipe, which she wanted to make for our next book club meeting. Leaving it under her mat didn't end up saving me any time after all. She kept me on the line for forty-five minutes just to thank me for the recipe."

I had to laugh at how her clever idea to avoid a long conversation turned out not to be so clever after all. "That's too funny!"

"It might be now," Ruth said, "but it sure wasn't at the time."

After chuckling at her response, I tried to remember the few times I'd been in Lillian's house. Although there were enough newspapers and magazines to fill the Library of Congress building in her home, I didn't recall seeing one actual book. I take that back, she *had* saved every Rockdale phone book from the mid-eighties through this year's edition, which was still lying on the kitchen counter. Funny how the phone book was now less than a quarter the size it was thirty years ago, thanks to the invention of the mobile phone. If not for the businesses in town, it wouldn't have required more than a half-dozen pages.

"Belonging to a book club sounds like fun." I was hoping to find out why someone who'd join a group like that and had never thrown a single item away in her lifetime didn't own a single novel. I did find out the reason, even though it wasn't quite what I'd expected. "Was Lillian an avid reader?"

"No, but I am."

"Okay. That's nice." I shrugged with my palms up to make it plain I was confused by Ruth's response. "And so . . .?"

"I'd taken her to my book club meeting the last four or five months because I felt it would be good for her to get out of her house more and maybe make some new friends. Since Gary's sudden and unexpected death, she'd become somewhat of a loner. Everyone always brings a dish to the monthly meeting, and we spend more time eating and drinking wine than we do discussing the book of the month. It's really of no consequence if you've read the book or not. I assured Lillian she didn't need to worry about that aspect of it if she didn't particularly like to read. Still, she seemed to enjoy our meetings and always wanted to take a dish she thought everyone would like. She'd move in on some poor, unsuspecting gal the moment we'd arrive at the hostess of the month's house. She'd then proceed to bend the ear of that poor lady for the entire two or three hours the meeting lasted. I believe her reclusiveness was making for a sad and lonely existence."

I have definitely misjudged this kind lady, I thought. *She's caring, thoughtful, and compassionate. But, just in case I'm wrong . . .*

I hacked and coughed a couple of times like I'd swallowed a June bug flying around in her living room, then picked up her phone to look as though I was going to review the next saved video. "Could I trouble you for a glass of water, dear? I've got a tickle in the back of my throat that won't seem to go away."

"Of course. Would you like ice in it?"

I began to decline the ice, but then realized putting ice in the glass would require more of her time. "Yes, please."

While Ruth was in the kitchen getting a glass of ice-cold water for me, I saved and shared the video of her taking the cream pie recipe across the street to my own phone. At this stage of the game, it was better not to let Lexie think I had any doubts at all about Ruth. It was then I realized the video was time-stamped 05:14.

When Ruth returned with the glass of water, I thanked her, and said, "You must really be a morning person. You took that recipe over to Lillian before dawn."

"You know what they say about the early bird getting the worm. Not that I have any hankering for a worm, mind you." She stopped speaking as though she'd just had an epiphany and studied me for an uncomfortably long time. "Rapella, you surely don't think I'd do anything to harm my dear friend, do you? Lillian and I have been close for years. I'm really going to miss her. My youngest daughter Lori lives in Missouri, about an hour from here, and Cindi, my oldest, lives in Texas. I don't get to see either of them very often so it's been nice having Lillian and Lexie just across the street from me."

"My hometown is Rockport, Texas, even though my husband

and I are now full-time RVers," I told her. In an effort to lighten the tension, I asked, "Where in Texas does Cindi live?"

"Plano." Ruth smiled as she thought about her daughters. It was apparent she felt the same kind of affection for both Lexie and Lillian.

"That's a nice area to live. Plano is known for its friendly people and great academics." I reached over to grasp Ruth's hand as she eyed me warily. "I don't think you would've hurt Lillian any more than you'd have sliced your own wrists, Ruth. That thought never crossed my mind. I was just admiring the fact you were such an early riser. My husband is too. He beats me up every single morning. And please don't think I meant that literally."

The uneasiness on Ruth's face faded instantly. After she chuckled in reaction to my wisecrack, I teased, "I bet you were hoping that putting the card under Lillian's welcome mat again would work better the second time you tried it."

"Actually," she began, "I'd already decided if Lillian were to call to thank me for sharing another recipe with her, I would let my voice mail pick up the call. It gives you a limited amount of time to leave your message before cutting you off. Sadly, she died before she could phone me."

"I'm so very sorry for your loss, Ruth." And I truly was saddened by the fact she'd lost a beloved friend so pointlessly. The flood gate opened and tears began to flow unchecked down Ruth's cheeks. I gave the grieving woman a long, warm embrace. After Ruth's tears dried up and she was able to collect herself, I asked, "If we are still here on the day of your next book club meeting, would you mind if I attend the meeting with you?"

"Heavens no, I wouldn't mind at all. In fact, I'd love to have you join me, Rapella. The meeting is actually this Saturday at my house, which will be convenient for you. I'll even send you home with this month's book titled *The Will of the Enemy* by Jody Shee. It's a page-turner that involves a resilient woman who's the victim of domestic abuse. If you don't get it read by Saturday, it's no big deal. But you can keep it regardless, because I've finished with it and I'm confident you'll enjoy it. Having witnessed how cluttered Lillian's house was many, many times, I now throw away anything I won't read, use, eat, or wear in the next six months. Except for wine, of course. Wine is eternal."

"Not always," I replied. "Not when it comes in a box rather than a bottle like ours usually does."

"You are so funny," Ruth clasped my hands in hers as though we'd been friends forever. "I wish you lived in Rockdale. We'd have a lot of fun together, I believe."

"I know we would!" Despite the fact I'd basically invited myself, I said, "Thank you so much for extending an invitation to the meeting this Saturday. I appreciate it more than I can say and am really looking forward to it. What dish should I bring? Should we rope Lexie into coming too?"

"You should absolutely drag Lexie to it, as well. But you two girls are going to be too busy trying to determine who killed my dear friend to worry about bringing dishes to the meeting, or even reading this month's book, for that matter. And that's an order! I want her killer brought to justice, Rapella, and I will do anything I can do to help you and Lexie catch him or her."

"Thank you, Ruth, but I can investigate the case *and* come up with a dish to bring. I want to be able to contribute to the club's potluck meal and know Lexie will feel the same."

"I'll be making a fruit salad for my own dish. I will also whip up some deviled eggs as Lexie's dish and a coconut and banana cream pie as yours. The pie will be in honor of Lillian Sparrow. It will be kind of like she's at the meeting with us since that's what she'd planned to bring."

"I love it," I said with a smile. "That sounds like such an awesome idea. Thank you, Ruth. I can't wait."

"Me neither."

We got back to the business of looking through videos on Ruth's Ring app. One was of a shorter than average man who arrived on foot and walked straight to a maintenance shed beside the home. He carried what looked like a rolled-up tarp in one hand and hand-held clippers in the other.

"That's just Narciso," Ruth said. "He was Lillian's gardener. Nice fellow who was very conscientious about his work. Lillian complained about him frequently but went out to eat with him, followed by a movie now and then, so her grumbling was all bark and no bite. I think she might've even enjoyed his company more than she was willing to admit."

"I'm sure it broke up the monotony of living alone too. So why didn't Narciso drive to her house?"

"He just lives on the next block so always walked over for the exercise. He kept all his lawn maintenance tools and supplies in the shed beside her house."

The video clip of Narciso arriving for work was followed by three or four more of him walking behind a push mower as he crisscrossed the part of the large lawn closest to the street. The motion-sensing camera's range seemed to extend only halfway up the sidewalk in front of Lillian's front porch.

"Too bad he couldn't afford a riding lawnmower," I said.

"He could've, but he didn't want one. Again, he enjoyed the exercise. I rent a post office box rather than have my mail delivered to the mail box on the curb for the same reason. I walk the two miles each way every morning to retrieve my mail at the post office in town."

"That is so admirable, Ruth. It must be the secret to your youthfulness," I said in awe before returning my concentration to the Ring videos. The next two were of Mickey arriving on his motorcycle at his mom's house at seven and leaving by eight. If he entered his mom's garage, the motion sensor in Ruth's doorbell didn't pick it up. Ruth explained that Lillian had told her she'd offered to cook him breakfast that morning if he wanted to stop by.

"I thought he lived with her at that point," I said.

"I did too, now that you mention it." Ruth looked puzzled She then shrugged, and added, "But what do I know? Keeping track of Mickey would've been a full-time job."

We found only one more video of interest, one that brought tears to both of our eyes. It showed Lillian getting into her car, looking absolutely giddy, having no idea what was about to happen to her. The car drove off and the video time-stamped at 09:17 ended. Sadly, she would be dead at 09:42.

Other than the video taken at 06:25, the two of Mickey arriving and departing on his bike, all the clips of the gardener arriving for work and mowing Lillian's yard, and the one that showed Ruth taking a recipe to her neighbor at 05:14, there were no other videos of anyone on the grounds of *Casa de Hermanas* who might've sliced Lillian's brake lines that morning. Clearly, it'd been the individual captured in the 06:25 video from that fateful morning who'd caused Lillian's death.

After I said goodbye to Ruth and stepped outside, I crossed her off the suspect list in my notebook. I felt bad I'd ever even considered her capable of perpetrating such a wicked crime. I could no longer imagine an evil bone in the kindhearted woman's entire body. *Having been involved in a number of murder cases in the last several years has made me cynical, and it's not a good look on me,* I thought.

As I crossed the street to walk down the inn's long driveway, I spotted an older Hispanic man dressed in overalls and a wide-brimmed straw hat coming out of a garden shed beside *Casa de Hermanas.* I knew it was the groundskeeper named Narciso Garcia.

I decided it'd be neighborly of me to pop over to greet him. He was carrying a weed eater and a tree trimmer and had a large box marked "RHS 2007" next to him on an ornate bronze bench.

"Good afternoon, sir. Are you the fellow who used to take care of Lillian's yard?" He nodded and after we'd introduced ourselves, I continued. "This property is stunning. I hope you got paid well for the remarkable job you've done here."

"I got paid enough," he said. "The property owner died owing me three weeks' pay, but her death was sudden and in no way predictable. It certainly wasn't Lillian's fault. With the cost of groceries shooting up—"

"No, of course it wasn't Lillian's fault," I said cutting him off because his voice had begun to rise as he spoke about the price of food. I didn't have the time or desire to listen to a tirade about the inflation plaguing our country. I had to listen to more than enough whining about the subject from Rip. "Lillian's son said you often complained about being underpaid for the work you performed here."

I was trying to spark a discussion about his relationship with his previous employer, and was surprised when he laughed, revealing a beautiful smile and straight white teeth. "That was an ongoing joke between Mickey's mother and me. She knew I was just a cranky old man and didn't mean anything by my grumbling. She griped about everything I did too, and I knew she didn't truly have any complaints about my work. As far as that worthless son of hers is concerned, he knows damn well I wasn't complaining, but rather making idle conversation with him."

"I've noticed the grounds are beginning to show signs of neglect."

"Yes, they are," he agreed. "And it's the pothead's fault. Lazy bum couldn't even work up enough gumption to feed Lillian's trea-sured koi fish."

"Yeah, I'd noticed that too." I wanted to tell Narciso the lazy bum wasn't a pot head. It would've been better for Mickey if he *was* a pothead instead of being a meth-head but felt it wasn't my business to spread rumors, even if I knew them to be true. "Why is it Mickey's fault the condition of the grounds is going downhill, Mr. Garcia?"

"After I retired from my job with the railroad, I got bored real fast. I needed a job to keep me busy a couple of days a week doing something I enjoyed and making a few bucks to boot. This part-time position, working eight hours on both Mondays and Thursdays, was perfect for me and I found I enjoyed Lillian's company as well. I miss working here, but I miss Lillian even more. I'm a widower, and she was alone too, so we'd go out for supper and take in a movie together every once in a while. Sometimes we'd go for a long walk when I felt she needed to get out of the house for some fresh air."

It sounds like a love story in the making, I thought. *Sadly, the relationship was nipped in the bud before it could bloom because of Lillian's untimely death.*

"I'm sorry I stirred up a painful memory for you, sir." I felt responsible for the tear that escaped the gentleman's right eye and cascaded down his cheek. He nodded slowly but didn't bother to try to wipe the tear off his face. His fondness for his former employer was evident.

"Don't be sorry. Remembering Lillian makes me happy at the same time it makes me sad. I cry a lot these days. If she'd have agreed to marry me, this never would've happened. I'd have driven her to her brunch date."

"But then you might have both died when the brakes gave out," I pointed out in a gentle voice.

"I always check the tires and the brake, coolant, oil, and wind-shield washer fluid levels before driving anywhere," he said, a bit indignantly, as though he couldn't believe I'd even question his atten-tion to details such as those. It sounded as if just driving to the store for a loaf of bread was a time-consuming chore for the man. *No wonder he always chose to walk to work*, I thought.

"If your work here at *Casa de Hermanas* is any indication of your fastidious nature, I'm sure you take exceptional care of your vehicles too," I said. "Do you have any ideas on who might've wanted to harm Lillian?"

"No." Both Narciso's voice and expression were intense. He looked disturbed and uncomfortable. I was about to leave him in peace, when his eyes misted over as he continued. "If I had any notion who cut her brake lines, I'd hunt them down and make them rue the day they stepped on this property."

Rue the day? I repeated his words in my mind. *I believe he truly would make the killer pay if he had any way of knowing who murdered his former boss.* Looking for a way to switch the topic to something less emotional, I looked at the lawn equipment he was holding. "You just here this morning to collect your lawn care equipment?"

"Yeah." The pain on his face instantly dissolved and was replaced by an expression of gratitude. I'm sure he was aware of why I'd quickly changed the subject. When I glanced at the large box on the bench, he said, "I'll have to come back later for the box of small hand tools when I'm out in my truck."

"Of course. It looks too unwieldy to carry far."

"Uh-huh." Narciso didn't look as if he knew what the word unwieldy meant, so instead of replying to my remark, he said, "When I heard the place was being put on the market, I decided I better stop in and get my tools before it sold."

"Glad you thought to do that as it's already been purchased by a couple named Buckley. They plan to turn it in to a lodging facility similar to the one next door. Mr. Garcia, you might want to speak with them about continuing on as the groundskeeper here. I can't see either one of them being enthused about mowing, thatching, edging or anything of that blue-collar nature."

I thought he'd be thrilled about my remarks but instead he just shook his head. He carried the heavy box back into the shed. After locking the padlock on its door, he leaned over and picked up a tiny toad off the concrete driveway. I was touched when he relocated it to a flowerbed and said, "It ain't as apt to get squashed amongst these Chrysanthemums."

"The mums are gorgeous when they're in full bloom like they are now. Would you like me to speak to the new owners about hiring you to take care of their lawn?" I asked.

"It wouldn't be the same working for the new owners," he finally said. "What'd you say their name was?"

"Buckley."

"Barron Buckley?"

"Yes," I replied. "Do you know him?"

"Not personally." Narciso shook his head. His expression was unreadable when he added, "Buckley was the fellow who offered to buy Lillian's place not long ago."

"So I've heard. I'm almost certain the Buckleys would pay you well."

Narciso waved his hand and said, "Oh, I don't care about the money. There are just too many memories here for me, I'm afraid. Maybe I'll volunteer at the VA hospital in Leavenworth. I can always find an old vet there who'll sit and gripe about life with me."

I soon found out he wasn't kidding about being a cranky old man. In the next ten minutes that I spent conversing with him, he complained about the price of gasoline, some pro football player who'd kneeled during the National Anthem, the fact the weather had been too pleasant for too long and we needed a good old winter storm to come along and shake things up, and even that they just don't make weed whackers the way they used to. He was a kind and thoughtful man, no doubt. But it'd been one of those conversations you walk away from wishing a boatload of asteroids would crash into Earth and end life as we know it on this miserable planet.

THIRTEEN

I heard Rip conversing with Barron Buckley as I neared the alcove where the four RV sites were located. The area was nestled in a grove of blue spruce trees which provided an abundance of shade. They were talking about the *Casa de Hermanas* and how Buckley didn't want to rush the previous owner's children but was hoping to gain full access to the property within the next few days. Again, he mentioned having court dates for several cases the following week.

"Gaining full possession in the next day or two shouldn't be a problem," I said, as I walked around the corner to find the two men sitting in lawn chairs outside our trailer, each with a beer in their hand. "You granted them a couple of days to remove the items they wanted and today's the second of the two allotted days."

"I know," he said. "But it's a huge and cluttered place to sort through in just a couple of days. More importantly, I realize it's a difficult time for the previous owner's children, having just lost their mother in such a violent fashion. Celia's in a red-hot hurry to get to work on the place, but she'll just have to cool her jets and show a little compassion. It won't hurt her to have to wait a couple of days."

"I can understand her excitement to get started on making the place her own. Even after Lillian's kids are done sorting out what they want to keep, there's gonna be a ton of meaningless stuff left to contend with. Getting the placed cleaned out is going to be a monumental task."

"I know, but I think we've found a company we can hire that does that kind of thing. They sort through the contents of the home and keep out anything of value to sell in an estate sale. Then they load up and haul off the rest. And surprisingly they do all that for whatever they're able to raise in the estate sale, which means no out-of-pocket expense for Celia and me."

"That's good," I said. "And speaking of that, if none of the kids take the sunflower quilt in that third floor bedroom with the hideous orange shag carpeting, can I buy it from you? As you can see, it's perfect for the Chartreuse Caboose."

"Buy it?" Barron asked, unable to suppress a chuckle after glancing at the trailer's paint job, of which I was inordinately proud. I didn't know whether to be pleased or insulted by his laughter. I chose to be flattered, especially after Barron's next remark. "This colorful RV and that quilt are indeed a perfect match. Please take the sunflower bedspread off our hands. The salvage company probably wouldn't get ten bucks for it in a sale, and I can almost guarantee you none of the siblings will want it either. Next time I'm over there, I'll grab the quilt and drop it off here for you."

"Thank you so much, Barron." As much as I liked the bed covering, I wasn't sure I'd have gone a full ten bucks for it either. I would have negotiated the man down to five or let the quilt go. "That's very kind of you."

"Especially considering the prank she pulled on you," Rip interjected, looking directly at me rather than the gentleman he was speaking to.

Where's a frying pan when you need one? I thought. *Thumping him on the head with my hand just wouldn't have the same impact, either physically or psychologically.*

"There are no hard feelings on my part, Rip," Barron replied. "I understand why Rapella and Lexie were determined to find that note before they turned the property over to a buyer. And speaking of that, Rapella, I found your bag of rancid potatoes in the foyer's coat closet, but for the life of me, I can't figure out what is reeking so pungently in the parlor."

The horror-stricken look Rip gave me made me hesitant to respond. In the end, I felt I owed it to Barron. "Oh, I'm sorry about that. If you take down those heavy drapes along the west wall of the parlor, you'll find a wad of smelly gunk crammed into the curtain rods."

"Ah-ha!" Rip exclaimed. "So that's where half my jar of stink bait went!"

"Stink bait?" Barron asked with a comical expression of disbelief. "You actually crammed stink bait in the curtain rods?"

Embarrassed, I nodded in confirmation. "While you're at it, you might want to put the seventy-five-watt bulbs back into the light fixtures in that room. The ones I removed to replace with twenty-five-watt bulbs are in a box on the fireplace mantel."

After a hearty laugh I hoped was more from amusement than disgust, Barron gave me the kindest compliment. "You are even shrewder and more conniving than I gave you credit for, Ms. Ripple."

"Thanks!" I couldn't help but be flattered by his praise.

I soon realized his remark was not meant as an accolade when he asked, "So did you also execute the fish that were belly-up in the koi pond so I'd be turned off by the property from the very beginning?"

The two men were still chortling as I walked into the Caboose and closed the door behind me.

Rip left soon after to help Stone change the filters in his lawn equipment. After making a few notations in my notepad, I decided to go check if Lexie had arrived home from Dr. Schultz's office. I found myself face to face with Celia Buckley as I opened the trailer door. She was holding the sunflower quilt at arm's length as if afraid whatever cooties it was riddled with could conceivably land her in the nearest hospital on life support.

"Barron asked me to drop this off with you. He said you wanted this quilt because it matches your trailer." She slowly scanned the exterior of the Caboose and remained silent. I couldn't be certain if it was because her mother had taught her that if she couldn't say something nice, it was better to say nothing at all, or if she'd become nauseous, as the green tint to her cheeks suggested. I sensed she, like my daughter Regina, thought the brightly painted trailer was an eyesore.

"Thank you, Celia. I appreciate it." As I spoke, I noticed Celia glance at the sling chairs on our little patio. I figured the only polite thing to do was to invite her to take a load off and visit for a while, while secretly hoping she'd decline the offer. Unfortunately, she was all too eager to accept my invitation. Always the skeptic, I thought, *is there a reason behind her eagerness to have a conversation with me?*

A few minutes later, the two of us were lounging in the chairs, sipping on freshly-steeped Darjeeling, a fruit-flavored black tea I'd picked up in Albuquerque during our recent visit. The tea had more caffeine than the green tea we usually preferred. Although I'd sworn off caffeine for the remainder of the day, how do you not offer someone a beverage in a situation like this? If I didn't pour myself a cup, as well, she'd likely wonder what I'd put in the tea that made me refuse to drink any of the brew myself.

After taking a dainty sip, Celia got right down to what I believe brought her to my door in the first place. "So, Barron tells me you and Lexie are looking into the death of the former owner of our new property. Why would you two go to all of that effort? Did you even know the lady?"

"No," I admitted, "but she was a friend of Lexie's and any friend of hers is a friend of mine."

"I'm not sure that old cliché works in this situation, but it's very admirable of you to help your friend try to find justice for a neighbor of hers."

"Neighbor *and* friend."

"Yes, well." Celia took another sip and set the cup down on the little table between our chairs. "Just be careful. You do realize whoever killed her won't appreciate your meddling and likely wouldn't hesitate to kill again, don't you?"

"Yes, I'm aware of that, but it won't stop the two of us from trying to get to the truth behind Lillian's death." I was seething internally at her use of the word "meddling" but trying to mask my irritation. The only way to accomplish that was to quickly change the subject, so I complimented her and Barron's motorhome. "It's gorgeous on the outside and I'm sure even more amazing inside."

"A Monaco Dynasty was our first choice, but Barron negotiated such a good deal on the Newmar we couldn't turn it down." I'd thought my remark would garner an offer to show me inside the fancy coach. Once again, I was wrong. I listened as Celia continued. "The owner of Wild Mustang RV Center felt he owed Barron a favor after Barron saved him a bundle on his divorce settlement. My husband's a family law attorney, if you weren't aware."

"I believe he mentioned that in passing. However, I'm curious how he saved the guy so much money."

"Barron had the guy's wife followed and the private detective snapped some photos of her shooting up heroin in the Acme parking lot. He then threatened his client's wife he'd make sure his client got full custody of their three kids if she didn't settle out of court. She jumped all over the deal and ended up with no alimony and minimal child support." Celia looked quite proud of her husband's ingenuity.

I'm not condoning the shooting up of heroin, particularly if you have three children in your care, but I felt Barron's tactics were underhanded and deceitful. And this is coming from someone who considers her own sneaky deviousness to be an advantageous gift.

"Barron must be very successful in his chosen field. I just don't think I'd have the stomach for it."

"He was also able to negotiate a great deal on *Casa de Hermanas* with the sellers."

"That's nice." I pretended to be impressed with her husband's negotiating skills. "How was he able to get the property for such a good price?"

"He'd learned from the real estate agent that the HVAC needs replaced, as does the leaky roof, the outdated appliances, and the septic system. There are a few other deficiencies in the house as well. Once confronted with these issues, the daughters were willing to come down substantially. They had no idea the house had developed so many problems."

If Celia noticed my face flushing as she spoke, she didn't mention it. I felt as if I'd been used, which was ludicrous. Barron had turned my ruse around and used it to his own advantage. Would I have done the same thing in his shoes? You're dang right I would have. But, for some reason, I still felt as if he had taken advantage of me and it had cost Lillian's children a heap load of money. Lillian's daughters had no clue I'd fabricated those issues to discourage Barron from purchasing their mother's house. And Barron was well aware of that fact, which made me think he wasn't as honest and forthcoming as he'd seemed to be. "Was the house as nice inside as you'd thought it'd be, Celia?"

"I have to say I was shocked when I first went inside."

"As was I."

"I've never seen so much worthless trash in all my life!" Celia shook her head so hard the tea sloshed over the brim of her cup and onto her white trousers. "Son-of-a-bit—"

"Oh, no!" I exclaimed, interrupting her expletive. "Let me grab a towel and some cold water."

I tried sopping up the spreading brownish stain from her slacks, but Celia waved me off. "Stop! You're only making it worse."

Mishaps like that are why I'd never waste hard-earned money on white clothes. I wouldn't get one wearing out of a white blouse, pair of pants, or jacket before I'd dropped or spilled something on them. Even high-society folks like Celia were not immune to clumsy accidents on occasion.

"You might be able to *Shout* it out," I suggested.

At Celia's dumbfounded expression, I had to wonder if the lady ever watched any television shows. *Has she really never seen the stain remover commercial I was referring to? Or is she so spoiled she has a housekeeper who takes care of her and Barron's laundry?*

After Celia resigned herself to the fact she may have ruined her nice pants, we continued chatting about the *Casa de Hermanas*. Out of curiosity, I asked, "Are you going to keep the name the same when you open up your B&B?"

"Heavens no! *Casa de Hermanas* sounds rather asinine to me. I'm changing it to *Casa de mis Sueños*, which means 'house of my dreams.' I decided to keep the name Spanish since Mediterranean homes are a blend of Spanish and Italian architecture. As you can probably tell, I'm of Italian heritage. The fact my parents met and married in Barcelona makes it the perfect investment home for me."

"It's awesome that you were able to acquire the property." Although I didn't say so, I didn't think *Casa de mis Sueños* was a name that rolled off the tongue as smoothly as *Casa de Hermanas*, or better yet, Alexandria Inn, but it did demonstrate to me how desperately Celia had wanted the place. "How did you come to find out the property was for sale?"

"I have family in the area and have visited Rockdale on a number of occasions in the past. I fell in love with the house the moment I laid eyes on it. I even had Barron try to purchase the place from the owner not long ago. He sent her a written offer, and then called her to encourage her to accept his proposal, but she responded that she couldn't part with it, even at the outrageous amount he'd offered her for it."

"I can't say I'm surprised. I'd imagine the thought of moving everything in her house to another location was overwhelming. I don't think Lillian could part with much of anything, from a McDonalds Happy Meal box to the huge mansion itself, which means she'd have had to purchase an equally or larger home to hold all of her stuff."

"That's true. But I think 'stuff' is a generous way to describe the majority of the items within the walls of the huge mansion. I think most of it would be best described as rubbish. Never-the-less, the place will be gorgeous when I'm done with it and I can hardly wait to get started. I was determined to own the property one way or the other and am relieved it worked out so ideally in the end."

"Yes," I began in my driest tone, "ideally, other than the fact it only became available because its owner died a horrible death at the hands of a killer."

"Well, yes, there was that sad tragic accident, which was just heartbreaking." *To some, but clearly not to you,* I could've said. *And, by the way, it was indeed sad and tragic, but it was anything but an accident.* After her less than sorrowful response, she stood up abruptly, as if she'd just received a tsunami alert on her phone and a wall of water was about to overtake us. "I need to get going. Lots of errands to tackle today, as you can imagine, and now I have to stop and change clothes before I get started on them."

With a look that indicated she blamed me for her having to spend precious time changing clothes, she sprinted to her motorhome as if the approaching tsunami was now but inches away. Having drunk no more than a few sips of the hot tea I'd made especially on her behalf, she was leaving with more of it on her than in her. In no more than a minute, Celia ran back out in a clean pair of slacks. She was apparently a slow learner because this pair of pants was white, as well. I preferred black slacks—not only were they thinning, they were also very forgiving when it came to stains.

Celia then jumped back into the car parked next to the motorhome. I was surprised to see she was driving the brown Ford Taurus we'd spotted at Lillian's house a couple of days ago. Lexie and I had originally thought it was Judy and Sammi's car once we discovered the HHR belonged to Rowdy. I gazed at the car, stunned that Celia would drive such a non-descript vehicle. My expression must have spoken volumes.

"Rental!" Celia hollered out of her partially rolled-down driver's window. "I threw a hissy fit at the rental agency, but it was to no avail. This piece of shit was the last car on their lot."

"It gets you from point A to point B, so I guess it's not all bad," I hollered back as she drove away. There was a dent in the back passenger-side bumper. *Since when did car rental companies lease out banged up, older model economy cars with a straightened-out clothes hanger where the radio antennae used to be?* I wondered. *And just how literally had Celia meant it when she said she was determined to own Lillian's home "one way or the other?" Could she have had something to do with how "ideally" the situation had worked out?*

My suspect list was beginning to groan from the growing pains it'd been experiencing the last few days.

I saw Lexie's Jeep pull in as Celia was driving away from the tiny RV park. In fact, they passed each other because Celia mistakenly went the wrong direction on the circle driveway. Lexie had been forced to pull off onto the lawn to let Celia squeeze by.

I had a lot to share with Lexie so I put the dirty cups in the sink, grabbed my purse in case she had somewhere in mind that the two of us should go, and locked up the trailer.

It was a shady, two-minute stroll to the back door of the inn which led into the kitchen. As expected, Lexie was holding a fresh cup of coffee. It felt like déjà vu when I saw a coffee stain down the front of her shirt. With an impish grin, she said, "I forgot my mouth was numb."

"We could try and sop it up with a wet rag unless you think it'll make it worse." I was thinking about Celia's reaction to my attempt to do the exact same thing just minutes earlier.

"No biggie. I'll go put on another shirt and throw this one in the laundry basket. If the coffee comes out in the wash, that's great. If not, I'll toss it in the trash and never even miss it." Lexie was a polar opposite of Celia's when it came to being laid back. I adored that unfussy manner of hers and did my best to emulate her. Sometimes I succeeded, but more often than not I failed miserably.

"Did you know Lillian's groundskeeper asked her to marry him?" I asked Lexie.

"Yeah," she replied with a laugh. "Narciso proposed about once a month, Lillian told me. She wasn't ready to dive into another serious relationship so soon after Gary's death and didn't really think Narciso was serious about getting married anyway. I think it was more of a running joke between the two."

"Oh, I beg to differ. I think he was definitely in love with her, even if she didn't care as deeply for him. In fact, he told me she'd still be alive today if she'd agreed to marry him. It's a shame she didn't accept his proposal."

"I agree," Lexie said. "Narciso is a bit on the cantankerous side, but as kind and dependable as they come. Once, when Stone was laid up with a sprained ankle, Narciso mowed our huge lawn with his push mower and wouldn't let us pay him. 'I was in the area anyway,' he said. I sent him home with a red velvet cake and some leftover chili as tokens of our appreciation. So, did you find out anything from the videos on Ruth's Ring app taken the day of Lillian's death?"

I explained that the only video of any interest other than the one taken at 06:25 had been the one captured at 09:17 of Lillian heading out to meet Rose in St. Joseph. I then had her pull it up on her phone where I'd forwarded it. Lexie studied it with a sorrowful expression. "I figured we'd find one of Lillian heading out in her car, and now I'm convinced it was the driver in the 06:25 video who severed her brake lines."

"Ruth and I agree. It could be no other because there were no video clips of anyone else arriving at her home that morning that we felt were suspects."

After a few moments of deep thought, Lexie said, "As Ruth suggested earlier, I think we should forward that 06:25 video to Wyatt to see if he can have someone in the department enhance it enough to get a tag number off the car. Hopefully, they can make it out with the light illuminating off the brake lights even though it was still dark outside."

"I think that's a good decision, Lexie, but won't that raise a red flag with the homicide detectives? We don't want to get shut down just as we are closing in on the killer, do we?" I asked.

"No, but I think I can convince Wyatt to get the video enhanced without letting on that you and I are looking into the matter on our own." Lexie looked unsure, and I was dubious as well, but she added, "It'd be worth the risk to be able to determine who owns that vehicle."

"I suppose I'd have to agree. So, how'd your appointment go with the dentist?"

"It was just as Dr. Schultz suspected. The molar was abscessed and after doing a root canal, he put a temporary crown in until the permanent one can replace it. There's infection in the gum around that tooth too, and he gave me some antibiotics to take. He warned it might be sore later, but it's numb as a stump right now. I thought it might be the perfect opportunity to go over to Lillian's house and casually chat with her kids. I think all three are there right now. I heard Mickey tell Barron the three of them should be out of there by noon tomorrow."

"I'm on board if you're sure you're up to it."

"I am. Give me a minute to change shirts." Lexie lifted her cup to her lips out of habit and coffee dribbled off her bottom lip, landing on her jeans. She rolled her eyes. "Ouch, that's hot! Make that two minutes so I can change out of these jeans as well."

FOURTEEN

As we exited the back door a few minutes later, Barron was walking briskly up the sidewalk. There was a bounce to his step as though he was anticipating a delightful day ahead.

"Good morning, ladies!' He stopped to check his watch. "I guess it's actually afternoon now. No wonder I'm getting hungry."

"Good afternoon, Barron." We returned the greeting in stereo. Then Lexie asked, "Did you need something to eat? I'd be happy to fix you a sandwich and a bowl of potato salad."

"Thank you for the offer, Lexie, but I'm meeting my wife for lunch at The Happy Hooker."

"Where?" I wasn't sure what to make of a restaurant with a name like that.

Lexie laughed, "It's a new seafood place in town. I love their stuffed flounder. It's Stone's favorite restaurant and apparently nearly everyone else's. We're planning to take you and Rip there for dinner later this week. Does Saturday night work for you two, Rapella? If so, I'll call and make reservations."

"Sure," I replied. "That sounds like fun."

Barron nodded in agreement and said, "I hope Celia and I can get a table at the seafood joint without reservations. I had no idea the place was so popular. Rose mentioned it when I asked her for a dining recommendation while I was making arrangements on the phone with her to schedule the closing. She said she took her mom there for dinner after the wedding they attended together."

"Now that you mention it," Lexie said, "I do remember seeing the two of them from the window above my kitchen sink pull out of Lillian's driveway around six that evening."

"Were they in the HHR?" I asked out of curiosity. I couldn't imagine Rose taking her mom to supper in that hunk of junk.

"No, Rose was driving her mom's Volvo." Lexie turned her attention back to Barron. "Getting a table for lunch shouldn't be a problem, particularly if you get there before eleven-thirty or after about one-thirty. Supper's another story, with a wait time of at least an hour if you don't have a table reserved."

"Thanks for the heads up, Lexie. We'll try to arrive after one-thirty. I was just stopping by to see about renting a suite for Celia to stay in for a few weeks while the place gets emptied out by Sampson Salvage Company. I'll need to be going back east with the motor coach in a few days. I have an appointment at Wild Mustang RV Center next week to replace the awning. The wind caught it just right going down I-70 on the way here. Or perhaps I should say the wind caught it just wrong. Regardless, it ripped the awning to shreds."

"Wow! Sorry to hear that. Hang on a sec." Lexie turned and reentered the inn.

"I bet that'll cost a pretty penny, Barron." I was trying to segue into a different subject while Lexie was retrieving a room key for his wife. "Speaking of being expensive, I hope they didn't overcharge you for that Ford Taurus at the car rental agency. I'd think you'd want to have a talk with the manager about renting out such a clunker."

"That clunker belongs to my wife, not a rental agency."

"Oh." I was left speechless. Clearly, Celia had been too embarrassed to "own up" to owning the Taurus.

When Barron recognized my embarrassment, he laughed. "I'm surprised when she drives it to the nearest boutique without breaking down. But she agreed to sell her brand-new Porsche convertible and use the funds toward furnishings for the new bed & breakfast. She then picked up the Taurus for a thousand dollars to replace it. Don't tell her, but I plan to surprise her with a new car on our thirtieth anniversary in a couple of weeks. I'm thinking about buying her a Mercedes. Selling the Porsche was kind of a test on my part to see just how much she really wanted to own and operate a B&B in the Midwest. I didn't want to invest that kind of money on a whim she'd be bored with in a matter of months. And to be honest, I'd like to see her in a safer vehicle."

"I guess Celia proved she wants it pretty bad. In fact, when I chatted with her earlier, she seemed as it's truly been a dream of hers for a long time."

"Yeah, I think you're right, Rapella. Now I feel a little guilty about letting her drive around in that old Ford."

"Judy and Sammi drive a convertible Porsche too. As you know, theirs is a red 911 with a white convertible top. What color was Celia's?"

"Celia's was red and white too." He replied with a wry grin. "In an ironic coincidence, Judy and Sammi saw Celia's Craigslist post on the Internet and bought the car from her. It's just another example of how small a world we live in."

I hoped I didn't look like I'd turned into a concrete statue, because I was so stunned I could hardly breathe much less move or talk. I swatted at an imaginary pigeon on top of my head out of pure instinct. "But, but—"

"Egg Harbor Township is only thirteen miles from Atlantic City."

"But, but," I repeated. I was saved from having to put a complete sentence together when Lexie walked out the back door with a key hanging from a keychain shaped like a porpoise.

"Celia will be in the dolphin suite on the second floor. There's a placard on the door with dolphins on it, as well. She can move in whenever she's ready. The front door of the inn is unlocked from eight in the morning until ten at night. If she or you need to get inside the inn during the timeframe that it's locked up, you can gain access through the parlor door with the code 1022."

"Thank you, Lexie. I'll let Celia know the code, just in case. I'll see you ladies later. Have a great afternoon."

With that, Barron strolled down the sidewalk, climbed inside his Lexus, and roared off, all within a matter of seconds. It was as though he was late to an important meeting. I was still trying to wrap my head around what Barron had just told me.

"Are you ready to go next door?" Lexie asked. When I didn't respond, she asked, "Cat got your tongue? I know it's not Trouble because I just put her out on the back porch. She'd been entertaining herself by ripping up a love seat in the parlor. Luckily for her I'd planned to replace that love seat with a full-sized couch anyway. The little rascal is definitely living up to her name."

Lexie's change of topic distracted me enough to get over my shock. "You're probably going to need to get her declawed, like we did Dolly after she'd shredded one too many throw pillows."

"Yes, I'm afraid you're right. We plan to have her spayed at the same time. I don't mind having a pet cat but the last thing I want is a kitten factory. Stone and I thought adopting Trouble would discourage mice from moving into the inn."

"I'm not certain Dolly wouldn't run from a mouse. She's definitely not the bravest creature in the world. Aerosol cans, balloons, ceiling fans, and my old Hoover are just a few of the things she's convinced would kill her and then devour her fat butt given the opportunity. Oh, and FYI, you and I are going to the book club meeting at Ruth's house at two o'clock Saturday afternoon. It should be over well before suppertime, but keep that in mind when you make reservations for The Happy Hooker."

"Yes, ma'am. You can explain how we got roped into attending a book club meeting later after you tell me what you've learned this morning while I was gone." I had to chuckle to myself, having used the same term when I recommended to Ruth we invite her as well.

"That sounds good. But let me first tell you what I just discovered from my short conversation with Barron." As we walked next door to *Casa de Hermanas*, I reiterated the exchange I'd had with him while Lexie was collecting the key for Celia.

"That's more than a coincidence, don't you think?" I asked Lexie. "I assumed he lived in Atlantic City or near Boston where Barron said his mother resides in an assisted living facility."

"That's what I would've thought too. I know the world can seem crazy small at times. But *that* small? I don't think so. Odder yet is that until now none of them have mentioned they'd met before."

"True, but we haven't been around them the entire time either. When Celia, Judy and Sammi all came together for the first time this week, they were in Lillian's house and we were across the street visiting with Ruth. We can't be sure they didn't exchange pleasantries and remarks like 'It's good to see you again' or 'How are you liking the Porsche so far?'"

"That's true too. But it wouldn't hurt to bring the subject up while we're over there."

"Oh, trust me, I'd already planned on bringing it up, along with some other things I'm interested in finding out more about." Something crossed my mind as we neared the Buckley's new property. I snatched my phone out of my back pocket and began tapping on it.

"What are you doing?" Lexie asked.

"Just Googling something I'm curious about." A few moments later I stuck the screen of my phone in Lexie's face. "Guess where Wild Mustang RV Center is located? The Buckleys bought their motorhome in Egg Harbor Township, as well. What are the chances the Buckleys would buy a piece of property in Missouri from folks who live in the same little town in New Jersey that they frequent? He told me they live in Atlantic City, but they sure spend a lot of time in Egg Harbor. Of course, he also told me the two towns are only thirteen miles apart. Even so, I find it hard to believe it's nothing but a coincidence. Don't you?"

"I do indeed, Rapella. What do you say we go mingle and ask some prying questions?"

"I am most definitely down with that, Lexie!"

We were surprised to see a U-Haul truck in front of Lillian's house. We hadn't expected Celia to be moving stuff into the mansion yet. Where she'd find room to put anything was anyone's guess. When we walked into the living room, we were even more astonished to see hardwood floor, and quite a lot of it. We soon discovered the three siblings, along with Sammi and Rowdy, had taken it upon themselves to rent the moving van and fill it up with boxes of frivolous junk. The box of Happy Meal boxes was gone, as were the *Better Homes and Garden* magazines. Even Lillian's basket of entertainment paraphernalia was missing, which I'd bet was the first container Mickey pitched into the truck to haul off. They'd also cleaned out much of the debris in the kitchen.

"We needed room to move around," Rose told us when we ran into her in the kitchen. "Mickey's going to haul the load of junk to the local dump. Then Rowdy's going to tow the HHR on a car dolly behind the U-Haul when we drive it back to New Jersey. It's just the right size to fit all of the furniture and miscellaneous keepsakes Judy and I want to keep. I'll move the furniture I've selected into a storage shed until we finally get a home on our own."

"I'm sure that something you're looking forward to," I said.

"More than you can imagine. Hopefully my share of Mom's

estate will help us toward that goal."

Although I'd never bring it up, I felt guilty the siblings had been swindled out of money by Barron, who'd used the prefabricated issues I'd made up about the house to talk them down on the sales price. I saw no reason they should have to clean the house out since that task had also been calculated into the sales figure, and I told Rose as much.

"We aren't cleaning out the entire house," Rose explained. "We only planned to haul off one truckload full of stuff to give ourselves room to sit down and take a break on occasion. We'll also need a decent path to move some of the larger furniture out of the house. We want to get done with this project so we can head home. Celia is getting impatient, and we all need to get back to our normal lives, as well. The Buckleys will still have nineteen rooms filled to the brim to empty out."

"I know Judy and Sammi had dealings with the Buckleys back in Egg Harbor Township before this real estate transaction took place. Did you and Rowdy also know them from back home?"

I could've slapped her in the face with a flyswatter and not gotten such a staggered expression in return. "What? What are you talking about? How did Judy and Sammi know the Buckleys?"

"For starters, your sister and Sammi bought their convertible from Celia. You didn't already know that?"

"They did?" Rose's reaction made it clear she had no idea her sister was already acquainted with the Buckleys. "Judy told me she bought it through a Craigslist ad. It was an anniversary gift for Sammi. Why would she never mention previously knowing the Buckleys?"

"I don't know. Judy did buy it through a Craigslist ad," Lexie said. "But the ad was placed by Celia. She plans to use the money from the car toward new furnishings for your mom's house. She bought that Ford Taurus to get around in for a thousand dollars."

"She told us she rented the Taurus and was unhappy they'd give her such a piece of you-know-what." Rose shook her head in puzzlement. "Why would Celia lie to us like that?"

"Humiliation most likely," Lexie replied. "She lied to Rapella about it too. She's accustomed to driving fancy cars, I'm sure. A clunky old economy car is quite a step down from that sports car she used to own that your sister and Sammi are now tooling around in."

"Why would Judy not tell me she already knew Barron and Celia?" Rose asked again, clearly disturbed by the idea her sister might have something to hide. "Celia told me they lived on the Jersey shore. She never mentioned Egg Harbor though. I didn't think there were any secrets between us, so why would Judy keep something like that from me? She's never been the secretive type, always sharing every little detail about her life with me, even when it made me uncomfortable at times."

"Actually, the Buckleys live in Atlantic City, which as you know, is not that far from Egg Harbor," I explained. I was touched when I saw Rose's eyes mist over. She was hurt by her sister's caginess, and I too had to wonder why Judy would keep Rose in the dark about something that appeared to be of no real consequence.

Or was it? I asked myself. *Is there a devious reason Judy and Celia don't want the others to know they've met before? Are they in collusion, having acted as a team in Lillian's death?*

Those were questions Lexie and I wanted to get answers to as soon as possible. Most of my potential suspects would be headed back to the East Coast before we knew it. Lexie patted Rose's shoulder tenderly. "I'm sure Judy has a very good reason and it's nothing personal."

"I hope you're right," Rose said. "Hey, Lexie, did Mom ever tell you she was supposed to go out on a date on the very evening of the day she was killed?"

"No, but I hadn't talked with her for at least a week before the tragic accident," Lexie replied.

"Was she going to see a movie with her groundskeeper, Narciso?"

I asked.

"Oh, God no," she replied with a grimace. "It was a first date with Kabir Bopanno, who is this really nice fellow we met at my second-cousin's wedding. The guy, who emigrated here from India, is a cardiac surgeon at the hospital in St. Joseph and unbelievably kind. He called her right before she left the house to meet me at Starbucks on the day of her death. She immediately sent me a text saying she was heading out to meet me and seemed excited when she told me Kabir asked her out for supper that night at the new seafood restaurant in town. It's too bad she died in the wreck because I think they'd have really hit it off."

Assuming the cardiologist wasn't mortified beyond belief when he took a step into Lillian's house, I thought. Out loud I said, "Her untimely death was such a shame, on so many fronts. I'm really sorry for your loss, dear."

"Thank you."

Lexie and I began to walk away, but I stopped abruptly and turned back toward Rose. "Oh, I meant to ask you what you thought about The Happy Hooker. Lexie and Stone are taking me and my husband there Saturday night for supper and Mr. Buckley mentioned you took your mom there for dinner after the wedding."

"Yes, it was her favorite restaurant and she wanted me to get to try it out too." Rose's eyes grew watery as she smiled at the memory. "I could see why she loved it. Ironically, we had dinner there just two nights before she was supposed to eat there with Dr. Bopanno. She told me she didn't tell Kabir she'd just eaten there when she agreed to go out with him. The atmosphere is awesome and the food was great too. The wait time is a bit long and the service could definitely be better, but all-in-all, it's a wonderful place. I'm sure you'll really enjoy eating there."

"Good to hear," I said amicably. "Oh, and by the way, guess who is now the proud owner of your mom's sunflower quilt? It's the one that used to be in the bedroom with the orange shag carpeting."

"I've seen your travel trailer," Rose said with a giggle. "So, the chartreuse bedspread absolutely has to belong to you now. Actually, I'm the one who removed it from the bed after Celia told me you'd like to have it. If I hadn't had to clear off the piles of stuff on top of that bed so I could sleep there the last time I visited Mom, you'd have never even seen it. I'm glad it worked out so well."

"Me too, Rose. I love it."

Lexie and I found Rowdy and Mickey circling each other in the kitchen, like boxers getting ready to rumble. I stepped in to distract the two men, who both were still healing from their last scuffle.

"Have either of you seen Judy and Sammi this morning?"

"I don't think they've been over here yet today," Mickey replied. "They probably slept in late after being up half the night fighting. I could hear them through the ceiling because they are staying in the suite right above mine."

"Oh, dear," Lexie said. "Would you like to move to a different suite? I still have several vacant ones available."

"Nah, I'm fine where I'm at, but thanks anyway."

And then, as if it was any of my business whatsoever, I asked Mickey. "Whatever would Judy and Sammi have to argue about?"

Mickey didn't seem to have any qualms about sharing what he'd heard. "Apparently Judy bought Sammi that Porsche as an anniversary present, and in exchange Sammi had promised Judy they'd begin the process of having a baby via surrogacy as soon as Judy's inheritance came through."

"When was their anniversary? How long ago did Judy buy the Porsche for Sammi?" I asked, doing the math in my head.

"I'm not sure." Mickey thought it over for a moment and said, "And I may have not heard her right. Their words were hard to make out at times when they weren't raising their voices. Judy might have just been suggesting they begin now that she had inheritance money coming soon. Not that it matters, because Sammi's having second thoughts. She thinks rather than pursue having a child they should pay off the Porsche and look at buying a waterfront home in Berkeley Shores, which I heard her say was in Bayville, New Jersey."

"I'll bet that went over like a pelican with two broken wings." As Lexie was responding, one word was echoing through my head. *Motive, motive, motive!*

Mickey nodded. "Finally, they agreed to just get through their time here and return to the subject once they got home. The last thing I heard Judy say was, 'I thought that's what this whole plan of yours was about.' I don't know what she meant by that, but she started weeping loudly after she made that remark. I had to put my pillow over my head so I could get some sleep."

Plan? What plan had Sammi proposed? I wondered. *Did it have to do with killing Lillian to hasten her wife's inheritance? Judy would have to want a baby pretty desperately to go along with a scheme such as that, wouldn't she?*

Those were the questions Lexie and I discussed as soon as we were alone in the kitchen. Mickey had left to drive the U-Haul to the dump and Rowdy had gone upstairs to help Rose carry down a small, but ornate, table she wanted to keep.

"We need to have a chat with Judy and Sammi, but pretend we know nothing about the quarrel Mickey overheard last night," Lexie said. "How should we approach the topic of having a baby?"

"Perhaps we can start the conversation with an innocent question like, 'Are you two hoping for a girl or a boy, or will you be content either way?' That will force them to talk about the subject that's in such dispute right now."

"Good idea, Rapella. We also want to bring up the subject of why they didn't want Rose to know they were already acquainted with the Buckleys. Let's go back to the inn and see if we can catch Judy and Sammi before they head over here."

FIFTEEN

We found the pair in the kitchen of the Alexandria Inn, searching for the toaster. They were in the process of putting together a simple breakfast of Raisin Bran and a toasted English muffin they planned to share.

"You girls don't have to do that," Lexie told Judy and Sammi. "Breakfast is part of the service we provide. In fact, it's what the second 'B' in 'B&B' stands for."

The gals chuckled politely at Lexie's remark, but in both cases their lightheartedness seemed to be forced. With a confrontational glare at her partner, Judy said, "It's not your fault we got up too late for breakfast, Lexie. You sure don't have to wait on us hand and foot. We know you gave us a huge discount on the suite, and we greatly appreciate it. We couldn't stay at the Rockdale Motel 6 for the rate you offered us."

"Well, I knew you two were saving up so your surrogate could begin IVF treatments as soon as possible." Lexie was slicker than black ice at times, a trait I greatly admired. "I just wanted to do my part to help out with your meaningful cause."

"Not meaningful enough, as it turns out," Judy mumbled,

glancing at Sammi as she spoke. At that point, I thought she was going to rehash the entire debate the two had engaged in the previous night. Unfortunately, Sammi nipped it in the bud before Judy could say any more.

"Judy's just joshing you," Sammi said. "She's understandably emotional about the subject. Having a child is bound to change our lives forever."

"You mean in a good way, of course." I wasn't trying to provoke another spat, but if my provocative remark caused one, we'd surely learn a lot in the argument that ensued.

Instead, all we got was an "Of course" response from Sammi in a tone that was even drier than the English muffin she was now spreading butter on. It was disappointing, but we weren't quite done with the conversation yet.

"We were surprised to hear Celia say she sold her Porsche 911 to you two. What an odd coincidence that she would end up buying your mom's house." Lexie was giving off a nonchalant vibe. Only I knew there was more to her probing than mere curiosity. "Whatever made you buy a two-seater sports car like that when you've got dreams of welcoming a young one into your family?"

Sammi was now glaring at Judy, almost daring her to respond. Which she did, with gusto! "I drive an older model SUV with plenty of room for a car seat—"

Sammi interrupted Judy to put her own twist on the remainder of Judy's remark, "—and all of the baby paraphernalia you have to drag along when you've got a small child. It's kind of like traveling with a rock band and all of their instruments. It can be such a hassle; it's almost not worth going anywhere." Sammi made her reservations about having a child obvious without actually saying she was no longer on board the baby bus. Now it was Judy's turn to get a dig in.

"I bought the convertible for Sammi for our anniversary."

"That was so sweet of you, Judy." I turned toward Sammi and asked, "What'd you get her?"

"A card," Judy answered before Sammi could even open her mouth to reply. "Apparently that's all I'm worth to her, even though we had made an agreement when I bought her the sports car."

The look on Sammi's face was one of regret. It was clear she loved Judy and had never meant to hurt her or make Judy think she didn't care about her.

"I gave you a card *and* the promise of a baby." Sammi clasped both of Judy's hands in hers as she lovingly spoke directly to her partner. "I'm sorry I've been such a horse's ass about having a baby. I guess the idea of being responsible for another human being terrifies me, especially one that's so tiny and fragile."

"You don't have to be afraid. Babies are not as fragile as they look. Besides, we'll be in this together. I'll take care of a lot of what goes into raising a child," Judy assured her spouse lovingly.

"I know. You're right." Sammi still had Judy's hands enveloped in hers. "Our surrogate is going to begin IVF treatments just as soon as I can sell the convertible, and get an older, but reliable car like Celia purchased. She had priorities and so do I. My number one priority is you, and to grow our family. I want to give you the baby you so richly deserve. I don't care if we never travel again, and I have to drive around in a twenty-year-old clunker until we are empty nesters again."

"Oh, babe," Judy said as tears flowed like tiny streams from her eyes. "Do you really mean it?"

"Yes, I'm totally serious. I can't wait to welcome our child. Boy or girl, I don't care. I just want it to be as special to you as you are to me. I will love both of you unconditionally for the rest of my life."

Soon they were both crying in their cereal, and Lexie and I were also wiping tears away. When Judy and Sammi had finally composed themselves and finished with their inevitable "I love you" and "I love you more" endearments, I asked, "Were you shocked when it turned out to be Celia and her husband who put in the offer on *Casa de Hermanas*?"

"No, not at all." Judy shook her head as she stuck a spoonful of Raisin Bran in her mouth. The milk had to be a little diluted from all the tears that had rained down on the cereal. After chewing for a while and swallowing, she said, "After I bought her car, I ran into Celia a couple of weeks later at a flea market in Absecon, a town about halfway between where we live in Egg Harbor and Atlantic City where the Buckleys reside. Celia says Barron's quite the gambler and up the street from several casinos is probably not the best location for his office to be."

"He doesn't seem to be hurting financially," Lexie said.

"Well, no. Not yet, anyway," Judy replied. "So, anyway, Celia and I got to talking and soon realized she had family back here just as I did. She told me it was her dream to own a B&B in a sleepy little town like Rockdale. She wanted to get away from the East Coast where she said the living was too hectic and stressful for her liking. I told her about Mom's place and how Rose and I wanted her to sell out and move to Egg Harbor to be near us. Celia knew exactly what property I was referring to, having admired it for several years, she said. It would've required a lot of downsizing on Mom's part, which she didn't want any part of, as you can imagine. But I thought if Mom was made an offer she couldn't refuse it might all work out perfectly."

"Yeah, we can imagine her reluctance to sell out and move," Lexie said. "Hoarding is a powerful addiction, probably not much easier to beat than drugs or gambling. That's too bad. Had she moved to New Jersey, this tragedy wouldn't have happened and she'd undoubtedly be alive and well today."

Judy's sobbing began anew and Lexie instantly regretted her comments. When Judy's tears dried up a second time, the young lady continued with her story. "Celia insisted Barron give Mom a written offer for the property. Even though it was probably several hundred thousand more than the place would've appraised for, Mom wouldn't even consider accepting the Buckleys' offer. It was almost as aggravating as it was heartbreaking to me. I didn't tell Rose about it because I didn't want to get her hopes up only to have them crushed when the sale fell through. With Rowdy's dad being in the condition he's in, and all, Rose has been on an emotional roller coaster as it is without having me add fuel to the fire."

"I totally understand." And I did. Rose was probably the most emotional of the sisters and I could see why Judy had wanted to protect her from a big disappointment. "So she still doesn't know you'd met the Buckleys before?"

"I decided it'd be best if I kept that to myself." Judy's explanation was brief and uninformative, but it explained why Rose was shocked when we opened the bag and let the cat out that Judy had wanted left in the dark forever. *Oops!* I thought. *I can already imagine the next conversation the two sisters will have when Judy and Sammi finally show up at their mom's house today.*

"I'm sure Rose would understand," Lexie replied. "Rapella and I will quit delaying you. Rose told us you all hope to finish loading up everything you want to keep and head home as soon as possible."

"Yes, that's the plan."

Witnessing the couple's reconciliation had been a touching moment and, truthfully, I was happy they'd worked things out. But lest you think I'd let my own emotions run away with me, I wasn't erasing the pair's names from my suspect list anytime soon.

SIXTEEN

Lexie's phone rang just after Judy and Sammi left to join the others next door. Lexie turned her phone on "speaker" so I could hear both sides of her conversation with Ruth.

"Listen, friends," Ruth began, "I was just thinking about something. Lillian worked as a legal assistant for a local law firm for years. She was almost obsessive when it came to keeping copious notes with both critical and non-essential details. That's why every recipe card I ever gave her has a notation on the back indicating where the recipe came from and on what date it was received."

When neither of us responded, she knew we were confused about the point she was trying to make. "I obviously already have most of the recipes in Lillian's recipe box. But it's something I think would make a good keepsake for Lexie as a reminder of her friend and neighbor and I truly believe Lillian would want you to have it."

"That's a sweet thought," Lexie said. "I would love to have it. But how are we going to find it?"

"I think between the three of us we could track it down. This idea is two-fold. Not only would I like to see Lexie have the recipe box, since she's always having to come up with ideas to feed her guests, I also think we might discover something useful from them. Lillian also jotted down notes on index cards when she was on the phone. Appointments and such she didn't want to forget. She'd file them in the front of her recipe box. She'd make out lists on those index cards too: things she needed to purchase, things she needed to get done, greeting cards she needed to mail out, to name a few examples. She'd keep them in her recipe box until the items were bought, the tasks were completed, or the cards were mailed before storing them in a larger cardboard box marked 'old lists,' which she kept in the parlor."

I remembered that box, laughing when I'd run across it while searching for the killer's note. On the very top of the stack inside the box was an alphabetized list of her old lists. I didn't feel very optimistic we'd discover anything pertinent to the case, but thought it wouldn't hurt to check the cards out. Lexie seemed anxious to get custody of the recipe box, as well. I knew she'd been as fond of Lillian as she was of Ruth. The box would actually be a memento of both neighbors. We agreed to meet Ruth on the back porch of Lillian's house after dinner that evening.

"I can't see where I'm going," I said as I led Lexie and Ruth through the back entrance of *Casa de Hermanas*. "Are you sure we can't turn on a light or two?"

"Use the light on your phone but don't aim it toward a window," Ruth said. "I'm afraid one of the neighbors would call the cops if they saw a light come on. I know I would, and some of them are even nosier than me."

"I agree with Ruth, Rapella. We don't want to draw any attention to ourselves." Lexie flicked on her cell phone light. "Ruth said she had a pretty good idea where Lillian kept the recipe box."

"Well, that might be stretching it a bit, Lexie," Ruth began, "I just meant she probably kept it in the kitchen."

"Duh," I replied. "Where else would she keep a recipe box? In a bathroom?"

We cackled like three old hens, until the eldest hen shushed us. "We don't want anyone to hear us either. The guy who lives next door, James Monaghan, might sneak over here and shoot us if he thinks we're intruders. He's got animals on his walls with bizarre skin and horns that he brought home from Africa. I don't want my head hanging next to that of a Grant's gazelle."

"Nor do I," I said with a snort. "The gazelle's head would undoubtedly be much prettier than mine."

With all of our phone lights illuminating the kitchen, it wasn't hard to sort through the drawers, pantry, cabinets, and counter tops. The siblings and their partners had hauled a lot of the debris out of the kitchen when they filled up the U-Haul to take a load to the dump. The one load had made a noticeable difference in the kitchen and living room. We searched for about ten minutes before Ruth sighed and said, "Maybe Lillian's recipe box was hauled to the dump with the other stuff. I doubt it would've have had any sentimental value to any of her three kids. What a shame. I know she'd have wanted you to have it, Lexie."

Just then we heard a loud thumping sound upstairs. It sounded like something fell over and crashed to the floor. All three of us hit the ground, put our hands over our heads, and looked for something to crawl under. We ducked and covered like we were participating in a grade school bomb drill in the early fifties.

"What the heck was that?" Ruth whispered from her prone position on the floor. I was impressed with the octogenarian's agility that had allowed her to get in that position to begin with. The fact Ruth was only three years away from becoming a nonagenarian made it even more remarkable. Her habit of walking to the post office and back every day made it clear she was in much better physical condition than me and I was confident Ruth would get back up off the floor with a lot fewer groans than I would too.

"It sounded like something fell over in one of the bedrooms," Lexie said in a soft voice.

Always the skeptical one, I whispered back. "Things don't just fall over on their own accord, and I didn't feel any trembling from an earthquake. Someone must be up there. They must've broken into the house before we did."

"What should we do?" Ruth asked. "You two are good at this sort of thing. Got any ideas?"

"They probably came in the front door," I surmised. "There should be some good hiding places in the parlor. Let's hide and wait for them to leave. Let's all try to video whoever it is so we have proof they were here and what, if anything, they take with them."

"Good idea," Lexie whispered. She pointed to the other side of the large kitchen. "How about I hide in the niche behind the pantry door over there? The intruder might decide to exit out this back door where he's less apt to be seen by any neighbors or passersby. We'll have both exits covered that way."

"How did the intruder get in?" Ruth asked. "Don't you still have Mickey's key, Lexie?"

"Yes, because he hasn't asked for it back yet," she replied.

"Lillian may have given a key to one, or both, of her daughters. Celia and Barron were surely given a set of keys too, even if the closing isn't until Friday." I was mentally going through my suspect list. "I don't think we can rule out anyone based on them having a key to the place. Rip can break into about any house using a credit card. He's pretty handy at picking locks too. Not to mention, according to Lillian's groundskeeper, everyone on the block knew she hid her house key under the welcome mat and I'm sure her children all knew about it, as well."

"Rapella's right," Lexie assured Ruth. "I'd forgotten about that.

Let's get in our hiding spots before whoever's upstairs comes back down. It might just be Barron and Celia."

"I didn't see any vehicles in the driveway when I walked across the street," Ruth replied. "But then it's just a two-minute walk from where their motorhome's parked."

It was about ten minutes later when we heard heavy footfalls on the stairs leading down from the second floor. We all had our phones prepared to take a video. There was just enough moonlight shining through the unobstructed window beside the staircase to illuminate the trespasser. The last person we suspected to be prowling around in the house in the dark suddenly descended the steps with his awkward gait. I heard Lexie breathing heavily in the kitchen, but it didn't appear Mickey did. He had a small wooden box in his hand.

Mickey? I thought. *Why in the world is Mickey sneaking around in his mom's dark house so furtively, as though he doesn't want anyone to know he's here? And, most importantly, what in the world is in the little box he's holding? Has he found some more jewelry to hock? Is he having withdrawal symptoms and willing to do anything to "score a rock," as he put it?*

Just then Ruth sneezed. Mickey fell to the ground as if he'd been shot between the eyes with a nine-millimeter Glock. Sadly, I knew it was his PTSD kicking in. When he hit the floor, so did the box. A hundred or more index cards scattered across the hardwood floor like they had wheels on them. Having heard the commotion, Lexie rushed into the parlor in a panic from her hiding spot in the kitchen. She had a cast iron skillet raised high above her head as if to wallop the intruder on the head if it became necessary. I shook my head at her and then caught Ruth's eye. "Seriously?"

"Sorry, I couldn't help it," Ruth said. "I'm allergic to dust mites. If there's anything this house has more of than old magazines, its dust mites."

Once Mickey was sure he hadn't had a heart attack, he asked, "What are you all doing in here in the dark?"

"That's what we were just going to ask you," Lexie responded.

"However, it looks like you were looking for the same thing we were: your mother's recipe box. Why would you want it, Mickey? For sentimental reasons? If so, why'd you wait until after dark to come get it? And why didn't you turn the lights on?"

"I didn't want to light the place up like a Christmas tree. Ma had some nosy neighbors. No offense, Ms. Petschl."

"None taken, Mickey," Ruth replied. "I'll freely admit I'm one of your ma's nosiest neighbors. It's called 'looking out for each other.' But why would you be so concerned about stirring up the neighbors? You're the homeowner's son."

"Not anymore. The Buckleys own this place now. I'd be illegally trespassing and the new owner's an attorney. Trust me, ladies; I don't want to be on the bad side of any lawyer right now. Rose, as Ma's executor, closed on the property with Barron this morning after the title company called him and told him the paperwork was all ready. He wanted to have plenty of time to get back to Egg Harbor for his appointment at Wild Mustang RV Center, so he was anxious to close as soon as possible."

Mickey then turned toward Ruth. "I'd been meaning to find this recipe box so I could return it to you. I know Ma got the box and most of these recipes from you. I thought it might have a special meaning to you, even if it didn't to me or my sisters. I knew if I didn't get over here this evening, it might be gone forever."

"I used the key I borrowed from you to get in," Lexie said. "How'd you get in?"

"I left a window in the parlor open earlier today, since you still had the key Ma always kept under the welcome mat," he said.

Lexie nodded. "I tried to talk her into finding a better spot to hide it."

"We all did," Ruth cut in.

"Yep!" He replied with a laugh. "I tried too, as did Rose and Judy. It was to no avail, at least until the prowler incident. After that, I convinced her to hide it under a rock by the koi pond instead. As soon as I moved in with her, the key went back under the mat. Speaking of the key, I need to give it to Barron or Celia."

"I'll give it to one of them if you'd like," Lexie offered.

"Thanks, Lexie. That'd be great." After speaking, Mickey's eyes shifted from Lexie to me and finally stopped on Ruth. It was as if he was waiting for the next shoe to drop. He shivered as beads of sweat begin to form on his forehead. I felt certain he was either jonesing again or on edge at having been caught snooping around his ma's house in the dark. Even he had to realize his story about finding the recipe box was implausible, if not downright unbelievable. Ruth must've been thinking the exact same thing.

"I'm astonished you were able to find your ma's recipe box," she said with her eyes misting over. "It was very thoughtful of you to go to so much trouble on my behalf. We were hoping to find the box because I wanted to give it to Lexie to keep as a keepsake. Obviously, I already have most of the recipes and I thought it might be handier for Lexie to have Lillian's collection of recipe cards. Where'd you find it?"

"I thought it'd be in the kitchen, but I actually found it in a bathroom upstairs."

"In a bathroom? You've got to be kidding!" I exclaimed. The three of us ladies looked at each other and began to laugh raucously, thinking back to our earlier exchange about where Lillian would keep a recipe box. "I stand corrected, Ruth. I guess she *did* keep it in a bathroom. Why would she put it there, Mickey?"

"Don't look at me. I'm as floored by it as you," Mickey said with a grin. "I never could figure out why Ma kept things the places she did. I found the box only because I had to take a leak, and—"

Mickey stopped immediately. Embarrassed, he said, "Sorry. I meant to say I needed to use the restroom and found it sitting on the top of the toilet tank. Maybe she put it there because it was the only available spot she could find. After all, I found a crowbar in her underwear drawer when I was searching for the anonymous note."

"Well, now that makes perfect sense, son," I said. Mickey looked at me as if I'd just been beat senselessly with the item he'd found amid his mother's undies. "She was a woman living alone until you moved in not all that long before her death. If she heard an intruder in or around her house, she'd want something nearby she could use to crack open a skull. A pair of Fruit of the Looms just wouldn't have made the same impact."

"Yeah," he said with a huge smile. "That does make sense. I assume that's why Lexie was waving an iron skillet when she rushed into the room."

We all chuckled at his observation. Lexie said, "You'd be wearing another row of stitches on your head if it hadn't been light enough in this room for me to recognize you."

Mickey rubbed his head and groaned in reaction to her comment. "Thank goodness for the full moon tonight. Now that I think about it, hiding a crowbar in her underwear drawer sounds just like something my ma would do. I'm glad I never snuck in after hours. In fact, I made a point not to so I wouldn't frighten her. I did so much sofa surfing for a while; I pretty much wore out my welcome at all of my friends' houses. I'm lucky Ma asked me to move in with her when she did. But not long before her death she made it clear she didn't want me here any longer so I moved into my tent out in the woods behind the rest area. It was ideal because they had both a shower and toilets - essential amenities even for homeless folks."

I'd never heard the term "sofa surfing" but would Google it later. It meant exactly what I'd figured it meant, judging by the context of Mickey's remarks. I understood why his friends got tired of him utilizing the practice. I wouldn't want some dude camping out on my couch indefinitely either. I'd either help him find an apartment or a job if it was money keeping him from having a place of his own. I'd help him move on just so he could move out. What puzzled me though was why his mom wanted him to move back out soon after she'd ask him to move in with her following the intruder incident. As Mickey began to speak again, I turned my attention back to him.

"Ladies," he began, "I was also interested in finding this recipe box because earlier today I recalled Ma's habit of writing notes on index cards and filing them in the box with the recipes cards until she didn't need the reminder anymore. Then she'd store them in her—"

"—in her 'old lists' box?" I interjected.

"Bingo!" I had to laugh at Lillian's idiosyncrasy.

"You and I must've been on the same wavelength," Ruth said. "That habit of hers just came to me today too."

We all began to pick up the index cards and returned them to the recipe box. We couldn't see them well in the dark, but we could make out that each index card had a floral design across the top and a recipe written on it in Ruth's handwriting. Except for one Lexie picked up, that is. It wasn't a recipe card though; it was a four by six-inch postcard the same size as the index cards Ruth used to write her recipes on. The picture on the front of the card was of a Ferris wheel at the 2018 State Fair in Augusta, New Jersey. She turned her phone's flashlight on to better read what had been written on the back of it.

Lexie's lower jaw just dropped as if she'd found a "recipe for murder," and in a way, she had. On the card was written, "You better give some serious thought to what I said earlier."

"Oh, my gosh!" Lexie exclaimed. "This sounds like another threat from the same individual who left the first one. But this one is handwritten, not typed, and has a cancelled stamp on it."

"And I knew who wrote it!" I exclaimed.

"You're surely not thinking Lillian's killer is one of Lillian's daughters or their significant others?"

"Nope! It's not any of those four." My remark sounded a little smug, even to my own ears. I noticed a look of relief on Mickey's face as I continued. "Lillian probably thought Mickey would never look in her recipe box for a second threatening note. But it's almost like she's helping us solve her murder from beyond."

"I didn't," Mickey asked. "So, who *did* write the note?"

"See the green ink?" I asked.

"Yeah." The threesome all responded. Mickey asked, "What about it?"

"It's from an old-fashioned fountain pen. I used to have one when I was younger. Notice the writing is in cursive?"

"Yeah." They all responded again.

"Cursive is not very prevalent these days and the teaching of it has nearly disappeared from public school."

"So?" Lexie asked. I was stalling to build up anticipation, and my irrational tactic was effective. In a chorus, the other three impatiently shouted, "Who wrote the note?"

"Barron Buckley," I answered simply. The reasoning behind Mickey's and our desire to look through the recipe cards had turned out to be sound. "When we get back to the inn I will show you a piece of paper I stuffed in my purse. On it, Barron wrote down his offer on the house, his name, address, and other information necessary to fill out an official purchase agreement. It was also written in cursive and matching handwriting. And it was written in identical green ink, which is not a common color to use in a fountain pen."

"Wow!" Lexie shook her head, as if trying to clear out cobwebs. "He was the last person I would've thought could do something so cruel."

"Me too," I said. "He was very kind to me, even after the trick I pulled on him."

"I'm going to call Wyatt and have him come over to the inn tonight," Lexie glanced at her watch to make sure it wasn't past the detective's bedtime. In the same vein as a yawn triggers others to do the same, I instinctively looked at my own watch. It was seven-thirty but seemed later. "We can fill the detective in on the details and let him interrogate Barron and/or arrest him. I'll think of a reason I need Barron to come inside the inn."

I had an idea and shared it with her. "Maybe you could ask him to come by on the pretense of wanting to say goodbye before he leaves in the morning."

"Perfect!" She replied. "How could he say 'no' to that?"

"He can't," Ruth said. "Wish I could be there, but that would look peculiar and might alert Buckley to the fact he was about to face the music for his crimes. Please let me know how the confrontation goes."

We both assured her we'd keep her in the loop, and Lexie thanked her again for seeing that she got Lillian's recipe box. After Ruth had parted ways with us, Lexie said what I'd been thinking earlier. Cuddling the recipe box in her arms as if it was an abused Chihuahua she was rescuing from an animal shelter, she said, "Seeing that the recipes were all handwritten by Ruth, another beloved friend and neighbor of mine, this box will serve as a keepsake to remember both her and Lillian should my older neighbor predecease me."

I'd thought of the two-fold significance myself and nodded in agreement just as Lexie's phone dinged. After reading the incoming text, she gasped, "I have to get to the hospital. Wendy's in labor!"

"How exciting!" I exclaimed. "Do you want me to contact Wyatt and tell him what we've discovered while you and Stone drive to the hospital?"

"Could you?" She asked. At my nod, she said, "Thank you. That'd be awesome."

"Hopefully we can catch up with you at the hospital before Chet makes his grand entrance into the world."

"Oh, golly! I can't believe my first grandchild is going to arrive soon," Lexie gushed. She took off in a dead run for the inn, leaving me to giggle to myself at her exuberance. I remembered feeling the same excitement when both of my grandchildren, Dusty and Tiffany, were born.

I called Detective Johnston and made arrangements for him to meet me at the Alexandria Inn in about twenty minutes. I could feel the excitement of having solved the mystery behind Lillian's death begin to envelope me like a gigantic soap bubble. *Now Lillian will have the justice she deserves and her children will have the necessary closure to help them move on with their lives.* The bubble grew expeditiously as that thought raced through my mind.

SEVENTEEN

I t didn't take long for Detective Johnston to bust my bubble. "I'm not sure this is enough evidence to get the judge to issue an arrest warrant."

"Are you kidding me?" I was stunned by his statement.

Wyatt shared a knowing look with my husband, who'd warned me I didn't have sufficient probable cause. My evidence was circumstantial, Rip had informed me earlier before adding, "And that man is no killer. You ladies have barked up the wrong tree, I'm afraid."

I'd pooh-poohed his opinion and was now having to eat a dish full of crow. Even pouring chocolate syrup over it wouldn't have made it taste any better. Crow was crow, after all.

"But, even so," I began, "doesn't it justify an interrogation into his whereabouts at the time of Lillian's death? Shouldn't you at least find out if the man has a verifiable alibi?"

"I suppose I could have a talk with Barron," Wyatt replied reluctantly. "But I'm not turning him over to be badgered by the homicide detectives just yet."

"I understand. But I appreciate you at least speaking to him about an alibi. Can I see if I can get Mr. Buckley to join us in the parlor for a moment?" I wasn't just being helpful. I wanted to be present when the detective grilled my prime suspect, who I was certain was a murderer. I was so convinced he'd killed Lillian Sparrow I couldn't even bring myself to call him Barron. It sounded too affable. "I'm pretty sure Mr. Buckley plans to head home to New Jersey tomorrow morning, so it has to be tonight."

"I guess so." Wyatt looked neither comfortable with the idea of speaking with Barron Buckley, nor confident a discussion with him would net any concrete indication of his guilt in the murder of Lillian Sparrow.

I had put Buckley's phone number in my contacts list, so quickly sent him a text before Wyatt could change his mind. I chose to text him because I was afraid my voice would give away the fact I felt we had him nailed to the cross for the vicious crime. Sometimes self-righteousness creeps into my voice when I least expect it.

Can you run over to the inn for a moment? A couple of us would like to say goodbye in case we don't get to see you before you head home tomorrow.

Sure, his return text read. *I'll see you in ten.*

As soon as I read his response, my palms began to sweat. I prayed my theory was on the money, as I didn't want to look like a moron for accusing the wrong person of murder. There'd been more than one occasion in the past when I thought for certain I'd pinpointed the person responsible in a murder case only to find out I was dead wrong.

Buckley cut his estimated arrival time in half and showed up in the parlor in five minutes flat. Following in his footsteps was Celia. They jaunted over to where Wyatt, Rip and I stood in front of the massive fireplace as though they were golden retriever pups wanting their heads scratched.

"Howdy folks!" Buckley tipped his ever-present fedora as he greeted us. He then glanced around, apparently surprised that neither Stone nor Lexie were there to greet them. "Where are the others?"

"Wendy's just gone into labor," I explained. "Stone and Lexie headed to the hospital in hopes of arriving before the baby does. They asked me to wish you safe travels and express regret they couldn't be here to say farewell."

"That's totally understandable! I hope Chet and Wendy both have an easy, uneventful delivery, and the baby is perfectly healthy. That's all anyone can ask for."

"Amen. I'll pass your sentiments on to them," I promised, amazed at how a stone-cold killer could be so charming when he wanted to. *Clearly, it's a facade to fool everyone into thinking he didn't have an evil bone in his body, when clearly, he's full of them*, I thought.

Wyatt was fiddling with his phone and Rip couldn't seem to take his eyes off his shoes. I sensed the reluctant detective wasn't going to approach the subject of murder any time soon. Granted, switching seamlessly from a heartwarming subject like childbirth to the topic of murder was near impossible. After giving Wyatt a few more moments to speak, I pulled the New Jersey State Fair postcard out of my back pocket, flashed it at Buckley, and asked, "Why did you send Lillian Sparrow this postcard warning her she better pay attention to your threat? Don't even try to deny writing it because I recognize both the color of the ink in your fountain pen as well as your handwriting in the note."

Celia laughed at my questioning as if it was ludicrous, Wyatt and Rip were now both mesmerized by their footwear, and Barron looked at me as if my eyeteeth had grown into fangs and I was baring them at him and snarling as I confronted him with the discovery. "Rapella, I have no intention of denying that I wrote and sent Ms. Sparrow that postcard. It was about a month ago that I mailed it to her. I'd earlier sent her a written offer of two million dollars for her property, which she'd declined. I only meant this message as a reminder it was my final bid and no one else was apt to come even close to proffering such an exorbitant amount. I wanted her to think about the fact she was apt to lose out on a lot of money if she didn't reconsider accepting my offer."

"How can you be sure she wouldn't get a larger offer if she decided later to sell her home and moved back east with her daughters?" I asked, already feeling uncertain about my earlier conclusion that Buckley was the killer.

"You've been inside that house; it's got more junk stacked up in it than there is in the rest of the homes on this block combined. I certainly never meant to imply I'd harm Lillian in any way if she didn't accept the offer. That's plum preposterous. Lillian and I spoke on the phone several times and I felt we had a congenial relationship. Ask Mickey. I would think he'd be aware his mom never felt as though I was a physical threat to her."

I stared at Buckley silently. Mickey had said nothing when I'd pointed out earlier I knew who'd penned the note on the postcard. I didn't know what to make of the fact he'd made no comment on my discovery so I stood there like a coat rack, unable to move or speak. When I didn't respond, Buckley continued.

"My guess is Lillian was afraid Mickey would encourage her to accept my offer, and she was dead set on staying in the house as long as she felt he needed her. Mickey surely realizes he was the only reason Lillian wouldn't sell the place and move back east to be closer to her girls."

"I'm not sure about that, Barron, but why send a handwritten postcard? Why not just call her if the two of you had formed a friendly relationship?"

"I only sent her the card because she didn't return my last three texts or a voice mail message I'd left the previous day. I didn't know if she was avoiding me, or what. I picked that particular postcard as a joke because Lillian had mentioned to me during one of our phone conversations that she was terrified of Ferris wheels." I had to smile at his reasoning behind the chosen postcard. "Besides, what kind of halfwit would handwrite a threat to kill someone, which could later be used as evidence of murder? Especially on a postcard, for goodness sake, in the green ink I am well known for preferring."

"That's kind of what I told her," Wyatt responded, clearly humiliated at even being in my presence as I'd leveled the thinly-veiled accusation. I wanted to poke the detective in the eye with the fireplace poker and then turn it on my husband. Both were supposed to have my back. Instead, they were making me look like the aforementioned moron I hadn't wanted to look like. Wyatt laughed and added, "As an attorney, I knew you'd be a lot wiser than to pull a boner like that."

"Good Lord, I would certainly hope so, Wyatt." Buckley then turned to me and explained, "Lillian called me a couple of weeks ago and told me she was considering accepting my offer and that she was thinking about moving in with one of her daughters back on the East Coast. Being from that area, we chatted for ten or fifteen minutes about Egg Harbor. Judy called me the next day and told me Lillian had been killed in a car accident. After expressing my sorrow and condolences on her loss, I hung up and called the Winnett Group Realty office who assured me they'd give me a call if the *Casa de Hermanas* was to go on the market, which they did."

"Thank you for explaining it all to me, Barron," I said sincerely. I'd been confident he was the killer when he'd first walked into the inn and now I was just as confident he could, and would, never do something so evil. I felt as though Lexie and I were back to square one and wondered if we'd ever know for sure who had killed Lillian. "I'm so sorry I ever doubted you."

Barron turned to stare at me. He wore a wounded expression that tore at my heartstrings. "Rapella, how could you seriously think I'd ever intentionally kill Lillian, or anyone else for that matter? Over nothing more than a piece of property, no less!"

"Well, I, I, I knew you, you, you practiced family law," I stuttered as I began to defend my theory. I couldn't make eye contact with either Barron or Celia as I struggled to speak coherently. "And I knew that, that as a, a, a divorce attorney, you'd be well aware of how, how much a divorce would, you know, would cost you. Celia had made it, it, it clear you'd better secure her dream house for her, no matter what it took for you, you, you to accomplish the feat."

Celia laughed again, and asked me, "Do you truly think I'd have divorced Barron if he couldn't buy the property for me? More importantly, do you honestly think he'd have ever married me in the first place without a pre-nup? You clearly have underestimated my husband! Don't you see, lady? It's *because* he's a family law attorney that I'd never ask for a divorce. I'd be lucky to walk away with enough money to buy dinner at McDonalds."

"Is that the only reason you'd never ask for a divorce?" Barron asked his wife in a feigned wounded tone.

"Don't be silly, darling. You know I love you." Celia ran her hand across his bottom as she spoke, causing Barron to blush. Then they both turned to stare at me.

"Well, but, but I—"

"Besides, when I said that I meant no matter how much it cost Barron to purchase the property, not how many people he had to knock off." Celia looked at me as if I was dense as a walnut stump. "This soft-hearted sap wouldn't hurt a flea. I'd be more apt to have killed Lillian to gain ownership of *Casa de Hermanas* than Barron."

I opened my mouth to inquire if she had indeed murdered the woman to get her dream home. She cut me off, and said, "And, before you ask me, no, I didn't wish any harm to Ms. Sparrow. Yes, I wanted her home, but no, I wouldn't have wanted anything bad to happen to her in order to make that goal attainable. And I certainly would never throw away my cushy life by divorcing Barron if owning the property turned out to be merely a pipe dream."

"Oh, come on, sweetie," Barron teased his wife. "Divorcing me wouldn't be all that bad. After all, I'd let you keep the Ford Taurus."

"Of course, you would," Celia said in a sarcastic tone. "*You* sure as heck wouldn't want to be seen driving around town in that piece of shit."

Wyatt had the audacity to laugh along with the Buckleys, much to my embarrassment. Then the detective asked Barron something I'd been wondering as well. "I'm just curious. How much did you end up giving for the Sparrow property?"

"A million-and-a-half, but I probably could've gotten it for less."

"Wow," Wyatt replied with a nod of approval. "That's half-a-million less than you'd previously offered for it."

"It most certainly is." The self-satisfied expression on Barron's face was nauseating. "I'd offered the two million before the real estate agent who showed it to me pointed out all of the things wrong with it."

Now my face stung with the shame I felt after his last cutting remark. My discomfiture didn't go unnoticed by Barron. "All right, Rapella. I'll cut you some slack. I actually offered less because the reason Ms. Sparrow turned down my previous offer is a moot point now that she's passed. And it was clear to me her heirs just wanted to be rid of the place. I agree I didn't word the note I sent to Lillian very tactfully. I can appreciate why you came to the conclusion you did. However, I assure you she didn't take it the way you did. She knew precisely what I was referring to. But that doesn't mean I don't believe someone else had it in for Lillian and devised a way to kill her. Why? I have no idea. The note Dolly helped us find on the kitchen cabinet was clearly left by the woman's killer."

"Thank you for understanding," I said. "You knew Lillian's daughters from back in Egg Harbor Township, didn't you?"

"We'd met Judy," he said, "but not Rose. We didn't meet her until she and Rowdy arrived a few days ago."

Celia added, "Having gotten acquainted with Judy is how we came to know about the *Casa de Hermanas*. She told me about the property when I ran into her at a flea market in Absecon a couple of weeks after she bought my Porsche. Once she figured out I was seriously interested in purchasing it, she showed me some photos she'd taken of the home and property. I'd driven past the place before but had never been inside. It was so unique, everything I'd dreamed about. I fell in love with it immediately. The land's like a stunningly beautiful park and I knew I could turn the old mansion into something special given time, money, and a lot of elbow grease."

"You're right about it being a unique piece of property, for sure," I agreed. "So, what happened next?"

Celia explained, "Judy called me one night to recommend I have Barron send her mother an offer. I think she wanted me to buy her mom's place even more than I wanted to. She said she and her sister were desperate to move their mother in with her and Sammi, or at least into a nearby home if she refused to give up her independence. Judy said Lillian would be happier at her place because Rose and Rowdy didn't have any spare room in Rowdy's dad's garage. Even though they've now moved into the house, Judy said she didn't think their mom would be comfortable there, because even Rose was uneasy living under Rowdy's father's roof. The driving force to get Lillian to sell the place was that the girls didn't like her living alone in Rockdale, and having their half-brother move in with her wasn't much of an improvement."

"I'd guess Rockdale to be as safe a town as any," I said.

"Yes, of course," Celia replied. "If it wasn't, I wouldn't be so keen to move here. It was more a matter of not really trusting Mickey. Knowing he was an addict, they thought it'd be better if she sold the property, moved to the East Coast, and forced him to find a place of his own. Judy even mentioned that he was undoubtedly stealing her mother out of house and home."

"I don't know if that's true," I said before I recalled Mickey admitting that after his mom's death he stole a diamond ring out of her jewelry box and hocked it for money "to score a rock of crystal meth." I decided not to press the issue. Whether he was stealing from her before her death was neither here nor there at this point.

My phone suddenly dinged and it was a text from Lexie letting me know that Wendy's cervix was dilated to four centimeters, which meant she was in active labor. Chet would likely arrive in short order, as the dilation was increasing at a rapid speed. The text concluded with, *You and Rip better get here soon if you want to be present for the birth. You can tell me what happened between Wyatt and Barron when you get here.*

After apologizing again, I bid Barron and Celia farewell and wished them a safe trip home. I felt certain now that neither of the pair was capable of killing someone, no matter how desperately they wished to own the victim's property. After the Buckleys headed to their motorhome, I thanked Wyatt for meeting us at the inn and apologized for bringing him over so late in the evening when it turned out to be unnecessary.

"No worries, Rapella," the detective said. "I can definitely see why you and Lexie thought he might've been behind Lillian's death. Please don't hesitate to call me again in the future if anything else disturbing pops up regarding this case. Just promise you'll bring the information to me and not to the homicide department. I don't want all three of us ending up in hot water over you and Lexie's interference with the case."

"We won't." I didn't appreciate his use of the word "interference" which ranked right up there with my dislike for the word "meddling" that Celia had used to describe Lexie's and my involvement in the case. But I did feel better about the situation due to Wyatt's sincerity. "Thank you."

As soon as Wyatt departed, I grabbed Rip and said, "We need to get to the Amberwell Atchison Hospital. Wendy's in active labor and Lexie said Chet's arrival is imminent."

"I hope you aren't planning on being in the delivery room when the boy is born."

"No, Rip, of course not. Only Lexie and Andy are going to be present. You and I will be keeping Stone company in the waiting room. Wendy and Andy would want us in the room during this intimate experience like they'd want ketchup on a grilled salmon filet."

"I don't know," Rip replied as he fired up the Chevy truck. "I might have to try that. Ketchup is kind of like bacon; it enhances the flavor of just about anything. Considering my dislike of salmon, adding ketchup might actually change my opinion about it."

We tooled along the interstate at such a slow speed I feared we'd never make it to the hospital in time. Usually when I made any comment about Rip's driving he teasingly responded, "Sit back, shut up, and leave the driving to me."

My patience wore off eventually. "Come on, Sam Safety. We just got passed by a ninety-year-old woman sitting on a booster seat so she can see over the steering wheel."

"Oh, so you can see in the dark now?" Rip sounded annoyed by my old lady remark. "I'm almost positive that was a middle-aged man behind the wheel. Besides, I'm nearly going the speed limit. I'm not going to risk a tragic accident just to make it to the hospital before Chuck is born."

"I think you could safely kick it up a few notches without causing a fatal pile-up. And, for God sakes, Rip, don't call their son Chuck in front of them. His name is Chet." I shook my head. I should be used to my husband's inability to recall names after over fifty years of being married to him, but it still aggravated me. "At this rate, we'll be lucky to get to Atchison in time to see Chet graduate from high school, much less be born."

Rip sped up to a lightning speed of two miles per hour over the speed limit. I sat back, shut up, and seethed internally until we arrived at the hospital. I guess you could take the law enforcement officer out of Texas, but you couldn't take following the law out of the lawman.

An hour later, while Stone, Rip and I were pacing around in the waiting room, Lexie rushed in and exclaimed, "The baby's here! He slid right out headfirst just like he was supposed to—all eight pounds, four ounces of him. Wendy sailed right through it too. We'll all get to see Chet after they get him cleaned up."

"Is he sporting ten fingers and ten toes?" Rip asked.

"Yep! Trust me, I counted them! He looks absolutely perfect. Chet has lots of dark curly hair like Wendy had when she was born and cheeks like a chipmunk after it'd filled them up with acorns. Of course they'll run all the standard tests, but the obstetrician doesn't foresee any issues with the baby." Lexie was as excited as I'd ever seen her. She'd long been anticipating spoiling her first grandchild. I was delighted she'd finally have the opportunity.

About forty-five minutes later, we got to see the new parents and congratulate them. Another ten minutes went by before a nurse walked into the room with the bundle of joy, wrapped up in a light blue blanket. She declared him fit as a fiddle. Chet was indeed a perfect specimen. He was cute as a baby hedgehog and clearly had a healthy pair of lungs. He howled as he was passed around the room from one set of arms to the next. He finally piped down when he made it back to his mama's loving embrace and the sound of her voice. It clearly hadn't taken Chet long to recognize his mother. I suppose nine long months curled up in her belly might've had something to do with it.

We all decided to head back to Alexandria Inn and let the new mama and baby rest. Only Andy stayed behind. The three of them deserved some time to themselves to bond.

Something had been flitting around in my mind since we'd

arrived at the hospital. I felt sure I now knew who was truly behind the tragic death of Lillian Sparrow, but it would take a little more digging. I wanted to run it by Lexie before I pursued the investigation into this individual any further. I'd already been wrong once, and basically accused an innocent man of murder. I didn't want to make the same humiliating mistake again.

EIGHTEEN

Both Rip and I slept in until nearly nine the next morning as we hadn't gotten home until the wee hours of the morning. I knew Lexie and Stone had planned to return to the hospital that morning, so I spent the day washing the bedclothes in Lexie's laundry room as she had told me I could. I remade the bed with fresh, clean linens, and scoured the sinks, toilet, and shower stall. I called Regina to check in with her, and then sent a message to my granddaughter. I knew Tiffany preferred to communicate via text.

It was afternoon before I saw Stone's truck pulling down the inn's driveway. I gave them a few minutes to unwind before walking over to speak to Lexie. She was bubbly from having spent time with her new grandson. After inquiring about Chet and Wendy's wellbeing, I asked, "Did you give the key from under Lillian's door mat to Barron?"

"No," Lexie responded. "But I did give it to Celia."

"Same difference, but it doesn't really matter. If worst comes to worst, Rip can use his credit card trick to break in. I'd rather not have to ask him to though, if at all possible. He always harps on the fact breaking and entering is a criminal offense in situations like this."

"We're going to break and enter into Lillian's old house?"

"Yes."

"Okay." I'd expected a query about why we needed to get into the house again before she agreed, but the question came afterward as if the thought of refusing to join me had never crossed her mind. "Are you going to tell me why we need to get into *Casa de Hermanas again*, or *Casa de mis Sueños*, as it's now called? Gee, I hope Celia rethinks that decision."

"Me too," I agreed. "It's such a mouthful. Anyway, I think it'd be better if I just showed you what's in there that I feel is incriminating evidence. I just need to check one thing to see if my suspicions are on target."

"Hopefully whatever it is hasn't been pitched or salvaged by one of Lillian's children," Lexie said. She knew me too well to bother asking who I felt the evidence incriminated. "And if it's still there, I hope it won't take us all night to find it."

"I know exactly where this item's at, if it's still there," I assured her. "I ran across it when we were searching for the typed threat. I think tying that note to the suspect is the key. I thought I'd done so when I saw the secondary note we found was written in green ink, but I was incorrect. I hope I'm not wrong this time."

"I'll give Ruth a call and have her meet us there if that's okay. She's been so helpful and asked to be kept in the loop."

"That'd be fine, Lexie." And it was. Ruth had proven to be helpful and had already been eliminated from my suspect list. The person I had in mind now hadn't been.

We were down in the dark, dank basement a short time later. I walked directly back to the far corner and switched on the light.

"It's gone!" I exclaimed.

"What's gone?" Lexie asked.

"When we were scouring through the house for the note that'd been left under Lillian's welcome mat, I walked down here to look around, more out of curiosity than anything. Next to this box labeled 'National Geographic Magazines 1980 through 1983' was an open box." I pointed to an empty spot on an old wooden sofa table. "The lid off the box was lying upside down on the floor as if someone had just been rifling through its contents."

"Did you see what was inside the box?" Ruth asked. I could tell both she and Lexie were still trying to figure out what had compelled me to bring them down to the house's creepy basement.

"I didn't really look at the items inside the box, but I did read through a list lying on top. You know how organized Lillian was, despite being a hoarder?"

Both ladies nodded and encouraged me to continue.

"The list read 'old Corona typewriter the girls used in high school, antique Malling-Hanson Writing Ball typewriter Aunt Linda left me in her will, test papers and school work, cheerleading uniform, and Rockdale High School yearbooks.' I took a quick glance inside the box and noticed the Malling-Hanson was a bizarre-looking contraption that defied description. I wouldn't have even known it was a typewriter had it not been designated as such on Lillian's list. I couldn't imagine how it operated, but I'm now more interested in the old Corona model anyway."

"I remember Lillian telling me that Rose was a cheerleader while Judy was in glee club and played the clarinet in the school band." Lexie was just being conversational, but I stored her remarks in my memory bank for future reference. "Are you sure this is where the box was located? Who would've removed it?"

"I don't know," I said, "but someone did. I'm positive it was right here. The box and the lid are gone. Maybe one of the girls loaded it up to take home with them."

"That has to be what happened," Lexie agreed as she picked up a dozen or so pieces of typing paper that were lying behind the box of old magazines. "It looks like they forgot to take some of their schoolwork. I remember having to type this exact same sentence when I took typing class many years ago."

"Oh, thank goodness!" I exclaimed as I took the small stack of typing paper from Lexie. Typed on the top piece of paper at least twenty times was `Now is the time for all good men to come to the aid of their country.` After studying the typed print for a few moments, I said, "This is exactly what I suspected and wanted to show you. I'm so relieved whoever took the box forgot to take these practice sheets."

"Why are they so important?" Lexie asked. "They're just from one of the sisters practicing with the typewriter the same way we did back in the Stone Age."

"I know!" I exclaimed. "And they're all the proof we need to get an arrest warrant for the murderer!"

Lexie and Ruth looked perplexed. They stared at the piece of paper as if waiting for the vanishing ink to disappear and reveal a hidden message that actually *did* make sense. Obviously, it was going to require a more elaborate explanation. "Look at the last letter, ladies."

"Okay," Lexie said before taking another glance at the paper. "It's a 'y'. So what?"

"Can you see how it's about twenty-five percent higher than the other letters in the sentence?" I asked.

"Yeah," Lexie said after Ruth nodded. She then repeated her original question. "So what?"

"I distinctly remember the seven y's in the typed message to Lillian were about a fourth higher than the other letters in the exact same way it is in this sentence. It's a characteristic flaw in this particular typewriter; the 'y' type bar is misaligned, which causes it to strike the paper at the wrong pitch. The fact this flaw matches the threatening note is not a coincidence. Rather, it's proof the note was typed by the exact same typewriter, which would be the old Corona, if I'm not mistaken."

"Okay," Lexie said. I could see her brain working in double-time, but she hadn't quite put all the pieces together yet.

Ruth stood by silently, looking totally baffled. I'm not sure she wasn't concerned about my cognitive abilities. "Are you saying you think Lillian typed an intimidating note to herself?"

"Of course not, Ruth," I said, waiting to see if she or Lexie came to the same conclusion I had.

Lexie mulled the situation over another few seconds and then exclaimed, "Oh, no! It was Mickey! He's really the most obvious person who could've used this particular typewriter to produce the note. I'm sure he either knew, or had an idea, where it was stored. After all, he claimed to have searched this place high and low for the threatening note his mother had received."

"Unfortunately, yes, it almost had to be Mickey who devised a way to kill his own mother! He clearly felt as though the note could not be tracked if it was typed, as opposed to a handwritten message. He hadn't considered the fact that typewritten notes can be linked to specific typewriters through brands of ink, or ribbons, individual characteristics like the misaligned 'y', among other defining factors."

"I guess I shouldn't be surprised," Lexie said. "When I put some clean sheets on Mickey's bed this morning, I found a dirty pair of jeans lying on the floor. When I picked them up, a small bag fell out of a front pocket."

"Are you referring to a little bag like the one with the meth in it that he buried in the woods behind the rest area?" I was hoping it was a totally unrelated bag, perhaps an empty, wadded-up potato chip bag. Lexie's solemn nod indicated it wasn't.

"Yep! It was identical to that bag." She shook her head slowly as she spoke.

"I will bet if we went back to the rest area, we'd find he has returned to the area and dug up the drugs he buried the day we found him there," I said.

"How would we know where to look?" Lexie asked. "And what purpose would it serve? Besides, I don't remember exactly where we were when he buried it. I was too busy praying we weren't going to be reduced to shreds by a wild and angry bobcat."

"I don't remember either," I admitted. "But I took a dime out of my pocket when he turned around and walked toward the parking lot that day. I set the dime heads-up directly on top of the spot the bag of drugs was buried in case we ever wanted to locate it."

"You were clearly not confident he'd succeed in kicking the habit," Lexie remarked. "That sure was quick thinking on your part though. I'm impressed."

"Me too," Ruth added.

"But what will it prove if the drugs are gone, and how will we find the spot if he did dig them up? My guess is he'd have taken the dime too." Lexie was thinking the same thing I had thought on the day I'd laid the dime on the ground.

"The spot he chose to bury the bag was right below the large cottonwood, on the opposite side of the tree from his tent. It was the largest cottonwood in the entire area, in fact. If the dime is not anywhere below the tree, within ten or fifteen square feet, the bag of drugs has clearly been dug up. As you recall, we weren't in a well-traversed area. It's not likely anyone else has been wading around in that neck of the woods anytime in the recent past," I explained.

"What would finding the drugs had been dug up prove?" Lexie asked.

"Nothing really, other than it'd prove that Mickey is still using and lying to us. I've asked him every morning how he's doing, and he always tells me he's doing good and maintaining his sobriety. If he's lying about his sobriety, he could be lying about killing his mom too.

If Mickey's still dependent on drugs he'd probably do just about anything to score them. As Rip said, it looks as though he actually did throw his mother under a bus, both figuratively, and in a weird way, literally as well. He acknowledged stealing some of her jewelry and hocking it. I'm sure he thought he'd have easier access to her jewelry if she was no longer around to prevent it. And the most enticing motive to him would be knowing his third of his mom's estate would buy a lot of meth."

"That's true." Lexie sighed and nodded. "I did think it was odd he was in his ma's old house, wandering around upstairs in the dark last night. Now I believe he was here to pick up that box containing the Corona typewriter before someone found it and put two and two together, if he hadn't already thrown it in the back of the U-Haul to take to the dump. One way or another, he got the box out of the house and disposed of it before the wrong person found it. And he did know the three of us were on the hunt for the killer. We're lucky he accidentally left behind these papers with the typing on them."

Ruth and I nodded and agreed there was more to Mickey being in her house late at night than trying to locate his mom's recipe box before Lexie continued. "He's a nice guy but I can't picture him going to all of that trouble just to find a box of recipes to give to me. Something didn't seem quite kosher about that."

"Actually, he said he was looking for it to return to me," Ruth reminded Lexie.

"Oh, that's right!" Lexie exclaimed. "That makes his actions even more curious, Ruth, because Mickey wasn't as well acquainted with you as he was with me. We need to go through that box of recipes card by card."

"Perhaps he knew, or just feared, that there's something else in that box he wanted to make sure got properly disposed of before it fell into the wrong hands," I said. "Like into our hands, for example. He knows how determined we are to make sure his mother's killer is brought to justice. I don't know how that boy could not be eaten up with guilt. Drugs, I reckon. They make a person numb to things like pain, guilt, and having a conscience."

"What a crying shame!" Ruth spoke up then with tears in her eyes. "It just breaks my heart to know her own son could've done something so horrible to her because of an addiction to drugs. But, yes, we do need to go through the cards in that box on the off-chance Mickey didn't already remove it before he headed down the stairs last night with the box. Like I told you before, I know Lillian had a habit of jotting important information down on an index card and placing it in with all of the recipe cards so she could find the critical info when she needed it. It was usually things along the line of doctors' appointments, phone numbers, and dates of social events she needed to remember. I knew of that inclination of hers and Mickey admitted he did too."

"Fortunately, we caught him trying to steal his mom's recipe box, so he had to make up a story about why he wanted so desperately to locate it." Lexie was speculating as she spoke, but I agreed with her presumption. "He probably planned to go through the cards as we plan to do and make sure there were no clues hidden within it that would point to him as the killer. If there was anything incriminating in that box, it should still be there. Unless, of course, Mickey had already removed it as Ruth just suggested."

"I hope I'm wrong," Ruth said.

"So do Lexie and I," I replied. "Is the recipe box on the kitchen table or anywhere else Mickey might have found it while we were gone?"

"Nope." Lexie laughed. "I put it in the oven."

"Now that sounds like a half-baked idea of where to hide a recipe box." I laughed at my own pun and shook my head.

"I wasn't really hiding it," Lexie explained. "I just wanted to put it someplace out of sight so it wouldn't clutter up the kitchen counter. If nothing else, I don't think Mickey would ever look there."

"I wouldn't think so." I was beginning to think that Lillian wasn't the only one who had an issue with OCD.

Before we approached Detective Johnston with the details of what we'd discovered, we decided we needed to do two things: make a trip to the rest area and carefully go through the box of recipe cards, one by one.

NINETEEN

"I don't know what to think now," Lexie said.

"Me neither," I replied. We were standing side-by-side in the woods behind the Highway 36 rest area outside Rockdale. "I can't believe the dime's still here, heads up just as I'd left it. The ground underneath it looks undisturbed."

"I guess we misjudged Mickey," Lexie said as she held the longest buck knife I'd ever seen. It served a dual purpose: to burrow into the ground to expose either the fact the drugs had been dug up by Mickey or were still there untouched and to potentially fend off a pissed-off bobcat should we be threatened by the protective mama again. "The drugs are obviously still buried. I don't see any reason to dig around in the dirt searching for them."

"I agree. It's possible Mickey truly is determined to be sober. Still, it's also conceivable he feels the drugs are easily replaced now that he's had unimpeded access to his mom's jewelry and has a substantial windfall coming in when the estate is settled."

"That's true too. Let's get the heck out of these spooky woods and go scour through the index cards in Lillian's recipe box. The entire incident regarding the box stymies me. For instance, Mickey slinking around in the house after dark, searching for the box, and then acting as if he'd just seen his mother's ghost when he walked down the stairs and spotted us. It just doesn't make sense to me."

"It doesn't seem logical to me either, Lexie. I barely know the boy but feel it was out of character for him to go to such efforts to retrieve the box of recipes for Ruth."

"I do, too," Lexie replied. "Mickey knew me a lot better than he knew Ruth. And he had to know Lillian was closer to me than she was to Ruth, even though they were good friends as well. I just can't picture him going to all of that effort to do something thoughtful like that for her."

"Yes, but you might also recall Mickey suggested we look carefully at the cards for something significant his mother might've jotted down on an index card and placed in the box with the recipes. He said he'd just remembered her penchant for doing such a thing."

"You're right again." Lexie nodded at me. "I'm glad you were along. I must've been too busy thinking about becoming a grandmother to pay attention to what Mickey was saying. But why would he suggest we scour through the cards in the box if there could be anything in there that might incriminate him?"

"Good question, Rapella. Let's go look through them and see if we can find any kind of clue that'd undeniably prove Mickey was the killer or—"

"Or prove somebody else was." I finished her sentence for her.

We nearly tripped over ourselves, racing back to the parking lot as if we seriously believed we could outrun a wild cat with babies to defend. And here we'd thought *Mickey* had acted illogically.

Lexie and I were giddy as we sat at her kitchen table, ready to sort through the index cards in the recipe box she'd just removed from her oven. Rowdy walked into the room just as we began to check the front and back of each card. His crooked nose brought to mind Owen Wilson. I don't know if the famous movie star's nose had ever been broken, but Rowdy's definitely had, thanks to his girlfriend's brother Mickey, with whom no love was lost.

"Can I get you something, Rowdy?" Lexie asked, ever the gracious hostess. "Would you like a bite to eat?"

"No thanks. Actually, I just wanted to stop in and let you know that the four of us are checking out a few days early. We'll be heading east first thing tomorrow morning."

"But you paid for ten days and will only end up staying a week," Lexie said. "I'll need to figure out how much of a refund you're due."

"I don't want to interrupt what you two are doing." Rowdy reached into his pocket and withdrew a post-it note. He set it down on the table. "I wasn't sure what your policy was about checking out early, but Rose wrote down our address just in case. You can just mail us a check at your convenience. She paid for both rooms."

"Yes, I remember that," Lexie said. "Why are you all heading home early?"

"We've done all we can do here. Besides, Judy and Sammi are anxious to start the process of having a baby as soon as possible."

"I can't blame them," Lexie said. "My first grandchild was born yesterday, and I'm already over the moon in love with him."

"As are Rip and I," I chipped in.

"Until you have your own child, you can never imagine how deeply you can love another human being." Lexie's beaming smile lit up the kitchen. It was almost as though she'd forgotten Rowdy was in the room.

"Amen to that!" I nodded in agreement before turning to Rowdy. "Are you and Rose planning to invest your inheritance money in a home of your own? Perhaps planning to have children?"

"I don't know about having kids. I don't know if Rose even wants children." Rowdy's response was surprising, considering the two had been together for a significant time. *Have the two never discussed their future together?* I wondered. Rowdy went on to say, "We may purchase a new home eventually, perhaps, but not as long as my father's alive. For now, we are content to stay where we're at. My mom passed about five years ago, and Pops is beginning to exhibit moderate dementia. Alzheimer's, the neurologist told us."

"I'm so sorry to hear that."

"Thank you. It's been challenging."

"I'm sure it has. Rose doesn't mind the living arrangements?" I asked Rowdy. "I'm not sure I would've been too enthusiastic about living in your dad's garage for an extended time. Or any garage, for that matter."

"No, she doesn't mind," he finally said after a long, uncomfortable pause. "I'm sure she's as happy living with Pops as I am. In fact, to be able to keep a closer eye on him, Rose suggested we move out of the garage and into his house. So we did just that before we headed back here. My sister took some vacation time off work and is staying with him while we're away because it's to the point every time he goes out to check the mailbox for mail, it becomes a potential silver-alert situation. The other day Pops ate a chicken pot pie straight out of the freezer. He forgot you have to cook it first."

"That's scary," I began, "and so awfully sad."

"It's not only scary and sad; it's also expensive."

"Expensive?" I asked. "How's that, Rowdy?"

"Pops broke his upper dentures in half when he bit into the pot pie, which was frozen solid." Rowdy laughed after his remark. I think he meant it to be humorous, but it was more heartbreaking than funny.

"What prompted you to rag Mickey at the fish fry the other night?" I asked out of curiosity. "Your nose looks painful, and the flesh around both eyes is a bit discolored. You could go trick-or-treating as a raccoon."

Rowdy didn't appear to be amused by my comment. His response was short and to the point. "I don't trust the junkie. I think he'd kill his mother to be able to afford drugs."

"I understand your mistrust." *So do we,* I could've said. "After all, a week ago, Mickey couldn't afford to buy a rock of crystal meth without hocking his mother's diamond ring."

"He hocked his mom's wedding ring to buy meth? That explains why Rose and Judy couldn't locate it in her house." Rowdy was livid at the news. "Why am I even surprised? Rose and Judy believed Mickey was stealing their mother blind, proving they were correct. I can't believe he openly admitted it."

"We were surprised, too," I replied.

"Lillian tried to convince herself her firstborn was no longer using," Rowdy explained. "But eventually, she couldn't ignore the truth, and she'd had enough. Lillian was even considering contacting the Buckleys and accepting their two-million-dollar offer. Judy was excited about the prospect but never told Rose not to disappoint her if the sale didn't transpire. Rose just heard about all this in the last day or two."

"Judy told us she didn't want Rose crushed if the deal fell through. She had her heart set on the two of you getting a place of your own," I said. I noticed Rowdy looked taken aback at my final comment. As if rendered speechless, he stared at me again in total bewilderment. *Can he seriously not know about Rose's desire to buy a new home and get out from under his Pop's roof?* I wondered. *Do these two lovers never talk to one another about anything of a personal nature?*

Oblivious that Rowdy seemed blindsided by my revelation, Lexie said, "I can't blame Lillian for standing her ground. I wish she'd talked to me about it. She never mentioned any of that in our frequent visits."

"Probably to save face." Rowdy had recovered his ability to speak but still gazed at me in confusion. "But she did kick Mickey out of her house and told him he'd have to pull up his bootstraps and find a way to make it on his own."

"So he truly did move into that tent in the woods *before* Lillian's death?" I asked Rowdy.

"Yeah, about a week or so before, I believe."

I thought that being booted out of his mother's house could've been the trigger that precipitated Mickey's decision to eliminate his mother. He could've gone down to the basement and typed up the threatening note the day she kicked him out, intending to return later to leave it under his mother's welcome mat. We did see a Ring Doorbell app video of him arriving at his mom's house the morning the note was left, as well as on the morning her brake lines were severed, but we hadn't considered him to be a viable suspect at the time. "Too bad it didn't work out the way Rose and Judy had hoped when they encouraged Lillian to ask Mickey to move in with their mother."

"Ha!" Rowdy laughed so hard that some of the hot tea he was drinking came out his nose, which had to hurt with that banged-up snout. "Ouch! They not only did not encourage it, they tried to talk Lillian out of asking Mickey to move in with her. Rose and Judy didn't trust Mickey at all. That's why they were so determined to get their mom to sell the property and move back east to live with Judy and Sammi or in her own home near Egg Harbor. We all believe it was Mickey who pretended to be an intruder one night. And believe it or not, the ploy worked! Lillian called the police, and when they couldn't apprehend the invader, she became frightened and asked Mickey to move in with her for a sense of protection. 'There's safety in numbers,' she told her daughters."

Not if one of them is a killer, I thought.

Lexie thanked Rowdy for letting her know the foursome would be checking out the following morning. She promised she'd mail out a refund check in the next day or two.

We were convinced that Mickey had killed his mother without scouring through the index cards. But we decided to do so anyway to have "sufficient evidence" to give Detective Johnston this time. I was determined not to look like a moron in his eyes again.

We returned to the task of sorting through the cards. Before contacting Wyatt, we wanted to make sure there wasn't more evidence against Mickey to be found in his mom's recipe box. It didn't take long to realize Ruth had an eclectic taste in food dishes. Not only did we find recipe cards for the broccoli-cheese casserole and coconut and banana cream pie, the last two Ruth had given her neighbor; we also found some off-the-wall recipes we couldn't imagine either woman cooking, much less eating. A few prime examples are Roadkill Burgoo—an entrée cooked with squirrel, possum, or raccoon as the main ingredient, and Turducken—chicken put into a duck, which is then stuffed into a turkey. That recipe sounded absolutely fowl to me.

As I was trying to imagine myself cramming a chicken-stuffed duck into a turkey, Lexie sniffed and inhaled loudly. My head jerked up instantly to see what had caused her to react this way. She handed me an index card, and although she already knew what it said, I read it out loud.

"Meet her at Starbucks at 10:00 in St. Joseph for coffee and breakfast." I was confused. "I don't get it."

"Turn the card over."

I did as Lexie requested. On the back was a notation showing how organized Lillian had to be to remember where anything in her cluttered house was. "Note from Rose inside new phone book."

"Thank goodness the woman was organized. But it's too bad she didn't forget about that brunch date with her daughter. The drive to Starbucks is what got her killed."

Just then, Lexie's phone rang. It was Wyatt, so she enabled the speaker again so I could listen to the conversation. Wyatt's deep voice said, "They were able to enhance the video from six-twenty-five on the morning of Lillian's accident well enough to get the tag number off the license plate. The car belongs to Verizon, and the dude in the video was taking this year's phone book up to her porch because Lillian had called and complained the previous two years after he'd pitched it into the bushes by the curb. What you two thought looked like several other people in the car were just towering stacks of phone books the guy had to deliver that day."

The results were disappointing; however, we couldn't help but chuckle at the idea Lillian had forced the guy to walk her phone book up to the porch. Most people step over a plastic-wrapped phone book in their driveway several times before making an effort to pick it up to pitch in the outdoor trash can or take it inside their home. Wyatt rang off then to respond to a call from the police dispatcher.

"So much for getting any evidence it was Mickey arriving at his mother's house in someone else's car from that video," Lexie said in resignation.

I thought about the video of Ruth walking a recipe to her neighbor's house at 05:14 in the morning, which I'd never shown or mentioned to Lexie, but decided to say nothing about it. At this point, I could no more imagine Ruth killing someone than I could believe Lexie giving up coffee for Lent. Another idea was flitting through my mind, and I wanted to check something out. "We need to get back into *Casa de Hermanas,* and I don't care who sees us."

The two of us hurried next door. I had Stone's crowbar in my hand, but we didn't have to use it to pry the back door open. Celia was in the kitchen making a list of things she wanted to get done by week's end and invited us in. Lexie explained the situation, and I retrieved the recently delivered phone book from where I'd recalled seeing it. Thank goodness it hadn't been pitched into the U-Haul when the siblings cleaned the kitchen. Sure enough, a handwritten note was still inside the thin directory, as Lillian had noted on the index card.

It read: Mom, can you meet me at ten o'clock this morning at the Starbucks in St. Joseph we went to last time I was in town? My schedule is really full today but I wanted to treat you to one of those pumpkin spice lattes you love, and we might even splurge on a breakfast sandwich. I have to head home this afternoon so this is my last chance to take you out while I'm in town. Plus, I think it'd be good for you to get out for a bit. Love you to the moon and back, Rose

"What a sweet girl," Lexie said. "It's so sad Lillian was killed on the way to meet her for brunch. I'm sure that's been hard for Rose to accept. The guilt must be overwhelming sometimes, even though she couldn't have predicted what was about to happen to her mother."

"I disagree," I said pointedly. "I think Rose might've known what was about to happen to Lillian, or at least likely to happen to her, because I think she could've planned it that way."

Lexie looked at me as though I'd just removed my dentures and placed them in the middle of her kitchen table. "What are you talking about?"

"It wasn't just Mickey who had access to Lillian's old typewriter. Rose did, too; she was in town, spending much of her time in this house. In fact, on the list inside the box's lid, it indicated the Corona was the typewriter used by Lillian's two daughters in high school. Although you said the girls usually stayed at a local motel when they were in town to visit their mother, Rose said that she cleaned off the bed with the sunflower quilt on it so she could sleep on it while she was in town visiting her mother. Rowdy must have stayed in a motel by himself because he and Lillian didn't exactly have a warm and loving relationship."

"Rose would never hurt her mother!" Lexie shouted, even though I was but four feet away. "I could believe Rowdy was involved, but not Rose."

"I'm not sure if he was involved or not," I admitted. "But I'm leaning toward the fact it was solely Rose behind the murder if the killer wasn't Mickey. And if so, my gut tells me Rowdy is in the dark about her horrific actions. It's obvious Rose is not as thrilled about living in his father's house as he seems to think she is. Rowdy was floored when I mentioned to him that Rose was anxious for them to buy their own place and move away from his pop's house."

"How can you be so convinced Rose could kill her mother? No matter how hard I try, I can't put two and two together and come up with Rose."

"Let me explain my theory to you."

At Lexie's nod, I continued. "I think Rose put up with the dismal living conditions for the sake of her relationship with Rowdy but might have secretly been devising a plot to get out of his dad's house and into one of their own. She knew if his father were to die, at her hands or otherwise, they'd end up living in his house, which might not have suited her at all. I think killing Pops was Plan B, because killing Lillian was more lucrative. Rose might've thought if they were to fall into a pot of money, she'd be able to talk him into buying a newer, nicer place, even if it meant his father would have to live with them for a while. Either way, I think she underestimated her boyfriend's love and concern for his father. I believe she could have hit the lottery, and Rowdy would not have left Pops to his own devices or put him through a big move to a new home, at least not with his father being in his current mental condition."

"I do have to agree with that," Lexie said. "Rowdy seems totally devoted to his father. But I still can't imagine Rose harming anyone. She's such a sweet gal."

"Think back to the videos off Ruth's doorbell camera," I advised Lexie. "The only car that pulled onto the *Casa de Hermanas* property all morning was the Verizon guy delivering phone books."

"Okay . . ."

"Don't you see, Lexie?" I asked. "Rose grew up in this house. She had to realize her mother would've never thrown away the typewriter her girls used in school."

"True."

"Rose had already told me she spent the night before her mother's death at *Casa de Hermanas*. I just realized something. The only clip we had of a vehicle stopping at Lillian's that morning, other than Mickey on his motorbike, was being driven by a delivery guy."

"And?"

"If the killer didn't come to slice Lillian's brake lines from outside the home, they had to have come from inside, which only left Mickey or Rose."

"Oh my God, Rapella," Lexie gasped. It was apparent she could no longer deny the obvious. "You're right! It could've been Rose! I'd almost believe she'd do it before Mickey would. But why didn't we find a video of her going from the house to Lillian's garage to slice the brake lines that morning?"

"It was because of the distance from Ruth's doorbell and the tree blocking the camera's view of this house's front porch. Rose could've slipped out the front door and into the garage without triggering the camera to begin recording. Remember how we only had videos of Narciso mowing when he was closer to the street than the house? All of the videos we viewed were initially triggered by movement much closer to the street. Any motion on the front porch of Lillian's house would not have activated the doorbell's camera from across the street."

"I suppose you're right. I don't want to believe it, but no one else had the opportunity to sabotage the Volvo other than Rose or Mickey. I wondered why Rose drove to Lillian's house to leave a handwritten note on the front porch inviting her mom to brunch when she could've sent her a text. She told us her mother sent her a text immediately after being asked out to supper on a date with the cardiologist, so they were accustomed to communicating that way."

"My guess is that Rose thought no one would suspect a daughter of murder who'd leave such a warm, loving note for her mother inviting her out for coffee. It was probably designed to be part of her alibi should she be questioned."

"Yeah, you might be right," Lexie said. "And Rose also had the perfect opportunity to get rid of the evidence by pitching the type-writer into the U-Haul to be taken to the dump." I could tell it was a painful awakening for Lexie. "But, if it was Rose, how could we ever prove it? We have no real evidence to hand over to the police department."

"Oh, but we do, Lexie," I said. "We have the piece of paper one of the girls practiced typing on in high school that has the same misaligned "y" type bar proving the threatening note was typed on that same typewriter. Wyatt may consider it circumstantial evidence, but it's a start. If we can convince the detectives to question Rose, they should be able to put the rest of the pieces of the puzzle together themselves. It's possible they could search the dump and still find the typewriter, as well."

"That's true. Rose might have even loaded that box into the trunk of the HHR since it had her school papers, yearbooks, and old cheerleading uniform in it. Those items might have some kind of sentimental value to her." Lexie was nodding as she spoke. "Should we call Wyatt?"

"Absolutely," I replied. "With Rose and Rowdy checking out first thing in the morning, we don't have much time to waste. If it was Rose, we must let Wyatt know so they can catch her before she leaves town."

"Good luck, ladies," Celia said. "I've felt Rose has acted almost as if she accepted her mother's death too readily. I've noticed Mickey and Judy have exhibited heartache, impatience at the police depart-ment for not arresting someone for their mother's death, and even anger at the unidentified killer this last week. But Rose has been nearly emotionless in comparison, it seemed. I realize that everyone handles grief and loss differently, in their unique ways, so I haven't thought much about it. But now, I think you are on to something.

Rose has the most compelling motive and the person who had the most convenient access to pull off such an act."

Looking back, Lexie and I agreed with her observation, even though we realized people handle grief in their own way. Rose's method of coping may be totally different from her siblings. We thanked Celia and headed back to the Alexandria Inn so the new homeowner could get started on the lengthy list she'd been in the process of making up.

TWENTY

As we were walking around the back of the Alexandria Inn, we saw Rose and Judy walking out onto the rear porch. The door led into the kitchen and was where Lexie and I had been heading. The fact they were walking arm in arm told us either an argument had not occurred regarding the secret between them, or they'd worked it out and were in good graces with each other. I'm sure if Rose was the killer, Judy had no idea about it. Otherwise, Judy wouldn't be acting so chummy with her sister now. From their furtive mannerisms, I got the impression the sisters were sneaking out. I motioned for Lexie to crouch behind a lilac bush next to me as we listened to their short exchange.

"Are you ready for this?" Rose asked as though whatever they were about to do was dangerous, exciting, scary, or all three. She was the shorter of the sisters, at around five foot tall, but only by an inch or two. Both had wavy blonde hair that hung down to their waists, although Judy's had some darker highlights and wispy bangs. Judy's eyes were green where Rose's were more of a light brown. They were beautiful young ladies and looked nothing at all like their half-brother. I could barely make out Rose's next remark, which was spoken in a whisper. "We don't have to do this if you're not comfortable with it."

"I'm okay with it." Judy didn't look okay with it, but rather nervous and distraught. "It's something I need to do, whether I'm ready for it or not."

"All right," Rose said. "If you're certain you're up for it."

"I am." Judy hugged her older sister before climbing into the convertible.

"They're acting kind of weird about going wherever they're going." I whispered to Lexie. "Let's get in the Jeep and follow them to see what they're up to, just in case it has something to do with their mother's death."

We would soon discover their excursion had everything in the world to do with their mother's death, just not what we'd anticipated.

A few minutes later we were traveling a safe distance behind the red sports car. The sisters, who looked as if they could be twins, had the convertible top down and their long blonde hair was blowing in the wind. From the back, they looked as carefree as a couple of teenagers on spring break.

It didn't take long for Judy and Rose to reach their destination. They pulled into the Rockdale Cemetery and Lexie pulled off into a daycare parking lot across the street so they wouldn't see that we'd been tailing them. She said, "Lillian was buried here. The girls have apparently come to visit her grave."

"Okay, it all makes sense now," I said. "Rose was concerned Judy wouldn't be able to handle their visit here on an emotional level."

"Rose knows her younger sister is already on edge and didn't want to make her even more anxious. I've been meaning to come and pay my respects at Lillian's gravesite too," Lexie began, "but I just haven't gotten around to it."

"Well, we're here now," I needlessly pointed out. "Why don't we wait until they're finished with their visit to their ma's grave and then we can do the same?"

"That's a good idea."

We got out of the Jeep and walked behind a row of oak trees that bordered the west edge of the cemetery to avoid being seen by the sisters. When we got within earshot, we used two side-by-side trees to shield us from their view.

We heard Judy ask Rose, "Is Rowdy's dad still as touchy-feely as he used to be?"

"Worse. Pops is like a horny sixteen-year-old, but I'm sure it has something to do with his dementia. I saw him reach under a nurse's gown when I took him to the doctor's office a few weeks ago. The young nurse just smiled and moved away from him as if she was used to that kind of behavior in old men like Pops."

"Why don't you say something to Rowdy about it?" Judy asked.

We couldn't make out Rose's response, but I sensed Judy had only brought the topic up as a way to dodge the true reason they were crouched down next to an unmarked patch of fresh dirt. There was no tombstone erected yet. No doubt they were waiting for it to be engraved. And there hadn't been enough time for grass to grow in the soil that'd been shoveled on top of their mother's casket. Judy began to sob and Rose also looked to be crying too as she comforted her sister. I felt tears form in my eyes too and I didn't really even know the deceased.

They left the gravesite about ten minutes later. We were surprised to see them stop and greet Mickey as they were walking toward the parking lot. He had just arrived on his junky bike.

"It looks like everyone wants to visit Lillian at the same time," Lexie said. "Should we wait until he leaves too? I hate to disturb his visit to his ma's gravesite."

I agreed and we waited while he staggered to her plot. He sat Indian-styled next to the rectangular dirt pile with a bottle of beer in his hand. He set the beer down and withdrew something from his pocket. Lexie shook her head, and said, "He appears to be messed up."

"Is that a prescription bottle in his hand?" I asked.

"Oh, no!" Lexie whispered in response. "I mentioned keeping that bottle of Oxycontin from my hand surgery in my nightstand while Mickey was in the kitchen with us, and I didn't lock our suite before we left."

"How many pills were left in the bottle?"

"I'd say a dozen at the very least, and probably more. I only took one of them for my toothache."

"You don't think he's planning to take them all at the same time, do you?" I asked. "Could the death of his mother have driven him to take his own life?"

"I don't know," Lexie admitted. "But he sure appears to be very agitated. I'm not positive but I think there are enough pills in that bottle to do the job if he's planning to kill himself. We better check it out."

"I agree we need to intervene."

As it turned out, committing suicide was just what Mickey had planned to do. He told us he'd already downed five bottles of beer to relax his nerves. He wanted to say goodbye to his mother and tell her he was sorry for what he was about to do before he swallowed all of the pills with the last beer in the six-pack he'd purchased that morning. He apologized to Lexie for stealing the pills. "I feel so guilty about my ma's death."

"Are you saying you had something to do with it?" Lexie asked.

"No, of course not!" Mickey was nearly shouting in anger. "I couldn't, nor wouldn't, have ever hurt my ma. I just feel if I hadn't screwed up and got kicked out of her house, I'd been there to protect her. I also feel like I should've forced her to show me the threatening message so I could go to the police with it."

Lexie patted his shoulder as she said, "I don't know if you could've ever talked her into showing you that note. Your mom was pretty obstinate when she wanted to be. You can't hold yourself responsible for her death."

"It doesn't matter anyway," Mickey said as tears streamed down his face. "I no longer have the will, or desire, to go on living."

It took a heap load of persuading on my part, and a lot of pleading on Lexie's, to get him to agree to let us take him to building 122 at the VA Hospital in Leavenworth, where veterans are treated for mental issues.

As we walked to the Jeep with Mickey twenty feet ahead of us, Lexie whispered to me, "I called the VA when Mickey couldn't get into rehab for a week. They told me if he went to that building at the VA Hospital, they would keep him under twenty-four-hour surveillance, or suicide watch, as they referred to it, while they treated him, and then transfer him to the rehab center when there was an opening."

I nodded in return so Mickey wouldn't hear what we were talking about, as we were now approaching the Jeep where he was leaning against the front bumper. Lexie called Stone to let him know where we were going. She asked him to let Rip know and take him along to the cemetery so the two of them could retrieve Mickey's motorcycle. Before she rang off, she said, "After we make sure Mickey is handed over to the mental health professionals, we'll head back to Rockdale."

"I'm praying they can help him turn his life around," I whispered to Lexie.

"Me too," she whispered back, "and I strongly believe in the power of prayer."

"You and me both, my friend!"

TWENTY-ONE

L exie and I felt bad for Mickey but were relieved to know he wasn't involved in his ma's death, even though we were upset that it appeared to be Rose who killed her own mother. We didn't mention our suspicions to Mickey. On the way to the VA Hospital, Mickey was pretty quiet in the back seat. He was depressed, somewhat intoxicated, and undoubtedly questioning his decision to let us take him to the mental health department at the VA for treatment.

But there was something I just had to say. "Mickey, we were pleasantly surprised you didn't go back and dig up the bag of meth you buried behind the rest area's facilities."

"Aha!" Mickey sounded upset. "So, you didn't trust me one little bit?"

"Should we have?" Lexie asked.

"No, I guess not." His irritation subsided instantly. "Sobriety is a tougher hill to climb than I ever realized, although I knew it'd be no picnic."

"It never is," I said. "But it will definitely be worth all the effort and willpower you put into it."

"I know. I keep telling myself that whenever I feel vulnerable,"

Mickey said. "And, by the way, Rapella, I saw you drop the dime on the spot where I'd buried the bag. What you didn't know was that I buried *only* the bag, after I palmed the meth and put it in my pocket. But I want you to know I really do appreciate your support and that I'm determined to beat my addiction this time. I'd truly rather be dead than be dependent on drugs the rest of my life."

I'd forgotten that Mickey was skilled at magic tricks and had performed tricks for veterans in the VA hospital. Sleight-of-hand is one of the very first skills a magician learns, so I'm sure palming the meth wasn't much of a challenge for him. I'm also certain he was amused we'd gone out to the rest area to see if the dime was still there.

That evening, I was thinking about Rose and wondering if she'd sent the box to the dump in the U-Haul truck or packed it away in the trunk of the HHR. If we didn't find out that evening, we never would. The sisters and their significant others were heading home to New Jersey in the morning. Then an idea hit me. I rushed over to talk to Lexie at the inn while Rip munched on popcorn and watch an old *Gunsmoke* rerun. Matt Dillon had just been shot in the shoulder for what had to have been the fifty-seventh time in his lawman career. Doc Adams had dug enough lead out of the United States Marshall in Dodge City, Kansas, to start his own fishing sinker business.

"What's up?" Lexie asked when she met me at the door. "You look like you've just had an inspiration."

"I have." I explained what I'd been thinking about and asked her if she'd go with me to speak to Rose.

"Of course."

"First of all, Barron ran across the sweetest note you wrote your mother about meeting you for coffee in St. Joseph. It was really touching. You might want to ask the Buckleys if you can have it back to keep as a memento." I was buttering her up to gain her confidence. We actually planned to turn the note over to the detectives as evidence.

Rose nodded before her face crumpled and she was overtaken with sorrow. She began sobbing so hard that Lexie and I were unsure what to do or say next. It was like it was the first she'd heard of her mom's tragic death. We silently waited for her to regain her composure. Once she had, she said, "I'm not sure I could ever read that note without breaking down. I would've just sent her invitation by text but I knew a handwritten note would mean more to her. I'd spent the first two nights at mom's house, but the last night with Rowdy at the Quality Inn. Before I left that evening, I put the note under her mat and then sent her a text to look for it the following morning before we were to meet for brunch."

"Was there a special reason behind asking her to meet you for coffee and brunch rather than picking her up on your way?" I asked.

"Yes," Rose began, "Rowdy was going to drop me off at Starbucks so he could use the car the rest of the day. Starbucks was on the way to a gun shop in St. Joseph he wanted to visit. He bought a scope for his hunting rifle that day. I was going to hitch a ride back to Rockdale with mom. Now I feel as if I'm partially to blame for her death. If I had picked her up, or hadn't invited her to meet me in St. Joseph in the first place, she wouldn't have been in the car when the brakes failed."

Rose began crying again. As Lexie was consoling Rose, I was wondering if the truth behind her mother's death was finally hitting home. *Is she playing us or is her anguish sincere? My gut tells me she's genuinely grief-stricken.*

"There was something else we wanted to tell you before you headed home," I said to Rose once I felt as though I could change the subject without looking dispassionate. "While Lexie and I were looking through your mother's house for the threatening note she received the day before her death so we could turn it over to the police department, I recall seeing a box that had your cheerleading uniform and high school yearbooks in it. We thought we better tell you about it in case it was something you wanted to take home with you, if you haven't already located and packed it. I wasn't sure you had enough time to thoroughly scour through the entire basement since your time in the house was so limited."

Rose looked shocked. I was pretty skilled at deciphering expressions, but hers had me baffled. She made her astonishment clear with her next few remarks.

"So you actually saw that box within the last few days?" At my nod, she continued. "I did want to take it home with me but haven't been able to locate it. It also contained my old typewriter and a lot of schoolwork I thought would be fun to go through all these years later. I ran across it the morning of my second cousin's wedding, which I attended with mom. But when I looked for it a couple of days ago, it was missing."

"Oh." My response was short because a lot of thoughts were going through my head. *The box must've disappeared soon after I'd seen it while looking for the threatening note. If it wasn't Rose who used that typewriter to type a threatening note to leave on her mom's doorstep, and we'd convinced ourselves it wasn't Mickey either, then who was it? Are we back to square one again in our investigation or is Rose lying to us? Did she send it to the dump to get rid of the evidence?*

"Could one of your siblings have taken it or have accidentally pitched it in the U-Haul to take to the dump?" I asked.

"I doubt it," Rose said. "I told both of them to keep an eye out for a large box with two old typewriters in it. The lid had 'RHS 2007' on it, so it should've been easy to spot."

I swallowed so hard I almost choked on my own saliva. The lid had been upside down on the floor when I'd first spotted the box in

Lillian's basement so I hadn't seen what was written on it. That was the box Narciso Garcia had been carrying the day I spotted him carrying some tools out of the maintenance shed. Now I realized RHS stood for Rockdale High School and Rose would've been a junior in 2007 if she graduated the same year as Wendy, which I knew to be 2008.

"Did you know your mom had a suitor?" I asked Rose. "Were you aware her groundskeeper asked her to marry him?"

She laughed. "Yeah, of course! We all knew about Narciso. He proposed on a regular basis. It was to the point she was getting a little creeped out by him. She described him as more of a stalker than a suitor. She fired him a couple of weeks before her death, but he kept showing up to work anyway. She refused to pay him, of course."

"Did you ever know him to work on any day but Mondays and Thursdays?" I asked.

"No, never," she replied. "His work schedule was pretty much set in stone. Mom swore the man had a compulsive-obsessive disorder, but we all thought she did too. Between the two of them, I can't imagine him ever working on any day but Monday or Thursday. Why do you ask?"

I recalled Narciso telling the sheriff he was at her house on the morning of her death. He had called for a wellness check on Lillian, he said, when he couldn't contact her. I also remembered Wyatt saying that Lillian died on a Tuesday. I'd known October twenty-second was a Tuesday because it was the exact same day we celebrated my granddaughter's thirtieth birthday in Albuquerque. *Why was Narciso there on a Tuesday?* I wondered. *To sever the brake lines on Lillian's car, perhaps?* It was something that had bothered me since the day I first spoke to Narciso.

I didn't want to say too much to Rose, but told her Lexie and I would look for the box of high school memorabilia and ushered Lexie quickly down the staircase.

I reiterated the visit I'd had with Lillian's groundskeeper while she was at the dentist a few days ago. I'd watched Narciso place the box back into the shed before I'd walked away from him. Lexie and I decided we needed to go check to see if the box was still in the shed before we called Detective Johnston. Lexie grabbed a pair of bolt cutters off of Stone's tool bench in the garage in case we needed it to remove the padlock on the shed. We called Ruth to give her an update and headed next door.

We heard a rustling sound inside the maintenance shed as we tiptoed toward it. Before we could sneak a peek inside, Narciso stepped out of the shed carrying the box we were intent on recovering. It was likely his first opportunity to retrieve it without being seen because there'd been nearly constant activity at *Casa de Hermanas* since the day I'd had a conversation with him. Our unexpected presence startled him so badly he dropped the box on his foot and let out a high-pitched yelp.

Before he could ask us what we were doing, I said, "I'm glad we caught you. That box you just dropped belongs to Lillian's daughter, Rose, and she'd like to take it home with her to New Jersey in the morning. So, if you don't mind, Lexie and I will carry it back to the inn to return to her."

Narciso *did* mind, and apparently very much so. When Lexie and I stepped toward the groundskeeper to pick up the box, he shoved both of us so roughly that we tumbled backward into the open outbuilding. Narciso grabbed a gas can out of the shed and shut the door as we were both still on our backsides, trying to assess if either of us had broken a hip or any other critical bone. The next thing we heard was the padlock being locked and the former groundskeeper muttering to himself. "I'll teach them to mind their own business."

"Oh, my God!" Lexie gasped. "We're trapped in here! And I'm not sure my kneecap isn't dislocated."

"Don't try to get up. I'll call 9-1-1 and ask them to also send EMS to assess your knee."

"Okay."

"I left my phone in the trailer," I said. "Let me use yours."

"I don't have my phone either," she said in a shaky voice. "I didn't know we were going to be going on a hazardous mission when I answered the door tonight."

"Well, crap!" I exclaimed as I unrolled a sleeping bag I'd found on a shelf in the rear of the shed for Lexie and me to sit on. I was wondering if the bag was what we'd mistaken as a rolled-up tarp in the video we'd seen on Ruth's Ring app. Not knowing he'd already been fired, we hadn't thought twice about it after we watched a number of video clips of Narciso mowing Lillian's front lawn, even though it wasn't on one of his normally scheduled work days to begin with. I figured he was going to use the tarp to gather up grass clippings.

"Hopefully someone can hear us if we scream while you bang on the door with that shovel beside you," Lexie recommended.

"All right," I replied, picking up the lawn tool. "I landed on this damn thing when I fell. The collision didn't hurt the shovel any, but it didn't do my backside a heck of a lot of good."

"Maybe you should ask that good-looking EMT who looks like Paul Newman to *assess* your tush after he looks at my knee." Lexie laughed and it tickled my funny bone too. We were giggling out of nervous energy when I stopped abruptly. "Do you smell what I smell, Lexie?"

"Oh, no!" She inhaled deeply and exclaimed. "Is that gasoline?"

"Yes," I replied. "I think Narciso is going to set the shed on fire with—"

"—us locked inside it!" We finished the sentence in unison.

I almost added, *and take off with the box, which we'll need as proof of Narciso's guilt*, before realizing that recovering the box as evidence was a moot point if Lexie and I were reduced to a pile of smoldering ashes inside the shed.

Between screams for help, Lexie and I were trying not to panic so we could come up with a way to escape the shed, but as the smell of gasoline fumes increased, it was hard to keep a clear head. We nearly lost hope when we heard the groundskeeper strike a match. We heard the "poof" sound of a fire igniting shortly afterward. The poof was then followed by a loud thudding noise.

Lexie and I clung together, praying and screaming as we waited to be burned to death. We both agreed we should've never stuck our noses into Lillian's death. It was kind of like wishing we'd closed and locked the barn door while we watched a dozen prized thoroughbreds racing down the street at a full bolt. Hindsight was indeed twenty-twenty, and it was useless to a couple of women whimpering in terror inside a burning maintenance shed.

Just then, the most angelic sound I ever heard rang out. It was the sound of Ruth's voice hollering to us to hold on because the first responders were on the way, including the fire department. We sighed in relief when we heard the sound of sirens approaching.

At first, Ruth had tried to cut off the padlock on the door using the bolt cutters Lexie had dropped outside the shed when she was pushed inside, but at eighty-seven she didn't have the strength to get the job done. She'd then noticed a water hose rolled up on a hoseholder beside the house. She turned the faucet on full bore and quickly spread the hose out toward the shed. For the next minute or two that it took for the fire truck to arrive, she sprayed a small stream of water on the shed which only made the fire more intense. Smothering the fire would've been more effective if Ruth had only had a way to do so.

"Stay low in the back left corner!" she shouted. "The fire is concentrated on the top and front and you won't inhale as many fumes if you keep as close to the floor as possible."

It seemed like forever until we heard men shouting and the exterior of the shed being hosed down by a strong stream of water. When the door swung open a short time later, Wyatt rushed inside. Behind him were Rip and Stone. All three wore matching looks of concern until they knew Lexie and I were all right, other than minor smoke inhalation, a sprained knee, and a large bruise on my left butt cheek that I would only discover later while taking a shower. I didn't mention landing on the shovel because I didn't want the handsome EMT "assessing" my rear end.

The EMT's who treated us were the same three men who'd responded after the hullaballoo that had ensued at the fish fry. Lexie and I both had oxygen masks strapped to our faces when Ruth walked over and squeezed Lexie's left hand and my right. We squeezed hers in return. Our smiles said it all. I turned to Ruth and asked, "How did you know to call 9-1-1?"

"I was walking across the street, following Lexie's call to update me, when I saw Narciso shove you two into the shed. He had a gas can in his hand when he closed the door, so I knew he was up to no good. I took a quick photo with my phone of the license plate on the back of the truck in the driveway and called 9-1-1. I also sent a quick text to Stone."

"Thank goodness," I said. "I'm impressed with your quick thinking and ever so thankful for it."

"At my age, I am too," she responded with a chuckle. "I was assured help was on the way and an all-points-bulletin would be sent out to area police departments on Narciso's green Ford pickup with the license number on the image I sent via text to the dispatcher."

"You sent an image via text?" I asked. "Now I'm really impressed! How did you know how to do that?"

"I'm not sure. Dumb luck, perhaps," Ruth said. "But more likely it was divine intervention."

"Whatever it was," I began, "Lexie and I are alive because of you."

"That's what friends are for," Ruth replied with a warm smile.

After Lexie and I were deemed good to go, I asked Wyatt if they had tracked down Mr. Garcia.

"The APB was unnecessary, as it turned out. His truck was still in the driveway when we got here with the EMT's. We found Mr. Garcia unconscious in the driver's seat of his truck, with the biggest hematoma on the side of his head I've ever seen. I swear it was the size of a goose egg."

His response confused all of us, except for Ruth. In contrast, her response made all of us erupt into laughter. She had turned toward the now destroyed garden shed and her words explained the thudding sound Lexie and I had heard right after the fire had ignited. "I'm glad you said that. I almost forgot the rolling pin I'd brought over with me. I was making bread when I got Lexie's text and had an inkling it might come in handy. After I walloped Narciso over the head with it, he crawled toward his truck. I would've continued beating him within an inch of his life with the rolling pin if I wasn't more concerned about my friends' lives at the time."

TWENTY-TWO

A fter a beautiful sunrise on Saturday, clouds rolled in and the temperature dropped substantially. Lexie and I bundled up to attend the book club meeting at Ruth's house. Although neither of us had been able to read *The Will of the Enemy*, we enjoyed the discussion about the novel and the huge array of delicious food. Lexie even agreed to join the book club and couldn't wait to read the following month's book they'd all voted on.

We both thanked Ruth for inviting us to the meeting and for all of her help during our personal investigation into Lillian's death. We were especially appreciative of her for saving our lives.

By dinner time, a cold rain was falling. We didn't let it dampen our spirits, however, or change our plans to eat at The Happy Hooker Saturday evening. Service was indeed slower than we were accustomed to, as Rose had warned, but the delicious seafood platter I'd ordered was worth the wait. Our lively conversation made the time pass quickly too.

The following day was Sunday and Detective Johnston's day off. Lexie invited him to the inn for supper. Together, she and I prepared an assortment of Italian dishes, including lasagna, eggplant parmesan, garlic bread sticks, and an antipasto salad. Thinking back to the anecdote Lexie had told me about running home to her mother after Chester insulted her first attempt at lasagna, I said, "I'm assuming you've improved on your lasagna-making skills over the years?"

"Probably not enough," she laughed, "but it's definitely better than that first attempt of mine. Even I knew the lasagna I'd made that day was inedible, but it still ticked me off when Chester insulted it."

"I understand completely," I said. "About five years into our marriage, Rip made an uncomplimentary remark about a special supper I'd prepared for his birthday. I didn't cook another meal for two weeks. At that point, he'd finally tired enough of his own cooking to bring me home a dozen roses."

"Knowing you," Lexie began, "you had to bite your tongue not to chastise Rip for spending so much on flowers."

I knew she was joking, but occasionally it stung when people teased me about how conservative I am. Still, her remark was spot on, so I laughed along with her and said, "A heartfelt apology is not only more meaningful than a bunch of over-priced flowers, but also a hell of a lot less expensive. A few days later, the costly roses looked so pitiful they had to be pitched in the trash. Seems like such a waste of money to me."

"I agree, my friend. I'll take a box of chocolates over flowers any day." Lexie smiled and my resentment at her tightwad jab disappeared like a platter full of hot wings on Super Bowl Sunday. "Let's cover these dishes with tin foil so we can heat them up for supper later on. I want to surprise the kids by taking dinner over to them."

"I wondered why we were making so much food," I replied. "That's a wonderful idea, Lexie. They will be delighted."

"I often volunteer to deliver food for the Meals on Wheels program. It's so nice to have people meet me at the door with smiles on their faces. It's also helped me get to know a lot of Rockdale citizens, which is nice."

"It doesn't surprise me that you volunteer for something so self-less," I said. "I'm sure a few of them have recommended the Alexandria Inn to family and friends in return."

"That's true. And the best type of promotion for a business is word-of-mouth advertising, so it's a win-win situation for me."

At three in the afternoon, the two of us hopped into Lexie's Jeep and drove to the kids' ranch in Atchison to deliver a full Italian dinner to them. The three of them had come home from the hospital earlier that morning and we thought Wendy and Andy would enjoy a tasty hot meal neither of them had to cook. It would be their first night alone with Chet and we felt all of their time should be focused on the baby, not on fixing a meal. After enduring hospital food for a couple of days, we knew Wendy would relish the meal we surprised them with.

As we pulled back in the circle driveway of the inn a couple of hours later, Wyatt arrived in his truck right behind us with his fiancée Victoria Prescott in the passenger seat. Lexie and I visited with Victoria as we reheated the food and set the table while the three men relaxed on the front porch, each with a bottle of beer in their hand.

After a well-received supper, Lexie and I joined the others on the covered back porch of the inn and Wyatt expanded on what had transpired since Narciso had been booked and charged with first-degree murder. I'd been anxious to hear about the case but hadn't wanted to interrupt the conversation the men had been enjoying about another fishing trip they planned to take with Ray Franklin on Wednesday morning. Victoria had occupied herself with filing a couple of fingernails while the men chatted.

"Mr. Garcia admitted killing his former boss, claiming it was a crime of passion. As I told you before, when first questioned, he told the sheriff he thought Lillian might have driven into the abutment intentionally because she'd mentioned to him she wished she was dead. During interrogation, Garcia told the detectives he made it all up to make them believe her death could be attributed to suicide. He said he used the key he knew Lillian always left under the welcome mat on her front porch to enter her house and type the threatening message on the typewriter in the basement while Lillian and Rose were attending a wedding on October twentieth. He spent that night in the shed and left the note under her door mat early the next morning."

"How'd he know where the typewriter was located?" I asked.

"Lillian had recently asked him to move a few of the boxes in the maintenance shed downstairs in fear the contents of those boxes would be ruined due to humidity and/or rodents. Narciso said most of the boxes in the shed contained old *Rockdale Gazette* newspapers, some as old as thirty years. He'd been all too happy to move them to the basement because it freed up some room in the maintenance shed for him to work and store his lawn tools in an orderly fashion. He admitted to having OCD and that the clutter had driven him crazy for far too long. While he was moving stuff around downstairs to make room for the boxes out of the shed, he came across the box containing the two old typewriters."

"I can see why the clutter drove him nuts," I said. "How did he get the box of typewriters out of the basement, Wyatt?"

"He would later sneak into the house one morning last week to lug the heavy box to the maintenance shed. He planned to retrieve the typewriter and haul it back to his house the first chance he had to do so undetected. He mentioned that some nosy old lady caught him with the box as he was putting it in the shed, so he pretended to be picking up some of his lawn tools." Wyatt winked at me and asked, "Would you be that nosy old lady he was referring to, Rapella?"

"Yep! That nosy old lady was me, but I had no idea I was looking the killer in the face at the time." I laughed at discovering I'd caught him red-handed and didn't know it. "I'd wondered if the shed was as stacked to the ceiling with 'stuff' as the house was, but had been reluctant to ask. Later, I was surprised that when Narciso set the shed on fire, all that was in there were a few lawn tools and a sleeping bag."

"And us!" Lexie cut in. "I'm glad there'd only been one can of gas in there for Narciso to grab before he closed the door and locked it, or the shed might've exploded like a propane tank."

"Oh, Lord. I don't even want to think about it," I replied. "Go on with your story, Wyatt."

"So, on the morning of the twenty-second, he showed up to work, even though he said it was a Monday and she'd recently let him go because she was unhappy with his work."

I interrupted Wyatt to say, "Rose told us she was creeped out by him and let him go because she felt as if he'd began stalking her after she refused his numerous marriage proposals."

"That makes more sense because he did a remarkable job on the grounds of that place," Wyatt said. "He must have been too embarrassed to tell us the real reason she fired him. Unrequited love can sometimes end badly, even tragically at times, such as it did in this case."

"Did Narciso say why he did what he did?" I asked. "When I talked to him about Lillian, he truly seemed to care deeply for her."

"Too deeply, perhaps," Wyatt replied. "He was upset about being fired and wrote the threatening note in an attempt to make her feel uncomfortable living alone. He got the idea after she asked Mickey to move in with her after she saw a Peeping Tom looking in her window. It was actually Narciso who was peeping in her window, and it pissed him off when she asked Mickey to live with her instead of him. But once Mickey was on the outs with his mom, Narciso thought he'd try to frighten her again and maybe this time she'd ask him to move in with her instead. He was convinced if Lillian got to know him better, she'd fall as deeply in love with him as he was with her."

"He sounds as if he's delusional," Lexie said.

"Most definitely," Wyatt agreed. "Narciso told the detectives

281

when he showed up to work early on the twenty-second, even after Lillian had fired him, she demanded he leave immediately. She told him she had a brunch date with her daughter that morning and a dinner date with a surgeon later in the evening. She said she didn't need him hanging around pestering her."

"And that's what set him off?" Lexie asked.

"Yeah, unfortunately," Wyatt said. "After he found out she was planning to go out with some surgeon she'd met at her cousin's wedding, he decided that if he couldn't have Lillian, then no one else was going to have her either. He then devised a way to kill her so he could, and I quote, 'have the last laugh.' He sprinted home to get his truck and about a block from Lillian's house he caught up with her in her Volvo and tailed her to the bank. While she took care of her transaction inside the bank, he made sure there were no security cameras aimed his direction in the parking lot. He had just enough time to sever two of her car's brake lines before she reemerged from the bank. He was able to slither away without her seeing him and, as they say, the rest is history. Narciso's story explained to the homicide detectives why there was no brake fluid on the floor of Lillian's garage."

Lexie and I looked at each other, both rolling our eyes. Neither of us had thought to check her garage for a puddle of brake fluid. Knowing the brake lines were not cut while the Volvo was in Lillian's garage may have altered the entire course of our investigation and spared us from nearly burning to death inside her maintenance shed. We all tend to learn from our mistakes, however, and that was one error in judgment neither one of us would ever forget.

"Wow!" I exclaimed. "Narciso seemed like a cranky but kind-hearted man when I talked to him. I could never have believed I was talking to a cold-blooded killer. Wyatt, we saw him mowing her lawn in one of Ruth's Ring app videos. Why did he do that?"

"Who knows," Wyatt replied. "He was probably stewing as he mowed, trying to decide how he was going to get back at her for casting him aside in lieu of some cardiac surgeon. And it's even possible he'd taken into account his arrival at her house might be picked up on a neighbor's security or doorbell camera and he wanted to have a reason for being at Lillian's house that morning. He may be the vindictive type of guy, but he's not stupid. He's had some mental problems in the past too, according to his records, so his behavior was not altogether uncharacteristic for the man. His OCD alone might have prompted his need to mow her lawn."

"Why did he keep a sleeping bag in the shed?" Lexie asked the detective. "It's toast now, but it struck me as odd when I saw it."

"He said he slept in the shed the night he typed the note," Wyatt said. "The guy actually was a stalker, so maybe he slept in the shed frequently so he could peek in her windows at night. He may have done that on numerous occasions, even though she only caught him the one time."

"I'm just relieved the truth has finally come out," Lexie said. "Thank you so much, Rapella, for helping me find justice for my friend. I'm glad it didn't end up getting us both reduced to a pile of ashes."

TWENTY-THREE

T he next few weeks passed quickly as Rip and I enjoyed visiting with Lexie, Stone, Andy, Wendy, and Ruth. We also fussed over Chet whenever the opportunity presented itself. I was able to attend another book club meeting with Ruth and Lexie, and Rip was thrilled to be able to go fishing with Stone and Ray a couple of more times before the weather turned cold. We were all delighted when Barron and Celia visited one afternoon with interesting news to share with us.

We were already aware that, as expected, the Corona typewriter found in the large box in the bed of Narciso Garcia's truck was tested by authorities and proven to be the machine the threatening note was typed on. What wasn't anticipated, however, was that the Malling-Hanson Writing Ball accompanying the Corona typewriter was not only extremely rare; it was also exceedingly valuable.

As per the real estate contract, the antique now legally belonged to the Buckleys. However, Barron said he wouldn't feel right claiming the family heirloom as his own. Instead, he found a buyer willing to pay one hundred grand for the hard-to-find antique that'd been manufactured in 1878 and gave the remaining contents of the box to Rose.

Barron used approximately thirty-two thousand of the proceeds to pay three years' rent on an apartment for Mickey so he would have a roof over his head while he got back on his feet. Barron also encouraged Mickey to invest his third of the proceeds from Lillian's estate with a friend of his who worked as an advisor for Morgan Stanley. Barron explained Mickey's future would be brighter if the money was invested. I suspect the attorney also figured the money wouldn't be as easily accessible should Mickey experience another setback. Barron had found a nice but inexpensive apartment in Atchison near Andy and Wendy's ranch. He'd thought Andy and Wendy would like the privacy of having their ranch hand living off-site, and Mickey would be happier being independent as well.

Because he was a disabled veteran, the VA covered Mickey's rehabilitation treatments. After a few days in the VA hospital under suicide watch, they transferred him to the Serenity Meadows Rehabilitation Center in St. Joseph to fill the vacancy that'd opened up there. He was released after a thirty-day stint in the rehab program and began attending Narcotics Anonymous meetings on a regular basis. But his motorbike had shot craps as Stone was driving it back to the inn from the cemetery and Barron wanted to make sure Mickey had a way to travel to his NA meetings. Mickey would also need transportation to Andy and Wendy's property where he was anxious to begin his ranch hand position. Mickey was given Celia's Ford Taurus. Not surprisingly, Celia's now tooling around Rockdale in a brand-new Mercedes convertible.

The same amount Barron spent on Mickey went into an account to be used toward eventual IVF treatments when Judy and Sammi were ready to proceed with having a baby via surrogacy. Rose and Barron then went car shopping together in Egg Harbor and Barron bought her a new yellow Hyundai Veloster with all of the bells and whistles. The pair settled on the Veloster because Barron liked its fuel efficiency, Rose adored its sporty appearance, and they both were impressed with Hyundai's ten-year new car warranty.

When all was said and done, there was three thousand, four-hundred, and seventy-two dollars of the one-hundred grand remaining. Barron used that amount to start a 529 college savings account in Chet's name with his financial advisor friend who always said, "Having money saved for college changes the conversation when the time comes." Lexie and Stone happily agreed to donate to the fund every year.

"Celia and I plan to do the same for our grandchildren, if we're ever blessed with any," Barron said. "We figure if for some reason the child decides not to use it for higher education, the fund should have grown enough by then for a handsome down payment on a first home."

And to think I'd once thought this man could've killed Lillian Sparrow just to gain access to her home. Barron Buckley was a saint, not the vicious monster I'd once imagined. I'd also suspected Rose Hamm, a warm, loving daughter who likely would've slashed her own wrists before harming her mother in any way, and even Ruth Petschl, who I now adored and to whom Lexie and I owed our lives. If not for her quick thinking, we wouldn't be alive to see Narciso Garcia be convicted of first-degree murder and sentenced to life without parole in prison. It was a lesson for me to always give a suspect benefit of the doubt until I had concrete evidence that the individual was guilty of a heinous crime. I had a tendency to be too judgmental and jump to conclusions too rashly. It was a bad habit I'd have to kick, just as Mickey Scott appeared to have kicked his substance abuse addiction. Only time would tell, I knew, but I was hopeful on both counts.

Now that the task of determining who committed the crime against Lillian was behind us, Rip and I planned to enjoy our time with friends before heading out on our new adventure in the Chartreuse Caboose.

One afternoon in mid-December, Stone planned to ride along with Rip to purchase a new spare tire for the truck. Stone claimed "he had a guy" who would give Rip a good deal.

Lexie and I decided to drive to the Legends area in Kansas City, Kansas, while the men were busy replacing the slashed tire with money Mickey had given Rip. It was the entirety of his first paycheck from his new ranch hand position, which we hoped was a lesson to the young man. With Christmas just over a week away, Lexie and I planned to finish our holiday shopping at the outlet mall and, naturally, stop for coffee and a pastry at The Dapper Doughnut while we were there. It promised to be a fun day.

After the holidays were over, Rip and I packed up the trailer to head out for our next destination while Willie Nelson's song, *On the Road Again*, played in our minds.

On our way out of town we stopped at the ranch just outside Atchison to say goodbye to Wendy, Andy, Chet, and Mickey, who was now fully engaged in his new job and was "loving every minute of it," according to the new cowpoke himself. To celebrate two months of sobriety, he told us he'd invested in a full set of dentures. When he smiled now, his handsomeness was astonishing. Helping his appearance was his new short hairstyle. The area that'd been shaved off to stitch up the laceration Rowdy had bestowed on him was the same length as the rest of his hair, which had been cut short while he was in rehab.

"Are you two heading out?" Mickey asked as we exited the Chevy truck.

"Yep," Rip replied. "We thought we should move on before we wore out our welcome at the Alexandria Inn."

Mickey grinned and then nodded at Andy and Wendy, who had just stepped out on the porch. Wendy was carrying a cooing Chet in her arms. Mickey turned his attention back to Rip and me. "I hate to see you two go. I apologize again for slicing your arm. I should be in jail for assaulting you and if not for your kindness, I would be. Thank you again for everything you've both done for me."

"It was our pleasure, son," Rip assured him. "Like I told Rapella from the beginning, it was no big rip."

"Yes, it was," Mickey countered. "But seeing what kind of monster I'd become, thanks to my addiction, helped me realize I needed to turn my life around. By the way, that new shirt I gave you for Christmas looks great on you."

"Thank you." Rip glanced down at the western-styled denim shirt he was wearing. I knew he was very proud of it. "I do look pretty good in it, don't I?"

After rolling my eyes at my husband, I added, "We are delighted to see you doing so well, Mickey. We have a ranch-themed gift to drop off for Chet."

I handed the cute crib mobile featuring horses and cows to Andy because Wendy's arms were full. Wendy thanked us and said, "That is so sweet of you guys. I love the mobile. It's adorable and fits the theme of the nursery perfectly. Like Mickey just said, Andy and I hate to see you go. Promise you'll stop by whenever you're in the area."

"Nothing could keep us away. You and your folks are like family to us." I hugged both Andy and Wendy before reaching into my shoulder bag.

I also had a gift for Mickey to show off the next time he told his traumatic account of getting a girl's toy at McDonalds. It was the Ariel the Mermaid doll I'd found in a box labeled "Happy Meal toys" while searching his mother's house for the note Narciso had left on her porch. Wendy and Andy were understandably puzzled by my present, but I'd never seen Mickey Scott laugh so heartily.

"Is there a story behind that doll?" Wendy asked.

"Yeah, but you'll have to have Mickey tell it to you," Rip replied with a grin. "We brought it for Mickey as a reminder to keep his hair cut short. He looks almost as handsome now as I do in this shirt he gave me."

As we drove away, we were waving at the three adults on the porch who were waving back at us and smiling. I swear I even saw a grin on Chet's pudgy little face. I was sad to be leaving our friends, but excited to head to Gatlinburg, Tennessee where we planned to spend a couple of weeks in the Great Smoky Mountains National Park. We were always excited to head off on a new adventure. I just prayed our time in Tennessee did not involve any murder case investigations. We were both badly in need of some serious rest and relaxation.

THE GRIM RIPPER

A RIPPLE EFFECT COZY MYSTERY, BOOK 8

I was putting three skinless, boneless chicken thighs in the oven when I looked out the window and saw my husband, Clyde Ripple—better known as Rip—slashing at the ground with a handheld weed whacker that resembled a small scythe. He looked like a man possessed. When we'd sold off nearly everything we owned to become full-time RVers, I'd questioned him about why he was packing the lawn tool in one of the undercarriage compartments of our thirty-foot travel trailer. Part of the reasoning behind our decision to become RVers was not having a yard to maintain. He'd replied, "It just seems like something that might come in handy some day on our travels." Finally, a decade later, he appeared to be using it to assault a figment of his imagination.

I opened the trailer door and asked, "What in the world are you doing, Rip?"

"I was getting ready to light the grill so I could charbroil the corn on the cob and zucchini when I noticed a snake right by my foot."

We were in Rochester, Minnesota for a visit to the Mayo Clinic, and I knew the venomous snakes could be found in the state's southeastern region. Visions of my husband being bit by a timber rattler flitted through my mind. I must have thought the snake was about to burst into flames because I grabbed the fire extinguisher we carried in the RV and rushed outside.

"Where is it?" I shouted, glancing around frantically. "I can't see it."

Rip used the sharp tip of the weed whacker to move some grass out of the way and expose what looked like pieces of a gooey jigsaw puzzle. Having grown up in a rural area of south Texas, I recognized the mutilated mess as a common garter snake.

"That poor little thing couldn't have harmed you if it'd tried, Rip," I said.

"I know *that's* right!" Rip sounded inordinately proud of the bravery, skill, and brute strength it took to maim a pencil-thin, harmless snake, no more than eighteen inches long. "You know what they say, don't you, Rapella? The only good snake is—"

"—a dead snake," I finished his sentence while rolling my eyes at him.

"Yes." Rip nodded. "A dead one that is diced into a hundred pieces, so there's no chance of it coming back to life."

Rip was wearing an old black and gray L.A. Raiders jersey and black sweatpants. Covering his bald head was a dark blue ball cap. I studied him as he stood over the mangled garter snake with a scythe in one hand and a bottle of lighter fluid in the other. Sarcastically, I asked, "Well, aren't you the Grim Ripper?"

I laughed at my clever pun but Rip just looked at me as if I'd suddenly begun speaking in Mandarin Chinese. Rather than bothering to explain my quip, I shook my head and turned my back to him. As I walked toward the trailer, I said, "The chicken will be ready at six."

We sat at the RV's booth-style table forty-five minutes later, dining on heart-healthy baked chicken, corn, and squash, and discussing Rip's upcoming appointment. He'd had a triple bypass in Seattle a couple of years prior and now needed a coronary stent. We'd been visiting my brother Billy in Mora, Minnesota when Rip suddenly experienced chest pains, very similar to the ones he'd had on the cruise ship in Alaska before his bypass surgery. At Welia Health Center, where the ambulance had transported Rip, it was determined he needed an angioplasty, which had led us to the Mayo Clinic.

Little did we know at the time that Rip's cardiac surgeon would suffer an untimely and highly suspicious demise in the parking lot of the clinic immediately following Rip's operation. When the police department ruled it a death by natural causes, Rip became incensed. As the retired sheriff of Aransas County, Texas, his gut told him the circumstances behind the physician's passing demanded further investigation.

I could never have imagined the day would come when it was my husband instead of me who'd insist we personally look into the truth behind a fatality.

Available in Paperback and eBook from Your Favorite Bookstore or Online Retailer

ABOUT THE AUTHOR

Jeanne Glidewell lives with her husband, Bob, in the small coastal town of Rockport, Texas, on Salt Lake, just off Copano Bay.

Besides writing, Jeanne enjoys fishing, wildlife photography, and traveling both here and abroad. She and Bob visited Ireland in March 2022 with Jeanne's sister and brother-in-law, Sarah and Bruce Goodman. Among other things, they kissed the Blarney Stone, drank Guinness in Irish pubs, and marched in Killarney's annual parade on St. Patrick's Day.

As a 2006 pancreas and kidney transplant recipient, Jeanne is an avid advocate for organ and tissue donation. Please consider giving the gift of life by opting to be an organ donor should you no longer need them, and let your family know of your decision because marking "organ donor" on your driver's license is not enough to ensure your final wishes are met.

Jeanne is the author of a romance/suspense novel, Soul Survivor, seven novels and one novella in her NY Times best-selling Lexie Starr cozy mystery series, and seven novels in her Ripple Effect cozy mystery series. She's currently writing Lexie Starr book eight titled *Looking for Trouble* and expects to have it released in the spring of 2023.

www.JeanneGlidewell.com